"YOU SAID YOU'LL help me get the keys from him," I force out. "With all the Order's knowledge, you must have asked your magic how to destroy it too. And it told you the same thing it told me—by sacrificing a conduit and returning it to the chasm?"

Rares nods slowly.

"And you're going to help me get the keys from Angra," I repeat. "You're going to help *me* destroy all magic. So—"

Memories flutter across my mind. The chasm and its electric, destructive fingers of magic that could only inhabit objects—when people attempted to let the magic touch them, it incinerated them as thoroughly as a lightning strike.

My anxiety is replaced by dread when Rares's gaze doesn't break from mine.

"There's no other way to destroy magic," I guess, the words coming from somewhere deep inside me, somewhere numb. "You're going to help me die."

FROST
LIKE
NIGHT

SARA RAASCH

BALZER + BRAY
An Imprint of HarperCollinsPublishers

To Doug and Mary Jo,
for being far less troublesome than Sir and Hannah.

Balzer + Bray is an imprint of HarperCollins Publishers.

Frost Like Night
Copyright © 2016 by Sara Raasch
Map art © 2014 by Jordan Saia
All rights reserved. Printed in the United States of America.

Library of Congress Control Number: 2016013281
ISBN 978-0-06-228699-4

Typography by Erin Fitzsimmons
17 18 19 20 21   PC/LSCH   10 9 8 7 6 5 4 3 2 1
❖
First paperback edition, 2017

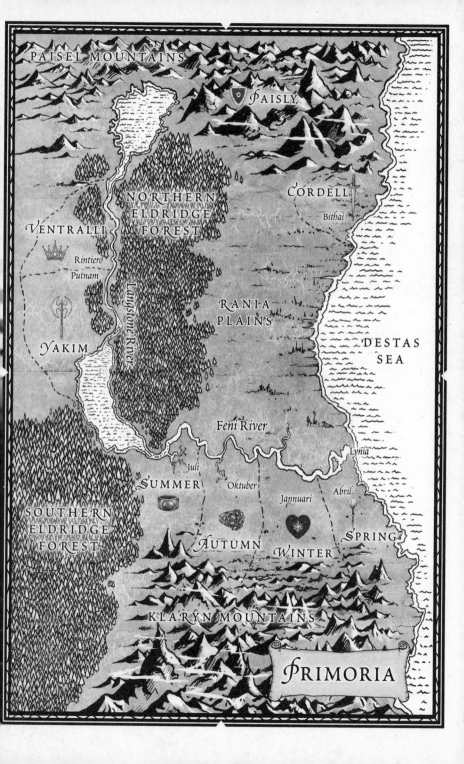

Meira

THIS IS WRONG.

I'm still hidden in the doorway of the Donati Palace's dungeon and already I can feel the change in Ventralli, like the darkness of a storm moving in. But instead of staying to fight with my handful of Winterians, I left them and followed the man in front of me.

And I have no idea who he really is.

Any guards who might have been posted outside the dungeon are gone, drawn into the chaos of Raelyn's takeover of the kingdom. Rooms open to our right and left, far enough away that the people within don't notice us, close enough for me to catch glimpses inside. Soldiers corral courtiers into groups against the gilded walls, servants weep—but even more terrifying are the bystanders who do nothing at all. The ones who watch the soldiers swing threats like blades, declaring King Jesse deposed and his wife, Raelyn, the ruler of Ventralli because she has a stronger power now, one everyone can use—power given to her by King Angra of Spring.

"He's alive?"

"His magic is stronger than that of the Royal Conduits?"

"Is that how he survived?"

These questions rise above the soldiers' threats, mixing with the pounding of my heart in my ears.

"Angra helped the Ventrallan queen depose its king. He"—my breath hitches—"already has his influence in Cordell. He seized Autumn and Winter and had the Summer king *murdered*, and yet somehow, this makes people feel wonder, not fear."

The man I've been following—Rares, if that's even his name—looks at me.

"Angra has probably been planning this conquest for the three months he's been gone, so his retribution isn't as swift as it would seem," he says. "And you more than anyone know how easy it is for people to choose wonder over fear."

"I, more than anyone?" I choke. "How could you possibly know that?"

"Do you truly want to have this discussion now?" The scar that runs along the right side of Rares's face, from his temple to his chin, creases with his squint. "I'd planned on at least getting us past any immediate threat of death first. . . ."

Swords clash and a soldier shouts from up the hall. Rares dives around the corner without waiting for my response, leaving me to scramble after him.

I shouldn't be trailing some mysterious Paislian—I should be helping Mather release the Winterians in the dungeons. Or planning a way to free my kingdom from the Cordellan coup. Or saving Ceridwen from Raelyn. Or finding a way to extract Theron from the grip of Angra's Decay.

I falter, tripping over my many worries. While I always suspected Angra's death was a ruse, I never, not in any of my most delirious fears, thought he could be strong enough to give magic to non-conduit-wielders.

But his power is tainted by the Decay, which was created when there were no rules binding magic to only royal bloodlines.

As Rares and I duck from hall to hall, I see the fruits of Angra's magic firsthand. The Ventralli of light and color that existed when we first arrived is gone, replaced by one that resembles the dark streets of Spring. Soldiers march with faces pinched tight by anger, their movements sharp. Courtiers huddle in trembling masses, fearful, with wide eyes and an eagerness to please their conquerors.

No one fights it. No one shouts retaliation or struggles against the soldiers.

This is Angra's doing. Though it looks as though he's only given his higher-ranking subordinates the ability to control magic, as Raelyn did when she killed the Summerian king. The people who crowd the halls simply appear fogged, influenced by something beyond themselves, as if they all got drunk on the same bad wine.

This is what Angra is creating, a world of infinite power, where everyone is possessed by a magic that makes them pliable, overcome by their deepest, darkest emotions.

How do I stop him? How do I save—

It claws at me, the question I asked my conduit magic, and I'm sucked back to that moment, when I was running through the streets of Rintiero with Lekan and Conall. My biggest worries then were trying to keep Ceridwen from murdering her brother, and figuring out how to form an alliance with Ventralli, and finding the Order of the Lustrate and their keys in order to keep Cordell from accessing the magic chasm.

Then I asked that question—*how do I save everyone?*—and the answer blistered itself onto my soul.

By sacrificing a Royal Conduit and returning it to the source of the magic.

But I am Winter's conduit. All of me. Thanks to my mother.

Rares yanks me behind a potted plant moments before a contingent of men jogs out of a room just ahead.

"Not now," he whispers. He fishes for something in his shirt and withdraws a key on a chain, the one he showed me in the dungeon—the final key to the magic chasm in the

Tadil Mine. "You found me. You found the Order of the Lustrate—and *yes*, we will help you defeat Angra and stop all this. But first, let's just get out of here alive."

His words offer much-needed comfort, so needed, in fact, that it isn't until he darts back into the hall that I wonder—how did he know I was worrying?

It doesn't matter. I swallow, resolute. I will do this. I will learn what I can from the Order, and use that knowledge: either I will face Angra in battle and destroy him and his magic—or I will get the keys from him, enter the chasm in the Tadil, and destroy all magic in the only way I know how.

Either way, this is what I need to do. Angra is too strong—I need help, and the Order of the Lustrate is the only resource I know of that could help me grasp my magic in the same unstoppable way that Angra does.

Rares leads me inside an empty kitchen filled with thick wooden tables and roaring fireplaces and food abandoned by servants who are most likely hiding from the frenzy of the takeover. He pulls out a water sack and fills it at a pump in the corner.

"Who are you?" I finally manage to ask.

He points to a block of knives on a counter. "Arm yourself."

"With kitchen knives?"

He doesn't break stride. "A blade is a blade. Blood can be drawn all the same."

I frown but slide a few knives into my belt. My empty

holster still hangs against my spine—my chakram is back in the ballroom. Back in Garrigan's chest.

I grip the edge of the counter.

A hand cups my shoulder, and when I look up, Rares is watching me.

"My name is Rares. I didn't mislead you about that," he says. "Rares Albescu of Paisly, a leader in the Order of the Lustrate."

He glances over my shoulder, at the kitchen door that leads into the palace. Footsteps echo, growing louder, and I know we'll have to run before he can explain more.

"I will tell you everything," he promises. "But first we must reach safety—in Paisly. Angra can't follow us there."

"Why not?" I face Rares. "What are you planning—*why* is this—"

Rares cuts me off with a squeeze to my shoulder. "Please, Your Majesty. It's the safest place for all I must show you, and I promise, I will tell you everything as soon as I am able."

"Meira," I correct. If I'm going to risk my life for the foreseeable future, then I'm going to be addressed how *I* want to be addressed.

Rares smiles. "Meira."

We move to the other kitchen door, the one leading to a garden. Rares starts to slip out when I'm caught by one last grip of remorse at all I'm leaving. By going with him, I *am* helping—the Order of the Lustrate is my best chance at stopping Angra—but it still feels like I'm running away.

Rares turns. "You can't save everyone by staying."

Other people have told me this before—*You can't save everyone; Winter is your priority.* Most loudly: Sir.

Grief stabs into me. Mather told me of Alysson's death, but what about Sir? Did he survive the Cordellan attack on Jannuari? What about the rest of Winter—what state is my kingdom in? I can't think about Sir being dead. He has to be alive, and if he is, he'll be doing everything he can to keep Winter together.

I hear what Rares said again, realizing now the exact meaning of his words, and I begin to see all the ways he differs from Sir. Rares's eyes are wider; his skin is darker; his hands are more scarred from years of fighting. And most of all, in Rares, I see something I never saw in Sir—something that made Rares add the two words that entirely changed the meaning of that sentence.

You can't save everyone by staying.

Not an end. A choice.

"Who are you?" I breathe again.

Rares smiles. "Someone who has been waiting for you for a long time, dear heart."

Soon after we leave the palace complex, a horn wails through the hazy gray sky.

They've discovered I'm gone. Which means they found

Theron, chained to the dungeon wall, and Mather and the rest—

No. Mather wouldn't let anything happen to anyone in his care. Not because I ordered him to keep them safe, but because that's who he's always been—a man who, even after he lost his throne, still found a way to be a ruler. The way his Children of the Thaw look at him, with the unquestioned loyalty earned by someone born to lead . . .

He is the one person in my life fully capable of standing on his own.

What about Theron?

The question makes me stumble as Rares and I sprint out of the city, wiggling between two bright, lopsided buildings and into the lush forest that borders Rintiero to the north.

That question. It wasn't *me*. It sounded almost like—

I slam to a halt, Rares making it a few paces farther before he realizes I've stopped. But the voice in my head holds me captive, and I brace my hands over my temples.

A terrible fate, isn't it, being part of the same magic? If only you were stronger.

My vision blurs until all I see is Angra's face in my mind.

"No!" I scream, buckling, my knees slamming into the moist earth. Angra could hear my thoughts when we were both in the Donati ballroom, but he's nowhere near me now. How is he able to talk to me, *within* me? I should be able to stop him—

But you can't stop me, can you, Highness? My soldiers are coming for you. Winter is finished. Spring has come.

A single word ekes out in response. *Why?*

I've already asked that question, back in the ballroom of the Donati Palace, surrounded by the carnage—the Summerian king's head, Garrigan's and Noam's bodies. But the only answer I got was the reason why Angra sought to destroy Winter's mines—he fears pure conduit magic countering his Decay, which is why he spent every moment he could working to undo that threat. That was why he attacked Winter for so long; that was why he turned on anyone who tried to open the chasm.

But what I ask now isn't even a conscious question—it's a whimper in the darkness as his face fills my mind.

Why is this happening . . . ?

I've seen my friends murdered for this war. I've watched my kingdom burn for this. I'm running for my life now for this, and after all these years, I still don't know *why*. What does he want?

Hands cover mine where I grip my head.

I open my eyes. Magic spreads down my limbs, cooling and deep and pure, turning my fear to shock.

Rares is pumping his magic into me.

His face tightens, beads of sweat breaking along his forehead. "Fight him!"

My heart knows I don't have to submit to Rares's magic, *shouldn't* submit to him, but everything else in me wants to, fear and panic coiling in a whip that tears apart my insides.

Fight! I will myself to stay open to whatever help Rares may offer.

A shock sends me flying backward. I slam against the ground, leaves sticking to my clothes, my head ringing as though someone has struck a bell inside my skull.

I see Rares mouth my name.

"You . . . ," I think I say. "What did you . . ."

Pain flares behind my eyes and it's all I can do not to vomit on the soggy undergrowth. But Rares puts his hand over mine again, even when I glare at him through the agony that turns everything a vibrant scarlet.

Rest now, a voice says. It isn't Angra—it's Rares, in my head. *Rest, and trust me.*

Trust you? What did you do? You haven't told me anything!

But even as I try to fight it, unconsciousness comes, lulling me like the tempting aromas that waft from a feast. I'm half aware of Rares lifting me, of the jostling sway of being carried at a run through the forest.

You're more like Sir than I thought are my final words before everything goes dark.

Mather

SHE LEFT.

Channeling every bit of his panic into the task at hand, Mather threw his weight against the bolt. It released with a squeal and the cell door opened, freeing Phil, who barreled out, fists ready, a breath ahead of the rest of the Thaw. But Mather spared them no orders before he heaved open the bolt on the next door, releasing Dendera, Nessa, and Conall. Theron's shouts for help from inside his own cell would alert his soldiers at any minute—and Meira had left them.

"We need to get out of here," Mather said to no one in particular, but as he pivoted toward the staircase, he hesitated. Leaving that way would almost certainly land them right back in the dungeon if they encountered any soldiers. Was there another way out?

Phil stepped forward. "We can split up. Some of us go

up the stairs, the rest go deeper into the dungeon, see if there's a way—"

Another voice spoke. "Or you could follow me."

Mather was too numbed by the day's events to feel anything but readiness as he leaped toward the voice. He reached for a sword, but his weapons had been taken before the descent into the dungeon, and all he had now was Cordell's Royal Conduit. His fingers brushed the jewel on the hilt, his lip curling as he remembered how Theron had tossed it away so carelessly—a part of him would take such joy in tarnishing Cordell's pretty blade.

The person who had appeared in the middle of the hall folded her hands against the skirt of her gown, the silver looking almost like armor. A matching silver mask obscured her face, and when she spoke, she lifted her chin as authoritatively as a commander.

"If you wish to live, that is," she said.

"You're Ventrallan," Mather countered, stopping just shy of her. "Why would we trust you?"

The woman scoffed. "And you have so many options at the moment?"

Mather didn't get in another word before Dendera croaked, her eyes narrowing, "You. You're Duchess Brigitte, the mother of the king. I saw you with Raelyn!"

Brigitte rolled her eyes. "If I agreed with her coup, do you think I would bother to be in this filthy place"—she turned up her nose at the walls— "*alone*? Either I can regale you with an explanation, or you can follow me. As I said, I personally do not care whether you live or die, but I think you can be useful to me, so make a decision quickly."

The door at the top of the dungeon's staircase rattled. Someone had finally heard Theron's shouts.

Mather lurched toward Brigitte. She took that as acceptance and spun on her heel, her silver gown flaring as she hurried down the hall. The rest of Mather's group followed without question—what other choice did they have? He had to get out of here to make sure Meira was all right, that whomever she'd left with wasn't part of a trap of Angra's. So many secrets had come to light—Cordell had turned on Winter, Theron had turned on Meira, and the Ventrallan queen had staged a coup. Could the man Meira left with be trusted? And beyond that, Winter was still under Cordellan control—how could they free it if they were Angra's prisoners?

Brigitte ducked into a cell on the right. Mather hesitated just long enough for his eyes to adjust to the dimness. If the old hag had led them into a trap—

But at the back of the room, a door cracked open, the stone on the outward side showing that, when closed, it would blend seamlessly into the wall.

"Shut the door behind you," Brigitte called before vanishing through the opening.

"Hollis," Mather hissed. "Take the rear. Stay alert."

Hollis positioned himself inside the room to let everyone

pass. Mather followed Brigitte, muscles humming with pent-up fight. The stone deadened most sound, leaving him with only the distant clicking of the duchess's shoes moving upward—stairs. He darted after her, hoping to put enough space between him and his group that if a trap did await them, he could give a warning with plenty of time for them to make it back down.

Alone in this narrow, dark space, a crack formed in his determination. It had all happened so abruptly—the man; Meira's unexpected trust; her desperate plea for Mather to free everyone. And he had agreed, only because he hadn't seen her look like that in months. Like the eye of a storm, terrifying and brilliant and severe.

The stairwell folded into a hall. One more hall led to another staircase, and at the top of that, Brigitte's footsteps stopped. Metal jingled, thin and light—keys. Mather waited a few steps back, bracing himself for soldiers, arrows . . . Angra.

He clenched and unclenched his hands, staring sightlessly down at them in the blackness. He had killed Angra himself. He had broken the deranged king's conduit on Abril's ground and seen his body vanish.

What had that truly done to him?

Brigitte opened a door. Mather forced his eyes to adjust, lingering long enough for the yellow light to reveal a little of the room beyond: a thick scarlet rug, a short table, blue walls. No soldiers that he could see.

Brigitte stepped inside and Mather followed, a beat behind.

"Grandmamma!" came a child's cry.

They were in a bedroom filled with mahogany furniture—a table and chairs, a wide bed, a few armoires positioned between floor-to-ceiling tapestries. This door stood behind one such tapestry while two more doors waited closed at other points in the room, unhidden.

Brigitte was the mother of Jesse Donati, the Ventrallan king. The king Mather had watched go from weak to infuriated and back while his wife seized control of his kingdom. The king who sat on a padded chair before Mather now, one child in his lap, another clinging to his arm as if it were a barrier she could hide behind.

A third child, the oldest but not by much, toddled forward. "Grandmamma," she said again, tears tumbling over her lace mask.

Brigitte stroked the girl's dark curls and looked over her shoulder at Mather. "I'll help you leave, but you'll take my son and grandchildren with you."

The Ventrallan king rose. The daughter who had been hiding behind him instantly latched onto his leg, and the boy in his arms, not more than a year old, stared with wide, calm eyes from behind a small green mask.

Phil moved beside Mather, and he felt the rest of the Thaw gather around. All the time they had spent in their clandestine trainings in Jannuari had let him learn each of them by heart, and he didn't need to look to know Trace's fingers twitched over his empty knife sheaths; Eli squared his jaw in a mimic of the glowers around him; Kiefer hesitated near the back, watching, cautiously ready to help; and Hollis and Feige hovered, quiet, on the edge of the group.

It was Dendera, Conall, and Nessa whom Mather had to check on. Dendera had her arms around Nessa, freeing Conall to stand alert, his face gray and hard. His brother had died as unexpectedly as Alysson.

Mather turned away from him. He wouldn't let his own grief rise any higher. Hopefully Conall could keep himself under control too.

"Mother," Jesse said, his surprise palpable even from behind his mask. "Who are—"

"Do we have a deal?" Brigitte asked Mather.

Mather narrowed his eyes. "You're saving us?" He had little to no experience with children, but even he could tell that getting them out of the palace would be nearly impossible.

Someone in his group stepped forward. Mather expected it to be Dendera—she, of all of them, was the most capable with children, but when Mather turned, he blinked in surprise.

Nessa faced Brigitte. "Of course we have a deal."

Mather had been on the verge of saying the same thing. Impossible or no, they wouldn't leave children here, defenseless. What surprised Mather was the ease with which Nessa moved forward and knelt in front of the oldest girl.

"Hi there," she said. "I'm Nessa. And that's my brother, Conall."

Conall gaped when his sister pointed up at him, but he managed a small bow at the princess.

"Melania," the girl told Nessa, rolling her *l* on an awkward tongue.

The smile Nessa gave her was impossibly soft for someone whose eyes still looked so haunted. "Well, Melania, how would you like to go on an adventure?"

Melania looked up at her grandmother. Brigitte's sternness melted as she smiled, and Melania placed her small fingers in Nessa's outstretched hand.

Things happened quickly after that. Brigitte pulled blankets and other meager supplies out of her armoires; Dendera and, more surprising still, Hollis eased forward to coax the other two children into coming on the same "adventure."

The room began to hum with movement, but the Ventrallan king stayed motionless before his chair. He didn't hold his son anymore—the boy now clung to Hollis—but instead stared at the floor with jaw-clenched ferocity.

"I have to go after her," the king said suddenly, echoing Mather's own looping thoughts.

Mather picked a dagger from the supplies, unsure of how to respond. No one else said a word. "Your wife sided with Angra," he tried. "Freeing her—"

"I don't give a damn about Raelyn," the king snapped, and something in his words made Brigitte, across the room, stop folding a blanket.

"No. I will not let you get yourself killed for—"

"For whom?" The king whirled on his mother. "You've called her many things over the years. Useless, harmful— a whore. But it would seem *Raelyn* is the one who most strongly embodies those attributes. So do not tell me not to go after Ceridwen."

By the time he finished, the room was silent. Mather felt that name dredge up memories of Meira's parting words. She had told him to save Ceridwen. Why would the Ventrallan king care about the Summerian princess too?

But the look on the king's face told Mather exactly why he cared.

Brigitte's lips puckered. She didn't utter another word before her son removed his dark green mask and pointed it at her.

"I'm not leaving until I break this mask and save Ceridwen."

Mather frowned. "Break your mask?"

The king didn't miss a beat, as though he had repeated this explanation to himself many times. "To break one's mask in the presence of someone you reject is an act of permanent separation. To say that you are finished with them in your life, so much so that you do not worry about them seeing your true face. You'll never see them again, so your secrets are nothing in their hands."

Mather nodded. It mattered little what the king wanted to do, honestly—if Jesse intended to confront his wife and save Ceridwen, Mather would follow, especially if it meant he could complete one of the tasks Meira had entrusted to him.

"Everyone else should escape while they can," Mather said, aiming the order at his group. "I'll accompany the king out of the palace. There's something I need to do as well."

"You're leaving us too?" Kiefer snapped.

But Phil stepped forward, his eyes on Mather's. "He's going after our queen."

Mather bowed his head in response. He expected more protest, but all that met him was silence, even from Kiefer. They realized the seriousness of Meira's situation—how she had left with someone none of them knew, and could at this moment be fighting for her life. . . .

Thankfully, Dendera picked up where he could not. "Bring her back. The rest of us"—she shrugged toward his Thaw, Nessa, and Conall—"will get the children to safety."

And then what? Mather held back the question, because he knew the answers too well. They would have to face the Cordellan takeover of Winter and whatever Angra was doing to the world, and bringing Meira back would put her at the center of those conflicts.

But she was the queen. She was *his* queen. Whatever she

wanted Winter to do in this brewing war, he would obey—but never again would he leave her to face any conflict alone.

Dendera turned to Brigitte. "How do we leave?"

It took visible force for Brigitte to look away from her son, and when she did, she ran a hand along her own mask as if making sure it was still in place. "There's another passageway, just through here," she said, and moved to a different tapestry.

But as Dendera neared it, Nessa put a hand on her arm.

"Where will we go?" she whispered. Melania clutched Nessa's skirts, burrowing into her, and Nessa straightened. "Winter is no longer safe."

"There's a Summerian refugee camp," Jesse offered, "a day's ride from where the Southern Eldridge Forest meets the Langstone River. You'll be safe there."

"Fine," Dendera said. "We'll steal some horses. A carriage, maybe, or a boat, and we'll meet you there." She pinned Mather with a gaze that told him it wasn't a suggestion. He *would* make it, with Meira, to that camp.

Dendera shifted the princess in her arms as the king bade a final farewell to his daughter. A kiss on her forehead, then one each for his son and other daughter, quickly, as if he didn't trust himself to linger over good-byes. When he turned away, his eyes were bloodshot, tears welling—there was pain on his face, but determination.

The king faced Brigitte, but she looked at Mather now. "Go down the way we came," she told him. "At the second landing, turn left—there's a door that will take you into the main hall."

"Thank you," Mather said as Dendera, Nessa, and Conall started moving for the other passage. Hollis held the Ventrallan prince, and it was plain on Hollis's face as well as Feige's that they knew they had to follow Dendera. The rest of the Thaw lingered, casting uncertain glances at Mather. He would have taken them in an instant if he didn't need to travel quickly, even faster than they had traveled here from Winter. Plus, the children needed all the protection they could get—of the group, only Dendera had ever truly fought, though Conall looked as deadly as any soldier Mather had seen.

Mather still swallowed a pang of reluctance. He felt stronger with his Thaw. More complete.

Hollis broke the Thaw's uncertainty with a grunt. "We will not be defeated," he said, a quiet declaration—the same pledge from their training.

Mather smiled. "We will not be defeated."

Hollis and Feige moved, with Eli closing in to coax his brother on. Kiefer jerked away and dove into the new passage, face dark, shoulders slumped.

Trace hesitated, sucking in a breath like he had questions prepared, but he just shrugged. "We'll race you to the camp," he teased with a flash of a smile.

Only Phil remained, motionless.

"Go," Mather told him. "The others need you."

Phil cocked a brow. "Sorry, Once-King—you're stuck with me."

"Phil, I'm serious."

Any further protest shriveled in the way Phil looked at him. "We're in this together. All of us. And if any of us splits off from the rest, he won't go alone."

Feige's head whipped up from where she followed Hollis into the passage. "Or *she*."

Phil smiled. "Or she. Point is, I'm coming with you."

His grin was infectious, his confidence resolute.

Mather found himself relenting.

In truth, he was glad not to be alone.

Moments later, the door to the new passage shut with a soft thud, leaving Mather alone with Jesse, Phil, and Brigitte.

Brigitte arranged herself on a chair, wrinkled mouth pursed. Jesse stepped up to her as Mather moved back to the first passage. He waved Phil through and hesitated.

"Thank you," Jesse said to his mother.

Brigitte shrugged. "Go. Raelyn will soon notice I had you moved to my chambers."

The king wrapped his fingers around his mother's shoulder with a delicate squeeze. Finally she looked up at him, the stoniness in her eyes dissipating in a tear-glazed rush.

"Go," she whispered. "I'll be fine."

Mather's throat swelled, and he looked away, eyes stinging.

Jesse pushed himself past Mather, into the passage.

Brigitte adjusted her gown and leveled her eyes at the door Raelyn would no doubt barrel through at any moment with a retaliation just as harsh as the one she had dealt the Summerian king. Mather had seen only the end of that fight, the Summerian king's neck snapping, but that had been enough to confirm that Raelyn showed no mercy.

Mather ducked into the stairwell and shut the door behind him. The bolt clicked.

There was no going back now. For anyone.

Ceridwen

THE INSIDE OF Simon's brothel wagon was musky with sweat and plumeria incense, the air hazy with smoke that hadn't been ventilated properly, the floor covered by silk pillows and satin quilts. Ceridwen had never been inside one of her brother's wagons, despite his endless prodding for her to "be a true Summerian" and join his exploits. As she drew her knees to her chin now, all she could hear were the teasing reprimands she had hated for so long.

And the grating pop of his neck when Raelyn had snapped it.

The wagon jostled, oxen tugging it through Rintiero's streets, and Ceridwen let her body sway with it, too exhausted to fight its movements.

"Cerie." Lekan crouched before her, wincing until he straightened his leg and dropped to the floor of the wagon. A gash cut across his knee, another stretched down his cheek, and she knew the rest of his body was just as covered in wounds. "Cerie—"

But his voice broke. What could he say? What could *she* say?

Ceridwen closed her eyes. In her mind, Simon's face flared purple from Raelyn's choking magic.

"Stop . . . Raelyn . . . leave her alone!"

Simon had pleaded for her life. Even though, minutes before, Ceridwen had barged into the square intent on murdering him herself.

And before she had been able to utter more than a feeble croak of protest, his head had jolted to the side, cracking his life away with it.

Ceridwen opened her eyes.

Lekan tore a section of blanket and worked at wiping the blood off her arms.

"Leave it," she bit through clenched teeth.

He didn't listen. "He was your brother. You loved him," he whispered quietly.

Ceridwen's muscles turned to stone. "I hated him."

Lekan's fingers tightened around the ragged strip of satin and he scrubbed harder at her shoulder. He stayed silent, eyes on his work, like he was just a normal slave and she a normal princess and the stains on her body weren't her brother's blood.

Ceridwen stared at the splatters. Raelyn's joy had been demented as she had ordered Simon's head to be severed.

And as a soldier had begun sawing at her brother's neck, Ceridwen hadn't been able to back away from the blood that had spurted under the pressure of the knife.

Simon was dead. His body, decapitated before her.

Ceridwen shoved Lekan away and tried to scramble to her feet. The shortness of the wagon's roof made it impossible and her back cut along the stained ceiling. She toppled forward, wrists popping as they caught her weight, the wagon rocking with her frenzy.

"Quiet in there!" a Ventrallan soldier shouted from outside.

Ceridwen leaped up again and slammed her whole body into the side of the wagon until it teetered even more, but it didn't break stride as it continued to haul them through the city. She screamed, reared back, slammed again, because if she didn't let it out in some form, her body wouldn't be able to sustain the misery within her.

She shouldn't feel miserable for Simon's death. She had *wanted* him to die—she had wanted him to feel just a piece of the terror he inflicted on his slaves. She had wanted that damned eternal smile of his to burn out so that he'd weep for forgiveness instead of brightening at the sight of her.

Ceridwen choked, sobs twisting in her throat.

He always brightened when he saw her. He'd smile like she was his favorite person in all of Summer, and that made her whole body feel like it was incinerating. She remembered when he'd first met Meira in his brothel in what should have been some show of politics, but his primary concern had been where Ceridwen was, whether he could see her.

Flame and heat, he had always *loved her*, even as he destroyed their kingdom and drove their people to destitution. She had wanted, more than anything, for him to hate her, because—

Then, maybe, she could hate *him*.

Lekan clamped his arms around Ceridwen and jerked her down as a blade shot through the narrow window, the one that had been boarded up shortly after they were tossed inside. A flash of silver licked the air above Ceridwen's head.

The remnants of her screams made her throat raw, pain shooting through her mouth. It was fitting for sorrow to hurt, especially this sorrow, this . . . betrayal.

That was what it was. She had turned her back on Simon. And he had still loved her.

Ceridwen desperately clutched Lekan, unable to relax for fear of what she might do again. There was nothing left in her, very little that Raelyn could take from her. Ceridwen had given up Jesse hours before, and now Raelyn had taken Simon and Summer, too.

But no, it hadn't been Raelyn. It had been Angra, if Raelyn's mad ramblings were to be believed. Ceridwen found herself wishing it *was* all Raelyn. She hadn't the slightest idea how to go about undoing what Angra had done. She didn't even entirely know the extent of all that had happened—he had given Raelyn *magic*. He had given Simon the power to control non-Summerians.

This war was so much bigger than her. Corrupt kings, she could handle; but *this*? Dark magic and webs of evil that stretched through all of Primoria?

Terror threatened to cripple her, but she inhaled the smoky, nauseatingly sweet air, using Lekan to orient herself.

"Meira got away," she told him, because she needed to believe it. "She'll stop . . . this."

One of Lekan's arms unhooked from her and dropped with a thud against the wagon floor. He flexed his fingers, rubbed his injured leg, and hissed in pain at one of the movements.

Ceridwen ripped sections from another quilt and made a pathetic compress before Lekan could protest. She tightened it over his knee and rubbed her hands on her thighs, working rational thoughts back into her mind.

"They locked the doors?" she asked, more of herself than him.

Lekan adjusted the compress. "Raelyn left five guards for us, took the rest with her." He paused, and Ceridwen knew what other piece of information flitted through his mind that he didn't voice aloud.

She also took Simon's head with her.

Ceridwen crawled to the doors at the back of the wagon and pressed on them. Sure enough, they held, so she fumbled around the edges for a weak point in the frame, or a splinter of wood she could pry free to replace the weapons they had been stripped of. She found nothing.

But the blankets and pillows—they could be tied together into something like rope, which could be used to choke unsuspecting soldiers when they opened the wagon doors. That would no doubt happen in the palace complex, where Raelyn would have many more than just five soldiers waiting to subdue her prisoners. Ceridwen could use one soldier as a hostage, keeping the satin rope tight around his windpipe until she and Lekan scrambled free.

But Raelyn still had control of the city. She was filled with Angra's dark magic.

And she intended to murder Jesse and his children.

Ceridwen grabbed the nearest blanket and started tearing. Lekan shifted to lean more completely against the wall, his gaze hard on the ceiling in an effort to ignore his pain. He was too injured to be of any use in a fight. Ceridwen needed to get him to safety, then come back, and—what? Take down the entire Ventrallan army on her own? Surely someone in Rintiero was still loyal to Jesse and would help her save him and his children. She would have to find them—or Meira. Meira would help her.

Unless Raelyn had already killed her. The entire city could have bowed to Raelyn's coup, and Jesse and his children could be dead, and every last trace of hope could have been snuffed out while Ceridwen sat helpless in a wagon.

Her hands stilled. The emptiness inside her whispered

that she shouldn't care so much what Raelyn did to Jesse. She had been pretending for four years that she didn't care what Raelyn did to him—why should she start now?

But every other part of her screamed in protest. This wasn't at all like it had been for those four years. This wasn't just ignoring the fact that Raelyn would sleep with Jesse in the same bed in which Ceridwen herself had slept with him—this was ignoring the fact that Raelyn would *kill him*. And not just him, but his children, and Ceridwen didn't care what had recently happened between herself and Jesse—she would not let his children die. Part of what had always made it so difficult to leave him was how much he loved his children. A man, a *king*, who crawled on the floor of his daughter's bedroom just to make her squeal with laughter . . .

Ceridwen would free Jesse and his children. That would be the first step in this war—free the Ventrallan king. Find the Winterian queen. Regroup against Angra, and make him pay for daring to claim Summer—and for letting Raelyn kill Simon.

She could do that.

"Halt!"

Ceridwen stiffened, her eyes flicking to the wagon door as the entire structure rolled to a stop. She flung herself at the one narrow crack in the patched-up window, soaking up what information she could before she jerked back in case another stray blade poked through. They weren't at the palace yet, but rather still in the city, surrounded by Rintiero's multicolored buildings, the magentas and olives mostly coated in shadow now.

Lekan frowned at Ceridwen. Why had they stopped?

They both stayed silent. Ceridwen shifted into a crouch, the quilt-braid taut between both of her wrists.

A horse whinnied. "We wish to purchase the contents of this wagon," a voice said, and Ceridwen strained to place it. Not someone she knew, and not one of the soldiers guarding them.

A man laughed. "Forget it—we have our orders."

"Orders, yes. But do you have gold?"

Coins jingled. *Lots* of coins, from what Ceridwen could tell. Someone was buying them?

Her nostrils flared. Probably a perverted Ventrallan lord who had seen the Summerian wagon and thought what all people thought when they saw Summer's flame—slaves for sale.

One of the soldiers whistled. Silence held for a beat.

"You can even keep the wagon," the purchaser prodded. "Don't want your queen finding out anything too soon."

Your queen. This person wasn't Ventrallan.

Finally the lead soldier snorted. The coins jingled again. "They're all yours."

Keys rattled. Footsteps moved toward the door. Ceridwen lifted higher, her body pivoted between Lekan and whoever might come at them. She slowed her breath, but her heart didn't listen, thumping against her ribs as a key slid into the lock.

The door creaked open.

She slid forward, ready to lunge—

The buyer, a soldier, blinked at her in the hazy light from lampposts along the road. His skin shone black against the encroaching shadows, and behind him, a woman stood among a cluster of horses and more soldiers. Her dark hair was knotted into a bun just above the stiff collar of her gray wool gown. On her back, glinting in the twilight, sat an ax.

The fight drained out of Ceridwen on a rush of breath.

"Giselle?"

The queen of Yakim had bought them.

Meira

THE FIRST THOUGHT that hits me when I wake up is: *I'm really tired of passing out because of magic.*

A small fire clicks and pops to my left, its smoke permeating the air. I force my eyes open, thankful I'm met with the manageable darkness of night instead of an explosion of sunlight, my head thumping in time with the passing seconds.

"You can heal yourself, you know," comes Rares's voice.

I roll onto my side, my fingers digging into my forehead in an attempt to push away the last remnants of agony. A ring of trees surrounds our clearing, thick foliage hanging from drooping branches. Rares doesn't look up from where he's running a sharpening stone against one of the kitchen knives I stole.

"If I knew how to control my magic that well, I wouldn't have followed you," I snap. "What did you even do to me? *How* did you do it?"

Rares tests the blade with his thumb and sighs. "I'd expect ill-cared-for knives in a pauper's kitchen, but the Ventrallan king's? This is a disgrace."

My glare deadens. He mutters that not even chickens deserve to be butchered by such blades.

Just as I draw in a breath to shout my questions at him, Rares looks up.

"Maybe I should teach you patience first."

I pull onto my knees, fighting a wave of dizziness. I'm so close to the fire that sparks shoot off the crackling branches and prickle against my skin.

"How do you have magic?" I demand, my voice flat. "And how can you use it on me?"

Rares rests his elbows on his knees, fiddling with the knife as he considers me. "You're worried I won't explain myself, and that even if I do, I won't tell you everything, and you'll be left with incomplete information. You're worried that you made a mistake in trusting me, but even more that you didn't find me soon enough. Did I cover everything, dear heart?"

"I—"

"And while I could assure you that I'm nothing like your previous mentors, I'll do you one better—now that we're safe, or as safe as we can be, I'll tell you everything, as I promised I would. Every detail, every reason, every flutter of a curtain that brought us to this moment. Well, not *every* curtain—some of them have been right gaudy."

"But . . . why?"

"Tassels, mostly."

"No," I groan. "Why would you tell me everything?"

He blinks. "Why not?"

I sink to the ground. Just this easily? I'm used to arguments—me begging Sir to explain things or me begging Hannah to tell more.

Rares goes back to sharpening the knife, and after a breath, he starts, his voice detached, as if he doesn't hear himself. "I know your mother told you how the Decay first ravaged the world. It was a byproduct of people using magic for evil acts, and Primoria's monarchs countered it by collecting their citizens' conduits through a violent purge."

I have to bite my tongue to keep from asking how he knows what Hannah told me, afraid that if I speak, he'll realize how freely he's giving me this information.

"Thousands died," he continues. "Even more were possessed by the Decay, lost to evil desires. It was a time of desperation—and that led the world's monarchs to create the Royal Conduits in the hope that such large amounts of magic would cleanse the world of the Decay—and they did, for a time. One for each kingdom, four linked to female heirs, four to male heirs. Paisly was no different, except in our refusal to bow to our monarch's power as easily as the rest of the world.

"We saw a violent cycle beginning. We saw magic still

in use, great stores of it connected to eight people who could become power-hungry. How could they be trusted not to turn corrupt and reintroduce the Decay to our world? Magic had no place here—its price was too high. We formed a rebel group, the Order of the Lustrate, that stood against our queen." Rares pauses, his gaze lifting from the knife to me. "And our rebellion was successful."

"Paisly has no queen?" I barely hear the question fill the space between us.

"We have a regent who plays the part of queen whenever such a figure is needed, but Paisly has no queen—or Royal Conduit.

"The night of the rebellion, the Paislian queen refused to negotiate," he continues. "She saw a threat against her kingdom, not the salvation we claimed. And in the battle, she sacrificed herself for her kingdom—moments after the Order broke her Royal Conduit, a shield."

"What?" I pant, folding my arms around my torso as if holding on to myself is the only way to make sure his words are real, not some bedtime story told around campfires.

Rares's dark eyes stay on mine. "No one realized what we had done until it was far too late. Everyone in Paisly, from the queen's supporters to the Order's members, became infused with magic. We all became conduits—just as your mother wanted for Winter."

Shock makes me rock forward. "How do you know that?"

But Rares presses on. "The queen's supporters were

badly outnumbered after the rebellion. The Order came into power and has ruled Paisly ever since. And it is still our belief that magic has no place in this world—which is why we have kept our kingdom as secret as possible. Of course, occasional interactions with other kingdoms are unavoidable, but it is amazing what you can hide when no one knows what to look for. Especially when your kingdom is in a mountain range." He winks. "Mighty easy to hide things in mountains."

My mouth bobs open. What Hannah wanted to happen in Winter *already* happened in another kingdom—magic spread to every citizen when their conduit broke and their queen sacrificed herself. An entire land of people like me, who are themselves conduits for a magic they never wanted. No wonder Rares said Paisly is safe from Angra.

I lean forward excitedly. "Then you can stop Angra. Paisly can rally an army and have him defeated in a matter of—"

Rares's look silences me. "Though every Paislian is a conduit, there weren't many of us left after the war. Which is why we took the approach we did—our members have been waiting all over Primoria for a conduit-wielder whose goals aligned with our own. The Order has been building a defense—but Angra's forces include the armies of at least three kingdoms now, and every soldier is infused with his magic. We could hold him off well enough in Paisly's mountains, but we do not have the manpower to defeat his threat on our own. But we will help you—the Order may believe that magic has no place in Primoria, but our circumstances have forced us to become experts in it. We'll help you learn how to control it so you can use it the way you plan to—to get the other keys to the chasm from Angra and destroy all magic."

My heart nearly ricochets out of my chest. "You know about that, too?"

Rares smiles sadly, the fire reflecting yellow in his dark eyes. "Being part of the same magic allows for a mental connection. Touching another conduit intensifies the reaction—you've experienced that through skin-to-skin contact with other conduit-wielders. But truly strong conduits can access thoughts and memories without physical touch—until you trust your magic enough to use it all the time, to block such intrusions. You're welcome, by the way, for getting Angra out of your mind. Someday you'll have to hold him off on your own, but for now, he can't access your thoughts."

I touch my temple. "Wait—could Angra hear my thoughts before I knew he was alive?"

Rares nods once. "Yes."

Nausea grips me and I reel forward, head in my hands. He could have heard anything—all my plans, all my feeble attempts to stop him. It had nothing to do with him touching me. He could have talked to me *whenever he wanted*. Who else could he do this to?

But I know. He did it to Theron—he could do this to

anyone who isn't actively protected from his Decay by pure conduit magic.

I glare at the flames before me. "So you fought him off for me. But *how*? I'm not Paislian, and Paisly's magic should only affect your people."

"Magic rules are different for human conduits," Rares says. "I couldn't affect a normal Winterian, but you are filled with the same magic that runs through my body. We're linked, just as I'm sure you've discovered you're connected to other conduit-bearers. Though the Royal Conduits were created to obey only certain bloodlines, the magic in them is, at its core, the same—and therefore, all conduit-wielders are connected. I'm sorry for the unconsciousness, but your endurance will increase. You were only out for about three hours, not even long enough for me to carry you out of Ventralli."

I gawk at him. I wasted three hours *sleeping*.

Anything could have happened in that time. Mather and the Winterians could be safely out of Rintiero—or everything I fear could have come to pass. And not only that, but if we're going to Paisly, the journey will take weeks—every moment we waste is another moment that Angra's grip on the world tightens.

And I don't even know his plan. I don't know what he intends to do next, who he will kill, which kingdom he wants to destroy first. . . .

Metallic anxiety fills my throat, making it impossible to swallow, to breathe, to do anything but stare at Rares as the thudding ache across my skull resumes.

No time to waste.

"You said you'll help me get the keys from him," I force out. "With all the Order's knowledge, you must have asked your magic how to destroy it too. And it told you the same thing it told me—by sacrificing a conduit and returning it to the chasm?"

Rares nods slowly.

"And you're going to help me get the keys from Angra," I repeat. "You're going to help *me* destroy all magic. So—"

Memories flutter across my mind. The chasm and its electric, destructive fingers of magic that could only inhabit objects—when people attempted to let the magic touch them, it incinerated them as thoroughly as a lightning strike.

My anxiety is replaced by dread when Rares's gaze doesn't break from mine.

"There's no other way to destroy magic," I guess, the words coming from somewhere deep inside me, somewhere numb. "You're going to help me die."

That makes Rares drop the knife and sharpening stone. He swings onto his hands and knees and closes the distance between him and me, moving close enough that I can feel the severity radiating off him as surely as I can feel the heat from the fire beside us.

"For nearly two thousand years, my people have lived in a state of regret for what the Order did to Paisly," he tells me. "By the time we could use our magic to figure out how to destroy it, we realized we would have had to get every Paislian to willingly throw themselves into the chasm. We are *all* Paisly's conduit now. So we have been observing the world's rulers in stealth through our link to their magic, hiding knowledge of the conduits' true limits from any who would seek to abuse them, hoping that a ruler would come to the same conclusion we had—that magic is too dangerous. We had hoped, of course, that this monarch would only need to throw their object conduit into the chasm. But you are the first conduit-wielder in centuries who has decided that the negatives of magic outweigh any benefits. Not even your mother sought such a thing."

I flinch at the mention of Hannah, expecting her voice in my head again—but no. She's gone. And that feels far more liberating than it should.

Even when she tried to help me, she never actually helped *me*—she merely scrambled to fix her own mistakes, and as I look at Rares now, hoping to see some other emotion beyond his odd mix of remorse and eagerness, all I see is a door. The same door Hannah guided me toward, one leading away from a world of chaos and pain, control and destruction.

But unlike Hannah, Rares is willing to help me understand all this. He can help me control my magic so I have a better weapon when I face Angra to get the other two chasm keys. Rares and his people have had centuries to study their magic—maybe they can help me come to a place where my fear evaporates into resolve.

"Are you sure telling me all this is a good idea?" I ask. "You don't want to hide it from me so I misinterpret something and make a mistake?"

Rares puts his hand on my shoulder, a steady pressure that makes me start. "You are not what you've done. Who you are right now, this moment, is who you choose to be."

"Who I choose to be," I echo. "I'm incapable of making the right choices lately."

I left everyone I care about in Rintiero's dungeon. I let three wasted hours pass. I—

Rares lifts his hand, coils his finger, and flicks me in the forehead.

I slap my palm over the stinging spot. "What—"

But he shakes the offending finger at me. "Consider this the first lesson as I teach you how to fully harness your magic: I will not stand for such talk about the person who will save us, especially from said person."

"How is that a lesson?" I squeak.

"You'll think twice before you try to be too hard on yourself next time. Now, since we've started our lessons, let's move on to lesson two, shall we?"

I let my hand drop. "What about everyone back in Rintiero? Can we find out what happened to them first? What if Angra—"

I can't finish the question.

Rares squints. "Angra hasn't found your friends in

Rintiero. At least, not all of them—if he had your allies, he wouldn't be bothering trying to track us. He'd just have them killed and let you seek him out in retaliation."

So much about that makes me anxious. "What? How do you know? And—wait, he's still tracking us? I thought you blocked him?"

"Blocked him from entering your mind—but his magic is still probing the world, searching for us. Once we get to Paisly, we should be safe from his intrusions entirely—the Order keeps a barrier in place. Now." Rares clucks his tongue as if chastising himself for letting me linger on my worries and picks a leaf from the ground beside him. "Lesson two." He lays the leaf across his palm. "Lift this leaf into the air. Your magic allows you to affect anything or anyone in existence. As you did in Putnam, when you not so gracefully threw your guards."

Conall and Garrigan. They flew through the air because of my desperation for them to get away from me so I wouldn't, ironically enough, use my magic on them.

"They were Winterians," I say. "But I shouldn't be able to affect people or objects unrelated to Winter."

But I *did* affect something unrelated to Winter—in Summer, when I panicked on the roof in the palace complex and made it snow.

"Normally Royal Conduits only have enough magic in them to do things like make crops grow or bring rain during droughts," Rares says, "and even then, only in their designated kingdoms. But *being* a conduit extends the limits, as you have seen through your skin-to-skin contact with other wielders—you *are* magic, and so are connected in a larger way. This enables you to affect other lands as well. Not other people who aren't connected to your kingdom, unless they have magic connections themselves, but objects. It allows you to manipulate what—"

"No," I snap. "I'm not going to *manipulate* anything."

"I don't mean manipulate as in an evil act that can feed the Decay. This leaf"—he shakes it—"knows nothing of good or evil. An evil act occurs only when it interferes with another's ability to make their own choice and thus results in pain, sorrow, fear, or the like. Murder, for instance, when someone would be killed and therefore robbed of their ability to choose to live."

I gape at him. "So when I threw Conall and Garrigan . . ."

Snow above, *no*. Did I inadvertently do something that fed the Decay?

"Your guards reeked of loyalty to you," Rares says. "What you did to them didn't interfere with their ability to make their own decisions—they would have chosen to do anything you asked of them. Though they did receive a few bumps and bruises, didn't they? But again, it was something they gladly accepted, however unconsciously."

That does shockingly little to alleviate my horror.

"Lift the leaf," Rares prods. "I won't let you lose control."

My magic has remained blissfully quiet since my earlier

collapse, and I'm in no hurry to awaken it. "I'd be able to stay in control if the barrier in the Tadil Mine hadn't done something to me. Every time I open up to my magic, it comes pouring out of me, and I—"

Rares stops me with a huff. "The magic barrier would've hurt, but it wouldn't have affected your magic in that way. Magic is all about choice, and somewhere in your mind, even if it was the quietest hint of wanting or panic or worry, you wanted all the things you did."

I wheeze as though his words punched me in the gut. "This was all . . . me?"

Rares's hand remains steady. "That's a different lesson. All you have to do for this one is look at this leaf and want it to lift into the air."

My mind thuds from these revelations and I twitch, rubbing my arms. Each passing minute burns my skin like the sparks from the fire. We need to *leave*—we need to get to Paisly so I can get what help the Order can offer, come back, get the keys from Angra, reach the magic chasm, and save everyone.

So I can die.

I grind my jaw as Rares meets my gaze.

When I filled Sir with strength in Gaos, when I blocked Hannah from speaking to me, when I made it snow in Juli, when I threw Conall and Garrigan—none of that was wanting. This *is wanting—and I want this shriveled bit of vegetation to smack Rares in the face.*

A chill vibrates in my chest, and all I have time to do is

blink before the leaf flies at Rares and slaps him straight across the forehead.

I smack both hands over my mouth.

Rares grins as the leaf flutters into his lap. "I suppose I deserved that," he admits. "But now you'll better understand the rest of our journey."

"How?"

He hops up to kick dirt over the fire. The flames extinguish with a hiss, leaving us in shadows. I barely make out Rares extending a hand to me.

"Because it will be just like what you did, only on a grander scale."

I'm so relieved to be leaving that I take his hand.

Rares drags me to my feet, but I don't see anything. Not just don't—*can't*, because the moment I'm standing, the forest evaporates into blackness, the moist warmth replaced by biting cold, the delicate breeze by stinging, icy wind. I gag on the sudden thinness of the air, and all I know beyond my shock is that we're no longer in Ventralli.

Rares is *moving* us. And not just up slightly and back down—I feel the distance flying beneath us as surely as I see blackness all around. We're spiraling in a surge of magic, the air sparking with electricity that eats at my skin. My heart lodges so tightly in my throat, I wonder if it will ever loosen; my palms are slick with so much sweat that I fear I'll lose my grip on Rares's hand and go spiraling into oblivion.

Rares must sense my terror, because he wraps his arms

around me. The silence of being suspended wherever we are, of being held tight in protective arms, pulls my mind to the last time someone wrapped me up like this—Sir, in Angra's cruel vision months ago. When I knelt on the floor of the cottage in Winter and he tucked me into his arms and everything was perfect.

No—everything was not perfect. The real Sir would never hug me like that. Like *this*.

I stumble back, trembling, on solid ground once again. We're not in the forest anymore—we're in a cave. Behind me, orange light dances.

Those details register in my mind as everything in my stomach rushes for my throat and I topple forward, retching.

Rares crouches next to me. "You handled it better than I did my first time. I vomited, passed out, woke up, and vomited again—all before I'd even reached the destination."

I heave once more. "Passing out doesn't feel that far off."

Rares takes my elbow. "Let's get you up, then. No time for unconsciousness here."

My blubber of protest goes unheard, and as soon as I'm vertical, he shifts, pointing into the tunnel. "Can't see it, but this leads to the widest valley on the western edge of the Paisels. Not many know of this route, but the tunnel cuts through the mountains and into Paisly—it's a two-week trip otherwise. This shortcut was my backup option if you hadn't been able to grasp the moving-leaf concept, but thank our lucky magic you did, because I right *hate* traveling, even if it'd only be a few days. The one thing about being a conduit I'll miss—the ease of transportation."

"You used magic to fly us to Paisly?" I choke down another roll of nausea. "Who else is capable of using their magic like that?"

But I know the answer before Rares looks at me.

"As I said, Paisly keeps a barrier up to prevent any outside magic from intruding. The only outsider who can use his magic to travel is Angra, as he's a conduit just as we are, but he can only use that ability on his Spring citizens or himself. It isn't technically an aspect of the Decay—not unless he intended to hurt someone with it. Basically, Angra would be a fool to use it, as he can't transport his entire army, and that plus the barrier means you're safe here."

Yet again, Rares's explanation does little to quench my terror. But I nod, accepting it.

Rares squishes his face. "Anyway. We're not quite in Paisly yet."

He turns. Behind us, a man stands in the glow of the torches. Exhaustion trembles in my every limb, but I hook my thumbs into the straps of my chakram's empty holster.

Rares waves at him. "Alin, Meira—Meira, Alin."

Alin tips his head at me but spins away to face a solid wall of rock—the end of the tunnel.

As Alin braces his hands against the wall, Rares leans over to me.

"He's a soldier under me in the Order. Don't worry; I can keep him from hearing your thoughts. This entrance has been under my guard for, well, ever. The whole kingdom is in a valley, which makes controlling who comes and goes a rather respected position."

My eyes flash wide when Alin shoves the wall, causing it to move. Like Conall and Garrigan when I threw them; like the leaf in Rares's palm; like us as we hurtled from Ventralli to the tunnel. What had once been a solid dead end shifts bit by bit to reveal—Paisly.

Night envelops the area, but thanks to the moon, I'm able to see the gray castle that sits just below this entrance and, even farther down, a village wrapped in shadow. Even the outline of distant peaks on the horizon is visible, a contrast of darkness against the paler black-gray sky.

Rares and Alin step ahead, talking on the cliff outside the entrance, giving me a much-needed reprieve, alone in the cave.

Meira.

My heart stops with a jolt.

Did Rares drop the protection he put on my mind? He said that the Order kept a barrier around Paisly, so Angra wouldn't be able to reach me here.

I look at the floor of the cave, then Rares outside, a stone sinking through my gut.

I'm not in Paisly yet.

Meira

RARES GLANCES BACK at me with a frown as I sprint for the entrance. I don't make it two paces before a force drives me to my knees.

You thought you could escape me? Angra jeers. *You've never escaped me, Highness, and you never will.*

My vision distorts, the twitching orange of this cave rippling away in favor of utter blackness. I fight it, getting patches of Rares and Alin racing back for me interspersed with Angra materializing in the gloom of my mind, his face contorted in a snarl.

Through my terror, one clarifying thought rises from Rares's earlier explanation: *"Being part of the same magic allows for a mental connection. Touching another conduit intensifies the reaction...."*

I ignore everything around me—Rares and Alin shouting, Rares's magic tingling on my skin—and see only

Angra's image in my mind. He's there, all of him, watching me from the shadows.

Without considering the ramifications, I reach out and grab his wrist.

Shock is clear on Angra's face. He may not be here physically, but he is in my head, and I am touching him now.

I use this one small opportunity to delve into his mind. I want to know so many things—if he caught my friends; what he made Cordell do to Winter; what his ultimate plan is—

I feel the last inquiry connect, and every other sensation dissolves around me.

A young Angra crouches in the halls of Abril's palace, a woman's head in his lap, her blood staining the obsidian.

I've seen this before—or, rather, I saw Theron's memory of this, one of the things Angra shared with him while he was a prisoner in Spring.

In Angra's lap, his mother's lips quiver. "Please," she moans. "Please stop him."

The scene changes and I see an older Angra, huddled in one of Yakim's universities, poring over books, then standing in Summer, beseeching their king to teach him about magic, anything he can use to overthrow his father. Because this is long ago, only the smaller conduits exist, and for every conduit Angra uses, his father has one to match. But the kingdoms of the world have no time to help a desperate Spring prince when their lands are being savaged by the Decay.

The solution to the Decay comes in the form of the Royal Conduits.

Angra sees his father gather every small conduit from Spring and return from the chasm with a staff of ultimate power.

Angra tries to combat the staff. Blood and punches and magic fly, and he crawls away in a bloody heap every time. His father is too powerful now—but his father is prideful and stupid, and Angra tricks him one night into releasing the staff. One moment is all he needs.

But his father still lives, lying broken on the floor of the throne room, and Angra can't use the staff until his father is dead. He doesn't want to kill his father—no, he wants his father to suffer first. But how, if Angra has no magic himself?

The Decay. The other Royal Conduits made it weak, but it is strong enough to infect one sad, broken man.

Angra keeps his father alive at first. But the Decay needs magic to feed off soon, so Angra kills his father in a glorious display of blood and revenge.

The staff links to Angra, and the Decay morphs with it. Angra rejoices in the power he and the Decay accumulate over decades of control.

From that, an image unfolds—the future he wants. One of control, where all who oppose him cower as his father cowered, slaves to their darkest emotion—which he will be sure is fear. Only fear. He made it so in his kingdom, and he will make it so the world over.

He wants to make all of Primoria his Spring.

Cold air fills my lungs.

I'm crouched on the cliff outside the cave's entrance, fingers tight on the ledge. Rares and Alin kneel on either side of me, their hands on my shoulders, panting as hard as I am.

"Meira," Rares says. "I'm so sorry. I dropped the protection too soon—"

"No." I shake my head, unable to get my breath under control. "I'm . . . glad for it."

Rares stares in disbelief. I stay there, fumbling for explanation, until I realize I don't have to explain at all.

Instead, I twist toward him and press my hand to his, willing him to open up and see what I saw.

He sits there, and all I can read on his dark face is an ancient horror. He flips his hand over to squeeze my fingers, his gaze moving to Alin.

"Stay on guard," he says. "If anyone approaches—*anyone*—notify me immediately."

Rares leaps up and starts down a sloping path carved into the mountain. I scramble to my feet as Alin returns to the cave, the wall closing behind him with a burst of air.

"Wait! We're going to stay here?" I chase after Rares. "We know what Angra wants now—we have to warn everyone—"

"To what purpose?" Rares doesn't stop, forcing us closer to the valley floor. "You still intend to fight him, don't you? All this does is add urgency to our training. We know now what Angra will be doing throughout the world—and he knows you know, so you'll be even more of a target once you reemerge." Now Rares does stop, swinging around to face me. "Which makes it even more imperative that you leave here as prepared as possible. Doesn't it?"

I pinch my lips together. My heartbeat eats a hole through my chest, and though my initial reaction is to scream at him, I force myself to process what he said, every word.

"Yes," I admit. But I hate it, and myself, and him, all of this, everything standing in the way of me helping everyone I care about. But *this* will help them.

If it doesn't, Angra will kill me, and any chance of ridding the world of his magic will be gone. He'll spread his control to every kingdom in Primoria as he's already started to do in Ventralli. I saw how much that kingdom had started to change after only one night under his rule—how long would it take him to conquer the world?

I blow past Rares, stomping ahead of him. Below, the castle sits, similar in style to Yakim's Langlais Castle. Gray stones snuggle alongside one another, beaten smooth from centuries of existence; windows of thick glass reflect flares of moonlight if the angle is right. At the top right corner of the wall, a flag flutters, its maroon background showing a mountain beneath a beam of light.

The symbol for the Order of the Lustrate.

"Why do you call yourselves the Order of the Lustrate?" I ask.

"*Lustrate* means to purify by sacrifice," Rares explains. "We thought ourselves noble in that regard—that we were willing to sacrifice magic to sustain our kingdom's purity."

I cross my arms over my chest. "Sacrifice," I echo. I haven't been able to say that word since I discovered that that was what the magic required. Saying it now, feeling each letter tumble out of my mouth . . . I don't feel anything.

But I have to, don't I? It has to be a willing sacrifice. It has to be something I *want*.

But I can think of only a handful of things I truly want. To be back in Winter, tucked away with Mather and Sir and Nessa and everyone I love; to hurl my chakram at something over and over until my heart doesn't ache anymore.

Rares jerks to a stop. I can see his eyes on me in the moonlight, and the gentleness there looks almost like sympathy.

"Wanting isn't weak," he says. The solid iron gate in the wall starts to creak open. "Wanting is a drive. A goal. Without wanting, what would we be? Empty, I think."

His mouth hangs open as he studies me, seeing through me.

"I know it's been a long trip. But . . . I think you'll need to talk to her, before you rest."

I frown. "Her?"

No sooner do I ask that than a door slams within the compound. Rares beckons me on.

The walls surround a complex illuminated by lanterns. Stables and a training ring take up the right, a garden fills the left—and in front of us, racing out of the castle, comes a woman just as old as Rares, with long, black hair in dozens of braids that sway against each other, beads jangling from the ends and feathers fluttering in the centers. She wears a ruby robe, the neckline and cuffs adorned with swirling gold designs, and a skirt splits at her knees, revealing a glimpse of brown boots and tan pants that show all the more when she gathers the robe in a fist to sprint faster.

"You're here!" she cries. Before I can object, she throws her arms around me, smashing me to her chest. She smells like well-worn fabric dried in the sun, like cinnamon and thyme and other, less familiar herbs. And when she pulls back, her dark eyes glittering, I can't help but smile. Something about her is all those things—well-worn and bright.

Rares hooks his arm around her neck. "What an impression, darling."

"Oh! I didn't frighten you, did I?" she asks me, eyes beseeching.

I shake my head. "You are by far the least threatening thing I've encountered in a while."

She laughs and plants a kiss on Rares. After a rather long, awkward moment of wondering if I should excuse myself while they reunite, Rares turns to me.

"Sorry, dear heart—Meira, this is my wife, Oana."

Oana sweeps up the bell sleeve of her robe so it wraps around her hand before she extends it to me. I stare at it, the fabric covering her skin.

She starts. "A formality in Paisly, you see. Can be rather intrusive, if either party is unable to block their mind. If you like, we don't have to—"

"No, it's fine." I put my hand in hers. "Perfect, actually."

She lets the shake go far longer than is customary, her

eyes sweeping over every part of my face. "You are lovely, sweetheart."

I pull out of her grip. "Um . . . thank you."

"*Now* you're scaring her," Rares chuckles.

Oana bats at her husband. "Nonsense—every woman likes to be told how lovely she is. You'd think after centuries of being married, you'd know that."

I gape. I had to have heard her wrong.

"You didn't think Angra was the only one gifted with long life?" Rares asks.

I study his face, then Oana's. "You can't be more than fifty."

Rares smirks. "I have a grueling beauty regimen."

When I don't respond, he sighs. "Magic, in any of its most powerful forms—the Decay, or *being* a conduit—preserves its host. Death can still find the particularly reckless, and we age, but slowly—imperceptibly slowly. Which was right good fun for the first few centuries, but . . ."

"But I age normally," I interject.

"You didn't access your power until recently—your magic was dormant until you consciously knew about it."

I marvel again at the ease with which Rares offers all this. Sir would have made me fight him for *months* to get this kind of information.

But I'm struck mute. Rares is like Angra. And this will be my fate too, now that I've awakened my magic from the dormant state it was in throughout my childhood. While the thought of never dying might be a glorious relief, the consequences hit me too.

I could watch everyone I love die. I could fall into Angra's hands and he could torture me *forever* with whatever horrible fate he wishes.

Rares bobs his head, his eyes on me. "This is why, before we continue with any training, I insist you speak to Oana. Not even the best teacher in the world can get a lesson to stick if you're not ready for it. Go with her. She'll help you. Consider it lesson three—and, truthfully, think of it as one of the most important lessons of all."

Wariness hums in my chest. "What are we going to talk about? Magic?"

Oana shakes her head. "No, sweetheart. *You.*"

Me. We're going to waste time talking about *me* when . . .

I clench my jaw to fight from glancing toward the wall and, beyond it, the waiting war. There are so many questions, so much to learn—what did I expect, though? To spend a few hours chatting with Rares and walk out of here a whole, strong queen capable of leading a victorious charge against Angra? That would be too easy.

And I know what happens when Winterian queens rush into things.

I take a deep breath and nod. I have to do this. Mather will keep everyone safe and my allies will keep Angra at bay while I myself become more capable, more skilled at controlling my magic so when I face Angra, I can get the final two keys from him with as little bloodshed as possible, and stop his war before it has a chance to take any more lives.

Oana offers me her arm, and I take it. She makes sure to wrap her hand in her sleeve before giving my fingers a tight squeeze and leads me up the path toward the castle.

"I'm glad you're here, Meira," she says. "We don't get many visitors."

It feels like she's grateful for more than my impending destruction of magic. The way she looks at me makes me feel . . . treasured. Valued.

I want to press her for more, but she flips her hand at the doors and the castle opens to us.

Inside, the iciness of the stones loosens some of the tension in my muscles. Chandeliers hang every few steps, casting yellow-white light on a décor just as warm and wild as Oana's style—maroon accents and comfortable wooden furniture. Rooms open off this hall, and Oana stops before one, the clacking of our shoes halting in abrupt silence.

I realize then—there are no other sounds here. No servants bustling through chores; no soldiers marching in drills.

Oana smiles at me. "We don't have much use for servants in Paisly." She nods toward the nearest chandelier, and as I watch, she uses magic to make the candles fade before raging to life.

My shock isn't as strong as it was before. But it spikes when I meet Oana's eyes.

I never asked about their lack of servants.

Her hand hesitates over the knob as she looks up through thick black lashes. "Rares can only block your thoughts when he's with you, sweetheart. No one can intrude on you through Paisly's barrier from a distance, but up close . . ."

My eyes widen when I realize what she means. Is this part of lesson three? Her poking into my head?

Snow, I hope not.

Oana opens the door. Gray and cold, the room holds a lumpy bed with a thick violet quilt, a trunk against a wall, and a dented table displaying dishes that make me weak with hunger.

"I assumed you'd prefer a room without a fireplace. The cold might bother others, but for you, it's comforting, yes?" Oana scrunches her nose in a knowing grin. "Eat, please."

I don't need further prodding. Two chairs sit at the table, and as I drop into one, I fear I may never be able to get up again. My arm shakes as I reach toward the nearest dish, hunger and stress and tiredness all washing over me.

Oana pulls out the other chair but doesn't sit, hovering over it, over me, as I sip brothy stew from a rough wooden cup.

I wipe the back of my hand over my mouth. "So . . . what is this lesson?"

Oana smiles softly, her shoulders folding forward. "You will only succeed in controlling your magic if you first have control of yourself. As I'm sure you've learned, magic is linked to your emotions; if they are unstable, your magic will be unstable too. I'm going to help you come to a state of acceptance—and readiness for Rares's training."

That was what I was afraid of, I think, then wince. She heard that, and gives me that look again, as if I'm a chunk of gold mined from the Klaryns.

"I hope, through this, you come to see how amazing you are," she whispers.

That look of hers, her words—it all suddenly creates a noose around my neck. I *know* I'm here to save them from their horrible existence of being all-powerful and, apparently, immortal; I *know* I'm here so they can tell me about magic and the chasm and help me die.

Isn't that enough? Does she need to make me feel even more like a sacrifice, untouchable and dehumanized? Do we really have to poke into *me*?

Oana steps forward. "That's not why—"

I drop the cup onto the table and bend forward, hands over my head. *"Stop."*

She doesn't move. "Don't hold back, sweetheart. Why is this something you fear?"

I choke into my hands, half a laugh, half a quiet plea.

I'm afraid of breaking.

I've been keeping every spare twitch of strength against the door in my mind, the one holding back all my crippling emotions. Keeping that door closed has been the only thing between a breakdown and me, but I'm tired, and the door is getting heavier, and Oana won't leave.

But this lesson is about *me*. We can't move on to the other lessons, the ones that will help me control my magic, until we confront this one. Damn Rares—but I know he's right.

I can't face Angra if half my strength is always spent on containing myself.

So I open the door, and let everything tumble out.

I should never have trusted Noam with my kingdom. I should have seen Theron's fall, but I pushed him out of my life—and as much as I should, I don't regret that. I can't remember what it felt like to love him without complication.

I do remember loving Mather. My memories of him are sharp and clear—I think of how, no matter what happened, who died, what evil we faced, he's always been in the background of my life.

Nessa—she grew up in a cage in Angra's prison camp; how terrified was she to be in a cage under his control again? I had no right leaving her or Conall, especially after . . . Garrigan. He sang Nessa to sleep when she awoke screaming from nightmares. He protected me with the same devotion he showed his sister. He didn't deserve to die.

But nothing in this world plays out as people deserve. Horrible things happen without cause or explanation, leaving slack-jawed horror in their wake. People make decisions without thinking about the results—they just do things, then run off into the dark, never admitting to their mistakes, never apologizing for *getting me killed*.

Hannah. *Hannah.*

Snow above, I hate her so much, and I hate most of all that she made me hate her. She was my mother—she should have loved me. She should have done a hundred other things that she didn't do, and now she's just one of the many pieces of my heart that hurt to touch.

Oana drops to her knees before me. "Meira, sweetheart . . ."

But I'm too lost in it now. I don't think I'm on the chair anymore, but rather curled into myself on the floor with my hands over my head and tears streaming down my face.

And now I know exactly what the world will look like if I fail. I suspected the sort of evil Angra would release, and I remember well the streets of Abril, how utterly empty they were, every person cowering except the soldiers, who wielded power like chained dogs at their master's feet. I have to stop that—but I don't want to do this. *I don't want to do this.* It's supposed to be a willing sacrifice, surrendering my conduit to the source of the magic. But it's all going to be in vain, because the last thought I think as I die will be *No, Hannah chose this.*

I want to live. I want to go back to Winter and grow old and—*I don't want to be used.*

Oana grabs my chin and eases my head up so she can look into my eyes. She must be blocking me, because she's touching my skin, running her fingers over my cheeks.

"We do not want to use you," she states, hard, despite the tears in her eyes. "We look at you like that because you are the first child we have had in our home in more than two thousand years. We age, slowly, but our bodies can only host one force—the magic makes it impossible for us to conceive. So we look at you like that both because Rares and I have wanted a child for so long and because it kills us what we have to help you do."

My heart spasms. The magic ruins that too? Another fate decided for me.

Oana forces a broken smile. "We look at you like this because we are *sorry*, Meira. We are so sorry. You deserve a better life than this."

Hannah never apologized. I'm not sure she ever saw me as more than a vessel to enact the things she'd put in place. Even now, it's been so long since I've spoken to her. A part of me *chose* not to talk to her, because I know what I am to her. Not a daughter—a conduit.

Sir never apologized. It was my duty and I should do whatever needed to be done, because I'd always wanted to help, so I had no right to complain when I was needed.

A vessel doesn't deserve an apology; a duty-bound soldier doesn't either.

But Oana, someone I barely know, says things that make me feel, for the first time in years, like someone who has a say in the horrible events around me. Like someone who *matters*.

I cling to Oana's heavy wool robes, burying my face in the crook of her arm, pouring out every emotion I've been keeping at bay. All the while, she holds me, and I sense, somewhere deep in my chest, the cracks starting to fill in—the faint, cool tingle of healing.

Mather

MATHER, PHIL, AND the Ventrallan king waited in the shadows of the cramped passage. Beyond the door, chaos filled the hall—orders shouted, soldiers marching.

Mather strained to catch more telltale sounds, shouts of protest or whimpers of victims, but if he hadn't known about the uprising, it would have been frighteningly easy to assume that Rintiero's army was merely practicing military drills. Had any dissenters been subdued already?

"Raelyn will be in the throne room," the Ventrallan king whispered. "Unless . . ."

His voice faded, but Mather felt his unspoken words.

Unless she's murdering my mother.

"Where would she keep Ceridwen?" Mather asked.

In the light from the cracks around the door, the king stilled. "I'll find out."

"How?" Phil asked. "Your wife is terrifying. I mean,

she's terrifying, *Your Highness.*"

"You have no idea. And it's Jesse." His eyes flashed. "I'm not king anymore, am I?"

Mather shrugged. "It's not so bad, being dethroned."

"Ah, but at least the woman who dethroned you wasn't a possessed murderer."

Mather laughed, but it only hollowed him even more. He sagged against the wall.

"I have no idea where Meira went," he admitted. Where would he even start looking for her? This city alone was huge. They could have gone anywhere, whether by boat or horse or on foot—

"Who was the man she left with?" Phil prodded.

"I don't know. I've never seen him before—or anyone like him. He was wearing a . . . robe?" Mather's brow pinched. "I haven't even—"

"A robe?" Jesse interrupted.

"Yes, why?"

"There are tapestries," Jesse said, his voice uncertain, "in our history hall. They were made centuries ago, ancient depictions of each kingdom's people. Ventrallans in masks and Yakimians with their copper and gadgetry and—"

"Is there a point?" Mather interrupted.

Armor jangled as soldiers passed their hidden door. Mather felt Phil and Jesse tense up.

Jesse exhaled as the footsteps faded. "And Paislians—in

robes. Did the man have a dark complexion, darker than Yakimians?"

Mather nodded, then realized Jesse couldn't see him. "Yes. He was Paislian?"

Jesse made a soft huff. "I have no idea why a Paislian would be in my palace, but it sounds as though one was."

"Wow." Phil whistled, soft and low. "Didn't see that one coming."

Neither had Mather. A Paislian had swept Meira away? Why?

"We can't hide in here forever," Mather said.

Jesse's ear angled toward the door. "It's clear. Follow me, but stay hidden—I think it best if Raelyn believes I'm alone. And . . . and try, as much as you can, to avoid Angra."

Mather snorted. "I'd nearly forgotten him."

"That's what makes him effective," Phil said. "He creates all these other threats, so many you forget to see the flower for all its bloody petals."

It was all too true.

Jesse said nothing as he eased open the door. The hall lay empty for a brief moment, and Jesse darted to the right. Mather tucked his weapons under his shirt—a knife in addition to Cordell's conduit, that horrifying reminder hooked in his belt—to make them inconspicuous. He and Phil swept after Jesse, shutting the door behind them and making sure to slip behind statues or other obstacles to be as unobtrusive as possible.

But Jesse went unnoticed. He had put his mask back on in the passage, and since no one expected their king to be anywhere but inside a prison cell, he was just another Ventrallan rushing down the halls.

They passed a number of rooms, many empty, others stuffed with royals. A quick sweep inside told Mather that, sure enough, they were all subdued, cowering in quiet groups as soldiers stood around them.

Had Angra done this to them somehow? Whatever the cause, it made creeping through the palace even easier, as there were few soldiers patrolling—no dissenters meant there was no need for a large guard.

Soon Jesse stopped before doors in an empty white hall lined with gilded mirrors. Mather tucked himself along the wall beside the doors, Phil at his side. Jesse met his eyes and gave a curt nod before he shoved the doors inward. To Mather's confusion, he didn't enter more than a few paces, and Mather peeked around the frame to survey the threat within.

At the end of the green and brown throne room stood a pair of mirrored chairs. One held Raelyn, lounging as she admired something in her hands.

Ventralli's broken conduit, the silver crown.

Jesse froze. "Where is Ceridwen?"

His shout rebounded through the room. Mather winced, certain soldiers would come running. Raelyn no doubt had a contingent waiting close by. He cursed softly, already regretting this decision. They should have

69

just left, run free of this palace—

But if it had been Meira whom Raelyn had captured, Mather would be standing exactly where Jesse stood, however foolish, however reckless it might be.

Raelyn laughed. "Oh, dear husband—why would you think she's still alive?"

"You wouldn't have killed her so easily."

Raelyn swung her legs around to sit upright. A smile crept across her face, slow and indulgent, like she meant to savor every lifted muscle. "You know me so well. Let's play a game, then. What would I do if I seized a kingdom from my worthless husband only to have that worthless husband's *mother* attempt to save him?"

Even before a door opened, Mather knew what was happening.

Raelyn's soldiers had discovered that that their imprisoned king had been moved; they had found Brigitte in her empty chambers. And they had brought her here to be killed by Raelyn.

Mather swayed, knees all but giving way beneath him.

Jesse would watch his mother die. And there was no way to save her.

The weight of that pressed on the agony in Mather's chest. He thought of Alysson, a bloody splotch staining her dress as she fell, limp and lifeless, into his arms.

Phil shot an arm across Mather's chest. Mather looked at him, exhaling. Phil knew. He knew, and he stood there, his eyes pleading yet sad.

"Hold on," Phil whispered.

Mather whipped his head back around the doorframe. Brigitte stood next to the dais looking no less than the severe opponent she was. All of Raelyn's attention was on Jesse, who shifted toward his mother, his fists trembling.

"What would I do, dear husband, since you know me so well?" Raelyn asked. "How would I reward traitors? Would I reward them like *that*?" Her hand shot out, pointing to something in the front corner of the room, to Jesse's left. Jesse turned, but Mather couldn't see anything from this position. Whatever it was sent a spasm of horror over Jesse's face.

"What did you . . ." Jesse stumbled backward. "*Why*, Raelyn?"

"Trophies of our victory. The old ways are dead—and Spring has come. And now I have one more to add to my collection! Well, four more, actually."

Soldiers swept into the hall, and before Mather had time to do more than swear at himself, he and Phil had been yanked into the throne room behind Jesse.

Mather could see them now, Raelyn's trophies. The sight made his stomach clench.

Bathed in shadows, three men loomed between the pillars in the back of the room, and at a glance it appeared as though they were merely soldiers hovering out of sight.

But they were far from soldiers. They were far from *alive*.

Spikes propped the bodies upright. The Summerian king's head cocked to the side, congealed blood wrapping around his neck in a thick band. Summer's conduit had been taken off his wrist and sat at the base of the spike, even more prominent a trophy. Beside him, Noam's neck bore a smaller slash, the mark of the chakram Theron had thrown. And next to him—

Mather hardened. Garrigan stood at the end of the row, Meira's chakram still in his chest.

"Aren't they marvelous?" Raelyn sighed. "A bit morbid, yes, but *so* satisfying."

"Raelyn . . ." Jesse's voice died as he finally realized Mather and Phil had been discovered. Phil kept his eyes fixed on the floor, shoulders pivoted away from the trophies, and though Mather wished he had the good sense to do the same, he couldn't.

He didn't know the Summerian king and cared little for his death. Noam he had hated, and he couldn't deny the gratification he felt at knowing the man was dead. But no one deserved to be paraded like this—no one except maybe Raelyn or Angra.

But especially not Garrigan.

Mather's eyes latched onto the chakram in Garrigan's chest.

"Now, who's first?" Raelyn's shoes clicked on the dais as she walked toward Brigitte. "You will be a wonderful addition to my collection, Duchess."

Jesse took a threatening step forward, but one of the soldiers met him before he could go far. A fist to the gut, and Jesse crumpled.

Phil hissed in warning, but Mather was already moving, drawing step by step toward the bodies as if they mesmerized him.

"Stop," one soldier grunted, his fist ramming toward Mather's stomach. Mather sidestepped, acting the part of the dazed prisoner as he stumbled closer to the bodies.

Raelyn's attention moved to them now. She had her arms out, fingers extended. He could practically taste Angra's evil radiating from her.

The soldier stomped toward him. Mather leaped the rest of the way to Garrigan, springing into the shadows between the columns and wrenching the chakram from its bloody holster. He tried not to think about the grating sound and the fleshy resistance that dragged against the blade. Using the same momentum that had flung him toward Garrigan, Mather swung back and sliced through the soldier's cheek, severing half his jaw from his face.

"No—" Raelyn's scream bit off as the old queen slammed into her, sending her toppling off the dais.

Brigitte whirled. "RUN!"

Mather let Meira's chakram soar, nicking the arm and chest of the two soldiers who held Jesse. Phil ducked to grab the now free Ventrallan king and hauled him toward the doors as the chakram returned to Mather. He caught it and used it at close range now, slicing enemies aside as Phil managed to wrestle a dagger from a soldier and slash back, hand flailing in jabs and frenzied thrusts. Jesse gaped at his mother still.

"Come on!" Mather shouted and gave him a solid shake. Raelyn could regain her composure at any moment—

Before Mather could blink, Jesse peeled the mask off his face, snapped it in half, and dropped those halves on the room's swirling marble floor.

"May this be one of your *trophies*," Jesse hissed, and swung around, sprinting out of the room. Mather tugged Phil along, both of them taking down the remaining few guards before they launched into the hall and hurled themselves after Jesse.

Not more than half a dozen breaths after they left, a scream pierced the air. Jesse faltered, losing his pace long enough that Mather caught up to him, hooked his arm through his, and hauled him on.

"Don't let her sacrifice be in vain," Mather said.

Jesse's face paled. "Turn . . . ," he managed. "There's a servants' entrance. . . ."

Mather pulled him to the left, Phil close behind, and the three of them burst into the chill night air. A narrow path careened around a stone wall that led to the front of the palace. Here the sounds of the coup racking the city were louder—the screams of innocents not yet subdued echoed alongside the shouts of soldiers, the stomping of booted feet, and the clashing of weapons.

Mather dragged Jesse around the wall before he smashed them back against it, hidden in a patch of shadows. The palace's courtyard fanned out, dim in the night, and five soldiers guarding one lone wagon stood near a cluster of torches. Mather's mind whirled through possible escape plans. They couldn't retreat into the palace—they couldn't cut across the courtyard without being seen—was that another door in the wall up ahead? Where did it lead? It didn't matter; it had to be better than—

Jesse stiffened. "That wagon . . . no. She wouldn't have . . ."

He stumbled forward, nearly into the light of the torches, when Mather grabbed his arm.

"Are you stupid—"

But his words were drowned by the sudden blast that echoed over the area. A warning siren sang out from the roof of the palace, delivering wordless orders to the five soldiers by the wagon. They shifted upright from their posts, revealing the gray Ventrallan crown silhouette on their purple uniforms, their silver masks glinting in the torchlight.

One nodded to two others. "You two, keep guard. We'll find out what's going on."

Mather pressed himself deeper into shadow as three of the guards broke off. Thankfully they turned toward the main entrance of the palace, jogging for orders from within.

The moment they were gone, Jesse launched forward. "You!"

The two remaining soldiers leaped to attention. When they saw Jesse, their eyes shifted from alert to amused.

Mather groaned and stepped out of the shadows, Phil following.

So much for stealth.

Jesse pointed at the wagon. "Who is in there?"

One of the soldiers smirked. "Queen Raelyn informed us you might—"

"We don't have time for this." Mather let the chakram fly. It sliced through the soldier's thigh, sending the man to his knees, and ricocheted back to Mather. The other soldier drew a blade in his right hand and Mather let the chakram cut through that shoulder. The soldier screeched, dropping his blade as Mather strode forward, bloody chakram pointed menacingly.

"Who. Is in. The wagon?"

The soldiers cowered, whether from Mather's merciless air or the equally withering glare Jesse threw at them. "The Summerian—"

That was all Jesse needed to hear. He dove forward, tugging at the locked doors. "Ceridwen! Cerie! Are you all right? Answer me!"

It took another slice of the chakram to get the soldiers to hand over the keys, and with the horn still crying over them, Jesse fumbled to unlock the wagon. The doors flew open.

But when light from the torches flickered inside, it revealed only walls stained the same wine color as the outside, and a few pillows and quilts on the floor.

Jesse whirled, grabbed the nearest soldier, and slammed him against the floor of the empty wagon. *"Where is she?"* he bellowed.

"Yakim!" the soldier cried. "A Yakimian paid us for her. Paid us to take the wagon back so Queen Raelyn wouldn't know—"

Jesse's mouth fell slack. "Yakim?" He looked to the wall of trees that formed the southern edge of the palace complex, as if he could see that kingdom from here.

"What?" Mather swung forward. "Why would Yakim take her?"

The soldier waved his hands again. "I swear it! They took her!"

When Jesse turned around, Mather expected him to be livid. These men were either lying or had sold Ceridwen to Yakim for no reason he could fathom—but Jesse's face was light, almost smiling, and he released the soldier to grab Mather's arm.

"I think I know where they would have taken her."

The soldier, still on the floor of the wagon, shot upright. "I can't let you—"

But Jesse spun, his fist slamming into the soldier's jaw. The man's head snapped backward, the jarring pop of his skull on the wood floor sending him into unconsciousness.

Jesse turned to the other soldier and chucked him inside the wagon. He relieved the man of his weapon—a bow and a quiver of arrows—before slamming the doors and throwing the lock. The wagon rocked, the one conscious soldier's shouts muffled by the wood.

Jesse looked back at Mather as he fastened the quiver to his back. "Yakim is an ally of Summer. In trade, at least— perhaps they heard of the takeover and sought to intercede."

"But intercede for which side?"

Jesse's fingers hung loose around the bow. The hope in his eyes guttered with doubt. "The river. Yakim is a short boat ride from here, and there's one dock reserved specifically for the queen's use. They're there." He paused. "They have to be."

"All right." Mather didn't need further explanation. This was Jesse's mission, and the sooner they completed it, the sooner Mather could listen to the tension in his muscles that compelled him to get to Paisly.

But Jesse blew out a steady breath. "No. You've done enough. Your queen needs you."

Though he felt a rush of relief at that release of duty, Mather didn't move. "Are you sure?"

Jesse nodded. "Yes. I'll see you at the camp." He flashed a smile. "Thank you."

He sprinted toward the southern wall of trees, vanishing into the shadows. Mather watched him go, waiting for shouts of alarm from any soldiers who might have been waiting, but none came.

He turned to Phil. "Now we—"

Every muscle in Mather's body sprang to readiness and he lifted Meira's chakram.

Phil, body rigid, stood with a blade making a threatening indentation across his neck. The hand that gripped the blade belonged to Theron.

All sensation drained out of Mather as soldiers rushed around them, filing out of the servants' entrance. But he didn't really see any of them, too consumed by the malice radiating from the new Cordellan king.

For once, Mather was grateful that Meira was far away from all of this.

The soldiers formed a ring, closing him alongside the wagon while more men worked to free their comrades imprisoned within. And when something moved on Mather's right, realization rushed back to him, letting him feel every stupid thing he'd done.

They'd been caught. They were surrounded. And it wouldn't be the dungeon for them this time, not with the madness in Theron's eyes—and especially not with the cloying smile Angra threw at him.

Angra stopped, studying Mather first, then Phil. Theron kept the blade to Phil's throat as if there was still a chance Mather might fight back, but they all knew who had won.

"Just the two of you?" Angra noted, one brow lifting.

Mather ground his jaw and lowered Meira's chakram. "You expected more?"

Angra's other brow lifted to match the first. He shook his head and a spark lit the air. As soldiers moved forward, Mather realized what it was.

Angra's magic. He'd sent a command to his men much as normal Royal Conduits sent commands to soldiers during battle—but Mather could feel this too. He imagined it snaking around each person in the area, diving into those who had already given themselves over to Angra—and coiling across Mather's skin when the magic recognized someone it had not yet possessed.

It slithered over his body, sending up images of power, strength, and unbreakable resolve. The magic whispered to him, a soft caress he fought to scrub off—fought more the urge to soak it in. If this was how Angra swayed people to his side, Mather almost couldn't blame them for surrendering.

Two of Angra's soldiers grabbed Mather and kicked him to his knees while the other two rid him of weapons. Meira's chakram—*damn it, damn it*—the Ventrallan knife, and—

"Now this is a surprise." Angra took Cordell's conduit from the soldier who found it. He glanced at Theron. "Yours, I believe."

Theron released Phil, shoving him to the ground. He took the conduit from Angra, the purple jewel on the hilt hazy in his palm. Mather, still held like a man bowing to his king, twitched in defiance when Theron bent to his level.

"I think this will be far more useful in your hands. I no longer have need of it." Theron pressed the tip of the blade to Mather's cheek, though not forcefully enough to break skin.

Mather jerked again, but the soldiers kept him pinned. Theron's threat didn't make sense—he'd let Mather keep the conduit, the *dagger*?

Theron twisted the blade. Blood trickled in a warm bead down Mather's face, and he imagined it draining the hatred out of him, releasing it to pool at Theron's feet.

A smile, and Theron pulled the blade away to lean still closer, angling his mouth to Mather's ear.

"And every time you see it, I want you to think of her with me. I want you to know that when I win this war, I will do so *without* this weak magic. And when this ends, and Meira is mine, there won't have been a damn thing you could have done to stop me."

Mather snapped his head into Theron's temple. The Cordellan king bellowed, but when he regained himself, he made to lunge again, the conduit's blade raised high.

Angra interceded with a touch on his arm. "That's enough. We can use him."

Mather snarled. Theron looked just as infuriated, but he pulled back, watching Angra.

"That was my mistake last time," Angra told Theron,

but the pitch of his voice made it clear that his words were meant to be as much a dagger in Mather's flesh as Theron's conduit. "I let weak rulers live even though I had the key to power greater than anything they could fathom. This time, I will strike until only those are left who will bring about a new, awakened world. And these boys will help me force the Winter queen to pick a side—especially him."

Mather panted. "There's nothing you can do that will make me help you."

Angra, still facing Theron, smiled. Then he looked down at Mather.

"And what makes you think I was talking about you?"

Understanding shattered what restraint Mather had left.

His eyes moved to Phil.

"No," Mather wheezed, then a shout, "Don't touch him!"

Phil's face broke. He scrambled back, trying to stand, but Angra's men descended on him first.

Mather wrenched against the soldiers, managing to get onto one foot so he propelled forward. But the men tackled him flat on the ground, and the wagon's wheels were all he could see, his arms bent against his spine.

He couldn't do anything when Phil started screaming.

Ceridwen

THE QUEEN OF Yakim had bought them from Raelyn's men.

The Ventrallan soldiers left them in a rush, and though Giselle had given her and Lekan a way out of Raelyn's clutches, the Yakimian queen never did anything without a calculated reason. As Ceridwen planted herself on the darkening street in Rintiero's south quarter, she folded her arms and glared at Giselle, who silently mounted her horse and arranged her heavy wool skirts around the saddle.

A distant yet powerful wail echoed down the street. Panic flared in Ceridwen's muscles. A warning siren? A call to arms?

She was intimately familiar with the everyday sounds of Rintiero, music and laughter and happy conversation so different from Juli's raucous bellowing. The siren called her attention to the way the noises of the city sounded suddenly . . . different. It was night, yes, but even at the latest hours, songs played from the music guild. The only things she could hear now were distant shouting, metal rattling—the noises of war.

A cold wave washed from her head to her toes.

Raelyn's coup had spread. Was finding Meira and stopping Angra even feasible anymore? She needed to get to the palace. Now.

Lekan, mounted with one of Giselle's soldiers, pressed his lips into a thin line and nodded. He understood. Whatever Giselle had in store, he could handle, and he was far safer with Yakim's uncertainty than Raelyn's guaranteed torture. Ceridwen could leave him here and—

A cold hand grasped her shoulder—Giselle, leaning down from her saddle. "Do not do anything foolish, Princess. Likely they're dead already."

She snarled. "Then I will obliterate Raelyn."

Giselle rolled her eyes skyward before kicking her horse. "Are you not exhausted by all this passion?"

Before Ceridwen could respond, Yakimian soldiers moved in. A few quick jerks, and they had her arms knotted in front of her, a rope tugging her wrists high where it connected to one soldier's saddle. Lekan snapped forward, but the soldier on his horse simply butted his wounded knee with the hilt of a sword, which made Lekan cry out.

"GISELLE!" Ceridwen's roar echoed off the buildings.

"The moment you untie me, I'll kill you!"

A few horses up, Giselle shook her head. "You are quite the terrible negotiator."

"And you are quite the terrible ally. For decades you sell to Summer, and *this* is how it ends—with you taking me prisoner? I knew Yakim was selfish, but I didn't think you were heartless."

That made Giselle yank her horse to a stop. After a moment, her party started on again, but Giselle drifted back until her horse kept step beside Ceridwen's fumbled mix of walking and being dragged.

"We are not heartless—we are practical." Giselle's back was rigid beneath the burnished, double-bladed ax that sat against her spine—Yakim's conduit. "And we are one of the few kingdoms, might I add, not currently involved in this war. Winter is here, Summer, Ventralli, Cordell—Spring. Autumn has been invaded, or so I heard, and Paisly has never bothered to be more than mountain rats. Being practical is what will keep my people alive. Don't pretend you wouldn't do the same for your kingdom, had you the foresight to protect it."

"I protect my people!"

"You had no idea this takeover would happen until it unfolded before your eyes."

"At least I'm still fighting it. What are you doing? Running away to barricade yourself in Putnam?" Ceridwen flinched. "How did you even know about any of this?"

Giselle tipped her head. "It took you far too long to ask that."

"Because I knew you wouldn't tell me."

"Won't I?" Giselle pulled her attention to the street. A hint of mildew tinged the air—they were drawing close to the Langstone River. "He came to Yakim. After your visit a few days ago." When Ceridwen didn't ask who, Giselle pressed on. "Angra. He came with a proposition to unite Primoria—but unlike the rest of the world, I realized what he truly offered. And it was not freedom, as he professed."

Ceridwen risked a glance up. Night had fully embraced them by this time, but she could still make out Giselle watching her with that maddeningly studious gaze Yakimians did so well.

"He left once I told him I would consider it, as is the nature of my people. To think and ponder and live in a world of ideas—which is the exact reason I cannot allow him to spread his magic."

Ceridwen's jaw went slack.

"I have seen the product of his rule. The entire world has." Giselle's grip on her reins tightened. "Spring festered for centuries—stagnant even by Season standards. And he wishes to spread the same to my kingdom? He honestly expected me to embrace something that would change my people from learned members of this world to mindless, possessed shells. I will not let my people's minds be marred by *him*."

Giselle smiled as if she were an adult speaking to a child. "Which is where you come in."

Ceridwen balked. "What? How?"

Giselle's smile softened. "When I asked who else was involved in his plans, he rattled off an impressive list, with even more impressive plans to choke the rest of the world into submission—except for Winter. 'That kingdom will burn,' he said. The only reason a man would destroy something like that is if he finds it a threat. They've been at war so long, Winter must know things about Angra that he fears. And the Winter queen calls you an ally."

"Yes. But—"

"And you have an army at your disposal." Giselle waved her hand before Ceridwen could say no, Simon had been killed, and Raelyn or Angra would no doubt seize Summer's assets. "No, child—*your* army. The one you think hidden from everyone else."

Ceridwen's face pinched before she tripped, slammed into Giselle's horse, and launched around so she swung as far from Giselle as she could get.

Her refugees. Her freedom fighters. Giselle knew about them?

"If you touched them—" Ceridwen spit.

Giselle stopped her with another flick of her wrist. Ceridwen wanted so badly to cut off that hand. "I care not for your survivors, but of course I know of them. Did you believe I had been selling people to your kingdom for *money* all these years? No, Princess, I sought a far greater prize—Summer itself."

Ceridwen blinked. "What are you talking about?"

"The people Summer bought from Yakim. Some were peasants, useless enough—but most were not so useless at all." Giselle's eyebrow arched high. "Soldiers, Princess. Spies, if you will, sent to build an army within your own walls. I hadn't planned the invasion to happen for a few more years, but recent events have forced me to reevaluate Yakim's priorities."

Sweat pooled along Ceridwen's spine.

"You were . . ." Her mind sputtered. "You sent your people to be tortured! Why would you think they would still be loyal to you after that? Children, Giselle. You sold my brother *children* so you could conquer Summer?"

Giselle clucked her tongue. "I did not tell you this so you could question me. I told you this because you have three hundred of my soldiers in your camp, and I want you to use them."

"Three *hundred*?"

Ceridwen couldn't see Giselle's face anymore. She couldn't see the street, or the shadows of night, or Rintiero at all—the only thing she could see was her refugee camp. The hundreds of freed slaves who lived on the border of the Southern Eldridge Forest in safety and anonymity—or so she had thought.

Ceridwen's blood caught fire.

Giselle fished for something in one of her gown's pockets and turned to Ceridwen, hand extended. "My royal seal, so you can convince them that I gave the order to fight for you."

The seal dropped from Giselle's palm and Ceridwen caught it. A small ring with an indentation on top, metal that curved into the outline of an ax.

Ceridwen glared down at it. She almost snapped at the Yakimian queen, almost shouted what she would really do with this information. She would use the help to stop Angra, yes—but she wouldn't let a moment pass after his fall before she swayed every Yakimian slave to her side. She would tell the innocents what their queen had done to them, and she would rally them against the callous bitch who had sought to use them. Conduits and magic be damned— everywhere she turned, it seemed, she met corrupt people misusing the power she would have given anything to have.

"You're sick," Ceridwen hissed. She tugged on the rope, drawing Giselle's attention to it. "If you did this to help, why am I your prisoner?"

They turned a corner and the docks stretched before them, long wooden fingers reaching into the blue-gray water of the Langstone River. Boats bobbed along the docks, small vessels beside large, mighty ones with sails coiled shut against the night wind and flags rippling over masts. One boat, sails unfurled, stood at the end of a short dock. Soldiers dashed across the deck and Ceridwen's eyes cut to the flag atop. An ax on a dark background.

"If I set you free now, you'll rush back in a futile attempt to save Ventralli, and I don't care about Ventralli," Giselle said. "You will be escorted to your camp to prepare for battle. I expect the Winter queen's own people are fast at work helping her escape as well—but even if she does not survive this night, I expect you to be an ally of Yakim. I'd accompany you myself, but I have a feeling Angra will try to worm his way into my kingdom, so I must leave."

"You'll have to kill me if you want to get me out of Ventralli," Ceridwen growled. "I'm not leaving anyone here to be slaughtered."

Giselle looked down at her. "You're far too useful alive. *Conscious*, though—"

Ceridwen ducked on a hot burst of instinct. As she dropped, the soldier who had crept up behind her swung forward, the hilt of his sword swinging where her head had been.

Lekan shouted, but his soldier didn't merely strike him this time—he dug his fingers into Lekan's wound, eliciting shrieks that spiraled through Ceridwen's ears.

"Stop!" she cried.

The soldier who held Lekan sat two horses ahead, unreachable. But if the attacking soldier swung, missed her, she could use the distraction to wrestle the sword out of his hands and arm herself.

Ceridwen angled, fists to her chest, legs splayed as she

held her place. The soldier swung again, hilt of his sword arching toward her, the blade flailing behind, and she counted out beats until the last possible moment—

Thwack.

The soldier grunted, his body spasming as an arrow sank into his shoulder. The blade dropped from his grip, clattering to the street, and it hadn't fully settled against the cobblestones before Ceridwen swiped it up, holding it in her two bound hands, and whirled toward Giselle.

"Let him go," Ceridwen demanded, her eyes flicking for a beat to Lekan. He was barely conscious now, but the soldier had stopped torturing him.

Most would feel panic that their prisoner had armed herself and someone had just shot one of their men, but Giselle looked only curious as she analyzed the street behind Ceridwen.

"I'd listen to her, Giselle," came a voice. "I thought I'd lost her twice today. That kind of stress does things to a man."

Ceridwen sobbed and bit her lips together before more could follow.

Jesse.

She couldn't bring herself to turn to see him, afraid she might be hallucinating, afraid if she looked away from Giselle she would lose her one small advantage. So Ceridwen stood there until Jesse stepped into her peripheral vision, a loaded bow stretched across him, one of his fingers anchoring by the corner of his mouth.

He had shot the soldier? And actually hit him?

That *that* was her thought made her want to laugh. But now she noticed the way he shook, the vibrations that trembled down the shaft of his arrow. Flame and heat, had he even been aiming for the soldier? Jesse was entirely useless when it came to weaponry.

Luckily, Giselle didn't know that.

"You escaped," Giselle noted.

Jesse pulled the bowstring tighter, this one aimed at the soldier holding Lekan. "Sorry to disappoint you."

Giselle laughed. "Disappointed? Certainly not. This makes things far easier."

She waved at Lekan's soldier, who deftly thrust Lekan off the horse.

Ceridwen sprang forward and looped Lekan's arm around her shoulder to help him up. He wobbled against her, his body cold with sweat, and she pressed him as close as she could, hoping some of her heat would flow into him. He had fallen in the center of Giselle's men, and Ceridwen struggled to keep him standing with one arm while holding the blade in her other. Jesse waited just outside the ring of soldiers.

"You will still use my boat. It will get you to the camp far more quickly," Giselle said.

Ceridwen snarled. "You can take your boat and shove it up your—"

"Camp?" Jesse lowered his bow slightly. "You were taking her to the refugee camp?"

Giselle nodded. "Now that you're here, she won't be tempted to run off to pursue less productive goals." Another curved eyebrow. "Unless someone else remains in the palace whom you feel the need to retrieve? Because the world is dissolving, King Jesse, and I have no qualms showing you the same force." Giselle bowed her head toward Lekan and Ceridwen.

Jesse shook his head. "No. We have no reason to return." He paused. "For now."

Giselle bobbed her head. "Excellent. Shall we?"

She pressed on to the dock, leaving a few of her men to make sure no one useful to her tried to scamper off into Rintiero. Ceridwen would have spared a few more scowls for her if not for Jesse, on this road, *here*.

The darkness of night and the appearance of storm clouds made it difficult for her to grasp his image, so she could almost dismiss him as a dream. His hair swung untamed and the sleeves of his black shirt were rolled to his elbows, showing the way his forearms clenched the bow.

He cleared his throat and slid the arrow back into his quiver.

The soldiers around them bore the usual Yakimian air of detachment and Lekan stood silent against her, which made Ceridwen feel suddenly as though she and Jesse were alone. Heat throbbed in her head, dizzying and unnameable.

Anger? Relief? She didn't know what she felt.

She just knew he looked . . . different.

Jesse cleared his throat again. "I found the wagon. I didn't think Giselle would be bold enough to dock where she always does when she visits, but I had to try. I had to . . . save you."

Ceridwen shifted Lekan's weight. "I don't need saving."

Jesse swung forward to hook Lekan's other arm around his neck, taking some of his weight.

"No, you don't need to help me," Lekan protested, leaning into Ceridwen more.

"Please," Jesse cut him off. "Let me."

But his eyes were on Ceridwen.

She couldn't breathe.

"Your . . . your children?" she dared ask. Her voice grew in strength. "And the Winterians? Did you hear anything of them? How did you even escape?"

She and Jesse started hobbling Lekan toward the dock, slow work that gnawed at Ceridwen's spine. The sooner they got onto Giselle's boat, the sooner she could find a place to be alone, away from Jesse.

She had ended her relationship with him. And the only reason she had intended to go back for him was to right Raelyn's injustices. Ceridwen had been prepared to see him under those circumstances, when she would have been the savior and he the one who needed her.

She was not prepared for . . . this.

Jesse winced at the mention of his children but seemed to physically force back his worry for them. "They're fine. The Winterians too, actually. They helped me escape. We all split apart, but we're to meet at your refugee camp."

The tension around his mouth lifted into his eyes.

Ceridwen choked.

That was why he looked different. He wasn't wearing a mask.

When he saw her studying him, the corners of his eyes lifted.

"I broke it," he whispered. "My mask. It's over, with Raelyn."

Ceridwen couldn't remember when she had last taken a full breath. Before Jesse had shown up, most likely, and she wheezed now, flashes of light spinning in her vision.

He had broken his mask. He had ended his relationship with Raelyn.

He did it. He finally did what she had wanted him to do for so long that the wish had become a permanent knot inside her heart.

But he hadn't done it until *now*. After Ceridwen had left him. After Raelyn had revealed herself to be dangerous.

They reached the boat, a plank of wood leading them from the dock to the ship's deck. A pile of empty sacks sat in a corner, and as they lowered Lekan onto it, Jesse squatted next to him, his eyes boring into Ceridwen's.

She couldn't look at him. Not now, while Lekan needed

her, while Angra's war still raged—while she wanted to hate Jesse. Flame and heat, she wanted to hate him so much—and as soon as she recognized that need, it roared strong and aching through her body.

She had waited for him for four years. And it had taken a coup and the return of dark magic to make him fight for her in return.

"Cerie," Jesse said. "Please, talk to me. Let me—"

"No." Ceridwen worked at checking on Lekan's leg. It needed a proper dressing, and she almost thanked him for getting injured so she had something to do.

Jesse didn't relent. "Please, I know I—"

"No!" Ceridwen snapped. "No, you don't know. Go away, Jesse. Leave me *alone.*"

Her final words lost their fire, dropping like rain falling halfheartedly from the sky.

Jesse's eyes shot to hers. A few lanterns hung around the deck of the ship, not enough to draw unwanted attention or do more than highlight the copper gleam of his skin.

"All right," he agreed, broken.

He hesitated, hoping maybe that she would change her mind. But finally he stood and took jolting steps across the deck to where Giselle talked with her men.

Lekan's cold fingers touched Ceridwen's arm. "He came for you."

Ceridwen stiffened. "Your wound needs dressing."

She started to flag down a passing soldier for supplies

when Lekan caught her hand.

"Yours does too," he whispered. A deep breath, a wince, and he relaxed his grip. "He sought an alliance with the Winter queen. Before the coup, just after you ended things with him. He intended to overthrow Raelyn before any of this happened."

Ceridwen's jaw popped open and she instantly snapped it closed. Lekan knew her too well, and that knowledge would force her to confront things she didn't have the strength for yet.

She had a war to plan for. Giselle's soldiers in her camp. Angra's threat spreading through the world. Dozens of other problems, all far more immediate and awful than . . . *Jesse.*

So she found bandages and water and cleaned Lekan's wound, all the while ignoring the way that Jesse watched her every move.

Meira

I WAKE IN the room Oana brought me to, unable to remember the last time I slept so well. Everything in me wavers like an empty sack in the wind, and I realize that's exactly what I am now—empty. I still remember every emotion, every worry, the faces of all the people I need to protect—but they're not consuming me anymore. They're just hovering in my mind.

I poke at them uncertainly. Sir—he's still in Winter, and who knows if he's alive or dead? Theron could be ransacking my kingdom now at Angra's behest. Mather . . . he might not have gotten everyone out of the dungeon. He might not have gotten away.

And while I'm aware of the concern each thought brings, I'm not crippled by it. The prevailing emotion in my head is just . . . nothing. Which allows me to focus on the small, insignificant things I'd all but forgotten.

Like the calluses on my hands, softening now because of how long it's been since I regularly threw my chakram. Or the shocking gauntness in my legs and stomach—have I been eating? I honestly can't remember.

So I do. Dishes sit on the table, fresh and steaming, and snow above, nothing has ever tasted so delicious. I don't even know what they are—something savory that looks like potatoes, and something sweet that has the texture of honey and cake all in one. I eat until my stomach bulges, and head for the washbasin in the corner.

After scrubbing my skin, I open the trunk against the wall and find clothes within. Robes; thin, airy pants; soft leather boots that stretch up past my knees; long scarves knotted into belts in a rainbow of colors. I sort through until I find a sky-blue robe with navy swirls on the sleeves and collar, the tones matching my one accessory, the locket. A silver belt completes the outfit, and as I stand in the center of the room, eyes closed, I allow myself a few moments of steady, silent breathing.

For the first time in months, years even, I can breathe. I can feel things beyond crippling doubt, beyond the consuming effort of keeping my emotions in check.

A knock on the door echoes at the edge of my awareness.

"You're ready for the next lesson," comes Rares's voice, and I know he means more than the fact that I am awake and dressed.

"Yes," I start, smiling. "I am."

It turns out, I slept for days. Three days, to be exact. No matter how good my body feels, my mind throbs with guilt at the thought of how much time I wasted.

I remember Angra's vision, his plan for the world. Is he still in Rintiero? Or has he moved on, spreading his fear and darkness to Yakim, Summer, Autumn . . . ?

I hurry after Rares, expecting him to lead me to the training yard I saw out front so we can dive into the sort of training I know I'll need against Angra. When he takes me into a room not far down from mine, I hover in the doorway, confused.

It's small, half the size of my room, with a cluttered desk spilling papers and books onto the floor. Maps cover the walls—maps of Summer, Ventralli, and Yakim; maps of Winter and Spring. Lines trace paths from Abril to Jannuari to Juli to—

"You were tracking me," I say, breathless.

Rares steps forward. "Once the Order knew Hannah was on the right path, we hoped someone in your line would come to the decision to get rid of magic entirely. I only kept an eye out for you to come into your power. Which you did, here." His finger goes to Abril on the map. "And here is where you found the door in the Tadil Mine"—he slides down to Gaos—"and here is where—"

"Okay, I get it." I slap his hand off the map. "You're a centuries-old magical man who's been using his spare time to spy on a teenage girl."

Rares chortles. "Someone got her fire back! But no, I haven't been spying—I was tracking. The only thoughts I ever got from you were magic related, and the occasional worry about war. Need I remind you that certain members of the Order have been tracking Primoria's monarchs for *thousands of years,* waiting for one to decide what you did."

I drop into a padded chair, all the others serving as more space for books and papers.

"Well, it's still strange."

He shrugs. "I'll let you take it out on me later. Until then . . ."

I lean forward, eagerness clearing my mind. Yes, training—*no time to waste.*

Rares takes a seat on the edge of his desk, moving a stack of books to the side. One catches my eye—*Magic of Primoria.*

"That book!"

Rares glances down at it before shooting me a grin. "You've seen this before?"

I nod, my eyes darting over the familiar gold lettering. This copy is just as worn as the one I read in Bithai months ago. The Order wrote it; it makes sense Rares would have a copy.

I shift in the chair, ready, waiting, *desperate.*

I slept for three days. It's been four days since Angra overtook Ventralli.

Be calm. I'm here. I'm doing what I need to be doing.

I square my shoulders and look up at him. "What's the next lesson?"

Rares's eyes brighten.

My lips unfold in the barest smile. "Have I surprised you?"

He laughs. "Have you surprised yourself?"

His question throws me and I shrug. "I'm . . . tired, mostly," I admit. "I'm tired of fighting every single thing in my life. I'm Winter's conduit; I'm Winter's queen; I'm the only one who can stop Angra and the Decay. Not that I've accepted my fate, I'm just done denying it. I've spent years analyzing every choice and resisting every change. I don't like who that's made me. That's not the person I want to be."

"Who do you want to be?" he asks, the one question I've been avoiding for weeks.

I didn't think it mattered. I *told* myself it didn't matter so I wouldn't crumble under how far I was from who I truly wanted to be. But I've already come so far, let go of so much, that maybe I can let go of my self-inflicted barriers too.

So I level a look at Rares. "I want to be enough."

His smile is soft. "You already are, dear heart. *Feeling* like you're enough has nothing to do with actually *being* enough—you choose whether or not you are."

Another choice. That eases me back to the matter at

hand, and I clear my throat, casting off this topic for an equally stifling one.

"The next lesson?" I try again, and Rares waves his hand in agreement.

"Yes, lesson four—do you know what happened to the magic chasm?"

I squint. "Aren't we ready to move on to magic use?" That's how Angra will be defeated, after all. He's too powerful to be taken down with a mere sword—I'll have to counter his Decay with magic, and block any of my people with magic, and save the world, *with magic*.

Rares cocks a brow at me. "Patience, dear heart. Do you know what happened to the magic chasm?"

Anxiety flutters in my stomach—*three days here, four days since the takeover* . . .

But I force my eyes to meet Rares's.

"It vanished centuries ago. No one knows how." I pause. "But I'm guessing you do."

He grins. "If one were to dig deep enough into the Klaryns—in any Season, not just Winter—they would find the same door you did. The only reason you found it is because of Winter's skill at mining; the Order originally constructed the door through Summer's mountains, with it triggered to appear wherever anyone digs past a certain spot, anywhere in the Klaryns. But that is only the first of many obstacles to prevent the magic chasm from being easily accessed. You encountered one other such obstacle in your search for the keys."

Rares fusses with his collar and draws out the key on a long chain. He pulls it off his neck and extends it to me, and I take it, holding it delicately by the chain as he presses on.

"The keys were left in Summer, Yakim, and Ventralli as the creators of the chasm traveled down through those kingdoms from Paisly—and to separate the keys in order to make sure, further, that finding the magic chasm was not easy, and that if someone attempted to open it, the search for the keys would give the Order time to make sure it was someone we *wanted* to reach the chasm. But the next difficulty you will encounter, beyond getting the two other keys back, is the labyrinth that lies behind the door."

A connection snaps into place. "The Order hid the magic chasm. *Paisly* hid it."

Rares sighs. "We only meant to keep the wrong sort from reaching the magic until we could destroy it. We didn't intend for your Seasons to take the blame for the chasm's disappearance. But much happened that we did not intend, dear heart."

A *Rhythm* is responsible for the act that made the rest of the world despise the Seasons.

And while I could easily nurture this spark of anger, I don't. I let it drift away, because it's part of yet more things that have already happened. All I have room for, all I can see, is what lies ahead. The one goal around which all others fizzle: destroying all magic.

"This labyrinth," I start, my fingers tight around the key's chain, "I'll need to use my magic for it too? But can't you come with me? You will, won't you?"

Rares whirls to a stack of books in the corner. When he turns back around, he holds an old, yellowed paper that looks one deep exhale away from fluttering into a million dusty pieces.

"The labyrinth was created by a small group of the Order's most powerful conduits to protect the magic from being easily accessed—and if it is accessed, it was made so only those worthy can reach it. They kept every detail of it secret. Even when they created it, they—" His voice falters and he purses his lips. "Well. They took their secrets to their graves."

My jaw tightens. I'm not the only one who sacrificed everything to protect Primoria. The Order of the Lustrate isn't expecting me to do anything they haven't done themselves.

"But"—Rares lifts an eyebrow—"they left us a clue."

He extends the paper to me and I stand to take it.

Three people the labyrinth demands
Who enter with genuine intent
To face a test of leadership,
A maze of humility,
And purification of the heart.
To be completed by only the true.

I read it twice. Three times. And before I can stop myself, I'm hit with an aching thought:

Theron would know what this means.

I drop the paper on the desk. "A riddle." I back up, legs bumping into the chair until I stumble and catch myself on the armrest. The key's chain bites into my palm, the key itself smacking against my thigh. "Is that all? Because I—I need—"

This room is far too small. For all my progress, I can't catch my breath, and I fall into the chair as I wheeze at the familiarity of reading ancient passages about magic. My memories of Theron rear high—sitting in his library, listening to him talk through that book, *Magic of Primoria*. I let myself dance with the idea of loving him because he was sweet, and kind, and we both wanted more of our lives. Even though it was an arranged marriage, even though it was political, even though I knew that I could never be the person I needed to be to love him.

He would always be Cordell's heir; I would always be bound to Winter.

I press my free hand against my forehead, swallowing the icy bursts of magic that swirl up my throat. I don't want to fight this guilt anymore, but I don't know how to fix it—because I can't save him. Everything that has happened to him will be with him forever, in the same way all Winterians still tremble from their years of enslavement.

So what can I do?

I could do what I've recently done with everything else. Acknowledge it, *feel* it, and let it bob out into the abyss, a constant presence, but not a crippling one.

Rares hasn't moved from his position beside the desk, giving me room, letting me breathe. And when I look up at him, he nods but stays quiet. Letting me heal on my own.

"What does this mean?" I wave at the paper, my voice croaking.

"For one thing, it means only two people can accompany you. The labyrinth accepts only three at a time, to limit those who can gain access to the magic."

"So you can come with me?"

"The door and the labyrinth were made so only the worthy reach the magic chasm. You noticed the barrier that repels anyone who tries to approach the door? The only way to pass that is for three people to cross together, all believing in their worthiness to reach the magic—the second part of the riddle, *Who enter with genuine intent*. A united effort. Simple enough, yes? But not entirely. For once you pass through the door, the labyrinth will make you prove that belief. It will test all three of you in ways that measure this worth—leadership, humility, and heart. I don't know what the tests are precisely, beyond the clues in the riddle, but when you face them, you should be as prepared as possible. Of all the people in the world, which two would you want at your side as you face such trials?"

Faces flash into my mind. *Mather and Sir.*

I frown. Mather, yes. Sir, though . . . there's a rift between us. But I do know that, if it came down to it, Sir would defend me with his life.

"Once you complete the labyrinth and reach the chasm, you will have only a few seconds to destroy it," Rares continues. "When the creators built the labyrinth, they started by forming an exit that opens only when someone accesses the chasm. A way for any worthy souls who reach the magic to leave. But the amount of magic needed to seal off this exit was tremendous, and the moment it opens, every conduit in Primoria will feel it. They will know where it is, and they will be able to access the magic too. You cannot hesitate in your mission, dear heart."

My mission. *Dying.*

I swallow. I can't think about it—can't give myself time to weaken.

"But to successfully complete the labyrinth's tasks, you will need what you came here for: control of your magic." Rares whips his hand out and a cabinet across the room opens. A dagger whizzes out, the hilt barreling into Rares's palm. He curls his fingers around it, beaming.

The noise I make is absolutely pathetic, somewhere between a squeal and a whimper.

I want to understand the ways in which he can control his magic—not only so I can face Angra and protect those I love, but because I had no idea I could use this infuriating energy so gracefully. Magic has done far more bad than good—but as Nessa pointed out in Putnam, we need all the weapons we can get. Any tool I can harness is valuable.

"Oh, dear heart," Rares says, his enthusiasm contagious. "You haven't yet learned the meaning of the word *valuable*."

Meira

AT LONG LAST, Rares leads me out to the training yard. The late-morning sun shines bright on the stables and the dirt rings worn into the earth. The grass billows in the cool air, infusing me with the smells of hay and crisp old wood—aromas that crafted so much of my childhood. All that's missing is the earthy tang of prairie grass and Sir shouting at me about my stance.

My heart knots and I survey Rares as he stops in the middle of the widest ring. Months ago, I wouldn't have questioned my instinct to want Sir with me in the labyrinth. But uncertainty wears a hole in my belly. So much has changed. My relationship with Sir isn't what it used to be—or what I want it to be. But what is it now?

Rares eyes me, ignoring my thoughts, and folds his hands behind his back.

"There are weapons in that crate." He bobs his head

toward a wooden box. "Get one."

I hook the key's chain around my neck and tuck the key itself into my robe, between it and my undershirt to avoid skin contact. When I touched the other keys, I got powerful visions of what I needed to know in order to access the magic chasm. Whatever this key might show me, I don't want it right now—I want to learn how to control my magic, to get one step closer to leaving and helping my friends.

No more distractions, no other lessons, no more emotional breakdowns. Only actions.

I start to walk toward the crate when Rares clucks his tongue.

"No," he chastises. "Without moving from that spot. You treat your magic with confusion, uncertainty, and fear, and as such it responds with chaos. To use conduit magic, you have to *know* what you want. You have to believe unswervingly that you want a sword from that box—just as, when you face the door to the magic chasm, you must know unswervingly that you are worthy. Confidence is essential to mastering magic, and you've already used your magic in such a way when you saw into Angra's mind. You used your magic to touch him—it was a channeled will. You're capable, dear heart. Trust yourself."

I roll my eyes. "Trust myself. You *have* met me, haven't you?"

Rares chuckles. "You can do it. And if you lose control,

don't worry—I'm more than capable of reining you in." He waves around the compound. "This is the one place in Primoria where you don't need to fear using your magic."

I square myself into a more solid stance and look at the crate, the warped lid that sits cocked open on top. I can do this. Even if I mess it up, Rares is right—this is the one place where I'm free to make mistakes. There aren't any Winterians around I could harm.

Or could I accidentally affect Rares and Oana somehow, since they are conduits too?

"Don't overthink," comes Rares's sharp reprimand. "Just *want.*"

I exhale, long and slow, and stretch out my hand.

I want to be able to face Angra and get those keys. I want to be able to protect Winter. I want to be able to stop this, all of this—

I want to survive.

In doing this, I'll protect everyone I love. I'll steal back the keys and get through the labyrinth and save the world from becoming a fearful prison ruled by Angra. But Mather will come with me into that labyrinth. He won't hesitate if I ask him, and he'll be there until the end. That is *not* the end I want for us.

I don't want an end with him at all.

I cup my hands over my face.

I want Sir there with me too. But will he come? I honestly don't know anymore. Last I spoke to him, I was so hurt—where do his loyalties lie now? I want—

I want, I want, I want—

With a tight snarl, I snap my hand out straight. The top on the box creaks open. And as my eyes widen, a sword comes hurtling out. The hilt smacks into my hand, but my shock is so consuming that I forget to grab it and the blade clanks against the dirt.

Rares applauds. "Took you a bit to get there, and your finish needs some work, but it's a start."

I stare at the sword, then at my hand. My fingers prickle, cool and stiff, with the magic that shot down my arm on my unspoken command.

It's a start.

Here I am, flopping swords around a training yard, when out there, beyond Paisly, the world could be burning.

"Not good enough," I snap and straighten my hand out over the sword. How did I do it? It wasn't even a thought, but it came on the back of emotion like all the other times I used my magic. What emotion?

Mather, Sir, the labyrinth, my fate . . .

I don't look away from the sword. "Have you received any word of Angra? The Order is still monitoring him, right? Have you received word from them about what he's doing?"

Rares realizes what I want and clears his throat. "The Order's barrier has kept him out of Paisly, and it appears he's given up attempting to break through—his magic has stopped prodding at our defenses. Which is good, but also worrisome. He knows you'll reemerge eventually, so for now he has turned his attention to the rest of the world. In the four days since the takeover, his forces have secured Ventralli, with Raelyn overseeing the kingdom in his stead. She's readying her army, presumably to join him—he's heading toward the Seasons with Theron, most likely to solidify their hold over Summer or—" Rares hesitates. "Or Winter."

My heart aches. Angra whisked Theron off like an ally, not a prisoner. What else has he made Theron do?

"His takeovers will hopefully be bloodless," Rares continues, his tone still hard and removed, as though he knows showing no emotion will give me room to foster my own. "His method is to approach a city, much as he did Rintiero, and spread his magic to the residents. Most will be taken willingly and bow to him, either joining his army or giving in to the fear his magic fosters in them—they don't know to resist it. Why would they? It happens so quickly, they don't have time to realize who he is. Those who resist, though . . ."

Those who resist. Mather. Ceridwen and Nessa and Conall . . .

I want to stop this. I WILL stop this. I will make myself even more powerful than he is and I will return every speck of worry he's heaped on me tenfold.

The sword wobbles, launches straight up, hilt-first, and I grab it.

Rares hoots in approval, and through the sweat now

beading down my face, I look over at him, frustration and anger and determination making for a toxic swirl that all but blinds me. I have to be in control of my emotions to best use magic—and these emotions are, right now, the easiest to control.

I do want to survive this. But I want to end this too.

I *need* to end this.

Unfortunately, I have to constantly keep that desire in my mind.

Rares doesn't move directly into fighting—for two days, he has me retrieve every sword from the crate and put them back to make sure I "understand the fundamentals of magic."

Two days.

Three that I spent sleeping.

Six, total, since Angra took Rintiero.

Each passing minute reminds me of all I'm letting happen in my absence, made more potent when I tell Rares to weave news of Angra into our training.

Rares can only give me updates based on what the Order observes—which means he can't tell me any specifics about my kingdom or my friends. Though this also means Angra hasn't spread his evil to them yet, which is infinitely preferable to having more concrete news of them. They escaped Rintiero. Angra hasn't yet reached Winter. I have to believe they're all okay.

The other news stays much the same—Angra approaches Summer; Ventralli is under his control, Raelyn's troops are readying to move out; Cordell has sent extra soldiers to supplement Angra's army; another force gathers in Spring, presumably to join Angra as well. Yakim remains untouched; Autumn is a mystery. Rares can tell me the state of citizens within each kingdom Angra has overtaken as he spreads his magic to them. It's faint—small currents of connection that only let Rares know they've succumbed to Angra—but it's enough that I become very, very good at retrieving swords.

By the time the last sword clanks against the others under the orange evening sky of the second day, sweat drips down my face despite the coolness of the proper spring air. I slam the lid closed with only the barest thought and throw a glare at Rares.

"How many more times—"

But he isn't looking at me. Through every clumsily lifted sword he watched me, arms folded, eyes bright, but now he stares at the main wall of his compound. For the first time since I met him, he looks worried, and panic flares in my heart.

I'm reaching for the crate to draw a sword back to me when Rares spins around.

"No," he says. "Alin found . . ."

He says a word that doesn't process, not here, so I shake my head.

"What did you—"

"Winterians," Rares repeats.

My muscles go slack.

"What?" is all I'm able to say.

"Two," he tells me. "Alin says one is hurt—he's unconscious."

All my incapacitating shock breaks away under that, letting turmoil rush in.

Winterians.

He's unconscious.

Mather?

I take off toward the gate, the iron bars already groaning open at my command. Before I make it two paces forward, Rares is there, his hands digging into my shoulders.

"Alin will bring them here," he assures me. "He's on his way."

I glare up at him. "But how did they even get here?"

The question hits Rares, making him wince.

"What?" I shake him. *"What?"*

"When we first arrived in Paisly," Rares says, "Angra found you right away. How did he know where to search for you? I simply assumed he'd figured out on his own where we'd be. But what if . . . someone told him?"

I'm numb. A river frozen solid.

I don't know the full story yet—it could be that Mather and one of his Thaw followed me on their own.

It isn't—it *can't be*—that Angra caught them, dug my

location out of them, and planted them here for me.

But my heart whispers the truth, and I look over the wall.

Rares squeezes my shoulders again. "Alin will bring them here," he promises me again.

I step out of Rares's grip and the gate thuds into the dirt. "Just get them here," I say before I square myself in front of the gate, arms crossed, chest humming with an emotion I know all too well—terror.

And this time, it isn't something I can let go, because the thought of Mather, unconscious, grows more unbearable with each heartbeat.

Mather

WHEN MATHER WAS a child, he could train every day in weaponry; he could listen with undivided attention to William's lessons on war strategy, economy, and history; he could be kind and fair and just. But not a single one of those things made him the female heir Winter needed, and through every lesson, he always felt that nagging pull in the back of his mind that whispered of his true worth—which was, at the time, merely to someday carry on the female lineage of his kingdom.

And in the dark, quiet nights, when the whole camp slept in their haphazard tents in whatever location William had selected, Mather would find himself wishing an impossible wish. One he didn't dare voice aloud, not when his kingdom's salvation depended on it:

He wished for magic to disappear. He wished for a world

free of it, where worth was based on a leader's true self, not on gender.

Mather had harbored this wish until Angra was over-thrown and Meira revealed as the true heir. Then, it seemed almost as if magic might be good after all—it had saved their kingdom. So he'd pushed that wish aside, and tried to accept the world as it was.

But when Phil's screams turned to wails that weren't so much heard as felt, Mather wished more than he ever had that magic didn't exist.

Mather was held on the ground through every tortured wail, unable to even see what they were doing to his friend. And when silence finally came, a bag was tugged over his head, his wrists shackled, his legs bound, everything tight and suffocating and *pain*.

He was thrown alone inside something wooden, the air tainted with the smell of mildew, telling him that either they were on the Langstone River or he was in some kind of box that had been on a ship. The rocking, reeling motion of his crate was too haphazard to guess whether he was being tugged along by wagon or boat. But they traveled, and traveled, and traveled some more, and just when Mather thought he might pass out from the improperly ventilated box, they stopped.

The heave of his crate sent him tumbling into one of the walls. His shoulder only connected with the wood for half a breath before the wall vanished, a door that opened and sent him plummeting out. Though Theron had shoved Cordell's conduit back into Mather's belt, he'd been unable to bend at the necessary angle to reach it, and therefore had been unable to get the manacles off during the trip. He had nothing to break his fall as he slammed into the ground.

Rocks. Gravel, mostly. No grass.

Where were they?

Hands lifted him by his upper arms, and after so long being bound, he hissed in pain at the further contortion. It would take weeks for his muscles to forgive him.

Such thoughts were all he'd let himself think during the journey. Anything else . . .

Mather squared his jaw.

His captors tore the bag off his head, cut the binding on his legs, even unlocked his manacles. The freedom died even before it had time to blossom—if they felt comfortable undoing his bonds, he had to be seriously outnumbered.

"*Ice above,*" he cursed, and bowed his head to his chest, his eyes watering at the stabbing intrusion of light. But he blinked, clearing his vision, and snapped his head up to take in his surroundings.

He had been in a wagon, for this part of the journey, at least. Cliffs loomed all around, and a bright-blue sky contrasted against the grim gray stones. If he hadn't known any better, he'd have said they were in the Klaryns, but they hadn't been traveling that long.

A *thump* pulled Mather's attention back to the wagon.

Some of the soldiers—ten in total, and neither Angra nor Theron among them, which was both a relief and horrifically unnerving—had opened another compartment near the back, out of which they dragged Phil.

Shockingly, no one stopped Mather as he scrambled to his feet, then dropped, knees folding with disuse. But determination won out, letting him half drag, half throw himself at Phil, who buckled on the stony ground without so much as a moan.

Mather held Phil upright, hands digging into his shoulders. One of Phil's eyes was swollen shut; the other blinked away blood that trickled from a cut over his brow.

But that was it. There were no other wounds that Mather could see, and Phil didn't favor any limbs or hold his hands over any gashes.

"What did they do to you?" Mather demanded.

Phil looked at him, tears welling. "I . . . told them . . . where she went. . . ."

Phil's face flashed with dread as the soldiers grabbed Mather and heaved him back, tossing him against one of the many boulders that lined the clearing. His hands were coated with the chalky grime of stones, and as he spun, he clenched his fists, legs in the best defensive stance his still-unsteady body could muster.

Phil only had three soldiers standing over him—the final seven had gathered around Mather.

One of the soldiers tossed something at Phil's feet.

Mather blinked. Was that . . .

Phil frowned at it, looked up at the soldiers, then at Mather.

It was Meira's chakram.

The soldier closest to Mather sneered. "Angra wants her to have it—consider it a gift, a mark of his leniency. He wants her to have *you*, too, so you can tell her something for him."

Exhaustion and hunger and a myriad of worries made Mather's brain slog through details like a horse in a muddy field. One soldier swung a fist, and Mather ducked, but another soldier met his movement with a punch to the gut. The air shot out of his lungs and he wheezed, doubling over.

The soldier bent over Mather as he slumped to his knees.

"If you live through this, tell her that this is what will happen to everyone who sides against Angra. And even if you don't survive—well, I suppose that will warn her all the same."

With that, he landed an elbow on the back of Mather's spine and dropped him to his stomach, where he landed with a broken grunt.

Phil sobbed, limp in the arms of the soldiers.

The others descended. Seven against him—Mather tried to fight back, but even as he did, he felt the hopelessness in every fist to his body.

Angra knew where Meira was. And Mather would lose this fight.

He wouldn't be there to help her.

Mather leaped up and dove at the closest man. A bright flash cut through his vision, a jolt of white that shocked every nerve into deadened silence.

He collapsed as a soldier swung another rock, but nothing else came—only pain.

Ceridwen

AFTER GISELLE DISEMBARKED in Putnam, the Yakimians dumped Ceridwen, Jesse, and Lekan where the Southern Eldridge Forest met the Langstone River, leaving them with horses, a day of supplies, and reminders of their queen's wishes—to stop Angra before he could destroy Yakim. No hint as to *how* they might do such a thing. Which was almost preferable—Ceridwen wasn't bound to follow any more of Giselle's orders—but she had no idea how to go about stopping Angra. Wait for Meira to show up and hope she had a plan? Track Angra's location and stage an assassination attempt?

Ceridwen kept Giselle's seal in her pocket and pretended the weight of the impending war was enough to distract her from Jesse's presence.

She knew her time of ignoring him wouldn't last. But,

flame and heat, she would fight to do so until the bitter end.

The refugee camp was only a day's ride from the Langstone, and Ceridwen was grateful that they didn't have to spend a night camping in the forest. Just as the sun and night sky warred on the horizon, they broke out of the trees into the Rania Plains.

Lekan's husband had helped pick this location. They had had a camp deeper in the Eldridge before, but with so many Summerian refugees, the wet, chill climate was less than ideal. Their camp now straddled the edge of the forest, close enough to the trees to allow for resources to be scavenged yet close enough to the plains to give the Summerians needed breaks of heat and dryness. Ceridwen breathed that arid wind, her chest aching at the memories such scents dredged up. Memories of Summer, of her cracked earth baking in the sun.

She squeezed Giselle's seal. The Yakimian queen wasn't the only one with a kingdom to protect from Angra. And now that Simon was dead, and Ceridwen Summer's only living heir . . .

Ceridwen closed her eyes, catching the gasp that rose in her throat. Her brother had *died*, Angra was slowly yet persistently enslaving the world, but some deep, sick place inside her reveled in knowing that one of her longest-kept goals had finally been achieved. For years she had bled to be the sole ruler of Summer.

She was a Summerian, through and through—able to find joy in any situation.

Ceridwen forced her eyes open. Through the dim blueness of night and the pale brown grass a few shapes moved toward them.

"Lekan!"

Kaleo leaped through the tall grass. A few soldiers followed—and Ceridwen sighed in relief to see they were Summerian, not Yakimians posing as refugees, *damn Giselle*—but they turned back to the camp when they heard Kaleo's confirmation of who approached.

Lekan kicked his horse but didn't let it get far before he heaved on the reins. His injured leg had stopped bleeding, but it still had to cause him pain when he dropped to the ground. He didn't hesitate in his mad rush to meet Kaleo in the grass, and the two collided, Kaleo's force sending Lekan toppling backward, their bodies vanishing in the waist-high grass amid a chorus of laughter—which quickly faded to a silence that made Ceridwen cut her eyes to Jesse.

He looked so different without a mask, and among the other things Ceridwen hadn't yet talked to him about was whether or not he wanted a new one. She couldn't deny the part of her that loved being able to see his emotions as he watched Lekan and Kaleo, a smile lifting his lips, consuming his whole face in light.

Then Jesse stiffened in his saddle, the muscles in his neck convulsing as he swallowed and looked at her. He bowed his head as if she had given him an order and kicked his horse on, fading into camp. She expected to be able to breathe easier with him gone. But nothing changed, not a single spark of relief.

Ceridwen pulled alongside Lekan and Kaleo. When her horse's hooves clomped just next to them, Kaleo whipped upright, straddling Lekan's waist.

"Princess! You brought him back injured. Again."

Ceridwen shrugged. "Only because I know how much he loves you taking care of him."

Lekan flopped out, arms splayed. "You'd better restrain me. Bed rest, for my own good, since I can't be trusted to stay safe and uninjured anywhere else."

Kaleo balled the fabric of Lekan's shirt in his fist, leaning deeper over him with a look that prompted Ceridwen to chuckle.

"I've slept in tents next to you two," she said. "I'm not sure your idea of *bed rest* is any safer."

Kaleo roared with laughter and Lekan used the distraction to flip on top of him, but the movement landed him wrong on his wound and he yelped in pain. As Kaleo moved to check Lekan's knee, their words softened, more teasing banter that, had Ceridwen been less used to them, would have made her blush.

She pushed forward, leaving them to their reunion. The camp stretched in a haphazard circle, more tents added whenever new refugees joined their group, creating uneven roads and paths. A messy, chaotic camp for a messy, chaotic group.

Ceridwen slid off her horse and eased it into a corral at the edge of camp. Everyone had settled in for the night, with only soldiers patrolling, casting nods as they recognized her. She studied each tent. Everything where it should be.

Her fists tightened involuntarily.

Well, everything almost where it should be. Three hundred of the refugees around her were Yakimian soldiers. There were no more than eight hundred people here in all.

Ceridwen growled. That meant there were three hundred places in this camp that could have been taken by slaves who actually needed saving.

Damn Giselle.

How many of the Yakimian spies had posed as soldiers here? How many had stayed hidden in the ranks of families and laborers? In the worst case, if every Yakimian soldier had taken up ranks as one of Ceridwen's fighters, she'd have only about a hundred and fifty non-Yakimian soldiers. *A hundred and fifty.* To make any sort of stand against Angra . . . that amount was laughable. She'd *have* to use the Yakimian soldiers. But for what?

The refugee fighters had been causing mayhem despite their small numbers for years—they could continue the sort of guerilla attacks that had frequently crippled Summer's forces. Surprise assaults from treetops, traps constructed on rough roads.

Ceridwen rubbed her forehead.

Would any of that really make a difference against Angra? Could she unseat whatever hold he had on Summer with guerilla fighters? Because she'd go after Summer first, regardless of Giselle's plea. Let Yakim sweat a little under Angra's threat.

"Wennie!"

Ceridwen grinned. Only one person had ever called her that, and the first time she had heard it, her nose had wrinkled. But that had only encouraged the now eight-year-old Amelie. The Yakimian girl had been just two when she had been sold to Summer, and it hadn't taken long for Kaleo and Lekan to fall in love with her and bring her into their family.

Lekan hadn't uttered a word about Giselle's revelation. Not once had he said, "My daughter's life was the currency that bitch used to finance her planned attack on Summer."

Though Ceridwen knew Lekan well enough to realize he'd never even think anything like that. Ceridwen would just have to be ragingly furious for him.

She opened her arms to Amelie, who slid into her hug. "Lekan's back," she said, and Amelie's already large brown eyes widened even more. The scar under her left eye, the branded *S*, wrinkled with her smile, the marking old enough to be smoother and less noticeable than that of those who had been branded as adults. But it was still there, a screaming testament that, if Amelie had returned to Yakim, would have earned her a quick trip back to Summer. She was Summer's property now—and so she, like all the others Ceridwen and her group had freed, had to remain in this hidden camp, safe from any who would force her into a life of nonexistence.

A mask would hide that brand. Ceridwen swallowed. Sending her refugees to Ventralli was an option she had once considered—but not for long.

Amelie clapped, her wild black hair bobbing around her shoulders, and she ran off.

"Papa!" she shrieked, and from out in the plains, Lekan's voice echoed back.

"Amy!"

Ceridwen smiled. It was refreshing to see a child still capable of being a *child*, happy and innocent in all the best ways.

A figure shifted on her left, and when Ceridwen turned, Jesse stepped into the light of a nearby lantern. The dark strands of his hair brushed around his shoulders, his collarbone, the dip of skin where he had unbuttoned his shirt. The angle of his jaw caught the light, sharp beneath a layer of beard that had sprouted after days without a proper shave. He had never looked so disheveled, but he wore his unkemptness like an outfit he had purposefully chosen, and Ceridwen's lips threatened a smile at how utterly Ventrallan that was of him. To make something beautiful despite the challenges.

"Are your children here yet?" Ceridwen asked, her voice croaking halfway through her question as she realized . . . she was talking to him.

Jesse seemed just as shocked. His already tense body jolted in surprise, hands in his pockets, shoulders caved in a state of meek surrender. "No—I checked with a few of the soldiers." Sorrow painted his features, but he shrugged it away, forcing optimism. "They might not have traveled by boat. It could be a few days."

"We can send someone out to search for them."

"Yes. Yes, please." He caught himself, his eagerness, and reined it back. Afraid of pushing too far, of showing too much emotion.

Four years, her mind argued. *I waited on him for four years.*

Four years, her heart countered. *I've waited for him for four years.*

"Have you . . ." She cleared her throat. "Have you been given a tent yet?"

He shook his head. "I should have asked when I went looking for my children." He scratched his neck. "I'm not thinking straight at the moment."

"Who is?" Ceridwen grumbled, and headed into the camp.

Jesse followed a pace behind. "Have you given any consideration to how you'll use Giselle's soldiers?"

Ceridwen clenched her hands and shot her words over her shoulder. "Really? *You* want to speak of war?"

"Simply because Ventralli hasn't seen war in years doesn't mean I can't be of service. I spent many nights watching you—"

Ceridwen spun on him. They were outside a tent not far from the exterior circle, one of the many reserved for refugees on their first nights before permanent housing could be arranged. Fabric draped from the pointed roof to the ground, overlapping strands nailed in place to allow breezes to enter while keeping prying eyes out.

"No," she snapped. "You wouldn't expect someone to know how to work with glass simply because he watched a glassblower for a few hours, would you? Whatever happens next won't concern you." Ceridwen grabbed the tent's flap and pulled it open. "There should be a cot and a bucket with fresh water—"

"That's not what I meant." Jesse's voice was brittle. "I spent years watching you fight for Summer, so I know what *you* need. And if you need someone to talk to, I can listen."

"So can Lekan."

"Fair point." Jesse bowed his head. "But I'm . . . here, Cerie."

She pinned her eyes on the road, one hand wound in the tent flap. This road was darker than most, only a single lantern nearby. It made everything indistinct, the trampled grass and the leaning tents and the sweep of star-speckled sky above.

"Soldiers come by every fifteen minutes," she said. "Any

of them will be able to help you if you need more—"

"*Cerie*."

She dropped the tent flap but couldn't make her feet move. There were a dozen different things she had to do—plan how to confront the Yakimian soldiers; send people to find news of Jesse's children, not to mention Meira; figure out what her next step should be. If Meira hadn't made it out of Ventralli, this war would come down to . . . her.

Jesse was right. She did need to talk to someone—but more than that, she just *needed* someone.

And that more than anything kept her rooted to the ground.

"Cerie." Jesse said her name again, as if it would mend every wound he had created. "I'm sorry. For Raelyn, for Summer, for . . . you. I'm sorry I hurt you, over and over." He managed a weak, dying chuckle. "I still don't understand why you tolerated me for so long."

Her breath hitched. *Me neither.*

But every reason was just as branded on her heart as all the pain he had caused. Each scar had a contradictory excuse to match, and she had fallen asleep so many nights counting them all.

I love you because you were the only one who heard me out when I came as a Summerian ambassador to Ventralli, and even though your council denied my country aid, you tried so hard for my people. I love you because you showed the kind of devotion I wish my king did. I love you because you love your children. I love you because you love the tradition of wearing masks and all the things your people create.

I love you for the same reason I loved my brother—because I'm weak, too.

"Stop," Ceridwen croaked.

"I don't deserve you," Jesse pressed. "That was why I went along with my mother's plea to marry Raelyn—I knew I didn't deserve you, and I thought it would be better for both of us if I married someone else. But you still loved me, even after, and I wanted to be worthy of you, so I kept you because I hoped that I would become the man I was when I was with you *always*."

"Stop," she said again, louder, and she knew he heard her this time.

"And I'm sorry, Ceridwen." His voice cracked. "When Raelyn broke my conduit, I didn't even care about the magic—all I wanted was you. I should have let that want be my guiding light all these years, but I didn't. I won't just apologize, though—I've said far too much that was empty over the years. The only thing I've ever said that truly mattered was that I love you. So I'll say that every moment of every day as I *do* things, not just *say* things, to prove how much I regret not treating you as you deserve. I love you, Ceridwen. *I love you*."

Ceridwen wanted to race to her tent and leave him here with his apologies. She wanted to shout at him to stop throwing emotions at her. She wanted far too much, tee-tered on the edge of a bottomless abyss, one that was black and putrid with the events of the past few days, and every word Jesse said nudged her closer and closer to falling.

Her brother had died before she'd gotten to say anything real to him. She'd wanted to scream at him about all the horrible things he'd done, about how he was the one who had forced her into a life of being alone. It was his fault—he chose to be her enemy.

She glared at Jesse. "You say this *now*. You needed the end of the world to figure out that I'm worth fighting for."

"I always knew you were worth fighting for," Jesse moaned. "I was just never worthy of fighting for you."

"I always knew you weren't worthy of me. I always knew you were weak, Jesse, and I don't want to have to put you together." The accusation cut into her own insecurities. "You are weak, and broken, and *you are alone*. Why did you ever think anyone would help you? You are nothing, and that's why you're alone, that's why you've failed *so many times*—because there was never anything in you to begin with."

The ground caught her as she dropped to her knees.

She was alone, in ways she couldn't entirely fathom. Her mother probably still lived, but what use had she ever been? Simon was dead, and honestly . . . what had she expected him to become? For him to wake up one day and realize how dangerous he was? No, there never would have been a happy resolution for her brother. Not for Summer, not for herself.

Arms stretched across her back. Tentative, shaking arms that eased her forward, rocking her into Jesse's chest. She knew this chest so well, every tense line of muscle, every expanse of skin. And he knew her body, too. He knew where to clasp his fingers around her arm, past the point on her left shoulder where a long-ago injury still ached if touched. He knew to stroke his thumb across the base of her jaw, just under her ear, steady, rhythmic caresses that rippled across her whole body.

She knew him, and he knew her, and he was *here*.

Ceridwen's body went limp.

"I don't trust you," she whispered.

"Don't," he said. "Let me prove myself. I owe you a lifetime of penance, Cerie."

A lifetime of penance could have meant any number of things. But what Ceridwen saw was her brother's head snapping on his neck. His lifetime had ended, so quickly, before she'd gotten a chance to tell him that she loved him, despite everything he had done, because he was *hers*, part of her kingdom, part of her family, and she couldn't help herself.

If she knew she would live a safe, long life, Ceridwen would be able to rationalize and convince herself that she needed better than Jesse. But now, this life she led—she knew how fragile it was, how she would most likely die too young in battle. In this kind of life, there was only time for wants, not needs. And she wanted Jesse.

She wanted him because she didn't want to wake up alone every morning. She didn't want to know he was out there and not hers when she could have him now. That was greedy, yes—it was also dangerous and careless and stupid.

But that was what war did. It made people realize the importance of stupid things.

A cot groaned under her. Jesse's lips brushed her forehead, his hands smoothed back her hair, and before she could piece together any words, she was gone.

Meira

THE TENSION IN the compound makes breathing impossible. All I can do is stand and stare at the wall, as Oana rushes out and threads an arm around my shoulders. Rares remains poised next to me, head tipped as if he's listening.

Rares can communicate with Alin—so should I be able to communicate with Mather and whoever came with him? They're not conduits, but rulers can use their magic to channel will and strength into their people, so maybe I could . . . what? Channel a random burst of strength into them? Or I could travel there and use my magic to bring them back to the compound instantly—but adding dizziness and vomiting to their injuries won't help anything.

I stagger closer to Rares. "Where are they? Did something happen?"

Rares opens his mouth and lifts a finger simultaneously.

After a beat, he points at the gate. "Now."

I send it slamming into the wall above as I sprint forward, eyes trained on Alin, who perches on the driver's seat of a wagon. By the time Rares and Oana guide the cart all the way into their compound and drop the gate, I'm already swinging around the cart.

Blue eyes blink up at me, one buried in a swelling mound of purple and red, the other under a cut that runs across his brow. He's one of Mather's Thaw, his white hair dangling around his face in matted clumps.

"Phil?" I guess.

He nods, trembling like a dog cowering from his master.

"My . . . my queen . . . ," he mumbles, and saying that breaks him. He flies out of the wagon, hands over his head and knees trembling until he drops, huddling in a ball on the ground.

"I'm sorry . . . I didn't want to . . . I tried so hard. . . ."

I watch him, unable to breathe.

What *happened*?

At the edge of my mind I hear Oana's soothing voice, the donkey bleating into the air, the wind hissing in my ears. It all fades to a muted hum when my eyes pin on Mather.

He lies in the bed of the cart, curled on his side as if they hauled his body in and drove off as fast as possible. Blood cakes the whole right side of his head, darkest near a wound on his temple. A saturated bandage hangs around his forehead and his chest rises in clipped breaths.

I've seen him injured before, after missions in our refugee camp; after particularly brutal sparring sessions. But through all those injuries, he winced and cried out in pain, but he was never unconscious. He was always able to look at me, and I never realized until now how necessary that was for my heartbeat to remain steady.

Oana touches my shoulder. "We need to get him inside, sweetheart," she pleads, and I realize I'm blocking Rares and Alin from lifting Mather out of the cart.

I leap back near Phil, who sobs, and when I turn, he's standing. His arms wrap so tightly around his torso that I fear he may snap himself in half.

"What happened?" My question slams into Phil, making him stagger.

"No . . ." He covers his eyes, the heels of his palms pressing deep. Each moment he doesn't speak lets possibilities thud in me. Images of Mather climbing the mountains in pursuit of me and falling; images of him trying to escape Rintiero and getting attacked by Angra's men—

Phil mumbles something into his wrists.

"What?"

He drops his hands. Looks at me. Then at Mather, now hanging limp between Alin and Rares as they haul him toward the castle.

"I had to make the voices stop," Phil whispers.

My body goes hot. "Angra?" I guess.

Phil moans softly and nods.

"I told them—where we were going," he says, gagging between words. "I told them—where you were—and they took us to the mountains—and Angra, he didn't come. He said—he said we'd be enough to make you come back. He had his men beat Mather to show you what Angra will do to everyone who stands against him." Phil doubles over, hands on his knees. "I told them where you were to make the voices stop, but they beat him in front of me, and I'd . . . I'd rather have the voices. . . ."

The door to the castle opens and Rares backs in, Mather's head lolling against his stomach.

I swallow Phil's words, my own agony, anything that makes me teeter on the edge of falling apart.

Through all I have to do, the sacrifice I have to make, my life is the only one that will be taken. I refuse to lose more people to this.

I throw that need deep into the magic, let it spread through the void.

Mather will live. Do you hear me?

He will live.

Rares and Alin put him on a cot in a narrow room with tables, a washbasin, blankets, and candles. Alin murmurs his apologies as he leaves, returning to his post, and Rares and I hover in the doorway, quiet enough that we can hear the muffled words of Oana caring for Phil a few rooms down.

Rares crosses his arms over his chest, and for the first time since I met him, I can't find a hint of levity anywhere in his demeanor.

I talk before he can. "Angra didn't come to Paisly."

Rares pulls his eyes away from Mather. "He knows he can't survive a direct attack—at least, not without the rest of Primoria's armies on his side. Which he's well on his way to having."

I look back at Mather. The blood on his head, pulsing fresh and bright.

"He won't heal without your help," Rares says.

"No." I shake my head. "I can't—I will *not* risk his life by hurting him more than he—"

Rares grabs my arms and the sorrow in his eyes undoes me. "The best I can do is make him comfortable while he slowly passes on. He's lost too much blood, the wound is too deep—the only way he will survive this is with Winterian magic."

One breath is all the time it takes—less than that, actually. One glimpse of Mather, broken, bleeding, out of the corner of my eye.

"I'll keep you from losing control," Rares assures me, but I'm already nodding. "It's the same as drawing objects to you. Relax your mind and let your choice echo out."

I push into the room until I slam to a halt just beside the cot. Mather's skin tone is gray instead of the vibrant, healthy gleam it should be. His chest moves almost imperceptibly, and my own aches in tandem with his tremulous breaths.

The cot squeals as I sit on it and take Mather's hand. Clammy sweat beads on his palm, but I weave my fingers with his, unrelenting against his limp grasp.

Rares was wrong, though. This use of magic is far different from drawing swords to me in the training yard. Then it was simply to understand how magic works.

Now it's war.

Angra brought the fight to me. He dragged me into it, whether or not I was ready.

But he will not win.

And next time, the fight will be on *my* terms.

I keep my eyes on Mather's closed lids, watching for any flutter of awareness, squeezing his hand tighter with each jerking thud of my heart.

He's always been in my life, and I never asked for more than that. Because our people needed saving; because I thought he was Winter's king; because of a hundred different reasons that always let me keep him at the edge of my life, constant and unchanged.

And with the weight of the magic chasm looming over me, I realize what I want now.

I want *him*.

I don't want him hovering at the edge of my life—I want him at the center, beaming that smile that has always shot through me. I want us to be *us* again, Meira and Mather.

I want him to look at me.

The magic glides forward and I open myself to it, willing every drop to pour out of me. Frigid tendrils snake all over his body. I'm amazed at how well I know every part of him, how easy it is to channel the magic away from minor injuries—that cut will heal on its own; that ache in his knee he got from a swordfight years ago, nothing life-threatening—and force all of it to hover over the wound on his head. I hold it there, staring at the bloody injury, squeezing his hand tighter, tighter, tighter—

Mather launches upright, sucking in breaths as though he's been held under water too long.

And he looks at me, finally looks at me, his sapphire eyes darting over my face in a way that feels like home.

"Meira," he breathes, relief draining the stress from his face. His eyes flash behind me, to Rares, and he shifts up a little straighter, wincing. "Where—what happened? Where's Phil?"

"He's fine." Rares steps forward. "He'll be patched up soon enough. Angra won't be able to add your lives to his death toll today."

I bite my lips, fighting the urge to delve into that topic. Rares doesn't give me a chance.

"I'll let you two have some privacy. I'm sure there's . . ." He stops, his gaze falling to where I still hold Mather's hand. I stiffen, unable to decide whether or not to pull away.

"We have time," Rares finishes. Those words leave a weight

on my heart as he shuts the door behind him, and when I pivot back to Mather, he's leaning toward me.

He hasn't looked at me this openly in months.

I swallow and prod gently at his wound, not trusting myself that it's really healed. He holds under my analysis, eyes dancing over mine, the barest beginnings of a smile on his lips. The musk of sweat radiates off him, but it does nothing to slow the sudden speed of my heart, licking all the way up my throat.

"You reek," I cough.

His smile expands. "I'm glad to see you too."

"You need . . . water." I fumble as I leap up and move to the washbasin. I grab a cloth and plunge it in, holding it there to occupy myself.

The cot shifts as Mather moves his legs to the floor. "Ice above, what did you do to me?"

I launch the towel at him. "Saved your life. You're welcome."

He removes the bandage and pats the towel against the caked blood, his eyes lifting to me. His attention holds, the silence weighing as if each second drops stones on my shoulders.

"Phil told me what happened," I manage. "Who else did Angra—"

The cot creaks as Mather rises. "Just us," he says softly, and I'm able to breathe, albeit only a little. "Dendera's leading everyone else to safety. Phil and I split off to—" He stops. "To find you. But don't you dare blame yourself, Meira—I didn't go after you twice before. No force in this world could have kept me from going after you a third time."

I gape at him. Whatever response I expected, this isn't it—him, blood-splattered, moments out from being close to death, but staring at me as if he's been beside me all along, just waiting for any word from me.

Mather swallows, the muscles in his neck convulsing. He takes tentative steps forward and leans next to me, against the washbasin's table. "Angra . . . he didn't come with us, when his men brought us here. He didn't stage a direct attack. Why? Why are you here?"

I run my fingers around the outside of the washbasin. Discussing magic and Paisly and my plans for Angra— it suddenly feels like the easiest topic of conversation, instead of talking about all the things I want when I look at Mather.

So I explain it all to him—but I leave out a few details. I tell him what I am now, what happened when Angra broke Winter's conduit. I tell him what Angra is too, what the Decay is, how it's spreading. I tell him about Rares and why I followed him—because he is part of the Order, and I couldn't control my magic, and I needed to know more so I can defeat Angra. I tell him about the labyrinth, about the three tasks and the magic chasm and the keys I need to get from Angra to open it.

But I don't tell Mather exactly what I need to do to destroy magic. Or even how the magic would keep me alive indefinitely, if I were to not die in the chasm.

Still, when I'm done, he stares at me with horror. Then it washes away with a shake of his head, and he turns, crossing his arms as he drops back against the table.

"We need to get to Winter. To the . . . labyrinth," he says, dazed. "Before Angra can take full advantage of the uprising Cordell started."

"Eventually. But I can't do this unprepared. Angra won't give me many chances." I stifle a sigh. "And he won't give me much time, either."

"Then we'll force him to give us time. We'll get an army—we have to have supporters somewhere." He shifts against the table, his eyes fluttering shut on a wobbling breath. "We'll attack him, pull his attention, buy as much time as you need."

I smile and wrap my hand around his arm. "We'll plan later—rest now."

He smiles. "Is that an order, my queen?"

I nudge him toward the bed, but his arm hardens under my touch to make himself immovable.

"Yes, it's an order," I say, shoving him futilely. "And might I add, I order you to never get so close to death again."

My teasing falls flat under his gaze. I think, at first, it's from the mention of what Angra did to him, but he lifts his other hand and grabs my fingers.

"I'm sorry," he says, his eyes heavy. "I'm sorry this was the only time I came after you."

I almost ask what he means, but the explanation hits me so hard I choke.

"I didn't go after you twice before," he said.

"You always did what was best for Winter," I say, breathless from the regret that fogs his face. He's been carrying this guilt around for months? "You couldn't have done anything to save me when Herod took me to Abril. Angra still thought you were Hannah's son. If he'd caught you . . . it would have been much worse than what he did now. You helped me by staying away—it would have destroyed me to see you in his hands. And I left Jannuari on political business. How were you to know it would end like it did? Besides, you helped me far more by staying in Winter and training your Thaw."

One side of Mather's mouth cocks up, his eyes racing over my face. "I knew you'd try to convince me I shouldn't feel bad. But duty aside, I should have done more. Been more. For you. I'm sorry, Meira."

I swallow, but the lump in my throat refuses to dissolve. He adjusts his fingers over my hand, and the bundled muscles in his arms coil tighter under my touch, making me all too aware of how tense his body is, and how close I am to him. The softness in his face coaxes a dizzy surge through me as his eyes drop to my mouth, staying there for long enough that I sway.

"You should rest," I tell him, but I barely hear myself.

"Rest," he echoes, like he only half heard me, like he's having trouble breathing too.

Snow, has he ever been this close to me before?

My lips part.

Should he be?

I back up, and it's enough to break the spell.

He runs a hand down his face. "Rest. I suppose I should."

He finally lets me help him to the cot, where he collapses on an exhausted groan. I don't let myself linger, backing up so I'm not tempted.

"If you need anything . . ." I trail off, because I'm pretty sure we *both* need something.

Mather lolls his head on the pillow to throw me a playful grin. "I'll come to you."

I stumble out the door, close it behind me, and collapse against it.

There is something wrong with me still. I didn't expect to instantly fix all my issues, but I thought I'd at least progressed enough to let myself love who I want to love. But when we fight this war, when I get to the magic chasm . . .

I don't want to hurt him.

"Maybe he wouldn't see it like that."

I jump, surprise flicking out to every limb. "Really?" I groan to Rares, already feeling heat rise to my cheeks. "You've been listening?"

He pulls away from where he had been leaning against the opposite wall. "Your thoughts are practically at a scream, dear heart."

"Liking you is hard sometimes."

"You and Oana can swap horrid stories about me later." He levels a penetrating stare at me. "You deserve happiness, Meira. No matter how brief."

I cross my arms. "It's not just about me."

"Ah, and therein lies an interesting development, I feel. I seem to recall a particularly strong emotion of yours. You hated Sir and Hannah for making decisions for you— but it would appear that you are doing the same thing to Mather. Making a decision regarding his future before he's even aware there's a decision to be made."

"I didn't . . ."

But I can't deny any of it.

Rares pats my shoulder. "I'm willing to bet that boy of yours thinks you're worth any sorrow. Because you *are*."

An ache pounds in me, one so deep I don't know if even Rares's words can soothe it.

"How can I love him," I ask, "when I'm not even sure I love *me* yet?"

Rares purses his lips and before I can back away, his

knuckle thunks against my forehead. I start, rubbing my skin, a frown working its way onto my face.

"Stop it," he chastises. "I told you I wouldn't stand for such talk about the person who will save us. You act as though love is a goal you only achieve after so long spent working at it. And yes, work is involved, but at the end of it all, love is a choice—the kind you have with a spouse, with your people, with *yourself*. If you acted on those things only when you felt them, you'd be like most people—eternally waiting for a feeling that may or may not come. But if you choose, every day, to love yourself no matter what—then, dear heart, nothing can stop you."

A breathy laugh comes. Everything really is about choice, even beyond the magic's rules. And I've already tried to choose myself, flaws and all.

I put my hand on Rares's arm. "You'll make a fantastic father."

He blinks, the faintest sheen of tears streaking across his eyes.

"I'm fighting for the chance," he says. "What are you fighting for?"

The answer doesn't come right away. I know what I'm fighting to *prevent*—the destruction of the world. That was the reason I made Rares tell me Angra's movements during training, using his threat to fuel me on. But that was all based on anger, fear, worry—dark, uncontrollable things.

When I healed Mather, it was instant and easy. It was . . . *peaceful*.

That's what I should focus on when I use my magic. Joyous, wondrous things, like standing here, talking with Rares, and Oana, who emerges from a room down the hall and puts a finger to her lips, mouthing *Phil's asleep*.

I understood long ago that this type of family was never mine to have. But another type, something odd but whole with Mather—I could have that. And the rest of the world deserves to have that too.

That's what I'm fighting for. Possibility.

Rares smiles. "You're ready now."

I squint. "Ready?"

But I feel it. An unraveling deep in my gut, the magic a gentle cascade of icy flakes that settles in me, soft and strong.

"Ready for the final lesson," he says.

I've been training until now under a blanket of anger, half my mind always focused on worrying for my friends and the rest of Primoria. But as I look at the door to Mather's room, I feel clearer than I have since I got here.

Angra wanted to break me.

But he only made me unbreakable.

Meira

I STAND AT the edge of the sparring circle, hands in the pockets of my robe. The overcast sky trickles soft light over Oana, Rares, and me, and as the clouds grumble, my heart joins in.

I'd assumed the final lesson would be fighting with magic, but the swirling gray storm clouds end at the edge of the compound, a perfect cluster over us and us alone. Another whisper of thunder rolls across the sky, moments away from releasing a deluge over the yard.

Rares made this storm.

Across the circle, he takes a relaxed stance, but I stiffen, even more alert.

"Your magic—it feels cold to you, yes?" he asks.

"Isn't it supposed to?"

Rares starts pacing, shifting around the circumference of the training ring, though I remain just outside. Oana watches from a bench at the edge of the yard. The amused quirk of her lips only makes me more confused, so when Rares stops directly in front of me, I'm practically humming with wonder.

"To me, magic feels . . . warm," he says. "Not hot, not cold, but a neutral, tingling sensation. To a Summerian, it feels the opposite of how it feels to you—raging heat. To an Autumnian, encroaching chill; to a Spring, rising warmth. I've always wondered why that is—why, through monitoring the monarchs of the world, I've sensed such drastic differences in how they perceive the magic. All Rhythms feel the magic as I do—as a neutral tingling. Why are the Seasons more extreme? Why do *you* find yourself swarmed with ice?"

I shrug. "I never considered it before."

Rares smiles. "I have a theory, dear heart. The Seasons are the only kingdoms that stand directly atop the magic. Their monarchs are the only ones whose blood is saturated with power, so much so that it affects their physical affinity for certain climates. What if the Seasons have more of a connection to magic than any other kingdom? What if they have the potential to be the strongest wielders of the Royal Conduits? For me, there is no natural magic—it takes equal effort to conjure rain as it would snow. But for you, I suspect it would be frighteningly easy to summon a blizzard, yes?"

I fiddle with the locket at my throat, the cold metal only

one more spot of chill on my body. The swirl of iciness in my chest is so constant by now that I almost don't notice. It makes sense for the Winterian monarch to be more adept at controlling winter weather. Our whole kingdom has a stronger affinity for it, so that talent should bleed over into me.

"But the Seasons have always been weak. We're stagnant while the Rhythms evolve." I quote the stereotype perpetuated by most of the Rhythms.

Rares's lips tighten. "That is in our nature, I believe. To recognize a threat and squash it, whether or not we consciously know why it is a threat. I think the Rhythms fear you. Or they would, if all the Seasons truly came into their powers. One already has, and he controls the Decay in a terrifying way—and you, dear heart, will be the next Season to change the world."

At that, Rares lifts his hands into the air and rain begins to slosh down onto us in heavy sheets. I'm drenched in seconds, my shoulders hunching against the drops.

Rares crouches into a stance I've seen enough now to know by instinct, and my muscles react by pulling me into a fighting pose too, hands up, legs stiff, shoulders relaxed.

"This lesson will be a culmination of everything I've begun teaching you. But we'll start first with a simple sparring session," he says. "You can use magic only as a defense in fighting. Using it to attack, with intent to harm, feeds the Decay. So attack me—without magic."

He waits. I purse my lips at the storage bin and call a

sword. Once armed, I swing at him.

Rares moves, hurling his body toward me. Confusion makes me hesitate—he's not using a weapon?

But no—he does have a weapon. And seeing it draws a startled chirp from my lungs.

A rope of water snaps against my blade, nearly cutting into my cheek. At Rares's command, the drops from the rain coil into a whip that tears the sword from my grasp and flings it across the yard.

Keeping magic within an object allows Royal Conduit-wielders to control weather and other elements needed to run their kingdoms; unlimited magic in a person-conduit lets them manipulate these things with greater accuracy. But understanding this doesn't stop my panic, and as Rares's whip snaps toward me again, I scramble back, terror shocking a reaction from me.

I lift my hands. A chill launches out of me and the water droplets of his whip crystallize into shards of ice that fall at our feet.

Rares's eyes sparkle. "Very good!"

My body vibrates with a mix of pride and power. Can I do it again? What else can I do?

Thunder explodes in an echoing pop and I plunge forward. Rares is right—snow, cold, and ice are my natural state, and I let myself feel all that. Every knot of chill I always kept so tight in my chest, afraid to use it, afraid to lose control. But for the first time since I found out what I am, I succumb to it, welcoming it as part of myself. Because it *is* part of myself—I am a Winterian. I am ice through every part of me.

Rares kicks my sword up into his hand and charges at me. Rain drips from each strand of hair, each piece of clothing. His gray robe hangs heavy, wool soaked through with rain, and one jerk of my fingers turns the wet edge into a solid block of ice, adding water in layers that drag him down. He stumbles, flailing for balance, and as I spin to get in one solid kick that will send his blade flying—

Oana appears between us, a delicate smile on her face as though she doesn't even realize we're fighting. Behind her, Rares smirks and brushes a hand over his cloak, freeing the ice, before he levels a stare at me and tosses the sword back into the bin.

"The coming trials will test you in other ways too," Rares calls over the roar and pulsing chaos of the storm, which grows in intensity with each passing breath. "Angra will throw everything he has at you as you try to retrieve the chasm keys. The labyrinth also. Physical challenges will be the least of your worries. Attack her, dear heart." He waves at his wife.

I hesitate but coil my fist for a jab. Before I get halfway to her, Oana moves.

Instead of calling a sword or water coils, Oana spins, arms tight to her body until she drops to her knees and slams her hands to the ground. With that comes—

Lightning.

I stumble backward, the blinding flash sizzling into the ground paces from me. Oana looks up at me, her delicate grin now just as wild as her husband's, and before I can get to my feet, she leaps up and jerks her arms down again, sending another blast into the ground between us. The air heats up in a burst of static and flame, my skin prickling with its energy. I pull myself to my feet and take off running, trying to put distance between the crazy, lightning-wielding Paislian and myself.

Oana prefers lightning. It's not as easy for her to call on as ice is for you, but what can I say? She loves her fire.

I stumble on the rain-soaked grass and go down in a puddle behind the barn, muddy water sloshing over me. Oana didn't follow me back here—yet—but when I look around, Rares isn't here either. It takes me a beat to realize he's in my head, and I leap to my feet.

Stop! I shout at him. *What are you doing? You can't—*

I can't? he says. *You have no defense for your mind, dear heart. There are only two defenses against the Decay—the protection of pure magic and strength of will—and strength of will can be broken down unless you build it up. You have pure magic to keep the Decay from infecting you, but Angra is still a conduit himself—you'll have to learn how to block him. The labyrinth is crafted of pure magic, and so will demand a higher strength of will as well. Oh, Oana's coming.*

A horse whinnies. I dig my fingers into the earth on either side of me until I connect with something—a stone.

Oana saunters into view and I let the stone whirl toward her. While she's distracted, I grab the barn's wall and use it to steady myself as I make my way through the mud, boots sliding until I connect with the only slightly less slippery grass. Lightning sizzles and cracks into the ground behind me and I fling myself around the next structure—the storage bins. From there, the castle is only a few paces away, and I can duck down its side to gain some ground on her.

But you can't hide from me, dear heart. Not until you block me.

I don't know how! How do I block this?

The same way you've done everything else. You blocked your mother, didn't you? How did you do that? Oh, this looks like an interesting memory—

Autumn. The little camp we had in the south for a short while, just before two more of our refugees, Crystalla and Gregg, set out on the disastrous mission to Spring that would enslave them both and ultimately kill them. I'm sitting in front of a campfire with Crystalla while she braids my hair, and Sir talks at the edge, some lesson on Winter's economy. It's too hard to pay attention because Crystalla's fingers are gentle on my scalp, and the smoky aroma of the campfire mixed with the coziness of being here urges my eyelids to sink down, down, down . . .

"Little sacrifice," she hums in my ear. "My little sacrifice."

She's not Crystalla anymore.

I whip around to see Hannah, covered in blood, gaping

wounds cleaved through her chest and up her face, thick patches of maroon-black gore. She writhes and slides back, her hands going up to her head, where Herod grips her bloody white hair in a tight fist, dragging her away from me, and all I can do is scream and scream.

STOP! I topple forward, mud sucking around my knees as the images fade. *That's not what happened! GET OUT OF MY HEAD!*

Make me, dear heart, Rares coos. *Hmm, what about this?*

Before he can use more memories against me, I launch out from behind the storage bins, eyes snapping over the yard to find him. He does *not* get to use my memories like that. Hannah was never gentle or caring or motherly at all.

My emotions toward Hannah come so easily. Not anger, exactly—something unnamable and resolute, a dark, cold mix of truth and realization. That was why I blocked her, however inadvertently. She was my mother, but she never tried to be anything but my queen.

Let's see if we can talk to her, yes?

I snarl and scan the yard again, still not finding Rares, but so ready to fight him. *I have nothing to say to her.*

And not because I still harbor anger; not because I'm still hopeful she'll change. Because I'm done with her, I don't need her, and if Rares brings her back into this mess she caused, only more problems will arise.

Intention coils in deadly springs in my chest, the air around me freezing with each breath. I realize my mistake too late—I'm on the offensive, planning an attack on Rares, which leaves me open to Oana's defense.

A sizzle, a snap, and I dive just as lightning incinerates the ground behind me. Oana runs out around the barn, her braids whipping.

I roll and fling my arms over my head, morphing all the raindrops around me into layer after layer of thick, hard ice. It curves over me, a convex barrier that flashes up half a heartbeat before Oana's lightning snaps out of the sky and hisses against it. The barrier explodes, the lightning continuing down to erupt into the ground at my feet. I'm launched backward, slamming onto my elbows as shards of ice cut across my face.

Block me, dear heart!

The Rania Plains. Sir standing over me in the meeting tent, his disappointment a palpable tang on the air. He holds the locket box in his hands.

"I never should have trusted you with that mission. Because of you, Angra found our camp. Because of you, we had to resort to an alliance with Cordell, and it is that alliance that led them to overtake our kingdom." He sighs. "I always knew you were a failure."

NO! I scream at Sir before the image vanishes, and that scream warps into a frantic plea to Rares. *No, stop!*

I can't breathe. Sir's image hangs all too real in my head, unraveling me as I roll to my feet. Oana closes in, but I can't draw a breath to fuel myself on, choking under the words I've feared for so long.

Block me! Rares shouts.

I launch at Oana. The training ring is a swamp by now, the deluge continuing to flood the area, so when I reach her, I slide to a stop by falling onto my backside. I catch her legs and she goes down too, mud splashing when she drops.

"I always knew you were a failure."

But it's just me. It isn't Sir saying that—*Sir has never said that.* I'm the one who says it, who keeps that phrase pressed to my heart even as it undoes every seam in my body.

I'm keeping myself restrained. It's only ever been *me.* And I know that—I've known that I'm the one to blame for months. But something about recognizing it now fills me with clarity.

If I'm the only one to blame, nothing else has power over me. Not memories of Sir; not memories of Hannah; not memories of anyone. It's all part of me—mistakes and horror and regrets, but also beauty and peace and love. Like the memory of sitting at the fire with Crystalla and Sir—that was glorious and calm. I can't pick or choose which to keep and which to ignore—it's all of them or none of them, and I *will not* give up my happiness.

I wobble to my feet, legs trembling, arms aching, face stinging with rain and gashes from the ice shards. Oana looks up at me, her smile no less dim though she remains in a helpless, defenseless position. But this isn't truly a fight—she *wants* me to win.

One last chance, Rares's voice comes again. *This next memory will not be so pleasant.*

No, it won't be. It will probably be crippling, dredging up every last one of my insecurities.

But I don't care. It's all a part of me, every horrific, squirming shadow—it's all *me*, and I will not hide from it anymore. *I do not deserve to be crippled by it*; I do not deserve to harbor this guilt, because yes, I messed up, but I learned from every mistake.

That was how I blocked Hannah. I outgrew her, because I am all of this. I am mistakes and victories and death and life. I am competent and powerful and *strong*, and whatever this war brings my way—even death—I will face it like the queen I am.

I shout at Rares. *I DON'T CARE.*

My magic beats with each breath, but I don't fear losing control. I *am* my magic, and it is me, and it will obey me as much as snow and ice.

I flick my wrist and a blade snaps into my hand from the storage bin, glinting as rain bounces off it. Oana's serenity drops into an amused glower and she rises to her feet.

When I fling my body at Oana, sword slashing, I let my body move, years of Sir's training rising from my memory; I let my magic flow, years of stifling it broken.

Oana pulls down small crackling bolts that dance between us as I stab at her, forcing her back. I'm too close to her for another large lightning strike, unless she wants to be fried herself. As I dance around each bolt, her smile widens, true effort showing in the way her eyes tighten and her breath comes in gasps.

She backs into the storage bins and teeters off-balance for one beat, two—then her hands go up. Not a call for another lightning bolt.

Surrender.

Because my blade is pressed to her throat.

Oana smiles, and in that smile, I feel what I did.

I didn't lose control of my magic. I didn't need to fuel myself with anger or negativity. I let everything happen, trusting in myself—and I won.

My arms fall limp and the sword thumps into the mud. At that moment the sky responds. The rain abates, the thunder stills, and all threat of lightning disappears as the clouds roll back on themselves in a ripple of blinding blue sky.

A slow, heavy applause starts off to my left, and I turn. Every muscle aches, stiffness spiraling through me in pain I'll feel for days. But it was worth it. Every bruise and cut— I'd take them a hundred times over to feel how I feel right now. And it didn't come through seeking gratification from Sir or Hannah or even Rares.

I made me whole. *I* am enough for me.

I face Rares on the stairs in front of the castle's main

door, my grin relentless. Mather and Phil stand next to him, Phil looking completely horrified yet amazed, and Mather . . .

Awed, stunned, bewildered—there is no word to describe how he looks at me. His eyes dart over me, from my soaked hair to my mud-stained robe, absorbing me in jerky motions as if he can't catch all of me at once. When he meets my gaze, his shock ebbs away in favor of a look I've never seen on him. One I always dreamed of seeing.

He's looking at me now like he loves me, and he doesn't care who sees.

Mather hobbles down the steps, his movements still a little delayed. As he starts toward me across the yard, my eyes catch on something in his hands.

I jog to meet him halfway, a new disbelief rushing through me.

"This was given to Phil," he says, lifting my chakram. "It was meant to be another threat, I think. But I'm not even sure you need a weapon anymore—that was amazing."

I reach out, fingers hesitating over the worn wood handle curling through the circular blade. With this much power, I don't need anything—and I could let that consume me.

But I want to need things, and people, and that choice feels far more powerful somehow. Choosing something regardless of what it can do for me. Regardless of who it can make me.

Choosing it because *I* want it.

I take the chakram, my eyes on Mather. "I'm not me without it, am I?"

A smile flips across his face before he shakes his head. "You're perfect the way you are."

And it thrills me to the Klaryns and back that I couldn't agree more.

Ceridwen

DESPITE THEIR INTERACTION the night of their arrival at the Summerian refugee camp, Ceridwen had found dozens of things to keep her distracted from Jesse. The largest of which was the one she had expected—and feared—the most: the news that Angra had seized Summer.

It had taken all of Ceridwen's not considerable store of patience to keep from screaming at the messenger who had shown up explaining that Angra was setting up a strong presence in her kingdom—mainly because she knew how receptive Summer would be to his magic. Every upper-class Summerian was so used to a constant influx of magic that Angra's would be no different—until their eternal joy was traded for the mindless terror and compliance Angra had unleashed in Rintiero.

But this gave her an advantage. Blindfolded, she could find any building in Juli. And if Angra was there, it would be easy—no, *enjoyable*—to sneak in with a small contingent of soldiers and end his reign of terror.

So that was exactly what they'd do: sneak into Juli and assassinate Angra.

They all knew—some had even seen firsthand—how Angra's magic spread. It didn't matter what kingdom anyone was from—it could affect people without limitation. But Ceridwen had been in Rintiero, and had left unscathed; Jesse and Lekan had done the same. So it was possible to resist Angra's magic. And of anyone in the world, Ceridwen's Summerian refugees had the most experience resisting magic. They had trained themselves to break free of Simon's stifling joy.

It was mad, to be sure, but possible—as long as they could use every tool at their disposal.

"What are you going to say to them?" Lekan asked, dust kicking up under their feet as they walked toward the Yakimian quarter of the camp.

Ceridwen's fingers tightened around the seal in her palm. She hadn't been able to bring herself to reveal it to the Yakimians when she'd confronted them; she wasn't Giselle's lackey, and any good that came from this would be her doing. But it was all she could think of to convince them to fight with her now.

"They're Yakimians. I'm sure standing against Angra will speak to their rational side as much as it did Giselle's."

Lekan grunted. "But will they agree that their first move

against him should be to help you reclaim Summer?"

"No—of course they won't. They're Rhythms. They'll laugh in my face, and I'll probably end up punching one of them."

The three hundred Yakimian soldiers had only revealed themselves once Ceridwen had stood on a platform and shouted Giselle's plan at her entire camp. As she had expected, not every Yakimian was aware of their queen's intent, so before an uprising could occur, the soldiers had stepped forward and spent the past two days trying to make their countrymen understand. This was an issue among the Yakimians, so Ceridwen had allowed them that time.

She came to a dead stop. The intensity of the plains' sun beat down, but the heat didn't have its usual comforting effect on her. Burn it all, what *would* she say to them now?

"Then you shouldn't present it like that," came a voice that did even less to comfort her.

Ceridwen spun around to find Jesse on the road behind them.

"Shouldn't you be with your children?" She squinted to hide her surprise.

Jesse's smile might have been hurt, but most of his face was covered with a mask crafted from burlap, the best he could do to hang on to Ventrallan tradition here. "They're asleep, and well watched over by the Winterians who brought them here," he said. "Which is why I thought I would join you. I heard you're off to confront the Yakimian soldiers? A

Rhythm monarch's presence could be useful to—"

"I can handle a few angry Rhythms," Ceridwen snapped.

"Handle them, yes. But convince them to fight for you?" Jesse pursed his lips. "I'm merely offering my presence as support. Nothing more. I won't say a word."

Lekan cleared his throat and didn't exactly whisper, "Having him there isn't a bad idea."

Jesse tipped his head. "Thank you, Lekan."

And that seemed to be all the permission he needed. Jesse walked around them, heading down the road toward their Yakimian meeting.

Ceridwen swung on Lekan when Jesse was out of earshot. *"Isn't a bad idea?"*

But Lekan didn't look the least bit apologetic. "We don't have time for your stubbornness. Who knows how long Angra will even be in Juli? This plan has to go into action *now*, and we need them on our side, Cerie. You know that."

"I'm sure they'll see our logic," Ceridwen countered as they continued walking, Jesse still a few good paces ahead. "Assassinating Angra will end all this."

Lekan gave her an exasperated look. "You expect a *Yakimian* to see Season logic? You're more stubborn than I thought."

"What's that supposed to mean?"

He cut his eyes toward Jesse's back, then raised his brows. When she shrugged in confusion, Lekan snorted. "You were willing to risk winning over the necessary support all because you don't want to have to deal with Jesse yet."

Her lips parted in an instinctual hiss. But Jesse didn't so much as turn to look back at them, and only the many people who clogged the area saved her from yelling at Lekan. Refugees moving about their day, scurrying to one of the market tents or carrying buckets for chores.

Ceridwen kept her voice low. "You want to talk about this *now*?"

Lekan angled closer to her. "Would you rather we talk about it while his children are around? Or Kaleo—I know he has opinions on your relationship too, but since this is the first time you and I have been alone since we got back, yes, I figured we should talk about this now. Because like it or not, Cerie, I love you, and I've watched you suffer far too long to let this go unaddressed. What exactly have you planned to do about Jesse?"

"Just because I wanted to handle this meeting without him doesn't mean I'm avoiding him," she spit. "My stubbornness has never been an issue before. I run this camp—"

"Kaleo runs this camp," Lekan cut in. "You won't get out of talking about Jesse this easily."

Ceridwen quickened her pace before he could dive back into that subject. Now Jesse did glance over his shoulder. She swallowed, then dropped back a beat, sweat breaking out across her spine.

After a moment, Lekan caught up with her, his gaze shooting across the tents around them. They were drastically different than the ones in the Summerian section of camp—heavier, perfectly defined angles with square frames. The Yakimian area.

"I just want you to be happy," Lekan whispered.

Ceridwen's grip on the seal was so tight that her arm all but went numb. "I know."

Lekan fell silent, waiting, perhaps, for her to open up to him, but what could she say?

I haven't really spoken with Jesse since the night we arrived.

I want a life with him. But I've taken no action toward that, because I'm afraid that his strength isn't permanent. That this will all get taken away from me again.

I've trusted weak men before.

That wasn't a fair comparison. Simon had never even been aware of how he "betrayed" her—he'd simply lived his life, ruining their kingdom, while she waited in the shadows for him to realize his folly.

But Jesse had realized his.

He looked back at her again, as if her thoughts spiced the air around them. One small smile, and he turned a corner, leading them on.

No—she didn't have room for such weaknesses. That was part of the reason she had been endlessly glad when Jesse's children had shown up with their Winterian escorts, a distraction that had taken all his time. She had her own distractions—planning their attack on Angra; Meira's fate to hope for; and she had spread word for the leaders of the Yakimian soldiers to meet them outside of camp.

She, Lekan, and Jesse emerged from the Yakimian area into the thigh-high golden stalks of the prairie. She almost expected to find it as empty as always—why would the soldiers listen to her?

So when she stopped on the border of the prairie and the handful of Yakimians waiting there turned with looks of hatred, she almost laughed. They had come—but come to murder her, it looked like. If they were surprised to see the deposed Rhythm king, they didn't show it.

One soldier stepped forward. "We've spent the past two days cleaning up a mess *you* made. You owe us an explanation."

Oh, yes, murder was what they'd come for. A few had weapons on their belts, their hands taut around the hilts of swords. But under each of their left eyes a brand sat, their flesh burned into the grotesque *S* that proclaimed what they were. Summer's property.

Ceridwen frowned. "The mess I made? Wasn't it your queen who sold you into slavery in the first place?"

The lead man's expression darkened. "Do not pretend to understand why a *Rhythm* queen would—"

Ceridwen lifted the seal to silence him. "I know the reason Giselle did what she did. She was the one who revealed your existence to me. She gave me her seal as confirmation of her new order—that you are to serve under me as we fight Angra."

The soldier narrowed his eyes. No retort yet.

"We don't have the numbers to stage an outright battle," she continued, and motioned to Lekan. "But my leaders and I have begun altering the tactics we used to rescue slave caravans. We're planning a small, direct attack while Angra is in Juli—"

The soldier laughed. "Juli? You expect us to risk our lives to reclaim Summer—for whom, exactly? Your brother is dead. Our queen revealed her plan to you, so you must know of her intentions, and if you expect us to retake Summer for *you*, a Season royal—and one of the wrong gender, at that—you're sadly mistaken."

Jesse stayed quiet beside her, true to his word, but she felt him tense, and she couldn't help but glance over at him. She wasn't used to him in these situations—it had always been Raelyn or his mother who had overseen similar meetings in the past. But now he stood here, arms crossed, eyes spitting daggers in her defense.

Was she dreaming?

The Yakimian soldiers grunted in agreement with their leader, a few fists thrown in the air.

"Steady, Cerie," Lekan murmured on her other side.

Ceridwen bit down on her tongue. Lekan was right—screaming at these men would do nothing. They were

Yakimian; they would respond to reason and logic. *Calm* reason and logic.

Flame and heat, that went against everything her Summerian blood begged her to do.

"The Spring king has risen up as a threat not only to Winter this time—he threatens the world," she started, her tone surprisingly level. "He has already taken Ventralli and Cordell, not to mention Winter and Summer. Summer is the closest and newest of his acquisitions, and the one that gives us the best chance of taking him down. My fighters know that kingdom better than Angra does. With your help, we can defeat Angra while he is there and, ultimately, keep him from adding Yakim to the list of kingdoms he's subdued."

The soldier took two quick steps forward and snatched the seal from Ceridwen's hand. He looked at it for a moment and then turned to his men. "The seal is Yakim's," he announced, as if Ceridwen might have forged it. He swung back to her. "And we will defeat Angra—but not for you. This war will only be won if those skilled in warfare lead. You will let my men and me take charge, and when Angra is killed, it will be done by Yakim's hand."

Ceridwen's calmness slipped away, a raging current sucking a boat downstream. "Absolutely not. My fighters and I are the ones who know Juli best, and I have far more experience in warfare than you."

"And how was anything you did warfare?" the soldier

returned. "The only thing you did was the usual Season barbarism. You know nothing of strategy or else you would have realized my queen's plot long ago. Now the threat facing us comes from *another Season*, and you expect me to let you lead the fight? That is the definition of pointless."

Not even Lekan's stern hiss could stop her. She lunged at the man, a hand's width from his face, so incensed she thought smoke should be billowing out of her mouth.

"You will not conquer Summer. I promise you, Giselle's plan will fail. I will never yield to that Rhythm bitch."

The soldier reared back, fist wound, and would've blackened her eye—

If not for the hand that stopped him, grabbing the soldier's wrist.

"You will not raise your hand to her."

The confrontation with the Yakimians had drawn attention. Heads poked out of tents, people lingered on the streets that led from the perimeter. But Jesse ignored them, his assertiveness making Ceridwen's mouth drop open.

Not a single speck of doubt emanated from anywhere in his posture. Even his mask did nothing to lessen the intensity of his glare.

He released the man. "I have seen the evil that started this war," Jesse told the soldier. "I watched Angra tear Ventralli apart. I know what it will take to defeat him—it will take leaders like Ceridwen, who have proven their resilience against oppression. She will stop at nothing to make the world a safe place for *everyone*, and someone like that is exactly who you want leading us. This war will not care if we are Rhythm or Season. It will affect us all, and so we must face it with a mind to save and protect equally."

Jesse shifted to Ceridwen and smiled at her.

"The world is changing." Jesse still spoke to the soldier, but his eyes remained on hers. "We cannot deal with problems as we have in the past, or we will always end up where we started."

The soldier shook his head. "Never thought I'd see the day when a Rhythm king would defend a Season royal."

Me neither, thought Ceridwen.

Jesse nodded. "That's only the first of the wonders that will come."

"Only after we defeat Angra," Ceridwen cut in, finding her voice again. "And we will need your help for that. We will need soldiers to sneak into Juli, but we will also need some to stay behind and guard the camp."

Her levelheadedness made the soldier cock a surprised look at her. Finally he lifted his queen's seal and pointed it at her. "I command my soldiers, but . . ." He gulped in a breath and blew it out with a quick shake of his head. "I will follow your lead."

"I—" Ceridwen stammered, blinked. "Thank you. My leaders and I will be meeting shortly, to discuss our strategy. In the Summerian section of camp." She hesitated, not able to believe she was actually saying this. "Join us."

The soldier touched his fist to his forehead in a show of acknowledgment before turning back to his men, who gathered around him with whispered questions.

This was not at all how she had expected this meeting to go—she'd thought it would take days to convince them. Not *minutes*.

But they had the Yakimians' support. They would finalize their attack, and then they'd go to Juli.

Home, a small place inside Ceridwen whispered.

She stepped closer to Jesse.

He instantly stiffened. "I know I promised I wouldn't speak—"

"Thank you," she said.

Jesse smiled, puncturing dimples into his cheeks. "I told you"—he put his hand on her arm—"I owe you this. You deserve someone who will fight for you." He hung there, his thumb rubbing circles on her bare shoulder. "I . . . ," he started again, seemed to think better of it, and straightened. "I should check on my children now."

He bowed his head but kept his eyes heavily, intently on hers.

She managed a feeble nod in return before he eased away, down one of the many roads that snaked through the camp.

"Well, damn." Lekan bumped her with his shoulder. "Was he always that sexy?"

Ceridwen smiled but knew he'd catch the rise of scarlet creeping up her cheeks. "Come on. We have soldiers to assemble."

Lekan smirked. "There's time. You know. If you need some time."

"Lekan."

"I'm just saying, *I'd* certainly want some time if Kaleo had just swept in and prevented a coup on my behalf."

"*Lekan.*"

"All right." His smirk wilted as Ceridwen headed into camp and he kept pace alongside her. "But we do have time now, Cerie. And we might not always have time."

She had told herself that already, but fear had kept her from acting. Fear always kept her from acting. Jesse's performance, though, had somehow thoroughly dissolved her fear, in ways that made her feel like a silly little girl. One act of bravery, and she was ready to throw herself at him?

But she could only afford to live in a world of wants, not needs.

For the first time in she couldn't remember how long, she hooked her arm through Lekan's as they walked through camp and smiled. Really smiled.

Until Kaleo came racing up the road, his face red with exertion.

Ceridwen's chest pulsed with a mix of panic and readiness. An attack? Angra?

Lekan intercepted him. "What happened?"

"There's something you need to see," Kaleo panted, hands on his knees. He peeked up at Ceridwen, mouth agape. "Or, well, people."

Ceridwen's panic receded into hope. "Meira?"

"Almost." Kaleo straightened. "Winterians. *Lots* of Winterians."

Meira

THE NEXT DAY brings more sparring, with Oana and Rares trading off who attacks physically and who attacks mentally. The initial few rounds begin the same as the first one—it takes a few attacks before I open fully to my magic. But by the end of the day, the sparring sessions start with me already blocking Rares from my mind as I counter Oana's sword, and it takes only a few short minutes to end each fight.

I have control of my magic. At least, the beginning of control.

As soon as I think that, I realize what it means. I could stay in Paisly, shielded from Angra, and train until I'm perfect—or I could latch onto the early blossoming of readiness and leave.

The decision feels like it's been in my heart all along. I

knew what I'd do the moment I got here.

A war awaits.

I kneel over the trunk in my room, hands on the edges, staring into the clothing. I know I need supplies—blankets, extra clothing, food—but I can't make myself move.

"We've almost got dinner—" Rares's voice cuts off when he enters my room, but I know he can't read my thoughts anymore. Maybe he just senses the change in me, sees the way I bite the inside of my cheek.

"I know what you're going to say," I whisper to the trunk. "That a few victories in a training ring don't mean I'm ready. But . . . this isn't normal training." I look up at him. "I know I've barely begun to understand all this, but I have what I came here for, and I don't have time to perfect it. This isn't in preparation for a war—the war has already begun. I—"

"I'm not going to stop you, dear heart." Rares leans against the doorframe, his eyes soft. "Where will you start?"

I stand. "I'll need support. Mather said everyone from Ventralli was planning to gather in a Summerian camp east of the Southern Eldridge Forest. They're removed enough from the world that the Decay might not have affected them yet."

"And then?"

"I'll use the support to help me get close to Angra. Get the keys from him. And . . ."

Rares studies me, and I watch him in turn, struck yet again by how different he is from Sir. I wouldn't be able to see a single emotion on Sir's face—just the stoic countenance of a general, immovable and solid.

Part of me wishes for Sir's emotionlessness, if only to avoid the pang of grief when Rares sniffs and rubs his eyes.

"Oana and I will do what we can here. The Order has already been at work readying our army—we'll join you as soon as we can." He steps forward, mouth open to say more, but whatever he's about to say is forgotten when he notices my empty hands. "You'll need supplies! Food, at least, and—oh, Oana's better at this than I am. Take what you need from the kitchen. I'll go get what supplies she thinks you should have."

He leaves, rushing out the door, and I don't breathe until he's gone.

Actions are always far easier than words.

I gather a nice assortment of food in the kitchen, but, unable to find a sack big enough to transport it in, I duck out in search of a storage closet.

A closed door sits just next to the kitchen. The knob sticks under my hand, but a firm bump from my shoulder sends the door groaning open. A window shines hazy evening light into the room, and that coupled with the light from behind lets me see enough that I freeze, hand on the knob.

This definitely isn't a closet.

A rocking chair wavers in the center of the room, its curved legs moaning at the air from the open door. Beside it, a wooden bassinet sits beneath a thick layer of cobwebs and dust. A moth-eaten quilt hangs limp over the chair, the colors faded from years of sitting in the sunlight through the window.

My heart convulses as I take cautious steps into the room. The last time I saw a bassinet—one made of fabric and covered in silk, not wood and delicate carvings—was in the dream Hannah showed me. Her memory of the night Winter fell.

My bassinet.

"They have a child?"

I spin to the door, where Mather stands, one shoulder slumped against the frame. The hazy light from the window casts him in grayness.

"No," I say. "But they want one."

Mather nods. His head hangs low against his chest. "I've been thinking about it lately more than I ever did before."

"About what?"

His head lifts. "Family." He waves at the room. "Parents. Everything we didn't get."

I'd forgotten how recently Alysson died, how fresh her absence still is. So many deaths crowd my heart, all overlapping each other with grief. But as I watch Mather now, he pivots to lean his back on the doorframe, the hall's light illuminating his face. He always looked more like Sir, but I can see Alysson's softness in the curve of his nose, the way he purses his lips.

"I never understood it," Mather starts. "That love, I mean. It was always so far removed from what we had. I saw families when we went out on missions, but I never—" His breath catches. "I didn't realize until too late how much I wanted it."

When Mather looks past me to the nursery again, there's no mistaking the tears in his eyes. He holds them back, jaw tight, arms digging mercilessly into his chest.

"What do you think it's like?" he whispers. "To love someone like that? Even the *hope* of someone? To keep a room locked away on the wish that someday they'll come? I can't fathom it."

"Alysson knew you loved her," I breathe, unable to make my voice any louder.

His smile is sad. "I know."

The memory of Oana's words, how being a conduit as we are makes us barren, shoots remorse through me that I didn't even know I'd had. I never thought about this—having children, a nursery—but Mather and I were forced to live a life without parents as much as Oana and Rares were forced to live a life without a child. Not that I can understand their pain, but I imagine it aches in a similar way. This is yet another area we're forced into without a choice.

If Mather could talk to his mother the way I used to talk to mine, he wouldn't hesitate. If Rares and Oana could talk to their child like Hannah could to me, they'd fight to reach me.

It's those two realizations that remind me just how fractured my relationship with Hannah was. Because I should want to talk to her, and she should be desperate to talk to me. But I haven't felt anything from her since I shut her out, no battering against my defenses when I weaken, no constant attempts to slip past the magic.

"I think I understand that love," I say. "At least, I'm beginning to. Family isn't always who you're born to. It's who you're with, who you love. Those families can be even stronger."

Mather exhales a laugh. "Like a chosen family?"

There it is again. *Choice.* The word that haunts my every action. "Yes."

"I'd still have chosen Alysson," Mather whispers.

I close my eyes, his words cocooned inside more emotion and more *want* than I've ever heard from him. My chest itches, already responding to my unconscious will, and as I open my eyes, I turn to face the room.

Dust lifts off the furniture. Cobwebs peel off the walls. The window pops open and all the grime and dirt undulates out on my command, leaving every surface gleaming like new. The quilt stretched over the chair remains ragged, but the filth is easy to remove, and the pillows and blankets in the bassinet sit fluffed and clean and ready to be used.

Because they *will* be used. Oana and Rares will someday soon be able to have the family they deserve. The family

Mather should have had; the family *I* should have had.

That's all I can do. Help create a world where the life I always wanted exists, even if I don't live it.

A place deep inside me aches every time I think like that, so close to fully accepting my fate.

"Meira?"

I scrub away any tears with my sleeve before I turn to him. All I want is to do what Rares suggested—give him a choice. Let him know what awaits me at the end of this journey, the reason for my tears.

But the moment my lips part, Phil appears. "Rares said we're leaving?"

I breathe, sending oxygen out to every muscle. "Yes." I'm caught by another piece of information I haven't shared with them, one that makes my own body sway with memory.

"And our route will be a little . . . unconventional."

Mather rises away from the door, intrigued. "How so?"

But I wave off any explanation. "Packing first." I wince. "Pain later."

That night, Oana loads us down with supplies—satchels, blankets, food, bandages, as well as a plethora of things we probably won't even need. As we all stand in the front yard of their compound, I grab her arms to prevent her from stuffing another apple in my bag.

Rares puts his hand on her waist, watching me. Dozens of words crowd in my mouth.

I'll see you again.

You two mean more to me than I know how to say.

The bassinet in that nursery will be used. I promise.

Oana wraps her sleeve around her hand and runs it down my cheek. "I know, sweetheart," she says, and somehow, that undoes me more than if she'd sobbed her farewell.

I hug her and Rares. "Thank you" is all I can get out, and it's weak and pathetic and not even half of what I want them to know. But they take it and pull back, eyes shining.

I turn to Mather and Phil, who are just as loaded down with supplies. They're barely healed, and already I'm pushing them on. But they don't question me or complain.

Though they might after what I'm about to do to them. "This will hurt," I warn. "And feel . . . terrifying."

Phil's eyebrows launch up. "What?"

But I don't give them a chance to worry. I take their hands and release the magic in my gut to take us to Ceridwen's refugee camp. An instant heaviness yanks down on my chest, the strain of magic use, but intensified—I haven't done this before, transported myself, let alone others, and the weight of it drags at my endurance as though I'm lifting a sword heavier than I'm used to. I falter, but hold.

The only problem is, I've never been to Ceridwen's refugee camp. The only location I have is what Mather told me—that it's a day's ride from where the Langstone meets the Southern Eldridge Forest. Is that all I need? Or do I need to have a specific place in mind? This isn't the best time to worry about this, I realize, as the whir of magic launches us into the void—but I refuse to let overthinking unsettle me, not when Mather's and Phil's lives depend on me. So with what concentration I can muster, I focus on the border of the forest where it meets the Rania Plains.

Half a heartbeat later, a solid *whoomph* ricochets through my body as my feet plant on the ground. Black sky gleams above me, dotted with stars, and stalks of prairie grass wave all around. The earthy, dried scent of the plains clashes with memories of the moist air of Rares's compound. I pause but, thankfully, the only dizziness that comes is minor, and no nausea incapacitates me this time.

I can't say the same for Mather and Phil.

I'm fairly certain Phil started retching before we even arrived. He heaves into the grass while Mather, seated on the ground, presses his face to his knees, hands over his head, emitting a low moan.

"What . . . did you . . ." Mather squints up. *"Do?"*

He notes the landscape. His eyes widen. He folds to the side, mimicking Phil.

I almost rush forward, but their nausea was caused by magic-induced travel—maybe magic can undo it?

A single thread of iciness launches out to them, and both Mather and Phil turn to me with looks of utter confusion. The ease of magic use still shocks me, how uncomplicated it is now—which makes me realize one other thing I need to do.

We're so far removed from anywhere Angra might know to look for me that his magic hasn't found me yet, not like it did in Paisly. But I still relax my mind, creating the same sort of protective barrier that kept Rares out of my head. Angra won't find me until I want him to.

Phil wobbles to his feet, hands out as though he doesn't trust his body. "What the actual snow above was that?"

I start to answer when Mather huffs a laugh.

"That is how we're going to win this war," he says. "The more I see what you're capable of, the more I start to fear for Angra."

Phil looks utterly horrified, his lips curled back before he catches Mather watching him and shakes it off, opting for a tight-lipped stare. "You're stronger than Angra?" he asks me.

I fight off a wince. "Magically? No. But in other ways . . . I hope so."

The edge of the Eldridge hovers a few paces to my left, shadowed in darkness, while the plains sweep outward on all other sides, ripples of grass as far as I can see. Heat rises from the earth, lingering from what was surely a warm day, and as I shift my chakram along with the satchel strapped across my shoulders, I groan.

"It isn't as useful as it would first appear," I say. "I have no idea where Ceridwen's camp is from here. Or if everyone else even got there. . . ."

Did Jesse free Ceridwen? Did the Winterians get the Ventrallan heirs out of the kingdom?

Mather squares himself in front of me as if he has the ability to hear the chaos in my mind as clearly as Rares did.

"We'll figure it out," he says.

"But—"

"We'll figure it out," he says again, putting both hands on my shoulders. "They're all there. I'm sure of it. Now—left or right?"

I swing my head in both directions. Prairielands one way; prairielands the other. I can't think of a way to use my magic to help me decide. For this, I'm just Meira.

That thought isn't nearly as terrifying as it once was.

"Left," I say. "Have to start somewhere."

Mather nods and swings his hand toward the horizon. "Lead on, my queen."

I squint. "Don't you dare."

"Don't I dare what?"

"Keep calling me that."

"What else should I call you, my queen?" Mather's voice lightens.

Phil stands, adjusting his travel pack. His horror seems to have retreated, at least as he eyes Mather. "I can think of a few things you want to call her," he mutters.

Even in the dark, the blush that creeps over Mather's face is the most adorable thing I've ever seen. And this is the first bit of levity Phil's shown since he appeared in Paisly.

Mather bumps Phil's shoulder as he passes, trudging through the grass.

"Come on," he says. "We should cover as much ground as we can tonight."

I grin, nearly bursting with how good it feels. "As you wish, Lord Mather."

That makes him roll his eyes, but he smiles, slow and small, and keeps marching to the left. Phil starts after him, and I fall in behind.

We spend two days walking, foraging for resources, and sleeping. We split into shifts to keep watch, one of us always alert for approaching enemies or lights on the horizon, signaling a camp.

Back in Paisly, for however brief a time, it didn't feel like the world was falling apart. Rares told me what Angra was doing, but I could still remove myself from it—here, though, each step I take draws me closer to war. Who knows what Ceridwen endured under Raelyn? I still don't know the state of Winter. And Theron . . . Angra has him.

Why would Angra ally with him at all, though? Cordell does have one of the most powerful armies in Primoria. But Angra wouldn't need Theron for that—the Decay's influence could sway anyone. Keeping Theron alive is a far bigger threat to Angra, because yet another person remains who is connected to pure conduit magic—the only way he can be defeated.

I haven't asked Mather what happened to Theron's conduit. Last I knew, Mather had taken it after Theron tossed it away in Rintiero's dungeon, but I doubt very much Angra let him keep it once they were captured again.

But that still poses the question—why would Angra want Theron at all? Angra loves having puppets to carry out commands for him—Herod was proof of that, Raelyn too. Is he planning to use Theron that same way?

My heart sinks. There's only one thing I can think of that Angra might need Theron for: me.

Theron knows things that could weaken me. Theron *himself* could weaken me, just by being who he is—someone I care about, possessed by the one thing I hate above all else.

And Angra knows that.

I wipe a bead of sweat from my forehead. Grass tangles around my boots, the sun beats down on me, but of all the emotions I could feel now—discomfort; fatigue; racking, consuming, fiery guilt—I only let myself wallow in one: acceptance.

This war will force me to confront Theron. I'll have to face whatever Angra made him into—someone just as cruel as Herod, just as dark as Angra. And I'll have to be ready.

Phil makes an *oof* as I bump into him. But he looks ahead, gaze fixed on the horizon.

Ahead of us, tucked around a bend in the line of trees, stand hundreds of tents in yellow, brown, and earthy green to camouflage against the plains and forest. Tendrils of smoke lift from campfires, movement shifts within, and the hum of voices hangs light on the air.

Mather spins to us. "That looks like a camp, right?" But he's already walking backward toward it, relief chasing off his discomfort at the plains' sweltering heat.

Phil throws his fist into the air. "Civilization! Well, sort of." He rushes forward, legs pumping over the grass.

Mather keeps walking steadily backward. My eyes roam past him to the camp, but I can't seem to make myself move.

"We're here," I say, throat dry. I grip the straps of my chakram's holster.

Suddenly *We're here* sounds more like a threat than the relieved statement it should be.

Mather steps toward me, his hand out.

War may loom, but I'm not alone.

I put my hand in his and let him lead me on.

All noises cease the moment we enter the camp. Conversation and laughter snuff out like candle flames guttering in a windstorm; pots clang idly over campfires as their users gape in shock.

I pull my shoulders straighter as I walk between Phil and Mather down one of the many makeshift roads, the grass worn by foot traffic in patchy stretches. People stare as we pass, mostly Summerians with their flame-red hair and tanned skin, but also Yakimians, even a few citizens of Spring. A hodgepodge of blond hair, brown hair, dark skin, light skin—but one common feature links most: the *S* brand of charred skin below every left eye.

We only make it past a few tents when the voices kick back up.

"Is that . . ."

"She's wearing the locket—look!"

"It's the Winter queen!"

I bite the inside of my cheek, trying with all my remaining strength not to wither under their assessments. I have no idea what these people think of me. What rumors have they heard? That I'm the girl who freed her kingdom only to have the same attacker come roaring back into the world? The girl who betrayed her only ally by seeking other allegiances behind his back? The girl who let these people's own savior, Ceridwen, become imprisoned?

My hand tightens around Mather's, drawing strength from the way he and Phil stay beside me.

More reactions come, echoing out from people as we pass. I stiffen, expecting the worst, but the people around us throw their hands in the air, shouting praise.

"Down with Angra!" they cry, and even more strongly, "We are Winter!"

That phrase hooks into my heart. These people have no reason to rejoice at my presence—their own problems have never intersected with mine. But that phrase—*We are*

Winter—only two people I know could have taught them that.

I tear ahead of Phil and Mather, hurtling into the camp. My heartbeat tramples my lungs, more people catching the cheer—*"The Winter queen is here! Down with Angra! We are Winter!"*—until those shouts are all I hear.

I spin around one more tent, sweat slicking down my back.

In the middle of the road, sprinting toward me, is Nessa. Behind her, Conall follows at a slower clip.

A beaming grin overtakes my face.

Nessa sees me and pushes faster just as I do, both of us racing until we collide in a tangle of arms and laughter and questions.

"How did you get here?"

"How long have you been at camp?"

"Where have you been?"

"Are you all right?"

I pull back and survey her for any injuries. She's fine—not even a bruise or a healing cut. Conall looks the same, and I tuck my arms back around Nessa.

"I'm so sorry," I gasp to her and Conall. "I'm so sorry I left you."

"You should be," Nessa snaps, but when I jerk back again, she's laughing. "You better have a good excuse for it."

I smile. Even her threat sounds delighted to see me. "I do, I promise."

"Meira!"

Dendera engulfs me, breaking her embrace only to give my shoulders a firm shake. "Don't you ever do that again. Do you hear me? *Never again.*"

Her command sobers me. I wish I could promise her that I'll never again leave without warning, but the lie gets stuck in my dusty throat.

"I missed you too" is all I manage.

But she's already moving past it, her eyes shooting to Mather and Phil, who hurry up behind me. Her face brightens and she tucks her hand into mine.

"Follow me," she says to us.

Nessa takes my other hand, bouncing alongside me as we turn down another grass-trampled road. Around us the cheering has dissipated, but the news still spreads—eyes watch me with interest, people point and call to friends that the Winter queen has arrived. I'm so distracted by the spreading news that I don't immediately realize who surrounds me.

Winterians. Dozens of them, holding bowls or food or buckets, but all turn toward me, staring with just as much wonder as I stare at them with.

"They're here." I tug at Dendera's hand. *"How?"*

"Henn heard about the camp while we were in Summer," Dendera explains. "He thought it would make a good safe spot for those who escaped the takeover."

"How many escaped?" I dare to ask. "Where is Henn? And—"

Did Sir not make it out? What about Finn and Greer and Deborah?

Dendera squeezes my shoulder. "William made it out. Finn and Greer—" She closes her eyes in a soft sigh. "They'll be free soon enough. William and Henn left yesterday morning."

"Left? For where? Are they going back to Jannuari?"

Mather closes in on one side, his expression just as dark as mine feels. My gut starts to throb as Dendera reads our concern and shakes her head.

"Not Jannuari. They'll be fine! You act as though they've never gone on a mission like this before. They went with Ceridwen and a small group of Summerians and Yakimians to Juli—it's Ceridwen's plan to assassinate Angra while he's—"

The noise I make is half a scream and half a sob.

"No," I say. "Tell me they aren't going to face Angra. Dendera, no—"

She squints, her pride in their mission flaking off the more I shake my head.

Ceridwen, Sir, Henn, and a group of soldiers went to Juli to face Angra. Without any magical protection.

They're all as good as dead.

Mather

MATHER LATCHED ONTO Meira's plan before she'd even spoken. All she did was look up at him, and he knew—they were going to Juli.

They had to do what they could to help William and the rest, who would be walking into a kingdom overtaken by Angra's Decay, possibly even more so than Ventralli by now. Ceridwen's group had more than a day of travel on them and could reach Juli the next night. They could attempt to face Angra and end up possessed by his Decay before they'd even raised their swords.

Meira whirled away from Dendera, her eyes going to the sword at Conall's waist. She pointed at it. "I need weapons," she told him. "Enough for—"

"Eight people," Mather cut in. "The Thaw and I will go with you." He nodded at Phil. "Go find them. They have to be here somewhere."

"I'll show you!" Nessa offered, and raced away so fast Phil had to scramble to keep up. Conall dispersed as well, ducking into a tent to start gathering weapons.

Meira pressed on. "We'll need medical supplies too—I can't heal any non-Winterians."

"Horses?"

"No, we'll travel as we did from Paisly."

Mather grimaced. "Great."

"Stop!"

The Winterians around them watched as Dendera stood with her hands spread.

"What are you doing?" she hissed, her voice low as she noted their audience. "If you wish to join them—"

Meira's face hardened. "Not join them. Save them."

Dendera blew out a breath. "What don't they know?"

But Meira shook her head. "No time to explain. Who's in charge of the camp in Ceridwen's absence? Send for whoever it is, now."

Dendera stood frozen for as long as it took Meira to turn away from her. Then she moved, her years of training as a soldier compelling her to obey orders even as Mather saw the gray hue of terror engulf her face. He knew what she was thinking, one worry pulsing like a brand across her mind—*Henn. He's in danger.*

Mather ground his jaw. *William. He'll die too.*

He growled at himself and spun after Meira.

Minutes later, Hollis, Feige, Trace, Kiefer, Eli, and even Jesse had gathered in the middle of what had become the Winterian section of the camp. There was little time for a reunion as a pile of supplies was deposited outside one tent. Mather and the Thaw picked through it, suiting up as best they could for battle. Meira knotted a sword's sheath to her belt as Dendera joined them with a man Mather didn't know, a Summerian who had the familiar *S* brand below his left eye.

"This is Kaleo Pikari, leader of the camp," Dendera introduced him. Her worry had been replaced with resolve, something she held as tightly as Meira gripped the sword she shoved into her belt.

Meira nodded. The way she stood there, head high, shoulders squared, she was every raging stubbornness from their childhood. She was the girl who had never relented in her arguments with William. She was the ferocity that had both terrified and entranced Mather as a child. She was all of that at once, fierce and bold and daring.

She was a queen.

Mather knew he was gaping. But ice above, looking at her was like staring at a snowbank under a midday sun— blinding and mesmerizing.

"I don't mean to come in and question your authority," she started to Kaleo, eyes softening. "But Ceridwen and her group are unaware of the severity of Angra's threat. All of you are—which is why you must trust me, though I realize this is a large request: you have to move this camp."

Mather shouldn't have been surprised. If anyone who knew of this camp's location became possessed by the Decay, they wouldn't hesitate to turn over that information to Angra.

More surprising still, Kaleo nodded. "We're already in the process of breaking down the camp. We were going to move for the same reason I suspect you have—if anyone in Summer who knows of this camp falls into Angra's hands . . ." His voice tapered off and he cleared his throat. "We figured it was safest to relocate."

"Where?" Meira refitted her chakram's holster over the leather vest she'd taken from the supply pile.

"Summer." Kaleo smiled sadly. "There are barren places there that not even Angra would dare go. It will be uncomfortable, but not impossible, living in the desert—and hopefully Angra won't think to look in a kingdom he's already overtaken."

Meira considered, her cheek caught between her teeth.

Kaleo pressed on. "We considered moving to Yakim, for instance, but we didn't want to risk becoming Giselle's prisoners when Angra falls."

"Angra won't fall so easily," she whispered. Kaleo's dark face paled enough that Mather recognized it as the same fear Dendera had shown—someone he cared about was in Ceridwen's group. "My soldiers and I will assist Ceridwen in Juli. Your camp should relocate, but I worry that anywhere in Summer will still be too close to Angra's reach. Anyplace you hide there will be known by *someone* in Juli, won't it?"

"Where do you suggest we go?" Kaleo's voice was clipped.

Meira turned to Dendera. "Did Henn and Sir pass through Autumn on their way here?"

She nodded. "They avoided main roads, so they didn't have much to say about it."

"Has anyone received word of them? Has Caspar sided with Angra?"

Mather heard the words she didn't say: *Has Angra killed Caspar yet?*

Kaleo was the one who answered. "We sent scouts who told us that Cordell turned on Autumn—but the royal family was never accounted for. So while the capital is under Angra's control, the rest of the kingdom is less certain. You want us to go to Autumn?"

Meira tipped her head, as though she was piecing together a plan as she talked. "An uncertain kingdom is better than one that Angra has definitely taken, and no one outside this camp will know any hiding spots there."

Mather expected Kaleo to show resistance, but clearly he had experience taking orders from young, passionate royals. Nevertheless, Kaleo weighed her words in turn, his lips parted.

"We can split the camp into small groups, able to travel faster, and take different routes through Summer to stagger our travel." He scratched his chin, thinking. "We'll make for the foothills—we'll go as far into the Klaryns as possible."

"How many soldiers do you have here?"

Kaleo sighed, and then he rolled his eyes. "Apparently Ceridwen had a conversation with the Yakimian queen. Giselle has been hiding soldiers among the people she sold to Summer. Seems she was planning to seize control of our kingdom—until Angra beat her to it. She's disgusted by the idea of a magic that infects her people's minds, so Yakim is no ally of Angra's." Kaleo waved at the camp. "There are three hundred Yakimian soldiers at our disposal, on her offer. Ours to use to defeat Angra."

Meira's eyebrows launched up. "You're joking."

"Unfortunately, no." Kaleo grunted. "But we have them, in addition to the hundred or so Summerian soldiers who stayed behind. Ceridwen only took a dozen with her. Since we'll split the camp into smaller groups, it should make patrolling easier."

"All right. Dendera, Nessa, Conall?" Meira turned to them. "You'll oversee the Winterians?"

All three nodded and instantly peeled away to help the Winterians around them.

"We'll reconvene with you once we get out of Juli," Meira told Kaleo.

Kaleo looked like he wanted to protest, maybe push her for more details, but his eyes slid up to the sun, noting the time. He pressed his lips together.

"Bring them back, Queen Meira" was all he said, and he vanished back into his camp. Jesse followed, offering his assistance, which left Mather, his Thaw, and Meira standing over the unused supplies.

Meira stared down at the pile, her eyes shifting back and forth. Mather stepped forward, close enough to take her hand and give it a protective, reassuring squeeze.

"We'll be in and out so fast, Angra won't even know anyone was there at all," Mather promised everyone, but mostly the girl whose icy blue eyes latched onto his. "This could be good, actually. Angra will be there. He'll have the keys."

Meira twitched in his grip as if she'd forgotten the bigger plan—get the keys, get to the chasm, destroy all magic and Angra with it.

"Yes. But—let's just make sure everyone's alive. That's all that matters."

Were those tears brimming on her lashes?

Meira pulled her hand free. Mather blinked in confusion as she turned to Nessa, who helped a Winterian family nearby pack their supplies. Meira glanced over her shoulder once and her eyes connected with Mather's again. The look that took over her expression—he knew that look like a fist to the gut.

Regret.

There was something she wasn't telling them. Something

that made her body sag as she turned around to talk to Nessa.

Phil stepped up next to him and shifted his pack, the one that made Mather's gut cramp even tighter. Within it lay Cordell's conduit—Mather couldn't yet decide what to do with it. Keep it? Get rid of it? Forget about it? Not that it would do much to help them. In truth, he wanted to destroy the damned thing and Theron's smugness along with it.

"Every time you see it, I want you to think of her with me. I want you to know that when I win this war, I will do so without this weak magic. And when this ends, and Meira is mine, there won't have been a damn thing you could have done to stop me."

Mather's gut lurched. Would Theron be in Juli too? He almost hoped so.

"You all right?" Phil asked.

Mather sniffed away his stony expression. "Yes." He looked over Phil again, noting the sunken circles under his eyes. "Are you?"

Phil shrugged. "Just not particularly looking forward to seeing Angra."

A stone nearly bored a hole in Mather's stomach. "He won't catch us again," he promised. "I swear. We won't be just the two of us this time either—we've got everyone now."

The Thaw, who had been talking quietly among themselves, turned to them. Trace looked like he might ask what had happened, while Hollis and Feige stayed silent and patient, Kiefer crossed his arms and wore his usual glower, and Eli looked almost excited to leave.

"So." Kiefer was the one to talk first, his voice sharp. "We're a group again? You're not going to leave us?"

Mather frowned. "We've always been a group. We've always been *her* group."

That made Kiefer blink, as if it had never before occurred to him that their purpose was to serve Meira as much as it was to serve Winter.

"But we're still us," Phil added. "We're still us, first and foremost. The Thaw."

"And we won't be defeated," Feige said.

Mather smiled at what had become their group's rallying cry. He looked at Phil, who toed the ground, but when he felt Mather watching him, he cracked a smile that looked a little too forced.

"We won't be defeated," Phil echoed. "I know, I know."

Meira stepped up beside Mather, joining their circle. Most of the group shifted at her presence, the unfamiliarity of being around their queen still making them unsteady. But there was determination behind their nerves, and even Kiefer stood with alertness.

Phil was the only one who didn't snap to attention, instead absently studying the grass. Mather nudged him, pinching his brows into an expression of concern.

Phil shook his head. Nodded. Forced a smile again.

Angra's torture was still too fresh. Mather almost told him to stay, but Phil made no move to leave the group, and indeed seemed to stand straighter with them around. He needed to be with them—even if that meant facing Angra again.

"I'll put us as close to Juli as I can," Meira said. "I don't want to risk getting too close to Angra and having him sense my magic."

Hollis frowned. "My queen?"

Mather stepped in. "About our journey—it won't actually be a *journey* so much as a . . ."

Phil moaned, his head thrown back. "Kill me. Someone, kill me now."

"Reassuring, Phil, thanks," Mather said.

But Phil just extended his groan. "Let's just get this over with."

Something in his reluctance made Meira's eyes widen, and she looked up at Mather before encompassing each of the Thaw with the same wary look.

"I wish I had time to explain what I'm going to do," she said. "I know the only magic you've ever been around was Angra's, in Spring, in the camps, and I— This isn't the same. It will hurt, but I promise, I'm not trying to change you, or force anything on you, and I—"

"It's all right, my queen," said Hollis, and he offered a smile. "We trust you."

She nodded, but she still looked loath to use her magic.

Even so, she held out her hands, encouraging everyone in the group to form a linked circle. Phil was the last to enter, his hand shaking as he grasped Mather's.

Maybe Meira can give him strength, Mather thought, but before he could ask her, she tightened her fingers on his. Mather staggered, unable to brace himself as her magic swept over them in a rush of frost and snow and sharp, stinging daggers of ice.

Meira

I SPLIT MY concentration among filling the Thaw with just enough magic to combat the nausea of travel, placing us close enough to Preben Palace but not so close that we catch Angra's attention, and keeping a shield around my mind so Angra can't feel me coming. But he could have the entire city in a barrier of some kind, waiting for me to break through—especially if he's already caught Ceridwen and Sir. He'd know I'd come for them, and he'd be waiting for me.

If he knows I'm coming, though, no amount of preparation will help.

The amount of magic I have to use to do everything I need saps my energy before I've even gotten us to Juli. The tributaries that branch off from the Feni sparkle in the fading sun, adding light against the endless orange and gold of Juli's sandstone buildings, and as I deposit everyone in an alley on the outermost ring of Juli, I fling another wave of iciness back at myself—strength, energy, keeping myself alert through the strain that makes me want to crumple in the dust.

The Thaw stumbles as we land, each of them gaping with awe and terror. Except for Mather and Phil, who clutch their stomachs and sigh in relief at the absence of vomiting.

"What now?" Mather asks, preventing the Thaw from lingering on anything but the task at hand: saving our friends. And getting the keys from Angra.

I shake my head at myself. Saving everyone is my first priority—if we can get the keys too, then we will, but not before everyone else is safe.

I step forward to peek out of the alley. Last time I was in Juli, parties raged up and down every street, wine and music and gyrating bodies oozing from the buildings.

Now evening approaches, but already the streets around us are almost empty. Shutters bang idly against windows; unattended flames simmer in the fire pits that line the street. Across from our alley, one lone wanderer flings himself into an inn and slams the door as if evil might follow; the building next to it shows only the faces of women and men pressed to the windows, watching the street with eyes that scream fear. They look so like the people I saw in Abril, long ago—hiding from the world, hoping the problem of fixing it will fall on someone else's shoulders.

If I had wondered before what Angra wants, the sight before me now would confirm it. He has taken the joyous, chaotic, beautiful riot of Summer and stamped it out until it resembles his controlled, fearful Abril.

I turn back to the Thaw, hands balled at my sides. "We need to get to the palace—that's where Angra will be, so that's our best chance of finding Ceridwen or anyone with her. And maybe, if we get close enough, I can use my magic to sense where Sir is."

"We're just going to traipse through Juli?" Trace's brows pinch over his nose and he tugs at his shaggy white hair. "We don't exactly blend in."

My eyes drop to the ground as I think—and the answer presents itself.

Summer's orange sand sticks everywhere—to the walls of buildings, the clothing of travelers. It coated everything we'd had when we passed through a sandstorm on our first visit to Juli—maybe it can serve as camouflage now.

I bend and start scrubbing the particles into my arms, my cheeks, my hair, and the Thaw follows my lead. Soon our Winterian features are covered, and by readjusting a few of our wraps and scarves, we might just go unnoticed. The empty streets work even more to our favor—if we hunch over and scurry from shadow to shadow, we could actually make it.

I take a deep breath in and lead everyone out into the nearly deserted streets.

Mather sidles up beside me, everyone else falling into line behind us. "What are we going to do if they've already been caught?" he whispers, his voice low against the eerie stillness around us. Wind whistles between buildings, causing Phil to hurry closer to us.

"Get them out," I reply, as if that's enough.

"Once Angra has been defeated, they'd be freed that way," Mather returns. "You know William would tell us to finish the war before saving him."

I glance over my shoulder, taking stock of the Thaw. "I don't think he— Oh, *really*?"

Mather turns to see what catches my attention. Phil, Hollis, Feige, Kiefer, and Eli crowd behind us, but back a few paces, Trace stands near the building with the faces pressed to the window. The front door is open, a girl leaning out, the drooping orange fabric of her shirt pushing recognition through me. That place is one of Summer's brothels.

And Trace is leaning against the doorframe, chatting with her as if we aren't trying to infiltrate an enemy city.

In panic, I fling a burst of magic at him, protecting him even more from Angra's Decay. I've been protecting all of the Thaw, though, haven't I? I refocus on keeping them safe, just in case, a cold funnel of magic pushing out of my chest and into them.

Trace doesn't react to the magic and only turns when Mather growls, "Trace!"

He jolts and looks at us, his eyes jerking from Mather to me. He chokes, realizing what we think, and waves his apologies to the girl as he jogs up the road toward us.

"I didn't—I mean, she was pretty, but—I figured she could help us," he says. "Tell us where Angra is, that sort of thing."

Mather frowns. "Did she?"

"Seems there's a gathering up at the palace tonight." Trace grins. "An announcement or something—guess Angra's been making such announcements every few nights. The first night, he presented the Summerian people with his magic, hence all the . . ." Trace waves at the desolate city. "The second night, the advisers, or whoever has been in charge of Summer since the king died, gave control of the kingdom to him. Tonight's supposed to be another one."

"Angra's held three separate gatherings since he's been here?" I squint. "It seems a little . . . excessive."

"Maybe." Mather tips his head. "Or maybe it's taken him that long to secure his power?"

"So it isn't a trap?" I press. "He hasn't been staging these gatherings to draw us out?"

Mather smiles in a way that's more a wince. "That's a given. Everything he does is probably, in some way, meant to squash his enemies."

I grunt but push past my worry—we know it's a trap. We knew from the beginning that this whole mission would be dangerous. Nothing's changed.

But it seems like every time I find out information that appears not to change anything, it does just the opposite.

The palace grounds echo the fear and apprehension that choke the city. Servants flit in and out of the gates, preparing for whatever gathering will be held tonight, which makes their panic easy to slip into, and we hide in a shadowed overhang by the stables. We stand in a tight group, the Thaw pressed in around me, and I reach out to my magic, the constant coldness reminding me that I'm keeping a shield around my Winterians and myself—Angra won't be able to sense us, and his Decay won't be able to infect us.

But we're here, on the grounds, and I'll have to risk using more magic now.

The Thaw is silent as I close my eyes, arms knotted across my chest. I let tendrils of magic snake over the ground and up to the palace, splitting apart and spreading out like frost crawling over a window. I should be able to sense Sir—his Winterian blood is connected to the magic within me, and he should be close enough to feel, the same way I pushed magic into the workers deep in the Tadil while I stood atop the mine.

"What is she doing?" Phil hisses.

"Searching for Mather's father, I'd imagine," Trace answers quietly.

"I don't know about you all," Feige starts, "but I'm ready for an enemy I can *see*. No more of this . . ."

My eyes are closed, but I take it she waves at what I'm doing. A few of the Thaw shift, their clothes rustling, and that's answer enough. They're uncomfortable with magic use, as I knew they would be—the bulk of their magic experience was Angra's control of Spring. The few months we were back in Winter, with me using magic sporadically to help crops along, did nothing to alter their already fearful view of it.

I almost tell them not to worry. It'll all be gone soon.

Mather shushes them, a sharp hiss between his teeth, and I bow my head to my chest.

Find him, I will my magic. I don't realize until I think those words how desperately I need it to work. Because if I can't sense Sir here . . . Angra might have already killed him.

A sharp jolt of connection makes me straighten.

"What?" Mather's hands go to my arm.

My eyes fly open.

"Sir," I pant, relief cooling my limbs. I look at Mather. "I know where he is."

I take off, led purely by the need in my heart. My magic doesn't sense any Decay in Sir—his strength of will must be enough to resist, for now at least.

Of course it is. Of course he'd hold out against Angra.

We slip into the palace through the servants' entrance, keeping our heads bowed, our features as obscured by scarves as possible. Luckily, every servant we pass keeps their shoulders hunched and faces to the ground as they rush to complete their tasks. I lead the Thaw through halls that once dripped with vibrant pink flowers and braids of silk—now the walls are bare, darkness serving almost as the only decoration. And, more than that, there's a heaviness to these halls, one that feels so reminiscent of Angra's palace in Abril that my heart can't stop galloping. *Pain*—that's what my body remembers most about Angra's home. Excruciating, shattering pain.

I stop before each corner, glancing down it to make sure Angra isn't lying in wait. I can't feel him anywhere around, which means he either isn't here—unlikely—or he's shielding himself as much as I am from him. He could be one wall away, and I wouldn't know.

Finally, I duck up one last staircase and come to a balcony overlooking the celebration hall. Four stories of arching sandstone balconies spiral around, the ceiling nothing but a great sweep of the night sky. Fire pits line the room, all burning low and casting just enough light to highlight the people below.

The gathering is a stark contrast to the last celebration I saw here. There is no music, no color—people stand in tight groups, talking in quiet, low voices, every so often casting wary glances at a balcony directly across from me.

We're on one of the second-floor balconies, the walkway empty of any other souls. Still we press to the wall, slinking through the shadows. My magic hums, compelling me forward—Sir should be here.

My breath hitches. *Trap,* I think. *It's a trap. Angra knew we'd come.*

But then I turn.

Sir crouches behind the railing, his body squished against a pillar. His attention is pinned on the balcony, centered across from him. No doubt Angra will appear there, and Ceridwen's planned assassination attempt will occur.

At the sight of Sir, images break apart in my mind, thoughts of him dead at Angra's hands, his body broken and bleeding on a battlefield. But he's all right—he's alive.

I hadn't realized how terrified I'd been until now.

The Thaw stops, hidden behind one of the larger pillars. I slide forward one step.

"Sir," I whisper.

He jolts and flies to his feet, utter shock scrawled across his usually stoic face, before he falls back to hide behind the pillar next to him.

His attention shifts to a movement at my left.

Mather steps away from the shadows and everything about Sir's demeanor softens. Where he had looked at me with shock, Sir looks at Mather as if he's staring at the most precious thing in the world.

Sir's arms drop limp. "You're all right," he mouths.

Mather hesitates, shrugs. But Sir doesn't give him a chance to respond—he stumbles into the space behind our pillar, and everything I ever thought I knew about Sir is proved wrong.

He hooks his arms around Mather's neck and hauls him forward, head bowing to tuck against his son.

Mather goes stiff.

Sir is hugging him—desperately, pleadingly.

Mather's eyes close and he dissolves, his fingers digging into Sir's back. A sob shakes through Mather's body, sorrow unleashed from his mother's recent death, from his tortured relationship with his parents, from the way I know he's always wanted this as much as I have. And while I am gloriously happy for him, a sharp flutter takes my breath away.

I've resigned myself to my relationship with Sir. I am his queen; that's all I'll ever be.

I clear my throat. "Where is Ceridwen?" I whisper.

Sir pulls away from Mather. When he faces me again, every bit of softness is gone.

He nods to the floor below us.

I press back against the pillar but angle forward so I can see the floor. My gut aches when my eyes land on Ceridwen, hidden in an alcove by a fire pit, her eyes cutting every so often to the same second-floor balcony across from us.

"We have archers," Sir whispers, nodding to the balconies above. "And swordsmen." He points at his own weapon, then to two more bodies hidden on this same level, on balconies closer to the one that holds all attention. One of the swordsmen is Henn.

I pause. They haven't yet been caught. They haven't yet been consumed with Decay.

This . . . might actually work.

"What can we do?" I ask, a breath against the music below.

But Sir can't answer—the moment I ask, a door opens on the main balcony. We all drop, crouching behind the thick sandstone railings and pillars.

The crowd pivots toward the open door. Their quiet whispering ceases, dead silence making the low-burning fire pits roar.

From the shadows of the opened door, Angra emerges.

Mather puts his hand on my knee. I grab his fingers, squeezing once, but the rest of my body has gone numb. I keep from looking at Ceridwen, knowing the pain that must be racking her. Angra is here, lording his power over her kingdom.

Summer is his.

Firelight cuts through the shadows around him, dancing off his black tunic and pale hair as he steps to the railing.

"Summer!" Angra bellows. The crowd shifts closer to him, drawn as flowers to the sun. "The world has transformed. I bring to each kingdom a chance at unity—a chance Summer has welcomed with great reception. . . ."

He drones on, a speech about unity and peace and things that set my insides on fire, so I ignore him in favor of studying him. Does he have the keys? They're more a threat to him than the locket ever was, and he kept that around his neck. There's no way he'd let those keys leave his person. So how do we get close enough to him without getting ourselves killed? Maybe, if Ceridwen's archers get a good shot, it will stun him enough for us to make a move. Or—could an arrow really assassinate him? Surely his magic wouldn't let him die so easily. But it could definitely distract him.

". . . will shift our world into a state of equality, where prejudices will die and new life will grow. Further"—Angra leans forward—"the Seasons and Rhythms will no longer hold to biased, childlike opinions. We are all equal, and as such, I, a Season king, present to Theron Haskar, a Rhythm king, a token of my trust and bond."

Every bit of blood in my body rushes for my head, wrapping me in a dizzy fog.

I knew he'd be here, but I hadn't let myself dwell on it, the same way I keep from looking at Ceridwen—I can't think about him now.

Movement from two places in the room cuts my attention.

One comes from below, where two men start walking across the back of the room. They're Yakimians, and I almost dismiss them as slaves—but they're armed, and they walk with a sudden purpose that stands out in the quiet crowd. Slowly at first, their footsteps gain traction with each step, and it isn't until they're halfway across the room that Sir, on the other side of Mather, grunts low in his throat.

This isn't part of the plan.

Another movement comes from the door behind Angra, the darkness unfurling around the figure of a man. He isn't injured, not a bruise or a scratch or anything to indicate he's been ill-treated—which is almost more horrible. He's whole and clean, dressed in a Cordellan military uniform, looking so normal that I have to squeeze my nails into my palms, the pain reminding me that this is real, not a nightmare.

Mather sucks in a ragged breath, his hand on my knee clenching tighter, grounding me.

Theron steps up to the railing. Angra reaches into a pocket on his black tunic to withdraw a chain from which two thick black keys hang.

I teeter forward, catching myself on the stone.

"These keys represent both our past mistakes and our future freedom," Angra continues, and holds them out.

Below, the two Yakimians reach Ceridwen's hiding place. She frowns at them.

I feel everything that happens next before it occurs, like the anticipation of watching a storm cloud roll in over the plains.

Theron takes the keys, opens his mouth to say something no doubt grand and rehearsed in response to Angra's display.

But the Yakimian men start shouting.

"You are unfit to lead us!" one cries. "We never should have trusted you!"

"You deserve death!" the other adds, and they draw their weapons and dive at Ceridwen.

The crowd dissolves into panic, their silence broken now

by horrified shrieking. They rush for the doors as soldiers advance from the side halls, Angra's men, their uniforms a mix of Cordell and Spring, their faces set with . . . amusement.

I send one more blast of protection to my Winterians, keeping them clear of Angra's Decay, and launch to my feet. No hesitation—the open-air room means dirt coats every tile of the floor, making it easy to lift the particles and create a haphazard version of a sandstorm. The air fills with blinding dirt as the crowd's chaos rears into terrified screams and the jostle of weapons.

Sir and Mather react without needing instruction, sprinting after me down the balcony. The Thaw trails behind us, their weapons drawn. The sand starts to settle, so I whip it up again, but another force snatches it away from me. The unexpected loss of control sends me stumbling into the railing.

The sand clears, controlled by Angra's outstretched hand.

I'm leaning over the room, so close to his balcony now that I could reach out and touch him. Henn stands next to me, having joined us as we raced past his hiding place.

Angra grins. Beside him, Theron smiles, just as pleased as Angra, albeit with more relief than satisfaction.

I push myself back from the railing and rip my chakram free, but the pillars make throwing it impossible. Soldiers appear behind us on the balcony, their booted feet shaking the walkway, and the Thaw turns to intercept them amid a chorus of shouts and clashing weapons. I send them bursts of strength and swing around the corner to come face-to-face with Angra. The keys are in his hand.

Angra doesn't bother with a weapon—a shadow engulfs his fist and his grin turns sickening. Below us, chaos still bubbles over, but the crowd has mostly departed—the only shouting comes from one source, a voice that triggers awareness.

Ceridwen.

She cries out, and I whip around to look for her.

Distracted, *distracted*—

That word consumes me as I blink and Angra punches the air, his shadow pummeling into my chest. I heave backward, hurtling into Sir and Henn, who jog up behind me.

Theron swings forward, catching Angra's arm. "She could be here to surrender!"

Angra holds and I fly to my feet, chakram still raised.

"Have you come to surrender, Winter queen?" Angra asks, but his voice says he knows I haven't. Another shadow gathers around his fist—

Before he can throw it, Mather climbs onto the railing and leaps to their balcony, careening into Angra, who slams back into Theron. The three of them drop to the floor in a collision of thuds and shouts.

I hesitate, eyes scrambling over the mess of bodies for the keys—did they get jostled loose? Does Theron still have them? Why did Angra give them to Theron at all?

But I know why.

Because I'd have no problem killing Angra to get the keys, but if I have to get them from Theron . . .

Angra is on his feet now, Mather between him and me with a dagger drawn. Angra doesn't toy with me this time—he jerks his hand to his chest, pulling the dagger from Mather's grip. Mather staggers forward with a cry of alarm, but Angra is already flinging his hand back out, hurling the dagger at me.

Theron flips onto his knees and reaches for Angra.

"No—she's *mine!*" he roars, and pulls Angra's aim off, the dagger plunging to the right to graze Mather's shoulder before it clatters into the room below.

Mather spins with the force of the blade. Behind me, Phil wails, and any last knot of concentration I had utterly unravels at the sight of blood spraying out of Mather's arm.

Go, I beg myself. *Get out of here, get out of here—*

Panic drives me, such fuel that I don't even need to touch the Winterians. Mather, Sir, Henn, the Thaw—I grab onto their bodies with the same snaking tendrils that let me find Sir, and on a pull that tears at my stomach, I use my magic to remove us from the balcony.

Ceridwen

TONIGHT THEY WOULD assassinate the king of Spring and end his magic-fueled reign of terror.

Ceridwen had felt Angra's Decay picking away at her mind the moment they set foot in Juli, but now, as he stood over her on the balcony, his magic pummeled her like raindrops beating against a parched ground.

But she had been parched for years—she had learned to live without rain.

She kept her place on the main floor, tucked on the outskirts of the quiet, waiting crowd. There was no denying Angra's influence in Summer as she watched the normally vivacious upper class stand in solemn, whispering groups. The trip through Juli had been just as wrong, the streets silent, even the brothels still. Everything about her kingdom was wrong, like a fire Angra had doused with water—no more light, no more passion, no more *life*.

Ceridwen shook her head and glared up at Angra. The archers above him were so well hidden that Ceridwen herself almost couldn't spot them—but she knew they were there, waiting for her signal.

Angra droned on, but still Ceridwen couldn't bring her hand to rise. He presented as good a shot as any.

Ceridwen clenched her fist.

Signal, she willed herself. *Give the signal—*

Her throat all but closed, her eyes glazing over in a sudden burst of dizziness. She staggered, tripping into a servant who held a tray of goblets for the crowd that hadn't drunk a single drop of wine all night. Once, that would have made her rejoice, that her court could be sober at an event—but now she found herself wishing for them to indulge as they used to.

The servant scurried away, outfit soaked with spilled wine. The scent flooded Ceridwen's mind with images of this room, memories of parties where wine had flowed and the courtiers had laughed, and drunk, and succumbed to Simon's magic.

Ceridwen righted herself, dazed. She needed to signal . . . something. Feasting to start, maybe—but no, that had always been Simon's duty. He loved announcing new festivities to the crowd.

Ceridwen shifted, turning to the tent he always erected in the middle of the room—

It wasn't there.

On the balcony, Angra beckoned to someone behind him, and Theron stepped forward.

Angra—kill him. Focus, Ceridwen!

She scrambled forward, her mind clouded, the crowd so close that she could feel each heartbeat egging her on, united in this one clarifying goal: to kill Simon.

A cry fought for life in her chest. She planned to kill her brother? Why would she do such a thing?

Her mind burned, magic prickling across her scalp with dozens of tiny, determined fingers. Simon's magic had never been this persistent—once she pushed it from her mind, it had seemed to sulk away as though even it was too drunk to press her more.

But Angra's magic was determined, and heavy, and warm. It cocooned around her body, waiting for one small window of weakness through which it could climb. It whispered in her ear, words dripping honey, *What do you want, Cerie?*

No one had ever asked her that before.

Do you want to join the courtiers? You've always wanted to be like them—so easily able to forget their worries and give themselves over to stronger powers, powers that know better. . . .

Ceridwen turned, bumping into someone else—one of the Yakimians who had come with her, the leader Jesse had had to subdue. One of his soldiers flanked him, their brows furrowed.

"You haven't given the signal," the leader growled.

Ceridwen swayed toward him. "Signal?" she asked, her

voice soft in the general silence of the room—only one voice rang out, giving some kind of speech. "Where is Simon?"

"I was right from the beginning." The Yakimian shook his head, lips peeling back as he bared his teeth. "You're weak, and I should have killed you long ago—this mission should have been mine. This victory will go to Yakim! You are unfit to lead us! We never should have trusted you!"

His comrade ripped his blade from its sheath. "You deserve death!"

They leaped for her, all biting iron weapons and rock-hard fists. She dodged their blows thanks only to the vacancy of shock.

The Yakimians are attacking me. Who armed the slaves? Where is Simon?

The crowd broke apart into terror, shoving this way and that as they dove for exits and soldiers moved in. Angra's magic seemed to dissipate from Ceridwen's mind in the sudden chaos.

Angra—she hadn't given the signal to attack. He was still alive, waiting for someone to kill him, just like when she had tried to kill Simon in Rintiero.

But no one else would come in and right Ceridwen's wrongs this time.

She had failed. Again.

Ceridwen screamed, but not from the threat of the attacking Yakimians.

There was no forgiveness to be had. Simon was *dead*.

A thought hit her, then. Some faint recollection of a time without pain, one of her only happy memories: Jesse, in the refugee camp, talking of fresh starts.

The Yakimians' own hatred compelled them to attack her, Angra's magic blinding them to any threat but the Summerian princess, so they didn't flinch as Cordellan soldiers swarmed the room and blades pierced their spines. Ceridwen dove for the first Cordellan, but he hurled her to the ground. She slid across the floor and slammed into a table overturned in the crowd's departure, her body rebounding limply.

She'd come back to Juli to stop Angra—and all she'd done was open more wounds.

A blast of ice cooled the scorching air of the celebration hall. All Ceridwen managed was a feeble acknowledgment—*Coldness in Summer? Meira?*—before hands heaved her upright.

"Ceridwen—" Meira started, but her voice cut off at the way Ceridwen could only stare at the floor. One of the Winterians who had come with her from the camp held her up, taking her weight. "Get her out of here," Meira told him, and they started moving, hobbling for the door as more blasts of ice warred with the hall's heat.

"Do you think Angra's magic got to her?"

"She'd be . . . doing something, then, wouldn't she?"

"Is she hurt? They hit her in the head?"

Meira knelt before her. Dirt streaked her face, sweat making a paste of the sand and grime from this hidden passage. Ceridwen hadn't been surprised at all when her group had found this former sewage tunnel still boarded up—it had made an easy, hidden entrance into the palace by way of the underground wine cellar.

She glanced around, taking quick stock of who was here and who was not. Meira, a new group of Winterians, General William, and Henn; none of the Yakimians; two of her Summerians. Lekan was one of them, and Ceridwen pinched her eyes shut against the burning tears of relief that he had made it out.

Flame and heat, what would she have done if he had died because of her?

"Ceridwen," Meira tried. "What happened?"

She didn't sound angry.

She should.

Five deaths had come because of this failed plan. A few of Meira's Winterians had been hurt too—one had a deep gash across his arm; another had a cut along his forehead; Henn had taken a sword to the ribs as he helped Ceridwen limp out of the hall. A single lantern cast shadows on their dirty faces, each of them straining for any sound of approach.

And all because Ceridwen had let guilt blind her.

She slammed her head back against the wall, the rough

stone threatening to puncture her skull.

"I'm sorry," she whispered.

Meira slumped to her knees. "It's all right."

"It *is?*" choked one of the Winterians—a boy, who was even now tying a bandage around the one with a cut arm.

"Phil," the injured one chastised him, and Phil dropped his head, scowling still.

Meira kept her eyes on Ceridwen, as if the mission hadn't been a disaster, as if there wasn't a barrage of injuries around them. "What happened?"

Even just hearing that question made the tears in Ceridwen's eyes overflow, and she pinched the skin above her nose, face contorting to push back a scream.

"Angra's magic," she started. "It got to me—"

"How?" Meira pressed.

She should have expected that. She owed them all the truth, why she, who should have been the most able to resist magic, fell at all. Was it because of her own weaknesses, or Angra's strength?

"It should have been Simon," she whimpered, "here tonight. And I hate that I think that, but I'd rather he be alive for me to keep fighting him than—"

She couldn't speak for the sob that gripped her throat. When it passed, she lowered her hand, sight blurring.

"I don't know how to move on," she said. "I don't know how to forgive him when he isn't here. *I hate him*—"

Meira just sat there, listening, while everyone else waited. Their silence made Ceridwen laugh, of all things, and she chuckled heartlessly through her tears.

"And I ruined everything," she finished, palms up, because what more could she say?

"You did not ruin everything," Meira said, but it was as empty as her smile. "Angra gave Theron something I'm searching for—those keys. If I can get them, I can defeat Angra, and we know who has them now."

"Angra gave the keys to Theron before we revealed ourselves." William leaned forward. "That was part of his plan. To make sure word spread that Theron has them."

Everyone heard the words he didn't say. *It's another trap.*

Meira's expression stayed the same.

Ceridwen locked eyes with her. "We'll be more prepared. I won't . . . fall apart next time."

Meira shook her head. "We should do our best to make sure none of us falls apart next time."

Midnight had long since passed by the time they left the hidden passage. It released them just outside the palace's walls, in an alley more akin to a garbage dump. That felt appropriate as they spilled into the night, covered in filth and blood and failure.

Juli had changed. The overhanging tension that had kept the city silent and nearly empty when they first arrived seemed enhanced. Fights broke out in taverns; warring groups tumbled through the streets; cries pierced the air from every direction, calling for help in an echoing rebound that made it impossible to track. Farther down the street, soldiers patrolled, barging into houses and demanding any residents turn over the Winter queen.

Ceridwen kept her head down, her muscles taut, and led the battered group out of Juli. They could stay and try to help where they could, but Angra's Decay would no doubt foster two more problems for every one they solved.

Ceridwen bit her lips together, inhaling the smells of the city one last time. Heat-soaked wood; bitter sweat; tangy wine; the grittiness of sand with every breath.

She was leaving. But she would return, and she would fix Summer—and maybe, through that, she would find a way to fix her relationship with Simon, too.

Meira

IT ISN'T UNTIL we leave Juli that the full weight of what happened settles over me.

Ceridwen's group stashed their horses in an abandoned barn south of the city. Now there are five riderless mounts, providing transport for the Thaw and me, who partner up to take them because we don't have our own. Mather eases up onto the saddle behind me and settles in, his arms loose around my waist. No one mentions how the former riders of these horses were left behind, bodies now at Angra's disposal. But I see Ceridwen stare at the horses as we ride out, her eyes tear glazed in the shadows.

As grim as a funeral procession, we head east, to the only Season that Angra hasn't had a chance to infiltrate yet: Autumn.

Angra was counting on us being in Juli. If he laid a trap

for us there, did he know we'd try to go to Autumn too?

I swallow the question. It doesn't matter. I'll do what needs to be done.

I will find a way to get those keys without having to kill Theron.

One afternoon later, the sun casts light over a long swath of something on the horizon—trees. And not Summer's dead, spindly trees, but plump ones bursting with red and yellow leaves. Beneath them lies crisp green grass and tangled brown undergrowth—such a welcome array of colors that I actually whimper.

As our horses burst into the Autumn forest, the air sweeps over me in a rush of coolness that, compared to Summer, feels like getting plunged into an ice bath.

Ceridwen pulls her horse to a stop in a small clearing.

I nod into the forest. "We should find water," I say. "Replenish our supplies before—"

But Ceridwen isn't looking at me. Her eyes narrow into slits looking over my shoulder, a frown wrinkling her brow before she pulls a dagger from her belt.

That's all the explanation we need—Mather draws a sword, the Thaw arm themselves, Sir and Henn and Ceridwen's remaining Summerians spin in their saddles, trying to find the source of the attack.

But it isn't an attack—at least, not immediately.

I guide my horse to face what Ceridwen sees, Mather pressing his body flat against my back, his sword held before me in defense. I'd thought all my adrenaline had been sucked dry by Summer's heat, but fresh energy surges, my muscles coiling for a fight.

A man moves out from the trees. He's Autumnian, his dark eyes wide against the smooth brown of his skin, his night-black hair tied away from his face in a frizzy knot. His armor is the heavy leather plating and his weapons the simple mix of wood and metal that Autumn is so known for—nature in its purest, deadliest forms. More warriors follow his lead, materializing from the trees around us, some on horseback, others, like the man, on foot.

He looks at me and flexes his hand against the hilt of a spear. "Queen Meira?"

I keep my jaw clamped shut. My horse paws at the grass under the tension.

If the Autumnians are on Angra's side, anything I say could feed back to him.

Sir pushes forward in my stead. "What do you want?"

"A darkness has fallen over Primoria," the man says. "My king wishes to know if it has affected the Winterian queen."

Sir's expression doesn't change, but I feel my own face flash with confusion.

"Your king?" Sir presses, just as I would have.

I stare at the side of his head. Sir, acting as my general.

This is how we're supposed to be, and it feels familiar—yet uncomfortable even so.

The warrior nods. "Caspar Abu Shazi Akbari."

Relief lets my muscles relax and I sag in my saddle. Mather twitches against me, and when I turn to him, he gives me a look like I've lost what's left of my mind. But Sir relaxes too, and he meets my eyes with a nod.

"Angra's Decay hasn't taken him," I explain to everyone else. "If it had, he wouldn't recognize Caspar as his king. He'd say Angra."

"Then why are we surrounded by armed soldiers?" Mather asks.

I turn back to the Autumnian. "We're also free of the Decay. Angra isn't our king either."

The warrior steps back, letting his spear drop against his shoulder as he puts his hands up in surrender. The others sheathe their weapons.

"We had to make sure you could be trusted. King Caspar has tasked us with watching the border. We received word to look out for you, but that you had gone to Juli—such a trip, so close to Angra, could have resulted in your being poisoned with his magic."

That grabs me. "You knew we were coming? How?"

The warrior smiles. "Caspar received word of you from several hundred refugees."

"What?" I ask. "Are they all right? Where are they?"

The warrior smiles again. "My king will be able to answer

those questions. He wishes to speak to you immediately." He bows his head. "If you please, Queen Meira, I'll take you to the Autumn court."

As we head into Autumn, the warrior explains that the Cordellans stationed in Oktuber turned on the Akbaris shortly after they received word of Theron's betrayal. The court managed to escape and regroup with half of their forces in the southern part of the kingdom, nestled against the Klaryns' foothills, stretching our trip to a day and half.

When I finally push my horse around one last aspen tree and catch a whiff of campfire smoke on the air, I sigh in relief. A few paces later, a group of Autumnian warriors stands on a narrow path, spears in their hands, swords at their waists, leather armor covering their chests and hanging in pleated skirts to their knees. They turn, alert.

"More refugees?" one of the warriors on guard calls. He motions to his right. "They've started a camp off in the—"

He pauses, his eyes catching on me again. My chakram, my locket.

He stiffens. "Queen Meira."

I smile, the last of my worry vanishing.

They've opened their kingdom to our refugees, who are no doubt still trickling in just as we are, creating a tight pocket of people who oppose Angra, tucked away in Autumn's forest. Even Sir's stoic face ripples slightly, and

I catch him studying me, a slight tilt to his mouth. In that moment I can almost see our past in his face—the last time we were in Autumn was years ago, when we were scraping by in our nomadic existence to hide from Angra. Now we're here, riding into Autumn as welcome allies.

Lifetimes have changed in what feels like heartbeats.

I tip my head at Sir and he straightens, pressing forward without a word.

The full bulk of Autumn's camp begins as a few orange and brown tents that camouflage into the earthy tones of the forest. The longer we ride, the more frequent the tents grow until blocks appear, carefully arranged streets, tents pressed into market areas and barracks and narrow houses. We see more people too, warriors mostly, men and women sharpening weapons or standing guard or eating at short tables along the road.

We slow to a stop just outside a large ruby-red tent. I slide off my horse, my eyes on the elaborate designs stitched into the fabric, leaves fluttering off trees and bonfires raging.

As the warrior who led us here approaches the tent, noises swarm out.

"Shazi, wait—"

A crash, the squeal of a child.

I laugh. At least this war hasn't dampened the Autumnian princess's spirits.

The tent flaps part, held by tiny fists.

"MEE-WAH!" Shazi screams, and I can't tell if she's

pleased or in dire pain. She launches at me and hooks her arms around my waist. I can only clutch her and laugh again.

Nikoletta flies out of the tent as if prepared to sprint after her daughter for what could have been the tenth time today. The moment she sees me, her brown eyes light up, drifting to Mather, Ceridwen, Sir, and the beaten group around us.

Shazi pulls back. "Mama! Mee-wah!"

Nikoletta stumbles forward. She says nothing at first, simply folds her arms around me, pressing me into the purple velvet of her outfit, the cozy aroma of wood fire lifting up off her.

"We heard terrible things," she whispers. "My brother . . . and Theron . . . and they said you'd gone to Juli. . . ."

Her voice fades, and I can't help but think she's embracing me now because she needs it, not simply because she's glad I'm alive. I hug her back.

"I'm so sorry," I whisper, and I hate how many times I've had to say that.

Nikoletta pulls away. Tears rim her eyes, and as more people exit the tent behind her, her features stand out. Gold hair and pale skin against the darkness of Autumn, marking her even more as Cordellan, as Noam's sister, as the aunt of Angra's latest puppet.

She lifts Shazi, who clutches the ring that hangs from the chain around her neck.

"Stwong, Mee-wah!" Shazi cheers. "Stwong!"

I smile. "Strong, Shazi."

She gurgles deep in her throat and buries her face in Nikoletta's shoulder.

Caspar emerges from courtiers and stops beside his wife, his eyes filled with a severity that sends a tremor through me.

"Your warrior told me you haven't sided with Angra," I start, and I feel my group move closer as I ask the one question that has been spinning around my mind since we entered Autumn. "But what are you planning?"

Caspar inclines his head. "Now that you're here," he says, "we're planning to beat him."

Checking for approaching enemies and throwing up a barrier has become instinctual now, and after sweeping the perimeter of the camp, I'm able to focus on the meeting awaiting me.

The main room of the tent is a large rectangle, lined with clusters of fabric and piles of pillows and dusty rugs unrolled over the floor. Incense releases rivulets of smoke that swirl around the ceiling. The air is cool, letting me breathe easy.

I hold that breath, reveling in it. We have allies; we're tucked away in one of the few kingdoms that Angra hasn't yet completely overtaken. We even know where the keys are, for the next step in this war.

We might just be all right.

Mather and Hollis stand in the corner; the rest of their group was sent away to assist our refugees. Apparently the Thaw designated themselves something of my own personal guard, taking up shifts watching me—and when Mather smiles at me from where he talks with Hollis, I find I don't mind.

Both Mather and Hollis shift when one of the tent's flaps rustles and Sir ducks inside. Mather instantly spins toward him, and I don't realize until I see his eagerness that I'm reacting the same way.

"No problems getting here," Sir says. "The refugees split into three groups. The farthest one has not yet arrived—should be a few days."

I swallow. The memory of Ceridwen's pain is vibrant: how she never had the chance to repair her relationship with Simon.

We should do our best to make sure none of us falls apart, I said.

I rub at my chest absently, lips pinched together.

"We can go after them," Mather offers. "Escort them safely in."

Sir nods. "I was going to suggest the same thing." His attention flicks to me, hesitation clear on his face. "If my queen wishes it."

I almost laugh. This is how we've been acting? Has it always sounded so absurd?

I smile at Sir. A real, normal smile, like the old me. "Of course. Who should go?"

Sir's face doesn't reveal anything he might be thinking. "You and I will be needed for whatever decisions must be made. I was thinking of sending Henn, along with—"

"We could go," Hollis offers. "A few of the Thaw, at least—if it's of importance to our queen, we should be involved."

Sir considers, then nods. Spots of pink stain Mather's cheeks, a rise of pride as he squares his shoulders.

"I'll send them out as soon as we're done here," Mather says.

As if on cue, the flaps part again and Caspar and Niko-letta file in. Moments later, we're joined by Ceridwen and Jesse, Dendera, Henn—representatives of four kingdoms; leaders of the armies of two. And a half. If our few hundred Winterian, Yakimian, and Summerian soldiers can even be counted as an army.

Caspar surveys the room, eyes moving from Mather to Sir, Dendera to Henn, like he can see each of their strengths and weaknesses written in vibrant ink across their foreheads. When he gets to me, I stiffen my spine to keep from withering.

"What was the last you heard of Angra's conquests?" he asks, straight to the point.

"In addition to Spring, he now has Ventralli, Summer,

Winter, and Cordell." I separate my emotions from my words, talking low and hard. Because I don't stop there—I've already gone too long without telling everyone the truth behind our war.

I explain what Angra is now, a host for the Royal Conduit's magic as well as the Decay, and how that magic will spread out from Angra and infect every living soul in Primoria until everyone is a slave to fear and their darkest desires. How I am a host for Winter's magic too; how Winter and Cordell discovered the entrance to the magic chasm. Nikoletta seems shocked to learn that we actually found the entrance, but Caspar doesn't even flinch, either because he doesn't care or because he already suspected it. I tell them about the keys we need to open it, about the labyrinth of three tasks built by Paislians.

And then I take a deep breath.

"Once I get through the labyrinth and reach the magic chasm, I can defeat Angra," I say. "But doing so won't just rid Angra of the Decay—it will rid the world of all magic."

Caspar is the first to understand, and he blinks slowly at me.

"We have to destroy all magic?" he asks. "Why? Couldn't we simply kill Angra?"

I shrug halfheartedly. "I would be the only person who could even get close enough to do that—but it wouldn't be guaranteed that the Decay would end with his death, and how many lives would be lost in the attempt? This way, though, is definite. It *will* end his reign."

"How is this definite?" Caspar asks. He isn't defensive; his tone is simply curious, though the expression on Nikoletta's face is more like horror.

"I . . . ," I start, then realize how absolutely insane this will sound. "My magic . . . showed me, in a way. Conduit magic's purpose is to protect its land—and I sought such help from mine. I asked it how to save everyone. Not even the Paislians knew of another way, and they've been searching for ways to undo magic far longer than we have."

"Those are our two options, then?" Nikoletta now. "Either we fight Angra as he is, and hope to defeat him by strength of arms—or your conduit told you we should destroy all magic?"

I wince and nod. The overall mood in the room is one of apprehension. The idea of a world without magic is one not many have considered, let alone the idea of asking conduits for help. There are only three other monarchs here besides me—Ceridwen, the Autumnian king, and Jesse. Ceridwen is the wrong gender to use Summer's conduit; Jesse's conduit is useless now, after Raelyn broke it in Rintiero and Jesse, in essence, let her; and in Autumn, they've lived without being able to use their conduit for generations. It wouldn't be such a far leap for them, for the world to be empty of magic. And they've all now experienced how expansive Angra's threat is—asking the conduit magic for help might not seem like such a farfetched thing.

In fact, Caspar looks almost like he'll agree with me. But he isn't the one who speaks up.

"We've all seen magic do far more mysterious things than give help when it was needed," Sir says. He crosses his arms, his stance telling the room that he expects his words to be heeded. "It doesn't appear we have a very difficult choice to make. We all have fallen victim to Angra's destruction—the Autumnians were ousted from their own city; the refugees around us were displaced from their homes; friends and family have been lost. Angra must be stopped. No matter the cost."

A pause, then slow murmurs of agreement pepper the room, coming first from Caspar, Ceridwen, and Jesse.

I glance quickly at Sir, who stares straight at me. He bows his head.

My heart squeezes, trampled beneath Sir's devotion and his last few words.

No matter the cost.

I didn't tell them what exactly I have to do to destroy magic. And I won't, for as long as I can avoid it.

"We know now who has the keys," I say, not lingering on the issue. "Angra presented them to Theron when we were in Juli. Which poses a number of problems, namely that he *wants* us to know that Theron has the keys—he's hoping we'll try to get them. Which we have to do. We have to figure out some way to get close to Theron."

When I finish, Caspar has a hand on his chin, his

mouth pursed in thought.

"All right. We can work with that."

"What are you thinking?" I ask.

It's Nikoletta who answers. "According to our spies, Angra has split the armies stationed in Winter—half he sent to fortify Jannuari and half to increase protection over the Tadil Mine. Which makes sense now—he's making sure you won't be able to easily access the entrance. Spring's army is at this moment marching toward Winter; the Ventrallans are boarding ships, and every missive we've intercepted in Summer has mentioned their own armies readying to leave. We suspect, then, that he is sending them all to focus his power in Winter."

My mouth drops open. When Angra took Winter last time, he at least left our land empty. Now, though, he has endless resources, and he knows that the only way to stop him lies under my kingdom.

Of course the final battle against Angra would take place in Winter.

"So we turn our focus to Winter too," I say. "But surely you can't mean to attack him, not directly?"

Caspar meets my gaze. "Perhaps not."

Nikoletta spins on him. "So we should let Angra gather his full strength?"

With a cocked brow, Caspar smiles. "Yes."

"What?" I frown at him.

"We have to assume that Angra will anticipate whatever

we plan—but if we *expect* him to get the advantage, we may be able to manipulate the outcome. Once Angra's armies are united, if we show our position, he'll know we're trying to draw him out on our terms. It's a risk, but I believe Angra will come after us himself and leave Theron to deal with *you*, thinking you will use the battle as cover to get the labyrinth's keys. It'll be a trap, but we can still control when and how it happens."

I mull over his plan long enough that the silence in the tent tells me everyone else is too. So when I speak, I know I'm throwing yet another twist into their swirling worries. "And if I present myself as leading the army, Angra will definitely come after us himself."

Nikoletta frowns. "Who would we send to retrieve the keys?"

"If Angra is occupied by the battle, I can use my magic to get myself and a few Winterians to wherever Theron is and then to the mine in minutes." I find Mather on the edge of the tent. "Mather and General William will accompany me—we'll get the keys from Theron, then instantly go to the Tadil. With a smaller group, we might even get the keys and get out before any traps can take hold."

"Where do you think Theron will be?" Mather asks, his face blank.

Caspar answers. "We'll have our scouts locate him for this. Though I suspect—"

"Jannuari," I say, as if from a distance, my voice low.

"Angra will put him in Jannuari."

If Angra truly does mean to use Theron against me, he'd put him in the one place that would most thoroughly unravel me: the heart of my kingdom.

My eyes stay on Mather. This isn't just a simple mission. This is everything I've been working toward from the first moment I heard of the war between our kingdoms: Angra's defeat.

For a moment, Rares and Oana flash through my mind, and I almost ask Caspar to send a scout to Paisly. But by the time anyone could travel there and back, the war would be long over, in whatever outcome.

I shiver. It's all happening too fast, yet too slowly.

I pivot back to Caspar and Nikoletta before glancing at Ceridwen. Their people are the ones who will suffer most in this, and though I don't know how many warriors Autumn has in this camp, I know it isn't nearly enough to actually win against Angra.

"As soon as the magic is destroyed, Angra will be powerless," I assure them, unable to keep the plea out of my voice. "I'll find the keys, then get to the chasm as quickly as I can. You won't have to hold him off for long. I promise, I'll make this battle as short as possible."

With as few deaths as possible.

The thought batters at me. People will die for this. For *me*.

Caspar puts his hand on my shoulder. "This war belongs

to all of us. We are all well aware of what will happen if we don't stand against Angra. You bear too much of the weight."

I almost dissolve under his comfort. But I nod, step back, and fumble with the hem of my shirt. The threads are entirely held together by dirt now, and the distraction gives me something easy to think about.

"We'll wait for Angra's forces to gather in Winter," I confirm. "In the meantime, can we borrow supplies?"

"Oh! Of course." Nikoletta signals to a few of the servants at the edge of the room, and as they duck outside, I follow. I don't think anyone expected me to leave the tent, but the orders have been given, decisions made, and I cannot stand around rehashing old news or picking apart our strategies.

"I'm coming with you to Winter, idiot. Not only do I have to redeem myself, but I'm not letting the three of you go alone."

Ceridwen keeps pace beside me as the servants weave into a tent across the clearing. While they shuffle through supplies inside, I face her.

"I'd take you if I could, believe me, but for this mission, I need to be able to use my magic on everyone. Besides, we'll need leaders like you in the battle."

"I won't sit here while you're off actually defeating Angra. He overtook my kingdom too."

Ceridwen's voice breaks. Her agony is a hot, sparking

wave that palpitates off her body.

"I know," I say. This isn't about packing down my weak feelings—this is about choosing what will strengthen me over what will break me, and right now, at this moment, I desperately need to be strong. "Please, don't argue this." My throat shrivels. "Go—spend time with Jesse. This war isn't done taking people from us."

Ceridwen pushes closer to me. "Get that look off your face right now."

I pull back. "What?"

"The look that says you don't expect to survive this. Because if you don't expect to survive this war, you *won't*. Death has a way of finding those who welcome it."

Her words heave at the balled knot in my chest. I turn from her, reaching for the tent.

"The servants should be—"

Ceridwen grabs my arm, holding me in place. "I'm not saying that that feeling isn't natural. Any fighter worries about it constantly. But don't let it consume you."

"I *don't* let it consume me," I snap. "You have no idea what it will take to end this. I do. I know exactly what has to happen, so don't lecture me on how to handle it. I'm doing the best I can, Ceridwen. I'm barely holding myself together."

Her grip on me loosens. I run a hand over my face, and when I look back at her, her anger has returned, a flash of hurt that makes me all too aware of how I yelled at her.

I slacken. The main tent's flaps part, and out come Sir, Dendera . . . Mather.

My chest deflates. "You've worried about not making it through battles before."

Ceridwen nods, sharp and short.

"Did you ever fear . . ." The question sticks in my mouth. "Did you ever fear what that would do to the people you love? Did you ever try to, I don't know . . . distance yourself, so it wouldn't hurt as much?"

Ceridwen doesn't respond right away, and when I look at her, her lips part.

"I got too good at distancing myself," she says. "Mostly it was because I was afraid. But I've come to understand things differently, after all this. And . . ." Her eyes stray to the camp around us. "And it's so ridiculous, these barriers we put up. We aren't hurting anyone but ourselves. Everyone involved in this knows that at any moment Angra could come sweeping in and obliterate everything. You think the people we love would be happier if we pushed them away? Flame and heat, *no*. Every moment we have is one more moment that can't be taken from us."

I look to Mather again—he's talking with his Thaw just outside the main tent, no doubt telling some of them to go with Henn to escort the last refugee group. His eyes jump to mine when he feels me looking at him, and even from paces away, his smile sends a tingling storm through my body.

Ceridwen follows my line of sight and looks back at me with a knowing grin. It softens into something serious, an absent longing dredged up from her own life.

"You'll only regret the time it took you to make the decision," she says.

That makes me shift a questioning smile to her. "And have you? Made a decision?"

Because the last time I saw her, she was distraught over ending things with Jesse. But they spent time together in her refugee camp—have they mended things since then?

By the slow, startled smile on her face, I know the answer.

She laughs at herself, palms going to her suddenly sheened eyes. "I don't know! I don't know. I just know that I—" Ceridwen shrugs, laughing again. "I love him. And that's all."

"Ventralli and Summer." I echo her smile. "It could work."

She rolls her eyes. "Believe me, this is not how I foresaw joining our two kingdoms—when neither of us really *has* a kingdom anymore. But . . ."

My eyes widen. "You really mean to join your kingdoms? You want to marry him?"

Ceridwen's cheeks tinge with spots of red, but I wave it off.

"I'm sorry—it's wonderful, Cerie. Really."

"Thank you." She recovers. "I'm glad my failed love life can be of some use to others."

"I wouldn't say it's failed." I motion toward the main tent. "Jesse's here. He chose you. That's certainly worth celebrating."

Ceridwen considers for a moment before she scrunches her nose and grins. "I guess I should take my own advice, shouldn't I? It *is* worth celebrating."

I cock my head, my sly smile returning. "What do you mean?"

But she shakes her head as the servants return, arms loaded with supplies.

"This way, Your Highness," they say and start down the nearest row of tents.

Ceridwen sprints back toward the main structure. I follow the servants, walking backward, half watching her go and half watching Mather move toward the western edge of camp with his Thaw. He doesn't notice me staring now, and my eyes slide over him, memorizing the dozens of details I've noticed for years. The way his shoulders cave when he's in a serious discussion; how the space over his nose creases on the left side when he frowns; the nervous twitch he gets when he's thinking, a shuddering shift in his jaw.

"You'll only regret the time it took you to make the decision."

Just before he turns down a row of tents, Mather looks at me over his shoulder. I smile at him.

Mather hesitates. Something catches in his eyes, loosening my feelings even more, as though he sees the difference in the way I smile at him. Phil says something to him, and it seems to take physical effort for Mather to break his curious eyes away from me.

This war will end with my death, but for now, I am alive. And Mather is alive. And we are here, somewhere safe for once, and if I'm to venture into the Klaryns and willingly sacrifice myself for this world, I will do so with no regrets. I will know what it is like to love, and love fully, with no reluctance or remorse or overthinking.

Just like I did with my conduit magic—I will harness all my life has to offer.

Meira

EVERY MINUTE OF every hour of the next three days is packed with readying the armies, settling the refugees, sending out scouts to watch Angra's movements, and discussing war strategies until everyone practically topples over from exhaustion. What moments I can steal, I spend pacing the perimeter of camp, straining my magic to double check that I'm shielding everyone as best as I can. What sleep I manage is light and fleeting, giving me just enough rest to get through the next day.

No one asks why I do what I do or says anything about how I stare off into the trees with my jaw clenched. I wonder about this for half a heartbeat one afternoon, long enough to realize that *everyone* is as stressed as I am. Everyone knows we have a few weeks at most before Angra's troops are fully gathered—which means we only have that much time to become a cohesive fighting unit.

And the more work we pack into each day, the fewer lives will be lost in the coming battle.

These thoughts fuel me when fatigue hits, and I need only glance at Nessa singing soft lullabies to the camp's children to force myself awake. When we break for the night and my legs ache from pacing, I need only spot Ceridwen running through drills with her refugee fighters to find the energy to take one more step, then another.

These tasks are infinitely preferable to what awaits us.

"Meira!"

I bolt upright, chakram in one hand, magic surging down my other arm in a bundled ball of defense. But it's only Nessa, bouncing in the middle of my tent.

"You're never going to believe what's happening!" she squeals.

I lower my chakram with a groan and scrub sleep from my eyes. "What's happening? How long have I been asleep?"

But even as I ask that, I think, *Not long enough.*

"Since..." Nessa's eyes drift upward as she thinks. "After midnight. It's just past noon now, and everyone wanted to let you rest, but I knew you wouldn't want to miss this!"

I twitch and lower my hands. It's past *noon?*

Nessa's face comes into focus, but my groggy confusion only intensifies when I see her outfit. Deep purple satin lined with gold trim curves around her body.

"I know we have to borrow things from Autumn, but

this is a bit fancy, isn't it?" I say.

Nessa spins to fluff the floor-length skirt around her sandals. "Isn't it lovely? You should see Ceridwen! She looks like a sunset."

I raise my brows. Nessa waves her hands.

"Oh, right, sorry!" She grabs my arm and yanks me out of bed, my chakram clanking to the floor, my tunic batting loosely at my knees. Only Nessa's giddy smile stops me from protesting as she hauls me outside.

Conall peels away from the threshold of my tent and drops in behind us, having taken up his task of guarding me again since most of Mather's Thaw left to escort our final refugee group. Where Nessa leads me isn't very far down the road, and considering the number of people we pass, I'm grateful. The Winterian queen should be a bit more dignified than to traipse around in little more than a nightgown.

A burgundy tent stands unadorned but for thin stripes of navy that run vertically down its fabric. Conall posts himself outside along with two Autumnian guards, and when Nessa tugs me in, a cloud of rose water and incense greets us. The narrow room houses a few dressing screens, open trunks overflowing with jewel-toned satin and silk, and pillows on which lounge Dendera, Nikoletta, Shazi, Kaleo, and his daughter, Amelie.

When Nessa and I stumble in, Shazi screeches and Dendera leaps up.

"She's here!"

That elicits a chirp from behind one of the dressing screens, and Ceridwen's head shoots out so quickly I catch only a flash of gold and a few bouncing red curls. "Finally! Flame, I was beginning to think you'd sleep through it."

"Through what?" I ask. Dendera holds a swath of blue satin up to my face just as a shoe flies out from behind Ceridwen's dressing screen, and I start to think I must still be asleep. "You all realize we have a war to prepare for? Unless you think we can settle our differences by throwing Angra a ball—"

Dendera squeezes my shoulder. "We *do* realize we have a war to prepare for, which is exactly why this needs to happen."

"*What* needs to happen?"

Ceridwen's head reappears for longer this time. Her curls are pinned in a gold headdress with dangling leaves glinting near her cheeks, accenting the gold and brown paint that forms curlicues across her dark skin.

"A wedding," she says, and the way the words come out on a giggle makes me smile. I don't think I've ever heard her *giggle*. "My wedding. To Jesse."

She ducks back behind the screen as Shazi tosses a length of orange silk into the air and squeals when it flows over her head.

"Your wedding?" I echo.

Dendera nods happily. "The latest reports put Angra's

forces five days out from being fully gathered. This"—she waves at the tent—"is necessary."

But I know what she means. We need this. We need it as much as every blade we will sharpen, every ration we will pack, every breastplate we will strap on.

Every moment of peace we gather here will help us stay sane later on.

I take the satin from Dendera. "I guess I should dress up too?"

She smiles and waves me behind another screen. "I'll help. Nessa?"

Nessa rushes to join us. The moment we're behind the screen, they both tug off my gray tunic and start wrapping blue satin in a pattern they must have learned from Nikoletta.

This is what Ceridwen meant a few days ago when she said she needed to follow her own advice. I know very little about her relationship with Jesse, beyond its scandalous beginning, but I do know she's loved him for a long time. And though a lot of horrible things have come from this war, if it forced them to move beyond their issues and reconcile their love . . . well.

I can think of no better counter to war than a wedding.

Dendera and Nessa finish with me in about half an hour, and when I shuffle out, Nikoletta and Shazi are gone, leaving only Kaleo, stretched out on a pillow, smiling lazily at Ceridwen's screen.

"Are you ready yet?" he calls.

"Art can't be rushed, Papa," comes Amelie's reprimand from behind the screen.

"You aren't the one marrying a Ventrallan—you don't have to talk like that."

Which comes just as Lekan ducks into the tent. He eyes Kaleo, then Amelie, who pops her head out and blows him a kiss. Lekan gives Kaleo a grin as he drops beside his husband.

"Already talking of marrying her off?" Lekan jokes.

Amelie giggles. "To a Ventrallan!"

She makes a gagging noise behind the screen, and Ceridwen laughs.

"Thank you for your support, Amelie. I must say, though—this *is* art, no matter what kingdom you're from."

The screen shifts, one panel folding back under Amelie's hand, and she bounces out, the smile in her eyes overshadowing the branded *S* on her left cheekbone.

"May I present—Princess Ceridwen!" She swings her hand out in an elaborate bow, her black hair dipping around her face as she pivots to make a small presentation area.

Ceridwen pops her hands onto her hips, the smile on her face causing ripples in the gold paint that swirls all the way down to her collarbone. Every strand of her hair shines scarlet, and Nessa is right—she does look like a sunset, her dark skin the hue of tan-brown hills in encroaching night, her hair the final trails of bleeding sunrays.

But her outfit completes the vision. Interlacing sections of scarlet silk fold over a sleeveless bodice and hem that glitter with gold beads.

"What do you think?" Ceridwen runs her hand across the beads. "Art, right?"

She sounds uncertain, as if she's afraid maybe it isn't enough to marry the monarch of the kingdom known for art.

I step forward as Nessa and Dendera whisper soft assurances, and when I take Ceridwen's hands, I see the same swirling gold designs fluttering down her arms.

"You're perfect," I tell her.

"*Perfect,*" she echoes with a roll of her eyes. "Far from it. Dead sexy, though, yes."

Amelie giggles, rocking back. And, as if sensing Ceridwen's finishing touches, the tent flaps part to reveal Nikoletta again, now in her own properly fancy outfit—layers of orange and teal overlapping in a weave of brightness.

She grins. "We're ready to start if you are."

Ceridwen pulls out of my hands and sucks in a breath. But when I look at her, she doesn't appear nervous or hesitant or anything but deliriously happy.

The suddenness of the ceremony means most of the camp is still busy with war preparations. As Nikoletta leads us through the dim streets, soldiers trot past, and people pound out weapons on anvils. And here we are, a cluster of royals dressed in glittering Autumnian finery, strolling through a war camp. Where did they even get these outfits? I can't imagine anyone thought to grab them in their rush to leave Oktuber. Could they be from Nikoletta's own wardrobe? I lift the hem higher off the dusty road regardless.

Nikoletta leads us deeper into the forest camp, snaking through patches of trees and wider blocks of tents. The Klaryns' foothills loom even higher, their sharp, spindly blackness stretching over us all.

At an intersection, Nikoletta turns to us.

"We've set up the ceremony site just beyond there." She nods around the corner. "Jesse is waiting in the middle of the group with Caspar. It's tradition in Autumn for the bride to weave her way through the crowd, emulating the path a leaf takes in its descent to the earth—your path to the one who is your true home."

Ceridwen shakes her hands in front of her face. "Stop! Burn it all, I'm crying already."

Nikoletta turns to the rest of us. "Follow me, please. We have a wedding to witness."

As everyone trails Nikoletta around the corner, I linger, my eyes on Ceridwen. She notices me next to her, and when her brow lifts, I put my hand on her arm.

"I'm glad you're happy, Cerie."

She laughs. "Me too. You have no idea how glad I am to be happy."

I squeeze her arm and back up a step.

"But . . . thank you," she adds.

The tears in her eyes are far too contagious. "Just don't trip," I call as I jog away.

"You're evil!"

But she's out of sight, and the only thing I see now is the ceremony set up at the end of this road, the rising foothills of the Klaryns capping the scene not far off. The tents stop after only a few paces, the path becoming a tunnel of lush green grass and rows of trees. Leaves flutter in slow spirals of orange and red and brown, and at the end, a small clearing opens. The ground is carpeted by still more leaves, an aromatic blanket that makes the area smell of long-asleep plants. People stand in a loose cluster, all facing the opposite direction from us, and Jesse's and Caspar's heads peek over the crowd. Musicians wait in a silent group on the edge, instruments poised to start playing at Ceridwen's arrival.

Leaves crunch under my slippers as I enter the clearing, and a few heads pivot to see who it is. But the musicians remain silent, so most people stay facing ahead. Ceridwen's friends Lekan, Kaleo, and Amelie stand with Jesse's children; an Autumnian maid holds a rare quiet Shazi; and my Winterians stand off to the right, each dressed in borrowed Autumnian finery, some as small as a satin sash over their regular clothes, others as elaborate as the head-to-toe outfit I'm in.

Nessa waves to me from where she stands with Dendera and Conall, and I go to her, drawn more by the person beside her, the one whose eyes widen at the sight of me. Mather wears a tunic so dark blue that it's nearly black. Gold thread creates elaborate patterns around the high collar and wrists, and the tight cut of it hugs close to his arms and chest. A few strands of hair hang around his face, the rest knotted in a ribbon.

I stop next to him. "Hi," I whisper.

His lips part. "Hi," he whispers back. His eyes sweep over my outfit, and he fingers the silver beads woven into fabric that drapes over my arms, a sort of shawl, the swift gust of movement toward me enough to send my heart launching up into my throat.

"You're beautiful," he adds.

My head goes dizzy. This is what I get, though, for letting myself admit to my feelings for him—incapacitating giddiness that makes me sure I'm smiling just as dreamily as Ceridwen was moments ago.

I want to pull some sense of control over myself, compose my features so I'm not quite so . . . off-balance? I can't think of the right word. I can't think of anything, actually, as Mather's eyes stay on mine. Suddenly he seems just as off-balance as I am.

When the musicians start to play, what was already a

perfect moment becomes even more idyllic. The clearing fills with a violin's rising hum, and as one the crowd turns.

I don't look over my shoulder, though. My eyes go to Jesse and Caspar, standing with arms clasped behind their backs at the head of the group, their eyes, like everyone else's, on Ceridwen. Jesse's tunic is sleeveless, the same deep red as Ceridwen's outfit. He wears a mask, this one crafted from red fabric, simple and unadorned.

But not even a full mask could hide the awe that soars across his face when he sees her.

His shoulders droop. His hands fall limp against his sides. The tense lines around his eyes smooth away. His dazed amazement is full of such pure love that I smile, because there's no other possible response.

Mather links one of his fingers with mine.

I can't draw a full breath, not as the instruments weave their bittersweet song, not as I look up at Mather and see the exact same look on his face. Dazed, with maybe just the slightest bit of fear. Seeing that flash of fear speaks to my own, and I think one unbearable thought.

I want this.

The song rises in volume as Ceridwen gets closer to Caspar and Jesse. She meanders through the crowd as Nikoletta instructed. When she steps free, Jesse lets out a choked breath and snatches her hands as if she were one of the leaves spiraling haphazardly through the air, uncatchable and chaotic and beautiful.

The song ebbs, leaving the clearing so still the wind practically roars. Caspar's dark eyes shift from Ceridwen to Jesse and back, his lips unfurling in the same smile we're all wearing.

"Ceridwen Preben, princess of Summer, and Jesse Donati, king of Ventralli, have asked that we witness them unite in the strongest bond of all," Caspar begins, raising his voice over the crowd. "We live in a time of great pain and fear. The only way to truly defeat that pain is to feel equally great joy in the face of it, and this"—Caspar smiles—"is undeniable joy."

He pulls a few items out of his pocket, holding them up for the crowd to see. A jar of black paint and a thick brush.

"In Autumn, marriages are celebrated as the rings of trees, each ring growing with time and dedication to create a union of just as much strength. Jesse." Caspar hands him the brush and uncorks the jar. "The first ring."

Jesse takes the brush and dips it into the paint. Hand steady, he paints a thick black ring around Ceridwen's upper arm.

"Ceridwen," Caspar continues, holding the jar out to her. "The first ring."

She takes the brush from Jesse, gathers up paint, and leans over his arm. Her line is less steady, her hand shaking, but the way Jesse watches her, it's clear neither of them cares.

When she finishes, Caspar takes the brush and steps

back from them. "You are now one ring, one tree. Whatever the world presents, you will meet it together. Ceridwen and Jesse." Caspar's voice drops out of formality and into joviality. "Congratulations."

He waves his arms, presenting the newlyweds to the crowd, and everyone breaks into applause as the musicians begin to play a faster melody. Ceridwen and Jesse leap at each other, practically toppling to the ground as they kiss.

Magic trickles out of me, calling the leaves on the ground to spin in a gentle spiral around Ceridwen and Jesse. They pull apart to gape at the swirl of color, but it only encourages their happiness and they dissolve against each other.

"No wedding is complete without a feast!" Nikoletta calls through the din. "Join us tonight."

Cheers rise up and the crowd starts to steadily move out of the clearing, trailing Nikoletta to whatever feast they arranged. The current pulls Mather away, but Nessa catches me, her arm linking through mine.

"That was perfect!" she exclaims. "I want an Autumnian wedding one day."

I laugh. "What about a Winterian wedding?"

Nessa smiles, dreamy. "Maybe I just want a *wedding*. Or, not so much a wedding as—"

She looks back at Ceridwen and Jesse, now whispering to each other as the crowd no longer watches them. They look even happier, if that's possible—their foreheads together, him stroking his fingers through her hair.

"That," Nessa says. "I want *that*."

I lean against her. "Me too."

A few hours later, the clearing in front of the main tent is just as beautiful, if not more so, than the ceremony site.

The evening light cuts through the trees, casting the camp into the hooded shadow of approaching night. A few of the tents have been removed to make room for tables and a crackling fire in the center of the area. Strands of braided fabric are tethered around the perimeter, creating a decorative foundation from which hang lanterns, golden glows flickering in the breeze. The musicians reposition themselves on the edge and start in on an upbeat song, one that encourages the regathered crowd's happiness. More people have joined now—off-duty soldiers, along with those of us who helped set up the last-minute celebration.

Conall, Nessa, and I stand on the edge of the clearing, watching the guests gather. A few begin dancing, and Nessa grabs Conall's hand. "Dance with me!"

He throws her a skeptical stare. "What?"

"Dance!" She tugs him toward the fire, the flames casting an orange glow on those already dancing.

Conall's eyes dart to me, back to Nessa, and he lowers his voice. "Not now, Ness."

Her face falls. "Please," she adds. "Please, Conall. We need this. He was my brother too."

Conall angles his shoulders as if to block the conversation from reaching me. "Nessa," he hisses. "This isn't appropriate—"

"Conall," I stop him. "She's right. You deserve to be happy."

Conall's expression falls. "All right, my queen," he says, and I hold back my annoyance at my title still on his lips. If that's what it takes to get him to accept Nessa's prodding, I won't fight him.

He lets Nessa drag him over to the dancers. She holds his arms out and tries to move to the rhythm, which urges the barest smile onto his face.

Sometime during all this, Ceridwen and Jesse sneak in, and they whirl past Nessa and Conall in their own frenzied dance. Kicks and twirls that fluff their clothing, the beat of the song picking up and coaxing everyone's intensity higher. I can't help but laugh at it all, the hodgepodge of colors around the licking flames, the steady ebbing of the guitar and violin and now a few bowl-shaped drums that send beats ricocheting around the clearing.

Someone appears next to me, their presence heavy, and I know who it is without needing to look.

"What did you think of the ceremony?" I ask, my eyes shifting to Sir.

He crosses his arms, his attention on the dancing. I almost expect him not to respond, or to start talking of war strategies, but some of the tension in his shoulders eases.

"I think Winterian weddings are more beautiful," he says.

I can't stop the way my eyes widen. The heat from the fire and the dancing bodies makes sweat break across my brow, and all of it goes ice cold beneath the glassiness in Sir's eyes.

He frowns. After a moment, his shoulders harden again and he nods toward the fire. "You'll get this. For yourself. Someday."

I choke on Sir's sincerity. "Thank you," I whisper, and every piece of my heart aches.

Fingers clamp around my arm.

"Come on!" Nessa sings, tugging me into the fray as Sir waves me off. I wish the temptation of losing myself to such a carefree activity was enough to distract me, but I feel the pressure of Sir behind me, of his words, the sort of thing I've wanted to hear from him for years.

This night makes such things possible.

So I fling my body into a spin, giggling when Nessa grabs both my hand and Conall's, knotting us into an awkward tangle. Conall smiles fully now and Nessa positively beams in the firelight and the pounding music and the wafting aroma of food—roasted pork, spicy mulled wine, and something so thickly coated in cinnamon that the air is heavy with the rich scent.

The song ends, switching to one that makes Ceridwen yelp in recognition from across the fire. By the intensity of the drumbeats, it sounds less like the lulling Autumnian music and more Summerian. And it must be, based on the way Ceridwen hurls her body into a set of choreographed movements, arms jolting, feet tapping a pattern on the ground.

Her Summerian friends are the first to join her dance. Jesse picks up on it next, and soon everyone around the fire is trying to follow, arms flapping, feet pounding, laughter roaring.

Conall hesitantly tries out the first few steps and Nessa doubles over, laughing so hard I fear she might splinter. His smile stretches even wider, and we both join him, moving our arms out, in, out, our feet sliding through the stomping pattern.

Ceridwen grabs Jesse, her Summerian friends split into pairs, and the dance grows closer, the music urging couples to bend into each other as the song continues.

Nessa's eyes flick around the dancers. Her lips curve into a sly grin, but when I spin to find what she's looking at, I see only more dancing bodies, nothing unusual.

"What is it?" I shout over the music.

She hooks her arm through Conall's and shoves me away. "He's my partner—you have to find your own."

The force of her shove sends me flailing into another body. I barely register Nessa's giggling before I notice the midnight-blue tunic under my hands, the chest heaving up and down, the arms on my elbows. Mather.

Heat flushes up my neck.

The music breaks, the drums beating with such ferocity that they're practically begging us to dance.

I press myself against Mather and imitate the waving, stomping chaos of the crowd. He seems stunned at first, but it doesn't take him long to fall into it too.

His body curves around me, his eyes just as bright as the bonfire. I've never been this close to him for this long, in a way that makes me breathless with more than exertion. His head angles down, our limbs keeping time to the beat even as our faces stay just shy of touching.

The music slows, quickens again, building in intensity. Each time it breaks, the crowd cheers, movements flailing ever more strongly. But the longer the song continues, the less I hear. The noises of the celebration lull, the sights and colors and smells ebb away, until there's only Mather, his body against mine, his breath tangling with my every exhale.

I always knew he was beautiful. But the way he moves, just as exuberant as Nessa, just as confident as Ceridwen— he's not just beautiful. He's . . . mine.

I stop as the song ends. Another picks up, not nearly as fast as the last one. Mather hesitates, panting, his joy easing into a heavy stare when I don't start dancing again.

One breath, just one, and he backs up a step. An invitation, an unspoken signal.

He weaves through the dancing crowd. When he reaches

the edge of the clearing, he stops, his sapphire eyes never leaving mine.

Mather's lips hover somewhere close to smiling and he plunges out toward the forest.

The magic in me tangles around my nerves until I'm walking. Slow steps, the drums thumping beats into me, the dark of the evening swallowing the firelight and the lanterns of the celebration.

I duck away from the dancers and follow Mather into the night.

Mather

EVERYTHING WAS SO clear here.

From where Mather perched on one of the lower ridges of the foothills that bordered Autumn, he could see the camp in its entirety. The moon had just become visible, its pale light spilling over the trees, the tents, and the clearing where the revelers still danced. The faint pounding of drums lit the air, the distance and encompassing night giving the illusion that this camp was all that existed. Not the shadow of evil that waited to devour them, not the jagged peaks of the Klaryns behind Mather, the mountains that would swallow them up in a few days.

The look on Meira's face today had all but ripped him apart. The way she had grabbed the image of Ceridwen and Jesse's happiness like a beggar scrambling to hoard a few last pieces of nourishment. Her brows pinched, her hands slack, those crystalline eyes showing how much she wanted exactly what Ceridwen and Jesse had.

And how much she knew she wasn't destined to have that.

That was what scared Mather most—her look of regret. Like she knew that despite her burning need to have that happiness, she never would, and she had accepted this sacrifice in return for whatever she had planned.

Mather dug his fingers into the earth. His legs dangled over the ledge and he closed his eyes, hunching down.

Leaves crunched behind him, and when he turned, the need in his stomach thrashed at the sight of her.

Meira stood at the entrance to the path that led up here, her fingers looped around a low-hanging tree branch next to a sheer wall of rock that shot up to the next ridge. She wore a traditional Autumnian outfit, but that didn't stop Mather from wondering if someone had designed it with the sole purpose of driving him insane. Light blue fabric cut around her body, leaving her stomach bare, skin gleaming in the delicate moonlight. A longer strand of fabric hung limp from her elbows and when she stepped forward, she let it drop to the ground, revealing her arms, her shoulders, in a way that made Mather's chest ache.

He flipped his attention back to the camp. Ice, something as simple as *skin* shouldn't send him into such a pathetic flurry. But when she sat beside him, her skirt catching around her legs, Mather didn't dare speak for fear of what might slip out of his mouth. He had a feeling it would be something inappropriate, like *That dance tonight will drive me crazy for months* or *We should keep dancing. Up here, on this ridge, with no one else to see.*

After a long pause, Meira turned to the forest below.

"Are you ready for the trip?" she asked, her voice as fragile as the leaves under them.

He shifted to face her. "Are you? Jannuari, then the Tadil. Should be easy enough, after everything else we've done." He paused, daring, pleading. "Right?"

Meira didn't agree with him immediately, and that was enough to make him feel a pang of alarm—then she sighed, the tears in her eyes barely visible in the darkness

"It was never enough," she said. "All the sacrifices we made for this war. None of it was ever enough, no matter how much it hurt. But this one"—she angled toward him, certainty giving her a slightly mad air—"this one will be, Mather. This one will defeat Angra."

She paused.

"A conduit must be sacrificed and returned to the chasm," she whispered, and it seemed to take physical effort for her to push out the words. "The sacrifice will destroy all magic, Angra's Decay included. I *am* Winter's conduit, and I will—"

"What?" Mather cut her off. "*Stop.* This is how you'll defeat him? You can't— Meira, *no.*"

But she didn't look convinced. If anything, she looked tired, as though she'd lost another ally.

"I don't need you to disagree with me." She pushed to her feet, and he followed her up as her hands formed tight knots at her sides, digging into the satin folds of her skirt when she whirled on him. "That's part of the reason I've hesitated to tell you, but I need you to understand what's waiting for me in the labyrinth, because . . ." Her mouth bobbed open, her eyes sheened with tears. "I want you. All of you, Mather, for however short a time I have left, but I need you to understand what that means. This isn't something that will last, and it will *hurt*, because I know what I'm asking you to do. I'm asking you to love me and let me . . . die."

Her words became muffled in his ears. It took Mather too long to figure out why he felt a sudden, heavy weight settling over his body.

She really was planning on dying for them.

Then he heard what else she said, and everything in him unraveled.

Longing balled in the pit of his stomach until he thought he might burst if he didn't do something he had dreamed of doing for a long, long time.

"What about . . . Theron?" Mather closed his eyes.

A cold palm cradled his cheek. He blinked down at her, wariness humming in the back of his throat as Meira looked up with the exact same wariness, as if she had no idea how she had come to stand before him, her hand on his face.

"I will do everything I can to save Theron," she stated.

"But there was always something wrong with us."

Mather sucked in sharp, short breaths, leaning into her palm more with each word she said, with each word she didn't say. "Why?"

Damn it all, *stop asking questions and just kiss her.*

Meira's hand trembled against his face.

"Because he wasn't you," she gasped.

That was it.

Mather wrapped his fingers around her wrist and pulled her forward, cupping the back of her head as he slid his face down to hers. He hovered just shy of her lips, panting, choking because, ice above, this moment—this was everything, the entirety of his life expanding from this one act, revolving around her because she was at the center of everything good that had ever happened to him.

His nose pressed into her cheek, his body vibrating with the compulsion to suck her up like the vortex of a blizzard, the numbing funnel that didn't allow coherent thought. Her lashes fluttered against his face, her skin glowed pearly in the rising moonlight, making her look so untouchably perfect that Mather's knees trembled.

She drew a breath and her lips parted in two words that rebounded through his body.

"Kiss me," she said.

So he did the only thing he could do, the only thing he had ever wanted to do, from the moment they had been children living a nomadic existence under the threat of war and she'd been this stubborn, determined force that had shocked him and scared him and invigorated him.

He kissed her.

Soft, careful, because he wanted to discover every contour of her lips. He closed his eyes and found her through the air between them, and she hooked onto his mouth. Mather scooped her into his arms, her chill radiating into his body and adding urgency to the pulsing need that made his abdomen tight.

They stumbled back until he felt the rock face under his palms, the jagged surface a contrast to the texture of Meira's lips, her lips, damn, it wasn't fair that anything could be that soft. He pushed her against the rock, one hand bracing himself on the rough stone because each kiss only made him want more as he drew in ragged breaths between kisses and cursed his need to breathe at all.

His fingers turned to claws, digging into the rock, crumbling chunks of stone and dirt off into his palm as his other hand stroked lines down Meira's arm, found her waist. He brushed over the gap in her dress, a moan echoing in his throat as his fingers connected with the tantalizing bare skin of her stomach, the curve of her hip. Her wearing this dress was too much and not enough all at once, and she didn't make it any easier when she knotted her fingers into his hair and echoed his moan, a low, intoxicating purr that made him grip the rock wall harder.

Mather emitted a strangled sound that was more pain

than pleasure. All his instincts screaming, he pulled away from her.

She blinked up at him, her hands on his chest. "What's wrong?"

What could possibly be wrong? He finally had her. He could finally touch her and kiss her and spend the rest of his life with his arms around her—

But that was exactly it. He wanted to spend the rest of his life like this, with her, but she would leave his life empty in a matter of days. Just the thought made agony snuff out most of the desire that swarmed him when he felt her move under his hands.

"I won't let you die," he told her.

She went slack against the rock. "It isn't your decision."

"It isn't?" He pitched toward her, but he didn't dare kiss her again, didn't dare lose himself in the way she watched him and touched her swollen lips. "How can you think you'll be the only one affected by this?"

Meira sagged even more. "I know I won't be. Why do you think it's so hard for me to do this? Why do you think I started to ask you to *help me?*" She pitched forward until her head fell against his chest, her fingers gripping his shirt like a tether keeping her from flying away. "I'm not strong enough to hurt you and everyone else like that. But I have to. Please, Mather," she begged, her head shooting back up. "I don't want to talk about this anymore. Let's just be here."

So many images of her being strong crowded his mind

that he had trouble seeing her like this, begging, broken, scared. But *he* was broken and scared, and ice above, if he didn't crumple at the thought of casting away everything bad in favor of one night. Just one.

Mather fell into her again, and he knew he'd never be able to regain control of himself. Tears burned his eyes but he didn't care; instead he lost everything in the way Meira met him with equal fervor, her body bending against his like they were two stalks of grass swaying with each other.

Their kisses went from gentle to chaotic, hands and tongues and sighs that could have been whimpers. And through it all, Mather wove words in a haven around them on the ridge.

"I love you," he said, and promised, over and over again. "I will always love you, and I should be able to protect you. . . ."

He felt Meira break under his words, tears streaming down her cheeks, mingling with his.

"I love you," she told him. "And I *will* protect you."

Meira

DON'T WAKE UP.

The camp had been quiet when we finally crept back last night, everyone safe and asleep in their various tents. Which made it far too easy to nod in passing at the soldiers and meander through the dusty paths, the tents the only audience as Mather and I . . .

We . . .

I'm fully awake now, a grin stretching my lips as I bury my face in the pillow. I lie facing the flaps of my small tent, and when I finally pull my face free, I thank last-night-me for her good sense to tie the flaps together, what with Nessa's propensity for diving in unannounced. The delicate, hazy light visible around the edges tells me it's not yet late morning.

My body cools, the iciness of magic reacting to my intense emotions, a sensation that roiled through me so often last night that I all but went numb with wonder. I press a hand to my lips, memory drawing up the feel of Mather's hands on my waist, my fingers nestled in the grooves of his muscles, my mouth finding his.

My grin widens and I roll onto my back, head lolling to the side.

A pair of jewel-blue eyes meets mine.

His smile is just as wide, maybe even more so, and he props himself up on his elbow.

"Hi," he says.

I dissolve into giggles, covering my mouth to mute the sound through the thin tent.

Mather's smile stretches. "What?"

"*Hi?* I don't know. It just feels a little too simple."

"What would be better?" He wraps an arm around me and nuzzles into my hair. "*Good morning, my queen?*" A kiss on my shoulder. "Or *lovely to see you this morning, Lady Meira?*" A kiss on my jaw. "Or *I had the most indecent dream about you last night, Your Highness?*"

That does nothing to help my laughter. "Odd, I had a rather indecent dream about you too."

He chuckles and goes back to lying on his propped elbow. The blanket tucked around us falls down to his waist, and despite everything, my cheeks flush at the sight of his bare chest.

"Oh?" he asks. "Maybe we had the same dream. What happened in yours?"

His mouth flutters in that smile he knows disarms me. But I can be just as disarming.

I roll over, burrowing against him, my fingers tracing every line of muscle honed from years of fighting, a few rough scars that knot his skin. "You know, I can't recall," I say. "It must not have been very memorable."

Mather howls and tackles me. I squeal, giving up on trying to stay quiet, and catch his lips with my own, our bodies aligning in a way that makes every touch from last night flash through me at once.

I knot my fingers in the hair at the nape of his neck and pull back to look at him. Another laugh spurts out, this one incredulous. "How did this even happen?"

Mather rolls back. "I can tell you *exactly* how it happened." He squints in a rather overdramatic show of thinking. "About twelve years ago, a five-year-old girl pushed me down in the training yard and stole my sword. That incident was only the beginning—eleven years ago she talked me into painting a tent with ink, six years ago she stole a bottle of wine and got me drunk . . ." He trails off, his eyes drifting down to my smirk, and he beams. "I was too stupid to realize that I willingly sauntered into whatever crazy plan she concocted. It was only a matter of time before she got me *here*."

"Oh, so this was my plan?" I lift up so I'm eye level with him. "You got all the dates wrong, though. The wine stealing was five years ago, and eleven years ago we were five."

Mather's brows twitch. "I knew I should have reminded you."

"Of what?"

"Our birthdays. Well, *yours* at the very least—it was a few months ago. You really missed it? You're seventeen now, Meira. We both are."

I pause. "Snow above. We *are* seventeen."

Mather laughs. "Afraid so."

"Alysson and Dendera always warned me to wait until I was older." I sigh. "So that makes me feel a little better about what happened."

"Better?" He tucks a hand around my waist, his fingers drawing absurdly distracting patterns on my hip through the blanket. "Why would you feel at all bad?"

His hand stops abruptly as his eyes snap open so wide I see my reflection.

"Ice above," he curses. "We . . . and I didn't . . . *damn it.*" He rocks back, hands over his face.

"What are you talking about?"

He peeks through his fingers, eyes still wide, and his attention drops to my stomach.

My own eyes stretch all the way open. "Oh. *Oh.* No. I can't—"

My mouth falls slack.

I can't . . . have children.

On that thought, Oana's sadness rises above my hazy delight. The dusty nursery she and Rares kept locked away, waiting for the day it would be used.

I sit up, curling my arms around my knees. And just like that, last night really is over.

Mather slides upright. "You can't?"

I force a smile. "Being a conduit makes certain things impossible."

Mather drops a hand around my bent legs. "I'm sorry I—"

"No." I push back, angling enough to stay in his arms but look into his eyes. "Don't apologize, for anything. I wanted this. *Want* this."

He smiles, but his eyes say he's slowly coming to terms with the night being over too. "You say that like it'll never happen again."

I droop against him. But I can't make myself repeat all the things I said last night, how this won't last, how it'll hurt, how in a few days, he'll be alone.

He shakes his head and tightens his hold on me. "We'll figure out something, and we'll both come out of that labyrinth alive, and we'll have many, *many* more nights like this one." After a breath, he smiles. "Besides, I need time to actually get *good* at it."

I snort, gripping his arm. I know he sees the tears rimming my eyes—but I cling desperately to his joke. Maybe because I'm weak and can't bear the thought of . . . everything. Maybe because I'm strong enough to push past what scares me.

Either way, I bump him with my shoulder. "I thought you were pretty good already."

He presses his forehead to my temple. "But who wouldn't want to improve?"

"What a goal to have."

"I know it'll keep *me* inspired."

I swing one leg out from under the blanket. "Well, we should get dressed at some point."

Mather grumbles against my skin as he brushes my hair over my shoulder. "Clothes," he mocks and lays kisses down the back of my neck. "That sounds like a bad idea."

Shivers prickle down my spine. And though the rest of me would gladly melt back into bed for the foreseeable future, I stand.

Mather's hands drop against the blankets. I grab the nearest article of clothing—a white tunic from the stack of clothes the servants gave me—and tug it over my head. By the time I'm dressed, a belt cinching the tunic to my waist, the boots from Paisly tight over my knees, my chakram in place, Mather is up too, the blanket tangled around his hips.

He steps forward, one hand holding the ivory and green wool at his waist. A gust of wind flutters the tent flaps, a gentle whoosh against their ties, and the motion sends a sliver of light across his face, curving down his neck, heaving over his chest.

I lower my gaze. "I'm going to check on everyone else. You can—"

"I'll be right behind you," he assures me. The tremble in his voice sounds like he's fighting to keep his tone level, and that undoes me even more, so much so that I undo the ties on the tent and get halfway out before I find myself looking back at him.

He's sitting on the bed now, hands in his hair and elbows on his knees.

This is breaking him, just like I knew it would, but I did it anyway.

The tent flaps tremble shut behind me. "I'm so—"

Mather stands, the blanket falling away as his hands dive to cradle my face. He slams his mouth against mine in a kiss that swallows my apology.

"You don't get to apologize either," he tells me. "No apologies. No matter what happens, I will *never*, not in a thousand tragic outcomes, *ever* regret loving you."

I loop my arms around his neck.

"I love you," I tell him for what must be the millionth time since the ridge.

He pushes his face into my hair. "I love you too."

The words press like brands into my neck, and I close my eyes, memorizing each letter as it lies along my body.

No matter what happens when I step out of this tent, when I go to Jannuari, when we reach the labyrinth, I have this.

I have *him*.

The area in front of the main tent still wears most of its decorations from last night. Unlit lanterns hang from the braided fabric, the fire pit sits black and charred. The food tables have been moved into the center of the ring, a few chairs gathered, and around the tables crowd most of the people from the celebration, all looking rather groggy.

Sir and Dendera chat at a table across the square, picking at plates of bread and fruit. At the table closest to me, Nessa slumps against Conall, yawning after every bite of food, and Ceridwen and Jesse shock me by being both here and awake. They're still wearing their celebration outfits, only drastically more rumpled, and as I slide into a chair across from them, I breathe a sigh of relief that I thought to grab new clothes this morning.

Ceridwen pops a blackberry into her mouth. "You certainly slept in," she notes.

I take the nearest bowl of fruit. "And why didn't you, newlyweds?"

"Who says we slept at all?"

Jesse chokes on a grape. "Cerie!"

She bats her eyes. "Oh, everyone knows what we spent the night doing."

Nessa straightens. "Why? What'd you do?"

It's Conall's turn to choke now. Jesse seems just as humiliated, but Ceridwen clucks her tongue at Conall in mock disapproval. Her eyes go to me and her brow lifts.

My lips tighten.

"Meira." Ceridwen tips forward, and I think I'm about to be glad that Sir and everyone else chose to sit at a table farther away. "Tell me you know what I'm talking about."

But even as she says that, her amusement recedes into shock.

"Do you? With your kingdom's fall, I guess you wouldn't have had time to—"

I clench my jaw, fiddling with an apple slice. "I . . . know," I squeak. And I do—well, especially now, but before last night too. The memory of Alysson and Dendera explaining certain things is one I try not to relive. Mostly because Dendera's face was flame-red through it all, and Alysson kept saying *It's perfectly normal* over and over.

I manage a coy smile. "I know," I repeat. "And I'm glad your wedding night was satisfying."

Jesse clunks his forehead into his palm. "This is what will kill me. Not the war. *This.*"

"Ohhhh," Nessa breathes, understanding turning her word into a song. She giggles, and Conall makes a sort of closemouthed screaming noise to his food.

"Good morning." Mather drops into the chair on my other side. Though it's only been a few moments since we saw each other, the giddiness in my chest feels like it's been lifetimes, and I bite my lip to stop from smiling too obviously. Mather smiles back, holding my gaze.

For too long.

Ceridwen chirps. "Oh my. Was our wedding night satis-fying for *someone else*?"

My face catches fire.

"What?" Nessa leans around Conall. "For who?"

Conall leaps up. "We have to go. Swords. Or something. Weapons. Nessa, come."

"Wait!" she protests as he lifts her to her feet. "What? Why?"

They get a few paces away and I cave forward. "I feel the sudden urge to bury my face in the fruit bowl."

Jesse lifts a goblet of water and tips it at me. "Try being married to her."

"Look at you, Winter queen," Ceridwen giggles. "You don't waste any time."

"Okay, I think we're done." I pivot toward Mather, expecting him to be as mortified as I am, but he's grin-ning. And not just an amused grin—a grin that screams confirmation as loudly as if he had stood on the table and shouted it into the air.

He reaches over to squeeze my fingers. "What?"

I fall back in my chair. "You want to talk about this, don't you? Snow above. Are you the Ceridwen in this relationship?"

Jesse laughs middrink and water sloshes down the front of his tunic.

Ceridwen angles toward Mather. "Yes, you are, because

I need details. I remember seeing you for the dancing, but only through the first few songs. When did you sneak off?"

"After that one song," Mather says. "When everyone danced the same movements."

"Ah, yes." Ceridwen sits back. "But they played that at the beginning of the evening. And it's two or so hours until noon now? That means you've been gone for twelve hours. . . ."

For once, distraction works in my favor, coming in the form of a trio of Autumnian soldiers. My eyes snap to their entrance across the clearing, noting their travel-beaten wear with a jolt of recognition. More of Caspar's spies. Do they have word of Angra? Or news of the last group of refugees? Henn and the Thaw should be back by now.

Everyone at my table turns to see what has my attention, their expressions dimming like candles in a harsh breeze.

"Do you any of you have news?" I ask.

"We should be ready to march out by early afternoon," Ceridwen says. "Once we decide on a location."

"How many are staying here?"

"About a hundred soldiers to protect those who can't fight, which leaves just shy of three thousand to stand against Angra."

I wither at the numbers, but it isn't meant to be a full-on war. Just a diversion.

A shadow falls over our table.

"If you're finished eating," Sir starts, and angles his head toward the main tent.

"We're just about done, General," Jesse says for us.

He nods, his eyes steady on me before he walks toward the main tent. The four of us stay seated for a beat longer, Mather's hand in mine, Jesse's arm around Ceridwen.

There's no room for emotions in war.

It's one of the many rules Sir beat into my head as a child. I see now that it's necessary. These are just numbers we're discussing; these are just fields we're mapping; these are just chunks of iron we're dividing. Not people, not battle sites, not weapons.

"My scouts put Angra's forces four days out from being fully gathered," Caspar says, and points to a map of the Autumn-Winter border, against the Klaryns. "This valley runs from Autumn into Winter. We could thin out Angra's army and prevent him from surrounding us all at once. He'd only be able to send a fraction of his soldiers at us at any time."

Ceridwen frowns. "But he could block us in. What if we need a retreat?"

"You won't," I promise. "Once the magic is destroyed, no one fighting for Angra will have magic to use against you."

Jesse slackens, his hand on Ceridwen's shoulder. "Angra's *entire army* will be able to use his Decay? I thought it was just a select group close to him."

"I don't expect he'd hold back in a battle," I say. "And . . .

there's a chance the Decay could infect you, too. If Angra is there, the only thing stopping him from sending his Decay to weaken you would be your own resilience—none of you have conduit protection. Even the Winterians will only have it as long as I'm there with them."

Ceridwen darkens. "Now that I know what his magic feels like, there's no way he's getting into my head again. Years of repelling Simon's magic should pay off somehow."

An idea flashes through me. "Wait—that's a good point. Maybe the principles you used to resist your brother's magic can help everyone else ward off the Decay. For a little while, at least?"

Ceridwen shrugs. "I can have the Summerians start teaching the methods we use, but I don't know how effective they'll be. It took us each years to be able to fully resist Simon, and I only lasted a few hours under Angra's influence in Juli."

"It's better than nothing," Caspar agrees.

No one else comments on this looming threat, the possibility of being swept up in Angra's war not by death, but by the Decay. Maybe it's something they've all considered, too. They've seen people fall to it—people who we already knew were dangerous, like Raelyn, and people who we never would have guessed could hurt us, like Theron.

We're all at risk, and they know that.

"How long is the march to this valley?" Sir interjects.

"With our army, three days." Caspar scratches his chin.

"We could press for two, but we'll still beat Angra to any attack."

"Three days," Sir echoes before he shifts to me. "Let's move out."

His face is weighted with the same awareness I feel digging into my chest.

We have a deadline.

I lean back from the table. "Yes. No time to waste."

Everyone else moves, darting off to their various tasks. I duck out of the tent and hesitate long enough for Mather to sweep out after me. When he does, I throw my arms around his neck, kissing him. There's no hiding now—Dendera emerges from the tent behind us, followed by Sir. They see, and I don't care to notice their reactions. I have only a handful of days left for moments like this, and if I spend even a blip of that time not with someone I love, none of this will matter at all.

I pull back from Mather, who drops his hands to my waist.

"They're all standing behind me, aren't they?" he asks.

I smile. "Afraid so. I think I'll leave you to explain it to them."

"So much for being a benevolent ruler."

"Where's the fun in that?" But I'm already backing away. Mather turns to Dendera and his father, who no doubt have a few things to say about this development.

But I have other people to see, and I head for the area of

camp where the Summerians, Yakimians, and Winterians have set up their tents.

Nessa sits by a small campfire, a book in her lap and a group of wide-eyed children around her. Behind her, Conall fits a new string in his bow. His attention catches on me first and he rolls to his feet as I near, but he isn't able to say a word before Nessa leaps up too.

The children groan. "Finish the story!" one whines—Jesse's oldest, Melania.

Nessa flaps her hands at them. "Later! Go help with chores now—some of the soldiers will be leaving on their own adventure soon, so we must do our part to help them!"

The look on Conall's face as the children cheer and disperse is nothing short of disbelief. That his sister is someone capable of turning a march to battle into an adventure; that he was the one who raised the bubbly girl who bounds over to me, her smile sticking on her face as the children wave their good-byes.

"Meira!" Nessa says. "Someone said you were called into another meeting. Have more details been decided? When are we leaving?"

"Today," I start, noting how her smile slowly hardens the farther away the children get.

Conall nods. "We can be packed within the hour."

"No," I tell Conall. "You two will stay here. You won't come with us to the battle."

Conall's head tilts. He doesn't say anything, but his expression is resistant.

I soften. "I appreciate all you have done for me. All you've lost." Emotions break through, squeezing around my throat. "But I need you to protect those who stay behind. Because if I fail . . ." I falter. "If this war ends badly, I can't think of anyone else I'd trust more to get those in this camp to safety."

Conall's jaw clenches, and after far too long, he looks down at me with narrow eyes. He's angry, but he's my soldier.

"All right," comes Nessa's soft agreement. I look at her, seeing an emotion I realize I expected. She's fine with staying behind—because she's found her place in this war.

I don't say anything, just step forward and wrap my arms around her neck.

"I don't want you to feel like you're alone in this, though. Like I'm abandoning you," she whispers into my shoulder.

A laugh bursts through the knot in my chest. "You *have* made me realize I'm not alone. And it's hardly abandonment if I tell you to stay."

Nessa pulls back. She looks older suddenly, like pieces of the innocent girl she was in Abril's work camp have splintered away over the past months. She takes Conall's hand and beams up at him.

Watching them together, I remember being in the Abril camp, meeting Nessa, Garrigan, and Conall, three survivors far stronger than I could ever be. I remember Nessa loving me instantly, Garrigan treating me with wary concern, and Conall outright hating me. He was afraid I'd stoke Nessa's hope too high and it would shatter her when Angra killed me.

I swallow the sorrow that almost makes me confess the future to them. How my death will come, and how I hope it doesn't break Nessa like Conall feared it would.

But a look of confusion descends over Conall and Nessa's faces.

Then I hear it again. The noise that cut off my confession.

Shouting.

Meira

"MY QUEEN!"

I squint at the rider who races up the road, and when he stops beside me, I blink dumbly.

"Trace?"

Both he and his horse look one swift gust away from collapsing in exhaustion. My eyes scramble behind him, looking for the rest of the Thaw or Henn—they should all be together, leading in the final group of refugees.

But it's just Trace, and he drops off his mount. "I rode— ahead—to warn—"

I grab his shoulders, holding him in place. He meets my gaze, his eyes holding such sadness I wonder how he hasn't cracked to pieces.

"We were escorting the refugees back," Trace says. "Three nights ago, we realized Phil had gone missing—"

"What?" I shake my head. "Missing? How?"

"Henn sent Phil to scout ahead—and he never came back. Hollis went out to search for him, but he was just *gone*." Trace gulps in a breath, steadying himself more. "We think Angra's soldiers got him, because—"

"Where?" My voice is shockingly level despite the panic that itches at the back of my throat. If they were too close to Oktuber, the Cordellan soldiers stationed there under Angra's command could have—

But Trace cuts off my analysis. "There's more, my queen," he says. "Hollis saw something when he went out searching. He came back with news of an army marching from Oktuber. Marching *here*."

I jolt back from him. "What?"

"We still haven't found Phil," Trace continues. "If the Oktuber soldiers got him—we don't know. We don't know, but they're coming. *Now*."

Conall is already moving, loading up the weapons scattered around his tent. Nessa stays beside me, steady and quiet.

If soldiers are marching from Oktuber, they aren't Angra's full forces. They'll be Cordellan, mostly, but still heavily armed. How do they even know where we are, though? This camp should be hidden—

Memories of Paisly nearly send me to my knees. Of Phil, broken, frantic, apologizing for what he told Angra.

And now, if he's been taken again . . . it won't be hard at all for Angra's men to break him even more.

My heart turns to lead and drops into my stomach, gagging me with the force. But no, no, I won't piece together any theories, not until I know for sure.

"How long until they arrive?" I ask Trace.

He shakes his head. "They should already be here."

My body goes cold. I take off running, Conall, Nessa, and Trace falling in behind me.

Screaming pulls at my awareness from the northeastern corner of camp. It's muffled at first, startled yelps that speak to the confusion in my own body—*too fast, this shouldn't be happening, how did this even happen?*

The northeastern corner of camp is already a battlefield. Conall, a sword in one hand and a dagger in the other, plasters himself on one side of me, Trace on the other, Nessa panting behind us.

Soldiers stream in from the forest beyond, pouring between tents, slicing through fabric, attempting to form battle lines in the camp's haphazard streets. They take advantage of the element of surprise by hurling themselves into each skirmish faster than our soldiers can keep up. Autumnians race around me where I stand, stricken, in the middle of the dusty road not five paces from the edge of the battle.

The battle, the fight we needed as the distraction, it's happening *now*, right now, in the middle of a camp filled with innocents.

I grab my chakram and hurl it into the fray, the magic in

my chest leaping after it. That push encourages the blade faster, harder, slicing through enemies in a swift arc of defense. The first line of soldiers falls, their armor clanging as they drop, and my chakram returns.

More soldiers come, more and more.

I grab Conall and Trace. "We need help!"

They nod over the cacophony. Nessa, her face blank, squares herself alongside me, and I hate the irony of this situation—we had just resolved to be apart for the final battle, and now here we are, she at my side. I expect her to run off to be with the children in the other part of camp, but she stays, rushing alongside me as I holster my chakram and push on.

The main tent isn't far—so close to the fight, *too* close— and I angle inside just as Caspar and Sir fly out, fury in Caspar's black eyes, severity in Sir's.

"Queen Meira," Caspar says. "Angra's soldiers have—"

"I know," I cut him off. "But they aren't Angra's."

Sir jerks to me, but one of Caspar's generals flies out of the tent and Caspar turns to him.

"What?" Sir presses me, his brow creasing.

"They aren't Angra's soldiers," I say. "They're Cordell's. From Oktuber."

Sir's face unravels and he whirls to grab Caspar's arm. Caspar turns with a startled frown, and when Sir repeats what I said, Caspar blinks at me, awareness registering on his face. He ducks back into his tent, shouting at more of his commanders that it isn't Angra's full army.

Sir's eyes sweep up and down my body, the familiar examination for injuries, before he does the same to each member of my group. When he gets to Trace, he pauses.

But Trace sags against one of the tent posts, his face ashen. "I didn't get here in time," he says to no one in particular.

We have scouts stationed all around camp who should have warned us of this attack long before Trace showed up. Someone would have seen such a large army coming.

This isn't right.

"Meira! Trace?"

Mather slides to a stop beside us. My eyes latch onto the bloody sword in his hand and all my instincts scream.

"The attackers," he says, his confusion at Trace's presence retreating in favor of the threat of bloodshed. He nods at Sir, grim. "They're coming this way."

This isn't right, this isn't right—

Sir already has a sword out by the time I feebly ask, "Here?"

My eyes go to the main tent, the clearing before it, filled with tables that will easily be overturned and wedding decorations that will easily be shredded. Of all the places in this camp, this offers the best chance at success—freedom to attack in larger groups, with the added benefit of being our command center.

How would the Cordellans even know this is here? This

camp is a maze of meandering streets and lopsided tents.

But it's too late for answers, too late to fix this, too late to do anything but gape at the soldiers who march down a street leading from the northeastern corner of camp, their Cordellan armor matted with signs of battle.

And at their lead stands someone the sight of whom makes Mather and Trace jolt forward.

"Phil!" they shout, warning him to get out of the way— but alarm flares so strongly in my heart that I all but gag.

Sir meets my eyes, and he knows too, and we stand there, sharing a look like we can both see an avalanche coming.

One who knew the exact location if this camp.

One who could have figured out the rotation of our scouts to let an attacking army avoid detection.

Phil stops, all the way across the square.

"Phil!" Mather screams again, less sure.

Trace comes to, and the look of rage on his face stabs grief through my stomach.

He grabs Mather's arm. "*He* did this."

Mather shakes his head. But the proof solidifies as Phil raises his hand and points.

At me.

The Cordellan soldiers behind him need no further instruction. They tear into the clearing, weapons ready. The scream of their attack draws our own fighters to the area, rushing in from side streets and spilling in a wall of defense against the dozens of Cordellans.

Sir, Mather, and Trace crash into the fight. Mather and Trace are driven by a warped mix of determination and agony that makes their movements toxic. I remain in a state of shock near the main tent with Conall and Nessa.

This wasn't the first time Phil told Angra of my location—according to Mather, that was how they ended up in Paisly at all. But then, Phil had been terrified and mournful.

Now—now he is beaming, pride practically leaking out of him.

Familiarity crashes into me and I stumble back, Conall catching me under the elbows.

I've seen this before—Angra torturing someone, only to have that torture plant the seed of betrayal. Theron.

I whirl on Nessa. "Get to safety!" I shout as I shove into the battle, Conall plummeting after me in a whirl of blades. Chakram in one hand, I slice my way through, sending spurts of magic where I can. Bursts of strength to the Winterians who fight; a perfect angle on my chakram to protect a Summerian. The Cordellan soldiers move quickly, slashing and stabbing as if each move brings air and they're suffocating. But we have greater numbers than them, a slight advantage. How long it will hold, though, I don't know.

I couldn't save Theron from Angra—but I can purge Phil of the Decay. The attacking army will no doubt keep on with the battle, but I can save him at least. I have to.

Phil stands at the entrance to the road the Cordellans

came down, watching the frenzy with delight. Before he even sees that I've drawn closer to him, I sheathe my chakram and use both hands to channel magic at him, a spiral of ice that flies from my body. I can practically taste the darkness in him.

But I've constantly purified my Winterians any time we were exposed to the Decay.

Except for when Phil and Mather were captured.

Except for whatever Phil underwent at Angra's hand.

I'm hit with the memory of Theron in Angra's cell, the mental torture he inflicted on Theron until, on the floor of Rintiero's dungeon, Theron told me that he *wanted* this.

Angra's doing it all over again.

No, no . . .

Phil howls as my magic pummels him. I break free of the fight, a handful of paces from him with Conall beside me.

Phil looks at me, his gaze fuming. "I don't want your help!"

Again I fling my magic and he slides back, howling through clenched teeth.

"I've seen what your magic can do," Phil barks. "It hurts everyone. You just keep fighting when it's been your fault all along—if you'd just surrender, we'd be free. *You* are the reason we were in those camps. *You* are the reason we all get hurt. I refuse to let you hurt us anymore."

"I'm not hurting you, Phil," I try, hands spread, my magic quiet. "I'm protecting you from Angra—he's the reason you're doing this! *You're* the one hurting people right now!"

I wave at the battle. As I do, Sir and Mather stumble out, their faces streaked with dirt and blood. Mather's weapons hang limp at his sides and he faces Phil, posture defeated.

"Phil," Mather tries, his voice coming like a gust of air from a punch. "Why?"

Behind him, a Cordellan turns from the fight and dives at us, but Sir intercepts, gliding back into the fray. His eyes cut to us when they can, a pinch in his expression I've only seen a handful of times: worry.

Sir is worried. For us.

I hold the tremor in my gut until it subsides.

Phil's fury boils over. "For *you*! For all of us! You got hurt, and she didn't care. You got hurt *again*, and she kept pushing on—she doesn't care about us. She doesn't care about anything but her stupid revenge! I won't let her hurt us anymore!"

He's screaming now, eyes bloodshot and crazed, skin stretched taut as though it can't contain the madness underneath.

My eyes flit to a movement behind Phil.

And my whole world dissolves.

Panic jerks me forward, one foolish burst of instinct, but that's all it takes to draw Phil's attention away from us to the figure who slips out from between two tents behind him. She raises a knife in her hand as though she intends to stab him in the back.

"Nessa!" I scream now, because Phil sees her—there's no point hiding. "RUN!"

She doesn't move when Phil turns, both of them freezing solid to the road. I realize then—Phil's a Winterian. I should be able to stop him. But I'd be forcing something on him, bending him to my will. It would be a negative use of magic.

Mather, Conall, and I take off toward them, but Phil is too close to Nessa, both of them standing in the road leading away from the clearing, free of the battle. The clearing around us holds the worst threats, blades puncturing the air, dying screams rippling through the breeze. All attention is here, so as we sprint forward, we fumble through parlaying enemies and have to duck weapons, while Phil and Nessa have only each other to worry about.

I hear a shout. "Meira!"

But I don't turn. I feel Sir's panic from where he's locked in battle, unable to break free and help us—but I can't think about it. Not the way he's worried, and showing it— not the way his voice splits in my ears, ragged and harsh, and makes me swallow a cry.

I fumble with my magic. I used it to relocate the Winterians in Juli without touching them, but I was driven by pure instinct, and before I can let myself go enough to try with Nessa, a Cordellan howls and dives for me. Conall twists, blade clashing with the Cordellan's.

I break free again, but Phil hears us running, or feels the ground shake, or senses my panic drawing near.

He has no problem using magic against us—which merely confirms that the Decay is in him. He launches his hand back at me. A knot of inky shadow barrels out of his fingers, polluting the air until it slams into me. I rear back into Conall just as he dispatches the Cordellan. Both of us go down, and Mather pauses, growls, and pushes himself forward.

A horn sounds, and shouts fill the air, feet stomping in a thunderous wave. But it's the Autumnians fighting who scream in recognition as their countrymen pour into the area, more of our soldiers finally organized and called in. It won't be long now—our numbers will overwhelm the Cordellans. Even behind Phil and Nessa, Autumnians appear, running toward them with weapons poised. They'll save her—they'll stop this.

I scramble against the ground to get to my feet. Magic swells out of me when my eyes find Nessa again, a command that burrows into her heart.

Go, GO! RUN!

Phil sees the Autumnians coming and rips a hatchet from a holster on his thigh. The weapon glints in his fist, and Nessa's eyes widen.

She turns, intending to run toward the Autumnians.

But Phil launches forward, one step, just one, and reaches her first.

She isn't a fighter. She's my Nessa, she's *mine*, and Phil's hatchet hooks into her neck before I can even start running again. But no, I don't run—I wrap the magic around me and fling myself beside Phil, who grins wickedly, and Nessa just gapes. She's confused, and shocked, and—

Her dagger clatters to her feet.

I slam my shoulder into Phil and send him thudding to the ground. His hatchet breaks free, trailing blood with it, and Nessa drops. I catch her, both of us falling.

The Autumnians surge around us, most barreling into the fight in the clearing, some pausing to survey that the enemy near us is down. But they keep going, even though I'm holding my whole world in my arms, watching it bleed out.

"Nessa!" I cry, magic gushing out of my body and into her, such waves of coldness that I know the ground around us has to be a swirl of frost and ice. "NESSA!"

Her head lolls against me. So much blood, not enough magic, so I pour more, but the magic just sloshes into her as blood flows out. I drive every speck of any power I have into *her*, to be hers, please, *please Nessa just take it, take anything you need, please Nessa—*

I couldn't save Garrigan, but I have to save you. Please, Nessa, let me save you.

Something moves. Phil.

He stands, snarling, but Mather, who stumbles up to him, saves me from having to kill him. No—Mather shouldn't have to do this, he shouldn't have this on his hands—

Conall heaves into Mather, who drops without a fight, eyes unblinking on Phil, lips parted as though he's begging Phil to stop. But Phil doesn't stop, *can't* stop, so frenzied that he roars at me like a beast.

It's Conall who pierces a blade into Phil's chest, plunging it in to the hilt.

Mather's hands go into his hair, a sob tearing from his throat that drowns my own.

Arms pull me back to Nessa. Arms that clamp around both of us, holding on so fiercely I think, almost, that we'll be all right. We're safe, safe in Conall's arms, and she'll be all right.

Conall's tears drip onto my face but he just holds me tighter as I scream his sister's name.

Ceridwen

CERIDWEN ONLY SAW the end of the battle.

After the final meeting, she had gone to split her fighters into those who would leave and those who would stay behind. So she was with Lekan when the first shouts went up. Running across the camp when the horn blew out. Gasping at the edge of the clearing when the Autumnian reinforcements reached it, their support bringing the fight to a decisive end.

And then she was running again, to the main tent, leaping over fallen victims and dodging the last desperate attempts of dying Cordellans to strike her down. She flew into the tent, only to see it empty, the table where they had made their battle plans still littered with maps.

Ceridwen whirled and ran again, the rank air that always came with a fight scraping down her throat.

Jesse hadn't left with her. He'd stayed to help

Caspar—he'd stayed *here*, in this tent, on the edge of a clearing that had all too recently been filled with joy and music.

Ceridwen raced for Jesse's tent. He slept with his children every night in the area given to the Winterians. Well, he'd slept there every night but one—last night, the one after their . . .

It was appropriate, too appropriate, for that clearing to be a battleground now. Perhaps it was punishment, on some level. As Ceridwen slid to a halt outside Jesse's tent, she felt that realization shatter the thin structure of happiness she'd built.

This was punishment, for believing in joy during a war.

This was punishment, for being happy when she had no right to be.

Ceridwen grabbed the flaps of his tent, drew in a breath, and ripped them open.

Let him be here, let him be here . . .

She saw Melania first. Then Geneva, and Cornelius, huddled together on the floor, wrapped in a single long wool blanket. They blinked up at her, their eyes wide behind their small, tattered masks, the only ones they'd been able to bring from Rintiero.

Melania put a finger to her lips.

"Shh, Cerie! You're interrupting."

And she settled back against her siblings, looking up

at Jesse, who paused over a book open in his lap. His eyes caught Ceridwen's, wide at first in a smile, then narrowing when he saw her tension.

He set the book aside and rose from his cot. Melania groaned.

"No, you have to finish it!" she begged. "Nessa didn't finish it either."

Jesse batted a hand at her and looked up at Ceridwen. "What's wrong?"

He didn't know. He didn't know about the battle. He was here, reading to his children.

A single laugh slipped free of Ceridwen's throat, but it dissolved on her tongue, and tears came with it, spilling down her face. Jesse rushed to her, and she knotted around his neck, heaving against him as she tried to keep from sobbing too loudly, if only so his children didn't worry.

"It's started," Ceridwen whispered to him. She felt him coil under her touch, his grip on her spasming. He hesitated, pressed a kiss to her cheek, and turned back to Melania, Geneva, and Cornelius.

"I need you to go play with Amelie," he told them. He looked at Ceridwen for confirmation that this was safe, and she nodded. From here, the Summerian section of the camp wasn't in the path of the battle, which had ended by now anyway.

Then Jesse turned to Ceridwen, and she put out her

hand, needing to hold on to him. A part of her ached as though she were still outside this tent, waiting to separate the flaps, unsure of what lay within.

That was how every moment would be from now on, she realized.

Uncertain.

Meira

"THE CORDELLANS WERE defeated by our forces."

". . . only half a battalion. Phil led a small group from those stationed in Oktuber."

"They were unprepared, as though they came in a hurry."

"Thankfully we only had minor losses—"

Minor losses.

My fingers tighten in the sleeve of Nessa's dress, her dried blood breaking across my skin. The voices around me stop, halted by my sharp twinge where I haven't moved in hours. Days, maybe, just here on the ground with her body in my arms.

"Meira."

I peel my eyes away from the gore-covered clearing that once hosted Ceridwen and Jesse's wedding celebration. Is that stain there blood, or wine someone spilled?

"Meira," Sir says again, crouching before me. He reaches

for Nessa. "We have to—"

"No!" I snarl. Sir flinches.

I can't blame him. I want to cower from myself, too.

Ceridwen is standing behind Sir. And beyond him, Autumnians, Summerians, and Yakimians alike work to clean up the carnage of the area. Caspar watches me, and Nikoletta, and Dendera—they all stand nearby with looks of sympathy.

A few steps away, Mather crouches over a body on the ground. The Thaw, Henn, and the remaining refugees got here sometime during the fight, so Hollis, Kiefer, Eli, Feige, and Trace surround Mather now. Some of them weep, some of them sit silent and ashen-faced around Phil's body.

My grip on Nessa tightens.

Someone else drops to his knees next to me. Conall. When did he leave?

He bends over Nessa, and I don't fight him off when he runs a hand down her gray face. His fingers shift over her arm, and he lifts it, slides something between it and her chest.

A book.

"I've been . . ." His voice cracks. "I've been writing down the engravings from the memory cave." He closes his eyes, and when he opens them, his gaze shifts to me. "It was supposed to be a gift for her. So she could carry Winter with her wherever she went. I wanted her to have a piece of our kingdom with her. I wanted her to . . ."

But he doesn't finish the thought. His blue eyes, mottled with tears, dart over my face, and the unhidden grief he shows destroys me.

"I'm so sorry, Conall," I hear myself say. It sounds weak, the blubbering apology of someone who failed. "I should have used my magic sooner. I should have stopped Phil, whatever the cost. I should have—I'm so sorry—"

Conall wobbles forward and yanks me to him, his forehead to mine. "Meira, don't."

That shocks me into silence more than anything he could have said.

He didn't call me *my queen*.

"They'll burn her," I whisper.

He swallows, nodding. "I know."

But it will be an Autumnian ceremony. For Nessa, the girl with the book of Winterian memories in her arms, the girl who should have gone on adventures all over the world and gathered pieces of herself from every kingdom in Primoria . . . it's fitting.

Conall eases his hands down, rocking his sister's body from my arms to his, and I let him take her. He stands, careful to keep the book on her chest. His eyes hook onto mine in one last look of understanding. Of pain—aching, disintegrating pain.

The moment he steps away, Sir pulls me to my feet. My legs crack from being huddled on the ground for so long, but he keeps me up, supporting me under one arm.

Weakly, I try to pull away. "You should be with your son."

He says nothing, just holds me up as I stare at Mather, kneeling over the body of one of his best friends.

The hand I used to push away Sir sits on his chest, and my fingers bend, clawing into his shirt. I push him again, or maybe hold him here, my throat so swollen with grief that I gag and sway, pushing and pulling Sir. He catches my other arm, pinning me to the ground, and I am pushing him now, beating on his chest.

"Let me go," I say, but it doesn't match the ferocity with which I hit him.

I still, open hands settling on his arms.

"Let me go," I repeat, a broken plea that I send to the dirt. "We could. We could go. We could leave, right now, before we lose anyone else. . . ."

The words bubble out of me, jagged wishes that shred my heart even as I utter them.

Sir's fingers tighten on my elbows. He'll yell at me now. He'll reprimand me for this kind of talk.

I clamp my eyes shut, bracing for the onslaught of guilt from him. A queen should be strong and resilient. A queen should face tragedy with hope.

But I have Nessa's blood on my body. I have the image of her death in my head. I have Mather's scream in my ears, when he saw Phil die. And we haven't even gotten close to defeating Angra yet.

How much worse will it get?

"You could leave," Sir says, his low voice rumbling up my arms. I flinch, then hear him. What? "But you won't, because you're stronger than even the worst thing that could happen, and that makes you undefeatable."

Panting, I look up at him, my eyes shifting over his features like I haven't seen him in months. Maybe I haven't—all the time I spent being angry with him never let me see how much this has changed him, too. Impossibly, the Sir I see now looks . . . soft. Comforting. And his words soothe the fire in my heart, one cold burst of air in the inferno of my grief.

He releases his hold on my arms as if to prove his point, that I can stand on my own. He steps to the side, clearing the way to Mather.

I swallow a shuddering breath. Nikoletta is helping Conall place Nessa's body with the others who died, while some of the Thaw now lift and carry Phil's body there too. Mather stays on the ground, hands over his face, back hunched. The whole area hums with sorrow, shock that can't be soothed.

Before today, this war was in our control. Some small part of it, at least. Now the looks on everyone's faces—they're afraid.

Angra found us. Whatever safety we thought we had is a lie.

I drop to my knees beside Mather and curl around him,

my face in his neck, my arms pulling him into me. He surrenders willingly. I think he apologizes, but I don't say anything.

This is the future I will have, if I keep moving forward. Nothing but tears and blood and pain, with the eventual hope of happiness—for everyone else. *Is it worth it?*

The question is covered in the blood I've seen, broken beneath the pain I feel. But I ask it nonetheless, my eyes squishing shut on fresh tears as Mather adjusts his arms on me.

My magic responds.

Yes.

In Autumn, the kingdom of endless trees and dry leaves, they have to take the bodies to a clearing wide and empty enough so as not to spread the flames beyond the dead. Which means properly burning all the bodies would take at least a day of travel that the army doesn't have.

So we leave Nessa's body with the eight others who fell during the attack. Nikoletta promises me she will be given an honorable funeral, one fit for Autumnian royalty.

And I will give her an honorable future, I think. *Her memory will live on in a world free from Angra.*

Hours later, we leave.

Those who won't join us at the final battle site gather on the eastern edge of camp to see us off. Nikoletta and Shazi; Jesse and his children; Kaleo and Amelie; all the

Autumnians, Winterians, Summerians, and Yakimians who can't fight along with a small cluster of soldiers who will remain to protect them.

But since Phil revealed this location to the Cordellans stationed in Oktuber, the camp will move too, for a new, safer location—only after we have gone. We've seen now, more than ever, the ruthlessness of Angra's magic. Should any of us fall to the Decay and have knowledge of the camp's new position . . . It's better we don't know where they are. We'll find them when it's over.

I wince at my own thought.

Caspar will find them when it's over. And Ceridwen. And Mather, and Sir, and everyone else who will survive this.

That's the only part of our plan that has changed now. The rest—march to the valley, reveal our location to Angra, and wait for the final battle to begin—stays the same.

It doesn't feel like it should, though. Nessa's death, Phil's betrayal, the shattering of our sense of security—it all feels like our lives should be irrevocably rocked by this.

I turn in my horse's saddle where I sit at the edge of camp. The space before me can't exactly be called a clearing, but the trees are thin enough to allow our army to gather in a mostly cohesive formation. The edge of the camp is lined with those bidding farewell, weeping families who cling to soldiers and whisper words of encouragement.

Conall stands in that group not far from me, his hands folded behind his back. He's still staying here, whether to fulfill my final order or because, unlike me, he cannot bear to not say farewell to his sister. He didn't get to mourn Garrigan either.

He's the only one left.

He meets my eyes as if he can sense what I'm thinking, or maybe he's thinking the same thing—*it shouldn't be me.*

I pull away from him, unable to hold his gaze without tears rushing back in. But when I look ahead, at the departing soldiers who fan out into the forest as they say their good-byes, I see the same emotion. Regret capped by mourning for the fate we're marching toward.

My eyes flit of their own volition to Sir. He sits on a horse beside Henn and Dendera, embodying the presence I knew so well growing up—a general marching to war.

Fear is a seed that, once planted, never stops growing.

Before, we knew the danger Angra presented to the world, but we still thought, foolishly, that we would be safe until we chose to march into it. Now I see, we all see, the truth of this war, how it will find us no matter where we hide or how safe we think we are.

And that is how Nessa's death and Phil's betrayal have changed our lives, I realize: we're afraid now. If we go into battle with such emotions that the Decay can latch onto . . .

We've already lost.

I kick my horse forward, pressing for the best vantage point between the departing soldiers and the remaining camp. Eyes shift to me as I slow my horse to a steady walk, pushing down the line of faces that hold the same fear that chokes the strength from me.

They don't expect to survive this. One of my own soldiers led Angra's men right to us—what other betrayals await us still? Who will be infected? Will they die not by an enemy blade, but at the hands of their own brothers or sisters?

I lift my hands over my head, mouth open to call for attention. But how do I address them? It isn't one kingdom I can call for.

That's just it, though.

"Angra seeks to unite the world," I start, my voice ringing out over the murmured farewells. Attention turns to me in a steady wave as I rise tall in my saddle, heart hammering. "We have seen the lengths he will go to in order to spread his control. But I see before me something much greater: *true* unity. I see an army of Autumn, Summer, Yakim, Ventralli, and Winter. I see Rhythm and Season side by side, marching together in defense of a collective dream. A world we have never known, but wish to build— one without threat of magic. One where each of us is free to live and love and *be* on our own.

"We have all lost something. Homes, loved ones, *freedom*—and that is why we march into battle at all. But today we suffered an equally great loss—a loss of innocence. You understand how the fight will go, that Angra will attack not only with weapons and soldiers, but with memories and regrets. The moment we meet him in battle, every pain you harbor, every fear that camps within you, will be used against you. And it would be easy to give in to his attacks."

My voice catches.

"But we are not here because we seek what is easy. We are here because we know we will achieve victory when we march to that battlefield. Angra wants to darken our world." I shake my head, grinning so wide that I begin to think I've gone insane. "But we cannot be extinguished, and our light will blind him."

The moment I finish, the crowd roars.

Fists rise into the air. Heads tip back. Shouts and cheers and whoops explode around me, each soldier casting off their fear in favor of this protective coat of belief. They feel it as much as I do—how much better it is to cling to words of hope than tremors of fear.

Not far from where I sit, Mather applauds alongside his Thaw, the smile on his face one of healing, one of hope. All I need is this. Mather, smiling. The soldiers, their mourning forgotten for a moment.

Everyone ready for war. Everyone ready for *victory*.

I pull my horse around, plunging into the gathered ranks of our armies to find Caspar and Ceridwen at the front lines. I pass by Dendera and Henn, who applaud with the crowd, Dendera's eyes glassy and her lips lifted in a proud smile. I tip my head at her, and my eyes flick to the side, pinning on Sir.

He sits straight up in his saddle, nearly a perfect mimic of Dendera, down to the glassy eyes and the quirk to his lips. That he's applauding would have been enough—but he's actually showing emotion. *To me.* Smiling. *At me.*

I exhale a shuddering breath, refusing to cry again.

I will face this war, we will *all* face this war, with the only weapons that truly matter: us, our strengths and weaknesses. Good or bad, awful or wonderful, these things have sculpted me, and I will use them to be the person the world needs me to be. The person Rares and Oana need me to be; the person Conall, Mather, Sir, and all the Winterians need me to be.

The person Nessa made me.

I will be Meira.

Mather

MEIRA'S SPEECH HAD taken the pain caused by the attack and smothered it like snow kicked over a fire. At least, the pain in the soldiers around Mather—even as he applauded, each clap of his hands thumped against the black grief in his heart.

He took stock of the Thaw without meaning to. Each of them was outfitted with weapons and dressed for fast travel. And each was solemn, applauding only because the energy of the crowd compelled them to ignore their grief for one sweet moment of clarity. But the moment would pass, and reality would crush them again, just as Mather knew it would crush him.

The look on Phil's face when Conall had stabbed him hadn't been regret or sorrow, nothing Mather had expected. It had been only anger.

Angra's magic had done that. Taken loyal, happy Phil and made him . . . feral.

Mather should have seen it happening. He knew Phil had been hurting after the torture in Rintiero, but he had never thought . . . he hadn't even *considered* . . .

But he was the leader of the Thaw. It was his job to see such things.

He had failed Phil. He had failed them all.

Mather swallowed as Meira's speech ended. She pressed past them, heading toward the front lines, and they, as her guards, should follow. But Mather watched William, Dendera, and Henn fall in behind her, and he breathed a sigh of relief that he had a moment to speak with his Thaw before duty swept in.

Only one moment. War never allowed for more than that.

Mather turned to the Thaw, who pressed tightly together as the soldiers moved around them, the cheering tapering off into murmured farewells.

"You have a choice," Mather started, his mouth dry. "I won't force any of you to go to war. Staying to protect the camp will be just as worthy—"

"Save it." It was Kiefer who cut him off, and Mather paused, meeting his eyes with a stern glare. If Kiefer had some objection to their plans that would leave him stomping off in a huff, Mather didn't have the energy to deal with it now.

But Kiefer's face was soft, almost. "We're going with you," he stated.

And that was all. No mention of how their trip to escort the refugees had led to Phil's death, and how Mather hadn't been with them for it—no mention of the other times they had been split apart, and the dire consequences of each.

Just unity, now. Unity and obedience, from Kiefer, no less.

"I'm sorry," Mather heard himself say. Two words that he hadn't meant to utter, though they had been in his mind ever since he'd seen Phil lead the soldiers into camp. Was it a sign of weakness to apologize to the Thaw like this? William had never once apologized for anything. Whatever it was, those two words rippled in the air, and he closed his eyes.

Silence didn't stay long before someone slapped him in the face. Hard.

Mather blinked down at Feige, her cheeks flame red and her lips pursed.

"No," she growled. "None of this is our fault. This is *Angra's* fault. All of it."

Her anger raged up into her eyes, and Mather felt that warning from when he'd first sparred with her. This wasn't just anger from Phil's betrayal. This was anger from every moment of living in Angra's work camp, from all the terrors she had endured under his reign. Phil's betrayal was sadly, horribly, one more nightmare in a long line of nightmares, all stemming from Angra.

Trace shifted, his fingers tight on the knife hilts sticking out of the holsters on his thighs. He bobbed his head in a quick nod, one echoed by Hollis, Kiefer, and Eli without hesitation.

Hollis stepped closer to his sister. "But let's agree, now, that the best way for us to get through this is by helping each other."

"We won't let each other get so consumed by the Decay that we're beyond help," Trace added. "We can bring each other back. The Summerians have been trying to teach people how to resist magic, so I know it's possible. We're never alone. No matter what Angra's magic tries to make us believe."

They didn't blame Mather. They didn't blame Phil. And as Mather looked into their eyes, the sorrow in his heart shredding anew, he saw beyond their own sorrow the same flicker of life that had first endeared them to him. They were fighters, through it all. They were survivors, and they would continue to survive, no matter the tragedies they faced.

"Well?"

Mather jumped. Trace lifted his brow.

"You're our leader, Once-King," he said. "Are we together or not?"

Mather hardened his shoulders. He felt their motto now more than he ever had before.

"We will not be defeated," he whispered. And he meant it.

Three thousand soldiers left the camp, a mix of Autumnians, Yakimians, Summerians, and Winterians.

As Mather marched alongside his Thaw, he couldn't stop himself from darting studious looks at the people around him. William, straight backed on his horse. Dendera, once again the reluctant warrior Mather remembered, fierce and deadly next to Henn.

And Meira, just as alert as William, just as fierce as Dendera. A heavier weight hung over her now, an even stronger fervor to keep everyone safe. While their massive army made camp each night, she walked the perimeter, almost unaware of how Mather and rotating members of the Thaw trailed her, once again her guards. And only when Mather coaxed her to bed did she go, reluctant until she got inside the tent—then she tumbled into the blankets and fell asleep beside him so fast that he knew she was draining herself, stretching the edges of her magic in some way.

But he just curled around her, his arm across her hip, his face tucked into her hair, and tried to make himself as calm as possible, a place she could go to every night for rest.

The preparation for the coming battle honed everyone's focuses. Which was why no one said anything about his sleeping arrangements with Meira—out loud, at least. William stared at Mather every night and every morning, and by the time they reached the valley, even William seemed unable to remain cloaked in his usual emotionlessness and stoicism.

Mather understood instantly why Caspar had recommended this site. The foothills of the Klaryns made up the right side, rising into the mountains beyond, while the left side was a hill coated in trees that created the illusion of a gold and orange wave cresting over the grassy plain through the middle. Halfway across the valley the emerald grass ended in such a deliberate break that it could only be caused by magic—the Winterian border of white and snow and evergreens.

This battle would happen on their terms, with no escape in any direction.

Caspar, Ceridwen, and Meira set to work immediately upon reaching the valley. Tents were erected at the westernmost end, effectively claiming the Autumnian side of the battlefield in their favor. Soldiers posed in lines across the grass, fanned out into the trees to start patrols for enemies advancing from the rear, and attempted daring escapades up the steep cliffs to attain more thorough vantage points.

Mather and his Thaw stayed clustered near Meira. She didn't seem to mind, too consumed by double-checking their plans with Caspar or going over a map with Ceridwen or casting sweeps for trouble. She caught Mather's eyes during one such sweep, and he smiled.

A pause, and she smiled back, then leaned over to say something to Ceridwen.

"She's your queen first and foremost."

Mather turned to William, who stood next to him just outside the largest open-air tent, the one for strategy and planning. When Meira had kissed him in the Autumnian camp, Dendera had managed to smile through her shock. But William hadn't reacted at all. Mather had tried to explain what it was—not something they should worry about, not something fleeting, but a true, lasting relationship he intended to fight for.

William had crossed his arms, narrowed his eyes, and walked away.

Mather shifted toward him now, brow lifted. "I know."

William pinned Mather with a look. "Do not lose sight of that. Especially now—she is your queen and you are her soldier."

Mather kept his voice low. "What do you think will happen? If anything, this makes me even *more* disposed to protect her, and I—"

"Protection isn't all she needs," William cut him off. "She is the queen of Winter, and you are a soldier of Winter. Both of your goals should be the well-being of our kingdom— regardless of how that would affect either of you, emotionally or physically. You will protect Winter beyond your feelings for her and I expect her to do the same."

Mather had heard similar speeches from William before, and he knew Meira had, too. *"Winter first, above everything"*; *"Your goal is our kingdom's salvation, nothing more."* He had never been on this end of such a speech, where he was the soldier and she the monarch. Was this what William had told Meira all those years, his reason for not wanting her to love Mather? So her feelings wouldn't interfere with their kingdom's progression?

Worse than that, Mather knew Meira agreed with William. He knew she would choose Winter over him, and try as he did to mute his constant worry, he couldn't stifle it now.

She would die for them. And William would expect Mather to let her.

He had already lost too many people to Angra—Alysson, Phil, and dozens more over the years. He might not have been able to save Alysson or Phil, but he'd be damned if he'd just sit back and let Meira die too.

Grief coated his mouth, metallic and rancid, almost forcing him to gag or scream or let it out in some way. No more deaths. *No more.*

"Someone needs to fight for her," Mather stated. "Alysson did the same for you. I'm hers first, and Winter's second."

"Family trouble?"

Mather swung to Meira, heat flashing up his neck.

"No, my queen," William told her. "Are you ready to leave?"

Mather balked. "Leave? Already?"

Meira balked, too, but recovered faster than him. It wasn't William's question that threw her—it was the way he stood there, distant and stoic as ever.

"Yes." She included Mather with a glance. "We received word of Theron's location. Angra is marching with his army, but . . ."

"Jannuari?" William guessed when Mather didn't trust himself to speak.

Meira nodded. She pointed toward a smaller tent off to their right. "Get your weapons and meet me back here in ten minutes."

"Angra hasn't arrived," Mather argued. Panic swelled in his chest. They were leaving for Jannuari in *minutes*. He thought they wouldn't leave until Angra marched on them, that he might have one last night with Meira, his body curled around hers in the tent they shared.

Meira's softness faded. "Angra is already close, and he knows where we are. We need every moment we can get."

Mather's mouth dropped open. "How do you—"

But he stopped when she absently touched the locket, the glittering piece of jewelry that was so out of place on a woman dressed in borrowed Autumnian leather armor, a Paislian robe and boots, and a chakram.

Her magic. She could use it to sense Angra—so could Angra sense her? Or could she protect herself from him, only let him know where she was when *she* chose it?

If she could do that, Angra could no doubt shield himself from her. So why was he letting Meira know where he was?

Mather bit back these worries. She knew what she was doing. He trusted her.

"All right," he agreed. The sooner they ended this, the sooner that bastard would no longer be a threat to her—and the sooner Angra would pay for everything he had done.

Mather jogged off toward the structure she had indicated, the one overflowing with weapons and gear. The rest of his Thaw stayed around the main tent, watching him go with a mix of worry and angst. He'd be leaving them again soon.

But this would all be over soon too.

Meira

THIS IS TOO easy.

I manage to block Angra for our entire journey. But when we make it to the valley with no ambushes, no change of plans, no bad news, I know something is wrong. Angra wouldn't let us get away with our plan if he knew about it—so either we somehow succeeded in making a move that surprised him . . .

Or we're in a lot of trouble.

Soon after I let down the barriers and unleash the hold I have on my magic, I know we don't have much time. Hunched over maps of the valley and surrounding mountains with Ceridwen and Caspar, I don't alert them to the fact that I'm prodding the area around us for Angra, my eyes on the table but my mind far, far away.

Just how far can I stretch my magic? I've been keeping

watch over our immediate area throughout the trip, but can I go farther?

I poke the forest around us. Nothing.

The Winter side of the valley. Nothing.

The mountains, the forest beyond—nothing.

But then—

I grip the edge of the table, feigning interest in whatever Ceridwen points at.

Angra falls into my awareness, a bead of water breaking the still surface of a lake. No direct contact, my mind still barricaded from any attacks, but I recognize him—and I'm entirely certain he's doing the same to me, latching onto my location now that I'm no longer blocking him.

Ah, there you are, I can almost hear him say. *So nice of you to join our war again.*

Angra isn't blocking me with magic like I did to him for so long—almost as though he's been waiting for me to try to find him. He wants me to know he's coming.

Because he's already on his way, no doubt leading an army toward us. At the very least, we did get to choose the location of the battle, but the fact that Angra is already on the move says he didn't wait for his full forces to gather before he left. He must still have enough to thoroughly destroy us.

His is the only presence I sense. Though Caspar just moments ago received word from his scouts that Theron is indeed in Jannuari, part of me hoped he was wrong. But Theron isn't with Angra, and I'd be able to feel his link to magic, at least—he's a conduit-wielder now, even if he doesn't have his conduit anymore.

My heart drops, but I stretch my magic toward Angra. Theron definitely isn't with him.

Does Theron even have the keys anymore? Angra could have taken them before this. But if I reach Theron, and he doesn't have the keys, there'd be no reason for me to stay. If Angra truly does want to lure me into a trap, his best way of doing it would still be for Theron to have the keys, and for me to have to get them from him.

If that's the way Angra wants this to play out, then Theron still has the keys, and he's waiting for me in Jannuari.

Angra's biggest weakness lies in my kingdom.

So he left one of my biggest weaknesses there too.

"He's coming," I announce, popping my head up. Ceridwen and Caspar pull back, cautious frowns easing across their features.

"How far?" Caspar asks, already bending over another map and tracing possible routes from Jannuari. The last report we got from Caspar's spies was little help—they nearly got caught and had to run before any information could be gleaned.

I knock his hand aside and point lower, to the area that tugs at my consciousness, the unnerving feeling of someone watching but at a distance. A spot just shy of the

Autumn-Winter border, north of us still, but not nearly as far as Caspar had been expecting. Angra's soldiers in Oktuber must have told him of our presence in Autumn.

Caspar rears away from the table and whirls on two of his warriors, posted outside the tent. "Call in our scouts. Tell them to fan out northeast. I want numbers, speed of travel—"

His voice fades as he stomps off into the camp, spouting orders at his soldiers without a backward glance. That's his tactic, I've learned: waste no time. Which fits the life Autumn leads—move, do, *be*, because at any moment, Angra could come crashing in.

Ceridwen leaves too, Lekan following, both of them bent in a quiet hum of discussion that fades once they exit the open-air tent. I'm left with the swishing of the afternoon breeze through the trees that hug the edge of our camp, the steady banging of smiths in the crude excuse for an armory we set up nearby.

I don't allow myself time for thought. I turn, seeking out my newly acquired shadows. Mather's Thaw lingers around the tent in a protective formation that made Sir nod approval. Whatever Mather did to train them in the short time he had, it was effective.

Mather talks with Sir at the edge of the tent, the two of them angled toward each other. I hesitate, struck yet again by how blind I was for so long not to realize they're related. They even argue identically—heads tipped to the right, eyes level and unblinking. The similarities bring up a much-needed breath of coolness, the gentle cascade of . . . home.

I cross the tent to them, branding their images into my memory with each footfall.

Moments later, Sir, Mather, and I stand in the main tent, as ready for war as three people can be.

Sir looks like he did every moment of my childhood—outfitted in black and weapons and severity. Mather tightens the strap of his leather breastplate, the deep russet material worn and pliable with age. He has two short swords on his back, a small pouch of supplies wrapped across his chest, and knives strapped over his boots and pants.

I'm far less armed. A short sword swings at my hip and my chakram sits on my back, but any other weapons felt too restrictive. If we're to do this, if I'm to use my magic, I want the freedom to move unhindered.

Most of my life I spent fighting to have weapons at all. Now I'm marching into war and choosing to go with only two.

But I'm a weapon on my own.

Ceridwen comes up beside me, herself already outfitted for war, only in far more Summerian style—bands hold skintight leather plating over airy orange pants and gruesome weapons I've never seen before, small daggers with guards that curve into deadly spikes of their own. She shakes her fingers through a few curls that have fallen loose of the strands of braided leather she wove her hair into.

"We have a farewell in Summer," she says in a tone I haven't heard from her in a while—the veil of political neutrality. "When someone goes on a long journey, those who stay behind wish them the energy of a wildfire. The power to take things that try to hinder you—wind, thrashing enemies—and use them to make you stronger. The power to burn so brightly that all who look will wonder how darkness ever existed in the same world as you." She puts a hand on my shoulder, but her resolve breaks, her eyes glassy. "Scorch this world, Winter queen."

I draw her into a hug, clearing my throat to strengthen my voice. "You're the ones who will do the hard work. I'm just taking a leisurely trip into the mountains."

Ceridwen pulls back and fixes me with a long, hard look. Her tear-rimmed eyes hold the barest threat. "We'll celebrate our victory *when* you return."

I want to thank her for everything she's done. Helping me in Summer, joining my crusade, and believing in me. I want to tell her how glad I am to count her among my friends, and that knowing she's alive to shepherd the world on makes what I have to do slightly easier.

But I can't say anything without confirming to her that I don't plan on returning. So I give her shoulder one final squeeze and bob my head in a vague bow.

"Scorch this world," I echo. *For both of us.*

Caspar bids me farewell in a far less emotional way. The sentiment from him is the same, though—speed, strength, victory. Dendera and Henn gather to say their own good-byes. We form a sort of procession, Mather and Sir moving down the line to receive well-wishes too. Mather's Thaw is last in line, waiting with straight shoulders, appearing more like soldiers than I've ever seen them.

Phil's betrayal did this. Or maybe every piece of this war has done this to them, chipped away at their exteriors until nothing is left but the resilient people who face me.

They pause, silent, and I swallow. Saying farewell to Caspar and Ceridwen was one thing. Even Dendera and Henn didn't trigger the flutter in my chest. But facing the Thaw is like facing all of Winter, all the people I've been fighting to protect my entire life.

"I won't let you down" is all I can think to say.

That softens a little of their severity, their expressions flashing with gratitude.

Trace inclines his head. "You never could, my queen," he says, brows pinched.

My jaw clamps shut, and I almost break, again. Thankfully, I'm saved by Mather, who moves in with final orders for them—they're to serve under Caspar during the battle, and give whatever help is needed.

I pull away, letting him have a moment alone with them, and step out of the tent, my eyes sweeping one last time over the area. Angra hasn't moved from where I last sensed him, which is . . . odd. He knows where our army is—he should be leading his own soldiers into position. Or does he intend to sit back and watch his puppets bring about the end of the world without him? I rub the back of my neck, scowling at the empty stretch of valley before me.

In a few hours, these tufts of grass will be nests for bodies. The untouched banks of snow at the opposite end will be macabre in their ivory and scarlet designs.

But the sooner I do this, the less blood will be shed. I just have to concentrate on the task at hand—one act, then another, then another. Right now, all I need to see is where we're going.

Mather and Sir step up beside me.

"I'll put us in Jannuari," I say. "We'll find Theron and get the keys from him. As soon as we have them, I'll get us to the Tadil—the quicker we do this, the shorter the battle will have to be. Angra put more guards on the mine, so there will probably be soldiers down there—but hopefully we'll have surprise on our side. Once they're down, face the door—we have to cross the barrier and get through it as soon as possible."

Mather nods. "Get the keys. Cross the barrier. Got it."

Sir is less ready. "The last time you tried to cross the barrier—"

"That's why I need you both," I say. "Three people have

to cross, all with the same will to reach the magic chasm. A united effort." I stretch my hands out to them, hoping they don't see how hard I'm shaking. "I don't know if the barrier will fall completely after that, and if soldiers will be able to follow us in and carry our fight into the labyrinth itself—"

I blow out a breath. One thing at a time.

Theron's face overtakes my memory, the look he gave me in Juli. Eyes vacant of all emotion, save for a possessive, dominating leer.

One thing at a time.

"A united effort," Sir echoes as he takes my hand. "I'm with you, my queen."

Mather takes my other hand. The moment the three of us are linked, I funnel all my concentration toward a single destination.

Winter.

Meira

LOCATIONS FLY THROUGH my mind as the familiar tension of the magic drags us into oblivion. The slightest exhaustion pulls at me, the exertion of having to transport multiple people, but adrenaline makes it easy to ignore.

If Angra sent Theron to Jannuari, he'll be in the biggest symbol of my city—the palace. And the sooner we reach him, the sooner we can get the keys.

I envision the maze of cold stone halls beneath the palace. The corridors toward the northwest corner were the least used, places no one had yet reached in the all too brief time we had to repair our kingdom.

My feet catch on worn cobblestones and I teeter forward. A wall of frigidity smacks me in the face, a drastic drop in temperature, even compared to the Autumn-Winter border. That drop eases my tight knot of worry.

The last time I was in Winter, my magic was a fearful, uncertain ball of power that thrashed against the barriers I put up. Now, it radiates down my every limb, cresting spirals that coil around my nerves and draw energy from the earth itself.

Home, every part of me says, each breath of cold air infusing me with joy.

If I thought my magic was powerful before, being back in Winter makes it feel . . . I can't even describe it. Invigorated; encouraged; *right,* the same unnameable sense of belonging that all Winterians feel being anywhere near snow.

My magic's purpose is to protect this kingdom, and it knows that.

Blackness coats the hall just as thoroughly as the chill, so I only hear Mather stumble back, still not entirely used to traveling this way. I send a blast of magic to them both, clearing their bodies of any ill effects. Sir wastes no time.

"Is he here?" he asks, a quick whisper that points out how quiet it is. No stomping footsteps from above or deeper in the halls; no shouting of orders or clanking of weapons. What did I expect, though? For an army to be lying in wait for us?

Yes. Because an army would be far more manageable than what I suspect Angra has planned—mind games like those he tortured me with in Abril, playing with my deepest fears.

But Sir's question prods me along. Is Theron even here?

I do exactly what I did to sense Angra: widen my awareness.

The halls around us—no sign of him.

The floor above us—

I jolt with recognition.

Theron is in the ballroom, almost directly overhead.

My magic senses his with frightening clarity. We're both connected to the Royal Conduits—mine is a stronger connection, but it's the same as when I sense Angra. Can Theron sense me too? Does Angra's Decay allow him that firm a grasp of magic?

But even as I wonder that, my magic responds with an answer of its own.

It doesn't matter what Angra made Theron capable of. It doesn't even matter what *Angra* is capable of. Because here, in Winter, is where I'm most powerful.

I've been blocking Angra for weeks now—so I do it again. Only this time, I block my entire city from him, a surge of magic flaring out over Jannuari in a shield. While we're here, Angra can't come. We'll get the keys from Theron without his interference. See how *that* works into Angra's plans.

Iciness streams from my veins, making me nearly giddy. Everything in me is a flurry of snow and ice and frost, my magic the center of a mighty blizzard that could level all the enemies in this city one by one.

Fingers tighten over my arm, and even in the dark, I turn

to Mather with a wicked smile.

"He's here. In the ballroom above. We can do this quickly—I didn't account for the extra boost of being back in Winter. Theron doesn't—"

"This is a trap, Meira." Mather's voice is soft. "Angra wanted you to come here. We have to assume he planned for this."

"Planned for me to become even *more* powerful?"

"Planned for you to be careless." Mather's fingers shift over my arm until he's holding both my hands. "Planned for something that would weaken you."

I swallow, tendrils of magic sinking back into my chest. A deep breath fills my lungs, and I squeeze Mather's hands in response.

"You're right." I take a step back. "Let's go, but slowly."

I start to give them more definite orders when a noise makes me pause. Two soft bangs, like metal tapping on metal.

Clank, clank.

"It's coming from up the hall," Sir says. The way toward the ballroom.

I grunt and start forward, boots swishing across the floor. The stone wall is grimy under my touch, but my fingers whisper across it, guiding me forward. Mather and Sir follow, noiseless but for the steady rustle of their clothing as they slip behind me.

Again the banging echoes toward us. *Clank, clank.*

The hall lightens shadow by shadow thanks to a single lit lantern two halls over—exactly in our path to the ballroom. My once invigorating power retreats in favor of unease as we near the lantern, all the shadows around me warping in the mesmerizing pull of the light.

And when I turn into the lantern's hallway, the two soldiers standing guard over one of the rooms face me like they've been waiting for us to appear.

They smile, blades already drawn, and waste no time in propelling themselves at me. Sir and Mather react faster than I do, diving forward with their own weapons as my eyes dart to the room the soldiers had been guarding. Rusted iron bars make up the door—a cell. Yellow sconce light plays with shadows that dart over mildew-covered walls and the body that smashes itself against the bars. Two taps echo over the clash of swords, eyes staring vacantly as the prisoner bangs a metal cup against the poles.

Clank, clank.

I jolt back to the fight as one of the soldiers drops at Mather's hand. Sir dispatches the second and doesn't break stride—he crouches an arm's length back from the cell.

"Greer," he whispers in relief.

Greer looks up. "William," he says as if he bumped into him on the street. He looks past him. "Mather." Then to me as I step into the light.

He smiles.

"My queen." *Clank, clank.* "He told me you'd come."

I look beyond him, into the cell. "Where's Finn?"

Greer smiles, a feverish grin. One quick flick of my magic, and I can feel the Decay inside him, a deep and thorough store that Angra no doubt spent days pumping into him. He's had free rein of Jannuari—any Winterian here would easily fall victim to the Decay without my magic's protection.

Clank, clank. "King Angra rid us of those who wish to bar the world from change," he coos, attention on the cup again. "King Angra killed the weak one. King Angra—"

He continues babbling, banging that cup harder with each word, but I block him out.

Angra killed Finn.

The pain of his death drops alongside all the others I've lost. So much loss, still, always, nothing but loss, even here.

I pull resolve over myself. Angra knew I'd find Greer, so he knew I wouldn't leave him here, possessed by the Decay, when I have the ability to purge him of it, since he's a Winterian. But I won't stop from helping my people just because Angra planned something. He's taken so much else from us—he won't take my ability to help them.

I launch a stream of magic at Greer, wiping the Decay from his body in one icy jolt. Clean and swift, as it should have been with Phil. But in the deepest, truest part of Greer, he doesn't want the Decay to possess him. He doesn't believe it will save him, not like Phil did.

Greer stops midsentence, gaping up at me.

"My queen," he says. His eyes scramble over Sir, Mather, and he drops the cup, coming onto his knees as he grips the bars in two tight fists. "Where are the others? Did you bring an army? Tell me you brought more than—"

"An army would have been impractical, under the circumstances," Sir answers.

Greer's laugh is almost a sob. "You've come to reclaim Winter."

"In a way."

He bends toward Sir. "I've heard footsteps for hours, marching above. Theron has soldiers in the ballroom with him." Greer's eyes turn to me. "He's waiting for you."

I clamp my jaw and glance up at the ceiling.

"Dozens of men," Greer says, as if reading the calculations on my face. "My queen, you need more help."

"Or a diversion." I look at Mather.

He darkens, the dancing light of the one sconce in this hall casting him even more concerned. "We're not letting you go in alone."

"Alone?" Sir rises, but by the time he's up, he realizes what I mean. "You want us to call the soldiers out of the ballroom."

I nod. "I can handle Theron. I can even purge the Decay from the Winterians in Jannuari like I did with Greer—you can have other fighters to help you—"

But Sir cuts his hand through the air. "No. No civilian causalities. Mather and I can keep the soldiers occupied for long enough on our own."

Mather eyes his father. "Two against dozens?" He smiles slightly and shrugs. "We've had worse odds."

Greer pulls himself up the bars. "*Three* against dozens." He pauses, leaning all his weight on the iron, and an almost imperceptible wince rocks his features as he meets my eyes again. "Finn. My queen, I'm sorry. Angra——"

"No," I say. I need to choose strength right now.

Sir is silent for a moment, no doubt pushing away his own memories of Finn. After a pause, he notes the injuries on Greer's body and looks at me. I move to work.

His injuries are easy to heal, though they churn my stomach as I pour magic into him. Angra has been torturing him with more than the Decay—far more. But I say nothing about it, and when I finish moments later, Greer grunts in relief and stretches.

"I haven't felt this good in years," he mumbles as Sir works to pick the lock on his cell.

I step down the hall before the door is even fully open. Angra tortured him. Truly, unrepentantly tortured him, and still the Decay made him mumble in devotion to Angra.

So what has Angra done to Theron? What state will I find him in? And, worse still, what state is the rest of my kingdom in? Are the Winterians in Jannuari all walking around with just as much mad passion for Angra as Greer showed?

I ball my hands into fists. It doesn't matter. Soon they'll

be free. Soon *everyone* will be free.

Mather puts his hand around one of my fists. "Don't go in until the room is clear."

"I know."

"We'll try to stay near the palace so you can find us when you're done. You can sense us with your magic. Or should we—"

"Mather." I turn to him just as we reach the staircase that will take us up to the first floor. "This is *our* kingdom. We can survive this."

He puts his other hand on my cheek, his thumb glancing back and forth over my temple. "That's not the part that worries me."

I kiss him, quick and hard. "I'll be all right."

He presses me even tighter against him. "Yes, you will," he tells me.

I pull back, unable to meet his eyes, so I look at Sir. "After you, General."

Sir pauses for a moment, lips parted as if he wants to say something. But he only nods and pushes ahead of me to lead Mather and Greer up the staircase. I trail behind them, keeping time with their quiet footsteps, all the while letting half of my focus float to the ballroom. Theron is still there, unmoved, waiting for me. I recheck the barrier over Jannuari—Angra can't come.

It will be just Theron and me.

At the top of the staircase, Sir darts to the right, forging a path toward a side door on the eastern edge of the palace. Mather shoots me one last look, weighted with purpose and surety in the way he tries to smile, and they're gone, leaving me alone in the dark, quiet hall.

There is one last thing I can do for them, though. I close my eyes, suck in a breath, and funnel a powerful surge of magic into Mather, Sir, and Greer, bleeding strength into their bodies.

I breathe in and turn down the hall, opposite them.

No soldiers guard these halls; no further traps lie in wait for me. The only noise is the creaking and groaning of the broken palace, occasional flurries of dust raining from the ceiling. When I catch glimpses out the windows, the roads are empty, the only inhabitants stray spirals of snowflakes that spin on gusts of wind.

If I couldn't sense Theron, I would almost believe this kingdom was deserted again.

Finally, the hall ends in looming double doors that hold the ballroom behind them. I stop, one hand on the curving knob and my ear to the crack between them.

Metal clanks. Someone whispers harsh orders before everything falls silent.

The soldiers are still within.

I pause, my attention split between listening to the ballroom and watching the hall behind me. After a few heartbeats of anticipation, each moment stacking atop the last to create a trembling wall of expectancy, it all comes crashing down when a shout echoes through the ballroom.

"Attack!"

"Intruders, spotted outside—"

A voice, then. One I know well.

"After them!"

Theron's order spurs the soldiers into action. The pounding of booted feet fills the ballroom in such a deliberate rush that I can't tell which direction they're marching. Panic sings through my chest and I fly back from the door, holding flat against the wall should they burst through this way. But a moment passes, and the chaos fades through the main doors, retreating into a battle for Mather, Sir, and Greer while I'm left with an empty ballroom.

And Theron.

Because he's still there. I can feel him, a sparking sensation that eats at my heart as my magic reacts to his. Close, so close . . .

I ease away from the wall and approach the door again, fingers around the handle. No time for hesitation—the longer this drags out, the longer the battle has to rage outside the palace.

So I pull open the door and march into my ballroom, head held high, muscles tense and ready for whatever might be awaiting me. An attack; a debilitating vision; a memory.

The ballroom is empty, the marble floor gleaming white. The windows carved into the southern wall have been covered with heavy black cloth that drips from the hole in the ceiling, cutting out most of the natural light. Tendrils of it peek through, though, slivers of white that let me see the only person still here.

Theron, in the middle of the room, arms behind his back and chin level.

His dark eyes latch onto mine as if he knew exactly where I'd be. The moment he sees me, his expression is so *him*, so happy and calm, that I almost forget what he is now, all he's done.

"My queen," he says. "Welcome home."

Ceridwen

EVERYTHING CERIDWEN KNEW about Autumnian warriors proved true.

Never had she seen such dedicated soldiers. The moment Meira and her group left—flame and heat, the moment they'd agreed to go to war at all—every body bound for fighting turned into a weapon, nothing more. The Autumnians were calm, their eyes alert, their muscles taut, so each of them resembled more a beast on a hunt than a person.

If they achieved ferocity like this without a female monarch who could use their conduit magic to give them strength, how much more intimidating would they be with one?

Ceridwen caught herself. Magic would never again be an influence in their lives after today—a welcome change that would level their out-of-balance world. But to have been able to see the Autumnians spurred by both natural and magical abilities would have been spectacular.

As Ceridwen jogged back to the main tent for one final meeting with Caspar, she couldn't stop herself from glancing west, toward wherever the new camp was that held the loved ones of every person in this army. Caspar's family, Lekan's family, her family.

Appreciation nestled inside her heart, and she shot wordless looks of thanks at every Autumnian soldier she passed. They would need such fierce, dedicated fighters on their side. They would need all the help they could get.

Lekan pulled his horse up alongside her and dismounted just outside the tent. "Our soldiers are centered in the valley; the Yakimians too. Caspar's infantry surrounds them. If Angra wants to break through, he'll have to pay dearly in blood."

"Angra has never been afraid to pay such a toll before."

Lekan winced. "You excel at motivational speeches."

"Everyone is well aware of what we're doing here." Ceridwen ducked into the open-air tent, weaving around tables strewn with maps and weapons. "And the cost that will come."

"In less than two hours now." Caspar didn't look up from the map he crouched over in the center of the tent. "My scouts got a more specific location—Angra's army should be here this afternoon. Are you fighting?"

Now he looked at Ceridwen.

"I'm not very good at letting my people risk their lives without me," she said.

Lekan cleared his throat. If Caspar wasn't intending to fight, she had as good as called him a coward.

But Caspar smiled. "Nor I," he said. "You'll be with your fighters, I take it?"

Ceridwen nodded. She and Lekan had worked this out already. "The front lines."

"And I'll be with my cavalry." Caspar rose, waving his hand to beckon someone forward. Winterians moved in, the same group that had escorted Jesse's children out of Rintiero—the Thaw, Meira had called them.

"But if we're both in the fray, we'll need a way to communicate." Caspar bobbed his head at the Winterians. "They have offered to run information between us during the battle."

Ceridwen bowed her head in gratitude. Such jobs often brought quicker deaths.

And when she opened her mouth to thank them, any words retreated deep behind her warrior's instinct, one built up over years of constant fighting and struggle.

A horn sounded. One of the many held by Autumnians posted around the perimeter of the valley, keeping watch for approaching attacks from the forward or rear. This one came blaring out from the Winter side of the valley, a distant blast that made everyone in the tent shift as one.

Caspar spun to face Ceridwen, his brows creasing.

"So soon?" Ceridwen was the one to ask.

But Caspar was already gathering what supplies he'd need from the tent. A few maps, assorted weapons scattered over the table. "Or Angra's reinforcements, arrived ahead of him," he said. When he looked back up at her, his eyes softened.

"You'll be at the front, so I'll leave the charge to you," he said. "To war, Princess Ceridwen—*Queen* Ceridwen."

That stabbed into her with more force than any physical blow. She *was* Summer's queen now, wasn't she? Or she would be, once Summer was actually hers again. And then there'd be the whole messy business of figuring out how to rule both Summer *and* Ventralli, now that she was married to Jesse. . . .

But that was a problem she would gladly face, once all this was over.

"To the future, King Caspar," she returned.

He nodded at her and left as more horns sounded, more scouts seeing the approaching threat and bellowing out warning. Some of the Thaw cut off to trail Caspar while the rest followed her and Lekan, making for a mismatched group that headed out of the tent. No horses now—they would fight on foot alongside the refugee warriors she had stood with for years.

The horns sent shock waves throughout their small camp. Medical tents prepared for the expected influx of wounded; weapons tents clanked with blacksmiths hurrying to sharpen every blade they had. It all bled into one goal—so much so that Ceridwen swore they all breathed on the same beat.

She clung to that as she led her group out of the camp area and into the valley. Bodies pressed side by side, stoic and ready soldiers who parted for her. She wove through them all—Summerians, Yakimians, Autumnians—her pride swelling with each resolute face she saw.

Maybe they could do this. Not only distract Angra long enough for Meira to succeed, but actually *defeat* his army.

Ceridwen reached the front line and stepped forward, her boots trampling the grass. Trees capped the opposite end, evergreens with bowing branches heavy with snow. Those trees held her attention for the next minutes, the next hours, her eyes snapping back and forth, looking for any sign of soldiers rushing to attack, of Angra thrusting his evil magic at them.

So she saw right away when the first rider emerged.

Caspar had placed Angra's soldiers a few hours away. It didn't make sense for them to be here so soon.

Now they were all Ceridwen could see. Her fingers tightened around the hilts of her knives. Caspar was right—these were reinforcements.

"That isn't Angra's army," she growled. "Again."

Lekan didn't move. He had come to the same conclusion she had. Just as in the attack a few days ago, Angra had sent others to do his bidding, like deluges of rain wearing away at a mountain, priming the area for a landslide.

The woman who led the army out of Winter's trees was, to Ceridwen, such a distraction. A deluge of rain and a landslide and a frigid, howling storm all in one.

Raelyn.

She was nothing more than a small form on a horse, but Ceridwen knew that form. She could feel the disdain that emanated from Jesse's ex-wife the moment she appeared. Ventrallan soldiers materialized from the forest, marching after her with measured steps.

"Run a message to Caspar," Ceridwen snapped at one of the Thaw near her. "Tell him this isn't all of it."

The boy nodded and slipped away.

Who knew how many soldiers Raelyn had brought with her? How many blades she had added to this war? Ventrallan soldiers had been reportedly coming to join Angra's forces, but they should have been still sailing down the Feni. Clearly, Raelyn had cut off from directly joining Angra and been sent here first.

It didn't matter. The only thing it changed was that now Ceridwen had a personal goal that sputtered fuel into her heart.

Meira had explained the magic they would face. Raelyn had *chosen* such magic when Ventralli's conduit could have kept her safe—everything she had done to Jesse, to her children, to Ceridwen, had been her choice.

And she would die for it.

Ceridwen stepped forward, sucking air deep into her lungs and holding it as the Ventrallan army drew steadily closer, Raelyn at their lead. She wasn't a fighter—which meant she wanted Ceridwen to see her. She wanted the coming confrontation.

That makes two of us.

The Ventrallans were paces from where the Winter side of the field ended. Nearly halfway across the valley.

The anticipation building in Ceridwen's chest grew painful, and she could feel the same need rippling through the soldiers.

Fight, fight, FIGHT—

Her fingers clenched around one of her knives. She lifted it, blade pointing at the approaching Ventrallans, arm straight and rigid while heartbeats fluttered through her.

The army behind her drew a collective breath. Weapons shifted into position, feet shuffled to brace against the ground.

Lekan brushed his fingers over her shoulder.

Ceridwen screamed. *Attack, go, fight, NOW*—some combination of all those words. It bubbled up from the depths of her as she tore out of the ranks of the infantry, the first to barrel headlong toward the Ventrallan army.

Meira

"MEIRA," THERON SAYS, easing forward, his hands extended.

I let the door swing shut behind me, the resounding thud matching the rhythm of my heart thumping against my ribs. He looks so happy.

He looks so *eager.*

"You've been expecting me," I say, a gentle poke to see how high the flames will go.

Another step closer. "I knew you'd come."

"You didn't go out with your men."

Theron's lips curve up. "Neither did you."

He stands there, watching, and the pieces click.

Greer, telling us that soldiers waited above. Theron, remaining in the ballroom. Me, sending my only support out to create a diversion.

It was part of Angra's trap. Getting me alone.

It really is just Theron and me—and suddenly the thought is terrifying.

Theron continues easing forward, his head tipped to one side so his golden hair makes a curtain across his shoulder. "You don't know the agony you've put me through," he says, only two arm's lengths away from me now.

I let him creep closer, my eyes pinned to his as I try to take stock of the situation. He has no weapons, his green and gold Cordellan uniform unadorned. A slight lump sits against his chest, just to the right of his collarbone. The keys?

A bit of my tension ripples away. He has them.

But a new worry quickly arises. Angra gave Theron the keys for the exact reason I knew he would—to get me to stay here. The longer I stay, talking with Theron, the better chance he has of weakening me. If those keys weren't here, I'd grab Sir, Mather, and Greer and be gone before we could fall into any traps.

Now, though, I'm stuck. Just like Angra wants.

"Likewise," I reply. But whatever meaning he takes from my words sends relief pooling over his features, beaming as he closes the space between us.

"I knew it," he declares and grabs my hand.

Touching him sparks the connection I feel whenever I come into skin-to-skin contact with another conduit-bearer. Seeing into their past, their memories, even their emotions at that moment—Theron opens himself to me when his skin touches mine.

I see Theron, waiting for me, pacing the halls of my palace, overseeing my kingdom with the same smugness I attributed to his father.

Theron, talking to Angra in Summer, in Winter; the two of them planning this moment, knowing I would come to him.

Reverence floods Theron with every memory of Angra. Adoration, devotion, so pure it breaks my heart.

I break free of Theron's touch, everything in me aching. He wants me—but this isn't human, this need. This is something fostered by the Decay. Even the expression on his face is one he would never wear, were he himself—a dark possession in the way his eyes follow me unblinking as I back away.

I force myself to meet his gaze. Force myself to stay calm, to ignore the hum of warning through my body. My instincts don't see just Theron—they see danger, a man who looks at me in a way that's almost familiar.

Herod.

Angra turned him into Herod.

My knees wobble and I buckle forward. Theron slides his arms around my waist, caging me against his body. He doesn't touch my skin again, but he's so close, *too close*—

I can't speak, can't move. I knew Angra infected him—ensnared him—but I never allowed myself to imagine that he would go this far. Of course he would—Angra knows my fears. He knows my weaknesses.

And he combined them in Theron.

"Meira," he says again, and his mouth is on mine before I can move. His arm around my waist is a vise; his lips insistent and hungry and bruising, the opposite of every other kiss I've gotten from him.

More emotions, so clear they're words spoken from his mind into my own.

This will be perfect. This is how it should be. She will love me with all the devotion I have earned from her.

Coldness wraps around me, the frigidity of my kingdom clawing at my rising panic. His touch sears me, his thoughts, the one wish he's harbored for so long that even in this brief whisper of it, every sensation feels *real*, too real, branding his body to mine—

A lump presses into my chest from his jacket. The keys. *Focus!*

I fumble with my magic to finally block his thoughts—never have I been so happy for Rares's training—and lay my hand on his jacket. Something hard and iron and distinctly key shaped sits within. The smooth velvet slides between my fingers as I reach into his pocket.

Theron's hands pinch against my shoulders and he jolts back from me. "You . . ." His eyes go to his pocket, then to my hand, fingers reaching toward it. "You didn't come for me," he states. His words echo around me, and the atmosphere of the ballroom goes from quiet and watchful to deadly. His fingers on my shoulders dig deeper. "You didn't come for me," he repeats. "You came for the keys. You came to stop Angra."

"He's infected you," I say, holding back my cry of pain as his grip nearly cracks bone. "But I promised I'd save you—"

"Promised." Theron's lips curl. "What other promises have you been making?"

He releases me by flinging me into the closed doors. I smack into the wood and use the momentum to dart away from him, not letting him keep me pinned in the corner. My shoulders scream at the new bruises he left as I stumble deeper into the ballroom.

"Angra is making the world sick," I try, hands out toward Theron in something like submission. But I ready myself as I take long, slow steps to keep him a few paces away from me.

The act of calling an object to me feels familiar now, and I launch my hand at Theron, hurling my magic at the keys to wrench them from his jacket. Theron sees me move and reacts, jolting his shoulder down and throwing up his hand to block me, a haze of Decay engulfing him in a shield.

"You don't understand his magic," he says, his eyes in slits. "You haven't seen how powerful we are now, how uninhibited. But you will understand—because I'll make you use it."

"Theron—"

He rears back as if to punch me, but he's too far away to

connect—until I note the shadow still engulfing his hand.

He's going to fight me with the Decay.

I cross my arms in front of me, flinging my magic out to draw snow from the sky—inside. It's my magic, my kingdom, and I will not be denied winter *in Winter*.

Clouds form above me, sheets of ice that respond to my call.

But too late.

Just as the first sheet of snow falls toward us, Theron's shadow barrels through the air and sends me crashing against the floor. I gag, the breath knocked out of me, but Theron is crossing the room, so I leap to my feet, tugging down a wall of ice as he sends another blast of Decay.

"Attack me!" he screams. "This is how Angra said it opened his mind—he used magic for *himself*. No one has ever let you do that, have they? Be selfish for once in your life, Meira. Fight me! You'll feel its power. You'll see how wrong you were."

My ice wall reverberates with the force of his blows, forming cracks that I cover with more ice. I can't stay here forever. I could fight him with magic—it would be defense, so it wouldn't feed the Decay.

But I don't want to fight him.

I drop the wall. It sloshes away, coating the floor with water. Theron waits, one hand drawn back in a fist.

I shake my head, letting some of my true exhaustion shine through. "I'm tired of fighting," I tell him, and it isn't a lie. "If peace is what you offer, I want it."

Theron relaxes, lowering his hand. I almost say more, feed into the lie, when he flicks his wrist and every muscle in my body sings out with pain.

He stalks forward, his lips cocked in a half smile.

I can't move—his magic keeps me pinned upright before him, muscles convulsing so I can't even wince as he stops, nearly pressed against me. I've used my magic only when I have a way to channel it, by pointing or shoving my arm out, and before I can try to use it without moving, Theron tips his head, his smile sending hot panic through me.

"This peace comes with a price—though it isn't a high price to pay, I assure you." He leans into me, his lips stopping a finger's width from mine.

The magic ebbs away from my head, holding the rest of my body firm. He doesn't kiss me, just stays there, waiting for me to initiate. To accept.

I pull back, just a twitch, enough to put a breath more space between us.

And this one flinch of a response is enough.

Theron knots his fingers around my braid and wrenches my head back so he stares down into my face. "It would be so easy for you," he spits, half a plea, half a snarl. "Yet you reject me *again*. Even when peace is so close—when the salvation of the world is within your grasp." His face darkens and he ducks to hold his lips by my ear, easing closer, the teasing, gentle movements of a lover. His magic holds me still, my body screaming with the need to fight, the same blinding, consuming panic that overtook me in Herod's room in Abril.

This is Theron, not Herod—this is Theron, not Herod—

But my heart doesn't believe that, as it thuds painfully against my ribs.

"It's the former Winter king, isn't it? Where have you been all this time, I wonder—with him?" Theron inhales along my cheek. "You reek of him. But you've always been mine, from the moment I saved you in Abril—you belong to me, and I'll remind you of that until you forget what it was like to be touched by him."

He backs up, all hint of joy gone, and in its place, resolve.

"One more chance," he tells me. "One more chance."

It's almost a plea, so close to begging that I wonder who he's more worried for—himself or me, if I don't listen to him.

The magic keeping my body motionless releases my right arm.

"Attack me," he orders. "Embrace this new world, Meira. Please."

He's definitely begging me. The strain on his face, the worry.

"All right, Theron." I lift my hand.

He starts to smile, hoping, wanting, *needing*.

Until I grab the chakram off my back.

His face falls. "With your magic!"

But I will use my magic—kind of.

The snowstorm still hangs over us, and I call down sheet after sheet of ice to wrap around my chakram's blade.

I'm so sorry, Theron.

My chakram flies at him as he leaps at me, and the two collide. The ice coating my chakram's blade turns it into a dense knot that cracks against Theron's head. He drops to the floor alongside it, falling unconscious at my feet.

His magic releases the moment he goes down, and I stagger toward him, my hand instantly scrambling to his neck. I sigh in relief—a pulse. Faint yet steady.

I reach for his pocket. Cold pieces of metal meet my palm, and I yank them out, staring down at the two keys I spent weeks searching for not so long ago. I wait, expecting relief to flood through me, but all I feel is the gentle nudge of duty.

To the labyrinth, now. This isn't over yet.

Then I realize—I'm touching the keys but receiving no visions. Nothing about what I need to do to access the magic; nothing to prepare me, as happened the first time I touched these keys. I check them, but they're definitely the ones I found weeks ago.

I guess that means . . . I must be ready.

I release the ice on my chakram and holster it. Theron doesn't so much as moan when I start for the doors, and each footstep I take away from him matches how many times I promise silently that I'll save him.

The courtyard is in chaos.

Shouting Cordellans cluster in groups, relaying information about where the Winterian attackers were last spotted. Some say west, some east—but thanks to my magic, I can tell they're spread out, one darting over rooftops north of the palace, one east, and one west, each of them flinging whatever projectiles they can to draw the soldiers into attack.

So when I step out onto the front steps, the already infuriated soldiers turn on me.

"The queen!"

"After her!"

The snow clouds over the city hang thick and gray, fat with condensation. I launch my hands up, calling down every flake in one furious pull.

Icy shards catch in breathtaking gales; gusts of white blind everyone in the courtyard. The Cordellans howl at the onslaught of the blizzard, armor clanking and feet stomping.

To Mather, Sir, and Greer, I fling one powerful will for them to meet me north of the palace, then I launch myself there as well. My magic dumps me into the street paces from flailing Cordellan soldiers, fists punching wildly in the storm. Other forms come into view through the onslaught of icy fury—Mather and Sir, crouching against a building across the road.

I send my magic shooting out, urging them in a wordless certainty to run to me. Mather stumbles forward blindly, and I can tell when my magic no longer needs to lead him— he makes me out in the blizzard and plummets forward, scooping me into a crushing hug so wondrously different from Theron's that I moan.

Sir reaches us, but I don't have time for words—I grab his hand.

"Where's Greer?" I shout over the gale.

Sir shakes his head. "He'll take care of things for us."

I don't have time to argue. I bury my face into Mather, tighten my fingers on Sir, and send us spiraling for the entrance to the chasm, leaving Theron and my city in the nothingness of the blizzard.

Meira

TORCHES ILLUMINATE A room that looks just as I remember it—the diamond-patterned floor; the moist condensation of magic in the air; the door with its elaborate carvings a few paces behind where I put us, just toward the front of the room beside the invisible barrier, our first obstacle to reaching the chasm.

The last time I was here, the world was a completely different place. Theron was with me, my ally instead of my enemy; I stood in front of this door with awe and apprehension, not determination and resolve.

The biggest difference now, though, is the soldiers who wait for us along the front wall.

I rip out my chakram and let it fly.

My blade is covered with blood before Mather and Sir have even oriented themselves in the room, a wave of magic again clearing their bodies of the effects of travel. They turn, join the fight, and in seconds the Cordellans are dead, their bodies flooding the diamond-shaped carvings in the floor with thick scarlet rivers.

I sheathe my weapon and stomp toward the looming door, hands balled, eyes level.

Fingers grab my arm. "Meira, wait—"

"Don't," I snap, unable to look at Mather. "If I stop to think, I'll fall apart. Please, Mather."

I can't think about Theron's desires or Ceridwen and Caspar fighting my war or Conall and Nikoletta back at camp or Rares and Oana—snow, what are they even doing? Have they succeeded in gathering support? Did something happen to them?

Mather holds, grip softening.

"All right. How do we get in?"

I scrub at my eyes and reel to the door. "Together."

Sir falls in on my other side, and where his silence would usually send me into a spiral of frustration, I'm unendingly grateful for it now.

The three of us line up, facing the door.

"Remember," I whisper, "we have to be united in our desire to reach the chasm."

Mather takes my hand, weaving our fingers together, and squeezes. "We're with you."

Sir takes my hand too. "To the end," he says. That's all. No *my queen*—just his support.

I know, then, that I made the right decision. There's no

one else I'd rather have with me.

We start walking, taking slow, deliberate steps across the room. Each draws us closer to the barrier, and I hold my breath, my body remembering the horrid sensation of the barrier shredding my nerves.

I fight to keep from wincing as we cross the middle of the room, the invisible barrier. But we keep walking, with no obstacles or pain, and the moment we pass, every particle of air seems to take a collective breath. The density of magic takes on a new aura—where it had felt present yet still, humidity choking the air with power, it sparks against my skin now, tiny bursts of alertness that flood me with an undeniable sense of purpose.

The labyrinth wants us here—the *magic* wants us here.

Maybe the whole time Primoria wanted to rediscover the magic chasm, the chasm wanted to be rediscovered itself.

We stop just before the door. Mather shivers next to me. "This is . . . incredible."

Sir echoes his wonder with a breathy snort. "Now what?"

Always the pragmatist. I release their hands and slide forward another cautious step. The door stands a few paces away, but there's no knob that I can see, just those keyholes in the carvings of vines, books, and masks near the symbol of the Order of the Lustrate in the center.

I take the keys off the chain around my neck and hand one to Sir, one to Mather. They approach the keyholes on either side of the one I pick and lift their keys.

Does it matter which key fits which hole? I guess we'll find out.

"On three," I say, and count it out. We plunge our keys into the holes, twist, and . . . wait. They all fit, but nothing happens.

I step back from the wall. "Maybe we need to—"

But my voice is ripped from my throat by a sudden onslaught of darkness.

Mather and Sir yelp. My body registers the weightlessness of falling as the torches' light fades above me. The fall makes my panic have to scramble to catch up with me as I smack into the wall of a tunnel sloping ever downward, careening me into the earth.

Mather and Sir aren't in this tunnel with me—not that I can tell, at least. By the time I catch my breath, the tunnel dumps me onto a smooth stone floor, the darkness giving way to harsh, bright light that's somehow . . . ancient.

I'm not sure there's a spot on my body that isn't bruised. A moan gurgles in my throat as I roll onto my elbows, head still spinning.

But that disorientation retracts on a burst of clarity when I turn over and find that the stone floor just *ends*.

I scramble back, heart galloping anew.

I'm on a ledge, at least seven stories in the air, over a long, rectangular room. The tunnel that dumped me here offers the only way off the ledge, but one glance at the smooth stone of the walls and I know climbing isn't an option.

I stand, one hand to a particularly nasty bruise on my temple. The residual panic from the fall leaves a metallic taste on my tongue. This has to be the first test of our worthiness. What did the Order's clue say?

Three people the labyrinth demands
Who enter with genuine intent
To face a test of leadership,
A maze of humility,
And purification of the heart.
To be completed by only the true.

This will be the test of leadership.

My arm drops. Rares said the Order wasn't told what the actual tasks would be, beyond this message, and I haven't wondered what they could be either. Partly because I had no idea where to even begin wondering, and partly because a piece of me didn't really believe I'd get here.

But I *am* here. In the labyrinth. A place no one else has reached in centuries.

I take a deep breath. I've come this far. I can make it through these tests too.

Roaring fire pits crown the room. A circular dais waits directly below me, too far to jump without receiving a number of broken bones, and beyond it, a wall rises halfway up, cutting the entire room down the middle.

I drop to my knees and bend over the edge, trying to

get a better view. Like the floor of the entrance chamber, this floor seems to be carved—but not into diamonds, into platforms. Mismatched shapes spread from wall to wall on either side of the divide, and the edges are carved deeper than normal, giving the illusion that each platform stands independent of the rest.

That would have been odd enough, but as I lean forward to get a better view, my fingers touch something cold on the ledge. I jerk back, hand tingling in a way I know all too well—conduit magic.

A small silver oval sits embedded in the rock, coated with the fine brown dust of years. I use the hem of my sleeve to wipe the dust clear—and laugh.

It's a mirror. At first glance, it looks like any other mirror, but as I tip my head to the side, the light catches and reveals a luminescent picture—the Order of the Lustrate's seal. Just like the one I found in Yakim's library. This one, though, is firmly planted in the stone; it's not a gear to be cranked as the one in Yakim was. I frown at it, then press my finger to its reflective surface.

Instantly the platforms below me start to softly glow—green, white, brown, red, maroon, silver, gold, and purple.

Snow above—these are the colors of the *conduits*. White for Winter, brown for Autumn, red for Summer, silver for Ventralli, gold for Yakim, and purple for Cordell. The green and maroon must be for Spring and Paisly.

Again my hand starts to tingle, and I know this mirrored

plate has been infused with magic as the keys were. When I touched those keys, they showed me visions of what I needed to do to reach the chasm. Maybe this plate will show me what I need to do next? It makes sense—if the Order created this labyrinth to keep unworthy souls out, they'd still want a worthy soul to pass it someday, to rid the world of magic, as was their original goal. But how to make sure a worthy soul would pass the tests when the time came?

I lower the barriers I have around my mind and open myself to whatever help the plate can offer.

A single scene flows into my mind—the platforms below me, the colors glowing brighter in pairs. One green platform on the left side; one green on the right side. And on and on, starting at the other end of the room and finishing below me, at the dais just under my ledge.

I pull back, confused. I'm not given long to think on it—shouting pulls me to my feet so I can peer down the length of the room. At the ends of both sides, small holes of black release two figures onto circular daises like the one below me. Mather and Sir tumble out, one on each side of the divide, separated from me by the long expanse of glowing platforms.

"Are you all right?" I call, my question echoing off the towering walls.

My voice jerks Mather's head up. "Yes." He leaps to his feet, stumbles to the edge of the dais. "Are you?"

Sir rises too, his eyes darting over the room. When he

looks at me, he squares his body as though he expects a fight to come storming in at any moment.

"I'm fine," I shout, ignoring every injury that says otherwise. "The labyrinth is testing us."

I glance over the room again. Mather is on the left side of the divide; Sir is on the right. The vision of the matching platforms created a haphazard path from them to me.

Realization sparks like a wildfire.

"I think you have to get to me." I point at the dais that sits where the divided wall ends below me.

Sir surveys the platforms. "This seems elaborate for such a simple task."

But Mather shrugs. "I'm not just going to stand here."

And he steps off the dais, onto a platform that glows silver. It drops under his weight. He stumbles, arms flailing, and as the floor sinks beneath him, the gaps around the platform release something that makes me shout a warning. Not that he needs the warning—the moment the flames burst around the platform, shooting up to his waist, Mather curses and stumbles back onto the dais, beating the fire that caught on his pants.

The platform returns to normal, the flames extinguishing as if they never existed at all.

I wobble forward, rocks skittering off under my boots and shattering on the ground below. I recognize this too. From where I found the key in Summer—the pit that opened up, the fire ring at the bottom. This is far more severe, though, and falling into these pits seems like a quick way to get incinerated.

Sir paces his platform, attention cutting from me to the wall that separates him and Mather. "What? What happened?"

"Fire happened," Mather shouts back. "It looks like we have to cross the room *without* stepping on the platforms."

Sir crosses his arms, analyzing the rest of the space around him. "We could—"

"Wait!" I shout. "You have to step on the same platforms on each side. I'll guide you."

Mather eyes me, hands still out like he expects the entire floor to give way. Sir looks equally pensive, but he steps to the edge of his dais. They both wait.

My heart sputters. This is the test—leadership. Testing my ability to lead, and their ability to follow.

Months ago—snow, even *weeks* ago—I would have shriveled at the thought of being the one to give orders and expect them to be followed. I'd have been weighed down by thoughts that Sir would be better than me in this situation, or Mather, and that I should have been the one following, the soldier meant to facelessly carry out missions.

But I can't afford doubt. Yes, I harbored fear the whole time, but being a competent, worthy leader doesn't mean being *only* competent and worthy—it means being so despite whatever emotions might arise.

I draw in a breath, my heart flapping until concentration

breaks away everything else.

"Mather—to the green platform. Sir—green, on your right. Mather—red, just ahead. Sir—jump over the brown platform and land on the other red one—"

My hands snap out to point at the corresponding platforms that I saw in the vision; my orders are clear and unwavering. Every muscle hums with adrenaline, every nerve flickers in alertness as I take stock of the platforms around them and calculate which ones they need to reach.

Mather and Sir hop from platform to platform, faltering as each one locks into place. They don't hesitate to listen to me, don't question how I know what they need to do, as if obeying orders from me is a natural state for them.

I hardly recognize the woman standing on the ledge over the room, spouting orders with all the confidence of a queen. Once, Mather lands on a platform a breath before Sir and the whole thing plummets down, fire bursting up around him in a spiral of orange and yellow heat. But I scream for Sir to jump, jump *now*, and he obeys in time so that both their platforms level out safely.

The fate of everyone I love hangs on me getting Mather and Sir through this.

And I know, above everything else, that I will not fail.

Finally, they leap simultaneously onto the circular dais below me. I drop to my knees, beaming at them as they share a relieved look.

I almost say something to them, but the labyrinth

doesn't allow us that luxury this time.

The ledge I'm on tips, along with their dais.

"Not again," Mather groans as the three of us go plummeting into another tunnel—this time together, a tangle of limbs and sheathed weapons and shouts that get muffled in the dusty darkness of the labyrinth.

32

Mather

THIS TUNNEL SPIT the three of them into a small square area enclosed by smooth walls. Torches flickered on three of the walls, casting enough light for Mather to sweep his eyes over Meira, checking for any injuries she might be hiding.

But she was the first on her feet, her hands absently beating her pants to remove the sheet of dust that had attached to every free space on all of them.

"That was too easy," she breathed.

Mather checked that none of his weapons had come loose during the fall and stepped beside her. "What did you expect?"

Meira shrugged and finally looked at him, holding his gaze. Looking at him, really looking at him, like she had in Autumn.

Mather weakened.

She broke the look with a tip of her head. "The next test will be of humility," she said, directing the statement to William as well, who walked deeper into the room with overly cautious steps. Two unexpected drops into mysterious tunnels had made them all a little distrustful of the floor.

"How did you know how to complete that test?" William asked her as he analyzed the room.

Meira too started looking around, though her gaze stayed on the floor. A moment passed, and she stopped, standing in the dead center of the room.

She crouched down and brushed away dirt. The torches caught whatever she had revealed—a mirror? And from this angle, Mather could see the symbol that had decorated Rares and Oana's compound carved into the reflective surface. The beam of light hitting a mountaintop.

Meira pressed her hand to the mirror and stayed there, body hard. Mather's gut cramped even tighter with anxiety. When she looked up, she shot William a steady gaze.

"The Order created the labyrinth to keep out anyone who would abuse magic," she said. "But they eventually wanted someone worthy to reach the chasm to destroy all magic—so they left these plates, just like they left the keys I found." She waved her hand when she saw both Mather and William's brows furrowed. "I never told you about that, but it doesn't matter—they're conduits, infused with enough magic to show a vision whenever a conduit-wielder intent on reaching the chasm touches them. The last mirror showed me the path you needed to take to get across the room."

"What did this one show you?" William asked. He accepted her explanation so easily. Not that Mather expected him to fight her; but Mather had to clamp his jaw shut to keep from making a lot of worthless statements, like *These people put a lot of faith in a pure conduit-wielder getting into the labyrinth* and *They're helping you die faster. I hate them.*

Meira stood, frowning at the walls of the room. Mather followed her gaze—

And nearly leaped back into the tunnel.

This place did terrible things to his soldier's instincts— his every muscle was poised for attack, his every thought was about drawing his weapons. But so far, they had seen no physical enemies, just the itching sensation of an ambush coming with every breath.

If this was how they were going to go out, lured to some fantastic end with no enemy save for mystical tunnels and glowing platforms, Mather would go mad long before death.

What Meira was frowning at, what Mather had *sworn* wasn't there moments ago, were doors. Three of them in the walls now, beside each torch.

Meira neared the door on the left, her hands slung idly in the straps of her chakram's holster.

"There are three doors," she said. "And three of us."

Mather balked. "We have to split up?"

The refusal must have been clear in his voice, because

Meira's shoulders drooped a little. Mather bit back further retort. This was hard enough on her without him questioning her every thought—but what did she expect from him? That he'd wordlessly agree to every idea that drew her closer to death?

There were three tasks, though. This was only the second. They would get through this and still have one more before Mather had to figure out a way to save her.

And maybe this damn labyrinth would produce an answer on its own.

"Fine," he conceded. "I'll take the middle one."

He started toward it, but Meira intercepted him. Her body pressed against him, her mouth on his in a still, frozen kiss, like she wanted to simply absorb how it felt.

"This is a maze of humility," she said. "We're on our own for it. That was all this plate showed me—a maze, each of us standing alone."

Mather chuckled. "Why do I get the feeling you're worried for me?"

"Well, you aren't the most humble man I know."

"My lady, I'm hurt that you have so little faith in me."

As Meira let him go, her face wore the same look she had given them in the last test—confident and serious and fiercely attentive.

She glared at William, who lingered at the door on the right, watching them with an expression that triggered Mather's need to defend his relationship with her again.

But William just dropped his head in a reverent bow.

"We'll see you on the other side," he told her. "Wherever that might be."

Meira and William each lifted the torch from beside their door and took it with them, ducking into darkness that abated in a steady pool of light from their flames. Mather drew in a breath and waited, motionless, until both Meira's and William's lights had been swallowed by the blackness farther on. When neither screamed for help, Mather squared his shoulders and approached the door in the center, the light twitching as he lifted the torch. Iron formed the base for a knot of fuel, oil most likely, and he shuddered to wonder how it had come to be here after so many thousands of years.

The flame licked heat onto his fingers, and he stepped through the door, creeping forward in small increments. Walls rose around him, ending before the ceiling but still too high for him to climb, and a thick layer of rubble and dust coated the floor.

He'd taken only two steps inside when a whoosh of air assaulted his back. Mather ripped a knife free and turned, crouched low, his eyes flying over the wall behind him.

The *wall* behind him? The door, the opening that led back to the room they had been dumped in, was gone.

Mather hurled his shoulder against the newly appeared wall, knowing even as he did that it wouldn't budge. This test really had meant to split them up.

The flame in his hand flared brighter for a flash as he whirled back to face the hall, his breath tight in his throat. Nowhere to go, now, but forward.

His steps became less cautious the farther he went, meandering deeper into the maze. Turns opened every so often, halls branching off to the left or right, forks splitting the path in two, dead ends popping up at blind corners.

Mather slapped the wall of another dead end, his fifth so far. Now he knew why Meira had feared for him—he'd never been good at things like this, tasks that required patience and analysis and a keen, clever mind. Meira would have no trouble with this. William wouldn't, either. They were probably both right now waiting for him wherever this test dumped them, conspiring about how best to go into the maze and save him.

Great—he'd come on this journey to save Meira, and she'd be the one who would have to save *him*.

Mather pivoted, stomping back to the last place he'd made a wrong turn. No—he'd get through this damn maze. He'd figure out this labyrinth's secrets and resolve some way to make this all nothing more than an adventurous story they'd tell their children one day.

He shifted a knife out to scrape an X into the left side of the wall where he made a left turn. Now if he passed it again, he'd know he was going in circles and to turn right instead.

A few more steps, then he carved another X.

A branch of four halls. Right this time. X.

Mather shifted the pack that clung to his chest, the contents scraping against his back. Sweat crept down his spine and smeared in greasy streaks over his face, but he brushed his dirt-matted hair back with his wrist and carved an X as he turned right again.

Another branching hall. Mather made to carve a marker as he turned left—

But growled at the stone when an X already stared up at him. He *was* going in circles.

Mather flung himself backward, dove at the right hall, stopping only to carve a shaky X on this one. Right, right, left, straight—

Until he met a hall with X's carved at every turn.

"Damn it!" he swore.

Mather took off at a run, jogging straight, left, straight, taking the most directly forward path he could. No more circles, no more turns if he could help it—

Back again to the hall with X's at every corner.

If the labyrinth wanted to play it like that . . .

He tossed the torch to the ground, the flame flaring up as it clattered on the stone, but the light held. He didn't think about it extinguishing; he didn't think about much of anything beyond the frustration of these halls, the darkness stretching ever onward, the walls pressing around in stances that seemed almost mocking. Could walls mock him? *These* walls could, and as Mather attacked the one closest to him, he swore he could hear it laughing.

His dagger chipped furiously at the stone, carving a rudimentary foothold. And another, slightly higher; still another, and another, until Mather had to lift himself up onto the first ones to carve more. Slowly he carved his way up, chipping rock in a flurry of projectiles.

Mather jammed his dagger into the wall about an arm's length from the top. One more foothold, and he'd be able to stand atop it and see this maze—at least as far as his light would show.

But as Mather wrestled to pull another chunk of rock free, the wall . . . *trembled*.

He stiffened, legs braced in his crude footholds, both his hands wrapped around the dagger embedded in the wall. A second shudder ran up the stone, this one more deliberate, and without further warning, every foothold Mather had carved vanished.

He scrambled against the now-smooth wall, only his knife remaining as support. But even that failed him as the wall seemed to eject it like an arrow from a bow. Mather dropped, his body bumping against the stone as he slid down at least twice his height before collapsing with a thud—

On his torch.

The light snuffed out beneath him, encasing the maze in darkness.

Mather had thought he understood darkness. The time

they'd spent in the Rania Plains had given new meaning to the word, when moonless nights would fall and their fires would go out. Storm clouds rolled in sometimes, casting gray hues to the blackness, and Mather remembered standing at the edge of camp, petrified, but forcing himself to endure the slithering feeling of being blind yet surrounded. Enemies could be right before his eyes but he, lost, disoriented, was unable to see them no matter how hard he strained.

That was what he feared most: being unable to perceive danger even if it was right before his eyes.

Like with Meira.

Mather leaped to his feet, fresh blades in both hands, ears straining to compensate for his lack of sight. Thoughts of her fueled his drive, urging him into a frenzy.

Yes, like with Meira. Like how, even as he lay next to her at night, even as he kissed her and touched her and had her *right beside him*, he couldn't see what danger possessed her. He couldn't protect her.

He couldn't protect her.

Mather slashed out at nothing.

"Damn it!" he screamed when he slammed into a wall, the stone tearing into his shoulder. "DAMN IT!"

He spun, stabbing, sweat pouring in waves down his body.

If he didn't get out of here, he wouldn't be able to protect her. She'd go on with William to the next test, and after that, William would let her die. She'd walk into whatever end she had planned, one Mather couldn't see, an enemy crouched in darkness and stealth, waiting with eager, unforgiving hands to destroy the best part of his life.

"No!" One of Mather's blades caught the wall and twisted out of his hand, clattering into the darkness. His muscles ached, his throat burned with thirst, and he slumped against the wall, forehead to the dusty stone.

No. She wouldn't die. *She wouldn't die.* He would save her. He would get out of here—damn it, *he would get out of here*—

Mather dropped to the ground, knees banging on the floor. He'd never felt this helpless, not even when Herod had captured Meira. Something about this place, this darkness, the looming threat of losing her, made every fear and doubt and hatred rear in his heart. Every bone in his body ached, and he caved forward, wanting to lash out, wanting to dissolve.

"You aren't the most humble man I know" came a voice.

Mather exhaled, dust puffing in a cloud that coated his face.

"This is a test of humility. You aren't the most humble man I know."

"Meira!" He launched to his feet, stumbling forward. "Meir—"

He stopped. It wasn't her—she had said that to him before they'd parted.

Mather gulped breaths to calm himself. Was he hallucinating?

A test of humility. The tests had been designed to ensure that only those who were worthy reached the magic chasm. And humility meant being able to acknowledge your own unworthiness and admit things like . . . defeat.

Mather's instinctual reaction to that was a rumbling *Never*. It went against everything he had ever been to admit that he couldn't do something, especially when that thing involved Meira. No—he'd figure out a way. He'd get out of this. *He'd save her.*

Mather dropped to his knees again, hands open and empty on his thighs.

Humility.

"I can't . . . ," he started, determination coiling around his words. He *could*, though. If he tried harder; if he could climb the damn walls; if, if, if . . .

If he admitted he couldn't do this, what other declarations would come streaming out of his mouth?

I can't save her.

I know I can't save her.

She'll die, and I'll stand there helpless to do anything but watch her go.

Mather doubled over, forehead to his knees.

This test was seeping into his mind. He just needed to get *out*. He'd get out and—she would still die.

"I can't do this," he spit, fury boiling in his gut.

Nothing happened. Mather pulled himself up, glaring

at the darkness. The magic here knew his heart. He had to be honest, *humble*.

Fine.

He might not be able to save her. But he wouldn't let her do it alone.

He swallowed, willing his lips to move and release the words with intention, with submission.

"I can't," he said, muscles hard, "do this."

The ground trembled again, a gust of air billowing coolness in a much-needed burst of relief. Mather's tension sloshed away the moment he saw the door open in the wall.

White light seeped into the maze, glaring after the utter darkness of the halls. Mather leaped to his feet and plunged into it.

"Meira!" he shouted. "William—"

The names echoed back to him much too loudly, a rebound of noise that spoke of far smoother walls than the carved stone of the labyrinth so far. His eyes adjusted to the light, pain lancing through his head as he took in the room. A tiled floor of black and white squares spanned in a perfect rectangle with pillars of white guarding either side. The ceiling—there was none. Just those pillars stretching on and on, ending in a cloud of brilliant ivory light.

Mather's instincts raged anew and he scrambled for more weapons. A dagger and one of the swords he wore across his spine. He spun, weapons raised, body yearning for a fight

while his mind tried to speak rationally against his eupho-
ria at having an enemy he could *see*.

Because . . . well, he could see this enemy.

And seeing it conflicted with every logical explanation
Mather could dredge up.

Three figures stood in the room. One was Meira, a
bit more dust-covered than she had been, but uninjured;
another was William, hands free of weapons and face completely blank in a frightening, deathlike sheen that Mather
couldn't understand.

Until he recognized the last person in the room with
them.

As a child, William had found a number of books on the
Winter Kingdom, and in one, a portrait of Queen Hannah
showed her as a small, pretty woman with long white hair
and a serene stare. Mather had stolen glances at that picture
whenever he could, desperate to feel some connection to the
woman who, at the time, he thought was his mother.

Now that painting came to life before him, and he found
himself staring at Queen Hannah Dynam.

"You've reached the end of the labyrinth," Hannah said,
smiling. "You've come so far."

33

Ceridwen

THE CLOSER CERIDWEN drew to the Ventrallan queen, the quieter everything became. As if all her other senses demanded her attention more, drowning out her ability to hear anything but the echoing *thump-thump* of her heart matching the cadence of her feet on the earth. The handles of her knives dug into her palms. The crisp, bitter air of Autumn met the frigid air of Winter, weaving into a blanket of iciness that burned Ceridwen's lungs.

This was war.

The Autumnian, Summerian, and Yakimian armies ran alongside her, the impact from their steps vibrating up her legs. But nothing penetrated her fog of concentration, the bumps sprouting along her arms the only thing telling her that her army shouted a war cry. True war cries didn't need to be heard—they were felt.

It had been too much to hope that Raelyn would surge

forward along with her soldiers—instead, she hung back at the rear. She'd make Ceridwen fight her way through until, by the time they met, she would be tired and bloodied while Raelyn remained poised and whole. And were this a normal fight, Raelyn would need such an advantage. But Ceridwen had seen the power Raelyn wielded now, how she had snapped Simon's neck with a flick of her wrist.

It was Ceridwen who would need any advantage she could get.

Lekan's shoulder jostled into Ceridwen's moments before they collided with the Ventrallan army. A wordless signal, one they had shared dozens of times—a swipe of his hand on her arm before an attack, a bump of her fist to his back before a rescue.

I'm here. I'm with you.

Ceridwen was never more grateful to have him by her side.

They fell into a routine as they always did, as if this wasn't a war, but rather one of their many missions to free Summerian slaves. Her left shoulder angled to his right, pivoted to create a deadly barrier with him slashing one side, her the other. When he ducked, she knew to duck too; when she deflected an enemy to take on another, the soldier stumbled into Lekan's blades. Against a dozen or so slavers, such maneuvers brought them quick victory—but never had they been forced to use it in a battle, where each soldier they felled was replaced by two more.

Nor had they ever used it on soldiers possessed by a deadly magic—not nearly as strong as Raelyn's grasp of it, but each enemy they met moved faster than they should, weapons puncturing the air in rapid blows that Ceridwen could barely see. Only her fighter's instincts kept her alive—she had no time to plan any attack.

These soldiers are using Angra's Decay.

But only Angra himself could spread the Decay. He was the source, as Meira had said. Until he showed up here, no one fighting against him needed to fear becoming like the soldiers they encountered, attacking as if they personally loathed each enemy they came upon.

One pause, a break in the wave of Ventrallan soldiers, and Ceridwen gasped icy air. They were in Winter now, snow matted and brown beneath the chaos, and the frigid air clung to Ceridwen's skin, making her nauseous with the discomfort. But these were prices she would willingly pay—for when she took stock of the area, she spotted Raelyn only four soldiers away.

Ceridwen met Lekan's eyes. He nodded and dove for the men, who advanced on him with howls of warning. He dropped the first two, ducked under the third, and impaled the fourth as Ceridwen dispatched the one he had avoided.

Raelyn watched this happen without moving. There was no weapon in her hands; she didn't even wear armor, just a simple black riding outfit and a small black mask, as if she had wandered into this battle while out on a leisurely gallop through Winter's ivory forest.

Lekan slid to his knees from the momentum of gutting the final soldier. He stabbed his blades into the frozen earth to free his hands so he could interlace his fingers into a solid cup against the snow.

Ceridwen backed up, then took off at a sprint. She landed one of her feet in the cradle Lekan made and he lifted, jolting her into the air. Her bloodied knives glinted as she reared, body arching to send her soaring toward Raelyn, high atop her horse.

For the smallest flash, Raelyn's eyes widened behind her mask. She shot her arm out and an invisible force smacked into Ceridwen, spinning her body to the side, her knives dipping just shy of plunging into the Ventrallan queen's chest. Ceridwen slammed into Raelyn, knocking both of them so they landed with a heavy thud on the trampled snow.

Ceridwen lost her grip on her knives, her fingers going numb in the snow's chill. She scrambled to her feet, shuddering from head to toe, holding her breath against the aching shivers that hammered her from the inside out.

Raelyn shot upright as well, the half skirt of her riding outfit swirling around her tight black pants. Her mask did little to hide her furious glare.

"I had no idea you were so anxious to follow in your brother's path," Raelyn snapped.

Ceridwen said nothing, partly because she had to grind

her jaw to keep from shaking to pieces, and partly because she hadn't expected to end up like this, facing Raelyn. The power the Ventrallan queen wielded was too much for her to take in this kind of confrontation—stabbing her quickly had been Ceridwen's only plan.

Now Raelyn would kill her.

Ceridwen darted her eyes around. The Ventrallan soldiers nearby gave them wide berth. Lekan had been drawn away, fighting alongside a group of Winterians who stood back to back, a knot of weapons that, even so, would soon be overwhelmed by the sheer number of Raelyn's troops. The only thing that Ceridwen and Lekan had had on their side was speed—and now that their momentum had been broken, reality set in.

They didn't have enough numbers to fight this battle. Especially when every attacking soldier could move so quickly. As Ceridwen watched, one of the Winterians in Lekan's group took a sword to the chest, causing another to cry out before Lekan corralled both of them into the middle of their circle, protected as much as they could be on a battlefield.

"Is my husband here?" Raelyn's voice scratched at Ceridwen.

"*Your* husband?" Ceridwen smiled. If she would die, flame and heat and burn it all, she'd die with a wicked grin on her face. "I'm fairly certain it wasn't your name he called out on our wedding night a few days back."

Raelyn snarled and punched the air, lurching Ceridwen back beneath a force that rammed into her chest, emptying her lungs of breath. She went down in the snow, wheezing as she rolled onto her side in time to see Raelyn stomp forward, punching the air again. Ceridwen's head crashed back into the ground, her limbs straightened, every muscle pinned as Raelyn stopped over her, one leg on either side of Ceridwen's chest.

"Dear girl, you *really* don't want to start sharing stories like that." Raelyn crouched down, her smile sickly sweet. "You're the one who truly cares, not me. You care so much, about so many things. Like your brother—shall I tell you what it felt like to kill him?"

Ceridwen jerked against the magic that held her, but nothing relented, and Raelyn leaned closer, stroking her finger across Ceridwen's cheek.

"It felt delicious," Raelyn purred. "To have the power to end a life with your own hands—" Her grip tightened, nails sinking into Ceridwen's face. "You can't imagine."

Raelyn pushed herself upright, standing directly over her again, and curled her hand into a fist. Raelyn's magic left Ceridwen's head free, so she turned to look at the battle around her, the last fleeting moments she would get to see the fate of her friends. Lekan and the Winterians had retreated beneath the swelling flood of Ventrallans. Which left her with Raelyn, alone, separated from any of her allies by lines of deadly soldiers.

She blinked, brow twitching.

Not all the soldiers around her wore Ventrallan armor.

She strained against the magic to look toward the line of Winterian trees. More fighters ran to join the Ventrallans, adding numbers alongside a few great iron contraptions rolling on creaking wheels.

Angra's army. And they had brought his cannons—not many, few enough to allow them to travel quickly, but even as Ceridwen analyzed this new addition, one sparked to life and shot a burst of black smoke behind a deadly stone ball that tore into the lines of fighters.

They had already been outnumbered against the Ventrallans. Now . . .

Ceridwen's heart shuddered, and it had nothing to do with the bed of snow cradling her.

Raelyn too noticed the influx of fighters. She cackled, giddy, and her eyes landed on something just as Ceridwen's did.

An impenetrable black cloud polluted the air at the line of trees.

Angra.

Ceridwen should have been incapacitated by horror.

But as she lay on that awful cold ground, pinned by Raelyn's unbeatable power and watching Angra drop into the valley, she saw a way, the only way, to fight the Ventrallan queen.

Angra strode forward, his Spring armor gleaming as he

moved from shadow to sunlight. A figured dropped out of the blackness behind him, the remnants of smoke wafting up into the trees.

No.

Theron caved forward, wailing as though every nerve had been frozen, burned, and frozen again. Angra had brought himself and Theron to this fight—by magic.

And if he had brought Theron, that meant Angra had first gone to Jannuari to retrieve him.

Ceridwen gagged. Meira—what had he done to her? How had Angra even used his magic to bring Theron here? She knew Meira could use her magic to transport other Winterians, but Angra shouldn't be able to affect Theron, a *Cordellan*, like that. Unless this was a further trick of the Decay? All Ceridwen knew was Theron screaming, rolling in the snow. Whatever Angra had done to get him here, it had worked, but it didn't seem . . . right.

Angra paid Theron no heed, simply marched toward the heat of the battle, his posture tall and his face livid.

That alleviated Ceridwen's worry. He wouldn't be this furious if he had succeeded in killing Meira.

Raelyn applauded his arrival. Clearly she hadn't yet figured out what Angra would do, but Ceridwen had. They had anticipated that Angra would attempt to infect the opposing army with his Decay, and Ceridwen had been ready to block him.

But the seed of an idea blossomed in her mind, making

her grit her teeth. Angra's Decay would latch onto everyone in this valley, and though most would fight it, it would eventually worm its way through and infect them with the same mad power that encouraged Raelyn's evil.

Please, Meira. Ceridwen sent the thought out into the void of her heart, holding it against the choice she was about to make. *Please hurry.*

Angra kept moving, gliding past Raelyn and Ceridwen. As he did, more of his cannons fired behind him and he stretched out his arms as a father would to intercept a child. But his face told a different story—lips curled, teeth bared, eyes ablaze.

He jerked his arms forward.

Murky blackness streamed out of him, snaking through the armies. One tendril broke off and barreled straight at Ceridwen, and Raelyn watched, waiting for her to writhe and struggle.

But she didn't fight it.

The magic collided with Ceridwen until she was nothing more than power and strength. Angra pumped as much into her as she wanted, poured it over her like bucket after bucket of water on a dry, dusty ground. She felt his desperation in that offering, how he wasn't holding back as he had with the small amounts of magic he had given to his soldiers.

This was the final war for both sides, and he would make the world his.

Ceridwen met Raelyn's eyes.

"When you want to kill someone, kill them, don't *taunt them*," Ceridwen grunted, and jammed her arms up at Raelyn, shattering the magic's hold with her own influx of Decay.

Raelyn's face took on a look of utter shock just before her neck popped. The Ventrallan queen's body dropped to the snow beside Ceridwen, her eyes frozen in a permanent state of surprise.

Ceridwen shoved to her feet. The Decay filled every corner of her body so thoroughly, she thought she might burst from the burden of it, full of such endless, glorious strength that the world would stand in awe of her destruction as they would a wildfire desecrating a forest.

She was a flame, and she was the fuel, and she was the light that would blind every sad, weak creature in Primoria.

If all of Angra's allies felt this good, no wonder they'd sided with him.

Ceridwen shook her head. *No; remember all he's done. Remember who he is.*

But this is power. THIS is strength. I've never had this before.

Ceridwen found herself running, barreling for the Autumn-Yakim-Summer army ahead. Any retreating had stopped, most soldiers now squirming in war with their minds as Angra's Decay pummeled for control. He still stood on the battlefield, black snakes of magic streaming out of him, his face swelling with demented joy.

This is power. This is strength. And these people are fighting it. They deserve to die.

No!

But Ceridwen's protest went unheard by her body, and she felt her legs propel her toward a group of Summerian fighters. They grunted and sweated but held, resisting Angra with more finesse than most, thanks to their years of fighting Simon's magic.

They need to die for it.

NO!

She leaped at them, and they saw her coming, their eyes registering their leader in a sweep of awareness. But they couldn't process her attacking them—she, of all of them, should have been the last to fall to Angra, and truly, that was the only reason she had any clarity at all now.

"*Run!*" she screamed at them, one garbled plea that shot through the hatred burning in her. Flame and heat, she hadn't even hated Raelyn with this much passion—but she hated *them*, these ignorant, righteous idiots who would keep the world weak.

Ceridwen punched one of the Summerians, who fell to the ground, stunned at her attack. The rest moved to help him, fighting as best they could, but she was augmented like all of Angra's other puppets now. She was unstoppable, and burn it all, she *felt* unstoppable.

Stop! They aren't your enemy!

A body slammed into her, tackling her on the Autumn side of the field.

"Ceridwen!" Lekan shouted and pinned her arms by her head. Others joined him, helped him hold her to the ground. "Cerie, stop!"

She wailed, thrashing under him. He was weak too. He'd never understand the *need* she felt, how this power came with the responsibility to use it—and use it she would.

"Cerie, we need you," Lekan pleaded. Blood spread across his forehead, mud caked in a tan-black coat down his neck. "This isn't you, but you're the strongest person I know. You can fight Angra."

That name spoke to the magic in her. Angra deserved this power. Only Angra could wield it.

"He's the enemy," she forced herself to say, out loud. Ceridwen dragged those words into her heart, compelling them to stay just as strong and relentless as the hatred that still urged her to attack Lekan and the Summerians.

Lekan nodded, but part of him slouched, defeated. "Bind her," he told one of the men holding her. "We can't afford to—"

They lifted Ceridwen, and Lekan continued giving orders, but she bade herself to ignore them. She didn't want to hear any information that the Decay could make her use against them.

The battle begged for her attention, anyway. What was left of their army had merged around them into a tight cluster of the most persistent fighters, those who could ward off Angra's Decay by strength of will. Caspar stood nearby, shouting with some of his remaining generals. Less than half of their original numbers still stood, which went beyond tragic—it was an exercise in suicide.

Their soldiers fought, but more fell than enemies. Their soldiers resisted, but every few seconds, one turned on their brethren in the same ferocious hatred that had possessed Ceridwen. Cannons tore through their cluster, leveling half a dozen soldiers at a time.

Angra stood in the center of his army, elevated on a stack of barrels or a crate or maybe the backs of the soldiers he had killed, his arms stretched, the Decay still gushing out of him. His joy had broken, the slightest strain showing, but that didn't stop him. Nothing would stop him.

Ceridwen realized that now—nothing could defeat him.

Not even Meira.

Meira

AS THE DOOR appears in the maze wall, I peer through it and search the exterior for another of those plates that will help me on the test. But there's only that door, white light streaming around me.

Then I remember what the final test will be.

Purification of the heart.

Even though they helped me on the other two tests, the Order would have wanted only those who are truly pure of heart to pass the labyrinth.

It's entirely possible they meant for everyone to face this test without help.

But help won't be necessary. I'm ready for this; I will pass whatever test gets thrown at me.

I clear my mind and enter the room.

And gape at who is inside.

Hannah.

I stand there for what feels like lifetimes before Sir's maze dumps him through a door on my right. He rushes forward, spots her, and stops as if the floor has grabbed onto his feet.

Seeing Sir and Hannah staring at each other jolts an image through my mind of Rares and Oana. How different they were from these two people before me. And though it has never been real, I can't help but see two versions of a life: Sir and Hannah, my parents; Rares and Oana, my parents. One pair always harsh and unloving; the other kind and gentle and everything I wanted.

A door opens on my left and Mather enters, weapons in hand and eyes darting over each of us as he steps closer to me.

Good—at least one of us is capable of movement.

"You've reached the end of the labyrinth. You've come so far," Hannah finally speaks, her eyes widening in encouragement.

"How are you here?" I manage.

I haven't talked to her since before I left on the tour of the world, before I thought the magic barrier in the chasm entrance had broken my connection to her—before I found out I was keeping her away on my own, because I didn't need her anymore.

And I had been fine not seeing her. I was *fine* when she was gone.

Seeing her now, smiling at me as if we're just an innocent

mother and daughter, as if I'm not moments away from dying for the mistakes she made, lights frustration that burns out to every limb. Why would she be here?

Purification of the heart.

I press a hand to my chest.

This is a test of heart. Anyone who harbors hatred, or anger, would be deemed unworthy.

But I thought I'd made my peace with Hannah at Rares and Oana's home. I let go of my anger at her and at Sir and realized that all the things I wanted from them were ill-placed expectations that could never be.

Sir lurches toward her, but his feet don't move, just his shoulders jolting before he straightens.

He's afraid.

Cold sweat washes down my body.

"I don't think it's really her," I tell him.

Hannah smiles. "Why would you think that, sweetheart?"

My hands curl into loose fists. "Because I've been blocking the real Hannah for weeks now, and I haven't stopped. You're a test. You're the magic playing tricks on us."

Her smile widens. "I've been magic all along, haven't I? Was I ever the real Hannah?"

I frown. "You—"

An explanation. Please, let there be an explanation.

But the longer I stare at her, the longer I realize she might be right.

I'd assumed the conduit that links us in our bloodline

kept her connected to me. Or has it ever really been her?

I shake my head. "Stop it! You're just trying to unsettle us." I turn to Sir so Hannah is almost behind me. "We have to get through this test—it's a test of heart."

Sir still stares at her, his lips in a thin line. He doesn't look at me, doesn't react at all.

"You could have imagined me, Meira." Hannah's voice is just as soft as I remember, invoking feelings of awe that make me want to listen with rapt attention to her every word.

"I didn't imagine you," I say to her, though I stay facing Sir, while beside me Mather remains poised. "I didn't even know you when you appeared to me. How could I have made up all those things you told me?"

"How can you be a conduit yourself?" Hannah counters. "How is anything in this labyrinth possible? When you touched the keys, you saw what you needed to see to get here. When you touched the plates in this labyrinth, they showed you pieces of the tests to help you pass them. Maybe the magic took what form it had to in order to help you during those early days as well. It created what you needed—a mother."

I spin on her, fingernails biting into my palms. "I made my peace with you in Paisly. I saw what real parents are like—I saw what a true family can be. And I know now that whatever relationship I had with you was *wrong*. Everything you did was your own doing, and none of it is my burden.

But I will fix your mistakes, Hannah. *I am better than you.*"

"I know," she says, and she smiles again. "Your heart isn't the one that needs peace."

My mouth cocks open.

"Who—"

Hannah pivots to face Sir. "I gave her to you for protection. She was forced to seek help from the magic because you failed me."

Sir.

Panic cracks through me and I take two reeling steps toward him, but he still won't look away from Hannah.

"Sir, don't listen to her! Look at me—"

"You failed me, General," she says, and this time, the bite in her voice is unmistakable. "You failed Winter."

"He did not fail Winter!" I whirl on her.

Mather appears beside me, his hand on my shoulder, trying to tug me away. "He has to pass this test."

I step directly in front of Sir, talking only to him. "Hannah caused all of this. *She* caused this."

Sir blinks. Movement that makes me sigh in relief, until he latches onto my face as if seeing me for the first time.

"I grew up with your mother. Did I ever tell you that?"

I freeze. Even Mather, still trying to coax me away, stops. We both recognize the melody in Sir's voice, the tone he's always taken when reciting history lessons.

"We were both children in Winter's court. Much like you two grew up together." He encompasses Mather with a glance. "I saw her awkwardness in youth. I saw her mistakes, her breakdowns, her faults—which made it harder than I expected to see her as a queen, once she was crowned."

He looks past me, at Hannah. "I made the mistake of not treating her with the respect owed to her position. And when she grew more solemn and distant as the war intensified, I comforted her as a friend would help a friend, not as a soldier would help his queen. I should have been only her general, and I wasn't. I should have guided Winter away from the path she was taking us down, and I didn't."

I grab Sir's arms. "You didn't know she had made a deal with Angra. You can't expect to—"

His eyes drop back to me and he lifts his hands to my arms. He's never touched me like this before—in a desperate way that feels all too much like he's begging. Delirium beats in his eyes the more he talks, awakened by Hannah, by this labyrinth, by everything we've endured for the past few decades, and as I watch him, the terror that shoots through me is unlike any I've ever experienced.

I'm afraid for him. *I'm* afraid for *Sir*.

"I swore to myself I wouldn't make that mistake again," he tells me, his fingers clamping around me. "I told myself I would see you as a queen, every moment of your life, so I would never lose focus. But I still failed."

Tears. On Sir's face.

"William." My voice cracks. "William, stop—"

"Angra took my kingdom," he continues. "I wasn't

allowed to raise my son as my own. I did everything I could, but it wasn't enough, and the only reason I could ever find was . . . you."

"Me?" Were Sir not holding on to my arms, I'd collapse at his feet.

"It was so foolish of me." Sir's grip spasms. "I realize that now, Meira. I blamed you for *years*. But you never accepted that blame, did you? Snow above, you fought it, fought *me*, every chance you got. And I think, somewhere in all that fighting, I realized my blame was misplaced. You weren't the reason for our past failure—you were the reason for our hope for the future. I may not have gotten to raise Mather as my son, but I got to raise both of you."

My heart surges against my ribs, full to the point of bursting.

"But you're right," he says, a laugh. "You're right. All this, everything that happened, was Hannah's doing. And Angra's doing. And I let them take even more of our lives by misplacing my blame for so long." His eyes cut to Mather. "I'm sorry I wasn't a better father."

He shifts back to me.

"I'm sorry I wasn't a better father to *both* of you," he tells me, his apology falling directly into my ear as he pulls me forward.

Sir is hugging me.

I made my peace with him too, in Paisly. I resigned myself to the roles he'd chosen for us, and I was fine.

But I wasn't fine.

Because wrapped in Sir's arms, I come undone.

I'm sixteen years old, hugging him in the vision Angra dredged up in Abril.

I'm ten years old, sobbing against him in the wake of Gregg's and Crystalla's deaths.

I'm six years old, rocking back and forth in his arms after a nightmare, the one time he ever willingly hugged me, the episode branded on my heart and held as a beacon for everything I wanted out of our lives.

I fling my arms around his waist now, bury my face into him. Dust from the labyrinth sticks to his shirt, the forms of small knives in sheaths across his chest press into my face. His heart thumps against my ear, his lungs fill with raspy breaths that match my own.

This is better than all those moments. This erases them and starts fresh.

I rise up to look at him and stretch one hand out to Mather, beckoning him in. "We'll fix this, together, and the world will be healed."

The tears that fall down Sir's face glisten on his cheeks, fold into the wrinkles that line his eyes. He lifts his head to look at Hannah again. Is she still there? It doesn't matter. We passed this test, all of us. We're healed now, and we can move forward. *Together.*

A crack forms in my joy.

No, it won't be together. But I will die knowing Sir loves

me. I will die knowing everything I wanted for us wasn't a hapless wish—it came true.

The crack splits so loudly that it rings in my ears when the look on Sir's face shifts from bittersweet happiness to nothing but sorrow.

Unrepentant, screaming sorrow.

"A test of heart," he whispers. "We're supposed to forgive her."

"We did," I tell him, but the look on his face . . . "We can go—"

The ground rumbles as the wall to my left grates, something black and tall forming in my peripheral vision.

"A door!" Mather cries. "Come on, we can—"

But the ground doesn't stop rumbling. And Sir won't move.

I heave on his arms, and Mather dives in to help, both of us pulling and shouting as the ground shakes. The pillars around the room react to the vibrations, chunks of rock chipping off and shattering in small explosions around us.

Sir grabs my shoulders, his eyes too calm, too knowing. "Run."

"You have to run too!" I shout over the building roar of the room quivering apart.

But Sir shakes his head. He motions to his legs, bends his knees in a jerk to demonstrate.

He stopped walking on his way into the room, as if the floor grabbed his feet. And it *did*.

He hasn't forgiven Hannah. The room won't let him leave until he does.

"You have to let her go!" My voice screeches in desperation, my fingers knotted in his shirt. Mather hangs on to Sir's arm, his eyes cutting between us and the door, the rubble gathering in collapsing bursts, the floor tiles breaking and—

Snow above—the floor is starting to disintegrate, like the other times it swallowed us. But these holes aren't tunnels to drop us into the next test or even ringed with flame like in the first room—they're just empty. Just blackness.

"No, Meira." Sir loosens my fingers from his shirt, still so calm. "I had to let *you* go. But I can't forgive Hannah, especially for the fate she made for you. For all of us." He shakes his head. "I can't. I'm sorry."

Mather balks. "You aren't . . . no. You have to come with us!"

Sir looks at him.

Puts a hand on his son's shoulder.

And pushes him toward the door.

Then he meets my eyes. *Go*, he mouths.

I slam my body into Mather, pinning my arms around him and propelling us toward the door. Gaping holes bar our path, making me tug him back and forth as we stumble in a flailing mess for the exit. Mather staggers along beside me and releases a raw scream that hammers into my heart.

We reach the door and I push Mather through, pausing just once.

The scene behind me is a mess of stones and tiles and yawning holes. In the midst of it all, Sir and Hannah stand, motionless, staring at each other.

A pillar falls, slamming down two paces from me, and I leap through the exit just as the whole floor drops into nothingness.

35

Meira

THE DOOR CLOSES the moment Mather and I are both through. It whooshes into place a hand's width from my face as I stand there, blinking away the debris, my chest heaving under labored breaths that might be sobs.

"Meira," Mather groans.

The sound of my name hauls me out of the protective shield I wore to get us out of there. I lift my hands to my face, shaking my head in a repetitive *No* because I can't make any words come out.

"*Meira,*" Mather repeats, tugging at my arm. I whirl, flinging myself on him, and he holds me as he says all the words I can't find. "No—maybe he survived—we can go back—"

His possibilities shatter before he even finishes saying them. I close my eyes, forcing each breath to counter the cries that rumble up my throat like waves in a storm.

Light beats against my eyelids, and I almost whimper with gratitude for the distraction.

But when I open my eyes, I only feel emptier.

We're in a long, narrow hall. The walls are lumpy black rock, the floor is uneven—and at the far end, a halo of light gleams orange and yellow and purple and blue in shifting hues.

"Mather," I whisper as I step away from him.

He pulls back, his head snapping to follow mine.

"The magic chasm," he says.

I nod.

He shakes his head in a long, slow rebuttal. "No."

"Mather—"

"It's too soon. My father—and now—" His voice cracks and he scrubs a palm over his forehead. I say nothing, motionless with my hands on his chest.

"I can't think of any way to save you," he finally says, all the pain in his life in those few small words.

I lift my hand to his cheek. "Once we get into that chamber, an exit will open—part of the labyrinth's magic. Run for it as fast as you can—when it opens, it means people can access it from the outside for a short time too. And I don't want to give Angra a chance to—"

"Meira, *no*."

But I keep talking, unable to let myself stop. "—I don't want to give Angra a chance to get down here. So run, don't stop running, and I'll run too."

"*Meira.*"

"Ceridwen and Caspar will need you. The world will need you to help pick up the pieces—"

He silences me by laying his lips over mine. I didn't think there was anything left in me to unravel, but his kiss dissolves my strength.

This moment—this is our last.

So I hold on to it for as long as I can, memorizing the rough edges of his lips and the way he tastes like salt and musk and joy, and the muscles that flex when I glide my fingers along his jaw.

We didn't have enough time. But the rest of the world will. Jesse and Ceridwen, Caspar and Nikoletta—even Theron, someday. And Mather. Snow above, Mather—he'll have this someday too. With someone better than me.

With someone who won't break his heart.

I pull back from him, tears rushing down my cheeks. He looks at me, those jewel-blue eyes so familiar and perfect in the way they feel like home.

He entwines his fingers with mine and smiles. The smile that defined so much of my life, melting me and filling me top to bottom with resilience. That he can smile here, now, chases away my last bits of fear and worry.

He's lost everything. His parents, and now me, too. And yet he's here with me, beside me, offering support and a hand to hold.

I turn with him to face the light at the end of the hall. It

pulses and ebbs, gleams bright and fades, an endless kaleidoscope of colors.

If I had to pick a way to die, it would be this—to go out
in a rainbow of life and energy. To know that my life was
valued by others.

I glance at the solid wall behind us.

To know that I was loved.

One step, then another, Mather and I walk side by side
down the jagged stone corridor.

Our steps accelerate the closer we get, until we're
sprinting.

As fast as I can. *As fast as I can.* This will all be over soon,
before Angra can even find the exit that appears, before the
battle above has to go on too long.

The hall ends, dumping us into a wide cavern that
stretches in rocky sweeps in every direction. A ceiling soars
untouchably high above; stalactites drip downward in gruesome teeth. The floor evens out into a solid cliff that ends
after a few paces in a wide, fathomless pit.

And in that pit, hanging down from the edge, waits the
source of magic.

I saw it once before, in one of the many visions Hannah showed—or whatever it was that showed me. The
magic looks just as it did then, a brilliant ball of energy
that snaps and sizzles as it hangs by sheer will in the pit.

Larger than the palace, larger than all of Jannuari itself, the magic seems to be a living, breathing creature bobbing just beyond the cliff, its fingers of energy snaking out to strike rocks and imbue them with the power that made the conduits so many thousands of years ago.

The product of that magic shines from every corner, rocks in orange, gold, purple, red tones, soft glows in every color. Just like at the entrance, the air hangs heavy and humid, each particle sizzling with magic. Conduits, magic, everywhere, a field of power ripe for harvest.

A field of power that will end soon.

The cliff loops around one side of the pit, and the moment our feet touch it, the familiar vibrations tell us a door opens where the cliff slopes toward the ceiling far on our left.

This is it.

I loosen my fingers and shake Mather free, unable to let myself do anything but angle for the cliff, plunging around stalagmites and leaping over piles of glowing debris.

I'll never see him again.

But I don't cry, or even falter in running. I press on, because I have to, because—

His hand slides back into mine.

I frown at him, but he pushes faster, matching my pace.

He didn't run for the exit.

Mather . . .

But I can't argue with him. No time, no words, nothing but my heart throbbing and a sob working through my pinched lips.

I could use the magic to transport him out of here, to safety. But he's *choosing* to be here with me—making him leave would be forcing him into something he doesn't want.

He wants this. And I'm helpless but to let him stay.

I think a part of me always knew he wouldn't leave me again.

Two paces to the edge of the cliff.

The magic sparks, crackling on the air, fizzling into my body with each breath I take.

One pace to the edge of the cliff.

Mather's fingers tighten on mine.

I return his squeeze as we both land on the cliff's edge. Rocks tumble off, normal, magic-free rocks that plummet into the source. They disintegrate in roaring bursts of consuming energy.

We will, too.

The magic intensifies, a wave of crystalizing heat reaching up for me, for us.

I'm ready, I think, building a shelter around myself with those words. *End this.*

All air leaves my lungs and I jump. The chasm below me shifts, drawing me in.

Then I'm flying backward.

Rock grates against my shoulder. Glowing pebbles scatter

around me, new bruises rupture in my skin as I'm slammed onto the ground near the hall we just ran through. My grip on Mather pulls him back to land on me, and he grunts as his shoulders connect with the rock wall.

I heave onto my elbows, disoriented.

Because when I look, the world is shifting.

The world is *screaming*.

Angra stands just inside the newly appeared exit, taking agonizing steps toward me. One of his hands stretches out, the shadow of his magic retracting around his arm in a black cloud.

He pulled us back.

He's here. He found the chasm.

And I'm still alive.

Ceridwen

CERIDWEN KNEW SOMETHING had changed only because Angra's manic glee lurched through his connection to the magic in her like a rider yanking back on his horse's reins.

Something had happened.

There was nothing controlled about his power now—it flowed from him in desperate surges of strength and magic and hatred, every need multiplied by a sudden pulsing thought.

No one will take this from me.

As Ceridwen thrashed against the Summerians holding her, fighting to keep from killing them and fighting *to* kill them—flame, she wanted nothing more than to scratch every piece of flesh from their bones, to sink her fingers into their hearts and *obliterate them*—she watched Angra, standing high over his army.

He lowered his arms, the tendrils of black magic ceasing.

Angra swayed but caught himself.

No one will take this from me.

He might have stopped pumping out magic, but that did not mean his hold had been broken. Like seeds buried warm and deep in the earth, the darkness would continue to grow in everyone he had infected, even after the sun set.

And set it did.

Angra grabbed someone next to him—Theron, whose gaze reflected the furious, livid hatred that Ceridwen felt burning in her own eyes—and together, they vanished without a final glance at the doomed battle. Theron cried out as the magic latched onto him in ways it wasn't meant for.

Few others noticed Angra's disappearance. Soldiers shouted, charging against Caspar's remaining infantry, swords trailing blood through the air. Their frenzy drove them to fight as they never had before, not just Spring and Ventrallans now but Autumnians and Yakimians too. Most Summerians had managed to resist Angra's magic and attempted to form lines of defense.

But they were so outnumbered, victory was impossible now. People they knew, former allies, now tore at them with desperation, eyes narrowed in tortured hatred. All around were nothing but enemies, weapons, death—from where Ceridwen stood, bound in the middle of Caspar's group, she couldn't find even one speck of hope in the carnage.

If Angra had left, it had to be to go after Meira.

If he found her, they had failed.

But the darkness in Ceridwen spiked with joy. *She will not take away this power. No one will take this from me.*

"Lekan," Ceridwen croaked, her body going limp against the soldiers who held her.

Lekan and Caspar conferred mere paces away, both streaked with blood and gashes and the telltale signs of men beaten by war. But Lekan swung to her. His eyes brightened, the light he reserved for Amelie when she asked if they would ever have a permanent home outside the refugee camp. The light of lying.

He knelt before her as the soldiers let her sink to the ground.

"Cerie—"

"I'm sorry," she panted. "I'm sorry . . . I let him in . . . I'm sorry . . . I—"

There was a wail from nearby as the lines of Angra's soldiers pressed closer, tearing down their defenses with the magic he had given them.

Kaleo would never forgive her if she let Lekan die.

And Jesse . . .

This was why she had married him. Because she knew her life would be too short.

Lekan put his hand on her shoulder. One squeeze, a wordless offering of comfort.

I'm here. I'm with you.

She met his eyes. It was all she could do.

An explosion punctuated the war cries in a sharp burst—cannons, all firing in rapid, deliberate succession from the Winter side of the valley. Dozens, at least. Had Angra's soldiers brought that many? Ceridwen moaned, braced for a cannon to come tearing through their group at any moment.

Lekan frowned, confused, and sprang to his feet to join Caspar, who stood on an overturned crate and peered down into the valley.

The explosions continued, eliciting mangled bellows of pain. Still Ceridwen waited. This many cannons meant one would surely rip through their ranks. . . .

The darkness in her roiled with fury. *I will not end this way. I have strength now.*

But beyond that, the small, clear part of her shrank, silent and tired and . . . ready.

"Soldiers," Caspar told Lekan, but his words carried all around, to every waiting, exhausted fighter hiding in this cluster. "Under Yakim's banner."

Only a handful of Yakimians remained with them, but they instantly cheered, waving their fists and hooting into the sky.

"They're firing weapons," Caspar continued. "Like Angra's cannons, only smaller."

"Angra's cannons?" Lekan's face contorted. "Are they fighting alongside his soldiers?"

But Caspar smiled. "No. Leave it to the Yakimians to

figure out a way to re-create Angra's own weapon and use it against him."

The area this group occupied was cramped with soldiers, but space had been made around Caspar, enough to allow movement to see the field. In this clearing a great ripple of maroon light fractured the empty air, bending and contracting until a man appeared.

A man *appeared*.

Even the magic in Ceridwen didn't react to it, her shock too potent.

It wasn't Angra. Soldiers instantly whirled on him, weapons upright, but the man didn't seem the least bit concerned. His dark skin stretched as he smiled, a scar through the right side of his face coaxing a memory into Ceridwen's beaten mind.

She had seen this man before, in Putnam. He was the servant who had escorted them to the university and showed her and Meira around the library.

Rares.

He looked straight at her. "You did a brave thing," he said, and encompassed the soldiers. "You all have. But the Winter queen has reached the chasm. The end is drawing near, and we have come to help usher it onward."

We?

Ceridwen stood again, her bound arms against her spine. As she rose, she saw more of that refracted maroon light throughout the battlefield. Nearby, within their soldiers;

far off, near the approaching army, who marched into the battle alongside small wheeled cannons. Everything Meira had told Ceridwen filtered through her mind like sunlight through a dirty window.

Paisly. The Order of the Lustrate.

Rares drew a blade from his belt, the long, heavy sleeves of his robe swaying as he lifted it into the air. "Those who still wish to fight, do so knowing this war will soon end," he shouted.

At Ceridwen, Rares leveled a single determined look.

"Hold on," he said before he dove away, toward Angra's soldiers. He met them with even greater speed than they showed, blocking their attacks with invisible bursts that sent them flying through the air. From somewhere down the valley, a crack of thunder erupted over the continuing explosions of the Yakimian weapons, and lightning plummeted out of the sky in a sizzling bolt that shattered one of the cannons.

The Paislians were fighting Angra's soldiers with magic. The Yakimians had come to help too—Giselle must have had a change of heart.

Ceridwen wavered as the voices around her rose from the murmurings of soldiers in the throes of defeat to the cheers of people given hope. This was what they needed—something to even the battle. An advantage to keep the fight going long enough to help Meira.

But Angra had gone after her.

Ceridwen took Rares's words, repeating them over and over to combat the tide of hatred and need that still filled her.

"Hold on," she said, a plea that rose until she was screaming, begging Meira to hear it and keep fighting. It was all she could do now. They had all come together to fight for this world, to fight for *Meira*, and, burn it all, *she would succeed.*

"Hold on," Ceridwen begged. *"Hold on."*

Meira

ANGRA IS HERE. And I'm still alive.

But I didn't come this far to live.

I pull myself to my feet and reach for my chakram, letting it soar at him before the new wounds scattered over
my body sing out a resounding chorus of pain. One of my
ribs aches; a slice in my thigh burns; blood trickles into my
eye, but I swipe it away as my chakram cuts through the air
at Angra.

It won't hit him. He knows I'll use it, but it will distract
him, just for a beat—so before it has time to reach him, I
run. The edge of the cliff is only a few paces from the wall
of the chasm, but it stretches before me as each footfall
draws me closer yet still too far. I pull at the coldness in
me, intending to hurl myself magically to the edge—

But a wave of Decay comes at me again. The cord of
shadow wraps around my body, straining taut as it snatches

me back. Angra deflects my chakram as the Decay yanks me away, and my blade drops out of the air, clanks against the cliff face—and falls over the edge.

I see my chakram fall as if in a dream. The ball of magic spikes with the electric, crackling destruction of an object falling into it.

My chakram is gone.

Pain screams up my arm as I drop like a sack of coal on the rock. Something popped, but I'm too desperate and blind to know where. This isn't how it was supposed to happen. I'm ready to end this—I *need* to end this—

"You will not defeat me!" Angra's bellow crashes through the chasm. Wrath emanates from each word, and when I roll to my feet, left arm pinned to my side, I face a madman.

His eyes sit crazed in his blotchy face as he rocks toward me. Mather hurls himself in front of me.

Angra chortles.

"So sweet," he rumbles. "But I've brought someone to take care of *that*."

I grab Mather's shoulder with my one good arm and try to tug him behind me—of the two of us, I'm better suited to fight Angra—but a shadow moves in the exit tunnel, one that makes both Mather and me stiffen instinctively.

The shadow hobbles into the chasm with just as much delirium as Angra. He's being fed Angra's emotions, I realize—every spark of anger, every flurry of rage. Angra pumps all of it into Theron, who doesn't waste a heartbeat.

He plunges down the cliff, both his fists wrapped around a blade. Mather shoves me back, but it isn't me Theron swings at.

He propels his blade straight at Mather. I stumble to the ground, screaming as Mather ducks, drops, and flips away to put space between him and Theron. A knife appears in Mather's hand, glinting off the magic chasm.

"I won't lose her to you," Theron snarls, and launches forward.

I scramble for my short sword, finally get it in my grip, but the choice to help Mather is taken away when the Decay snakes around me. Magic loops over my arm, wrenching the sword from my hand. My broken arm grates and I cry out as the Decay drags me over the uneven ground toward Angra.

My own magic responds with a surge of ice that shrivels the darkness, and I leap up. Angra stands not four paces away, between the edge of the cliff and me. My eyes scan the ground to look for my sword, and it's there, waiting behind a stalagmite—

I reach out toward the sword, magic bursting in an icy column from my fingers, but Angra sends a blast to match me. His reaches my sword first, a smoky shadow looping around the blade like vines eating up a tree, and with a harsh jerk of his arm, the sword flies behind him to drop off the edge of the cliff just like my chakram.

"Oh, no, Highness," Angra taunts. "I've seen all your

tricks. I've survived everything you've ever thrown at me. There is no ending where I don't emerge victorious."

I don't acknowledge him. I run, aiming to dart around him, racing on nothing but primal drive for the ball of magic. Nothing else is in me anymore, no pain or love or feeling at all. All I am is all I'm meant to be—a void from which anything could sprout. Goodness or evil, purity or darkness—whatever happens after this, it will be the world's glorious, unaffected choice.

Angra whips the shadow back and the line of magic barrels at me, blocking my path to the chasm. I scream—*no, no, NO*—and drop to my knees. The dense, humid particles of air that hang in the chasm fly to me, lengthening into a solid wall of ice that slams up in time to block me from the burst of Angra's magic.

He cackles, sends another whip that chips away at my ice barrier. "I told you, Highness—I know your tricks."

I grunt, arms up to keep the ice barrier reinforced with my magic. Nothing he says matters. *I will end this.*

"Every defense you have, every pathetic plan you made," Angra continues. Another knot of Decay slams into my barrier. "Nothing you do can stop me. Even your ally, the Summerian princess? She's mine now. *Mine.* And all the world will follow her, one by one, until it is as it was meant to be: *controlled by me.*"

Ceridwen fell to Angra? I choke on it. His words make me glance to the side, where my shield ends. Mather and

Theron fight still, back and forth across the cliff.

The last time they fought, months ago, lifetimes ago, they were matched skill for skill in Bithai's training yard. But now Theron has Angra's Decay fueling him, and he moves faster than any normal human could—slashing around Mather so quickly, I can barely keep track of him. And if I'm having trouble watching him, Mather has to be even more frenzied.

I swivel to Mather, ready to launch one invigorating burst of strength and energy to help him. But before the magic leaves my body, Mather turns, and Theron swipes his blade through the air, both of them arching toward each other. All breath leaves me, my throat closing in horror that Mather won't be able to duck Theron's blow.

But Theron's blade doesn't plunge into Mather as it should.

I blink, and Mather catches Theron's sword.

How did it—there was no way Mather could have moved that fast—

A glow of yellow emanates from Mather's other fist, one of the many rocks here imbued with the source's power over the years. Just like the original conduits that used to run rampant through the world, giving single jolts of magic that people eventually used for the evil acts that created the Decay. Compared to the Royal Conduits, individual conduits are laughably small and temporary, good only for quick influxes of power.

But quick influxes of power are just what Mather needs.

The stone in his hand dims to a muted shine and he tosses it, spins under Theron's next swing, and grabs a glowing blue stone that helps him catch Theron's jab. He's using the magic only to defend, not attack.

Snow above. He figured out on his own what Rares and Oana had to teach me through violent lightning strikes.

A split shakes my ears and I look up in time to see a crack in the top of my ice shield, plummeting down, straight for me. Angra's magic—he's breaking the ice barrier. I have no weapons left, nothing I could use to attack him.

Except the ice.

Angra gives me no further time to think. I launch back as my barrier explodes, slivers of ice cutting through the air and scraping my face in small frozen blades. One large shard whirls after me, and I catch it before it shatters on the stone.

"No," I snarl, at him, at myself, at this whole awful war, and it's the only thing I can say as I stand there, the skin on my palm breaking open as I grip the ice shard.

Angra stands, triumphant among the ruins of my ice barrier. "Go ahead and try, Winter queen. Spring will always win."

My useless broken arm stays clamped to my body, but the rest of me moves to fight without any prodding, knees bending, waist shifting, good arm coiling as I throw the ice shard at Angra. He slams one arm up, a shield of Decay incinerating the shard before it touches him. But I let another fly, scrambling through the debris around me to hurl any and all pieces I can find. A particularly large chunk drops into my palm, and my magic flares with recognition, wanting to break free, so I let it—but only to creep down my left arm and heal the break. No other magic use. I can't risk magic in what could be an attack on Angra, a negative action that could feed the Decay.

I'm too close to lose.

Ice shard after ice shard, and each one lets me take another step closer to Angra, to the edge. Closer and closer, my arm a repetition of grab, bend, throw—grab, bend, throw—ice flying toward Angra only to dissolve as he wrenches up barrier after barrier against my relentless attacks. His face bends with vehemence, brows caving over his eyes in a glare that matches the growl he unleashes.

A few more steps, just a few more—

One ice shard flies, smaller, and instead of dissolving in Angra's barrier, it hits him, only because he lets his defense fall to fling his arms straight out at me. The ice leaves a thin red line along his cheek, blood welling in beaded trickles as his magic flings me back, high into the wall, but instead of crashing to the ground again, I'm held there, pinned to the stone.

Angra pants, one hand lifted to keep me defenseless against the rock.

"If you kill me now," I say, "all of Winter will become

just like me. Conduits. There will always be someone to fight you."

"You think they can stop me?" Angra lowers his hand and I grind down the wall, serrated rocks cutting into my back. A sharp scream bursts from my lips before I can bite it away, and the noise makes Mather pause in his fight.

He turns toward me. Just a flinch.

Theron rakes his blade across Mather's stomach.

I feel the cut as if it happened to me, a hot sear that empties my body of rational thought.

"Winter welcomed me," Angra continues, unmoved by anything happening outside us. "Your kingdom opened its doors to me once I told them the truth of our power. Conduits or no, they worship me. The *world* worships me, Winter queen, and you cannot defeat me."

Mather crumples, one hand around his gut.

Theron circles him, grinning, his sword tinged red.

Watching Mather scramble for another conduit, his wound leaking scarlet blood down his thighs and Theron readying behind him, blade rising, all I can see is death.

Sir, and Nessa, and Garrigan, Alysson, Noam, Finn, myself—everyone I couldn't save.

Angra thinks this is his war, and maybe it once was. But it has become something far greater, something that makes him inconsequential by comparison.

This has nothing to do with him. This has nothing to do with his magic.

This is about all the people I couldn't save and all the people still out there now. This is about a future, a true future, the one that died when I was a child who had weapons instead of toys. The future that died when Mather had to grow up thinking he was the king of a lost kingdom, when Theron's father forced him to live a life by Cordell's rules, when Rares and Oana couldn't have a child, when Ceridwen had to bow to her brother's tyranny.

The future even Angra should have had. One that may have been worse than the one he lived, yes, but it could have been far better. And even if it was worse, it would have been by his own doing. It would have been fair and true and *human*, a future free of magic, a life formed apart from darkness or light.

This has brought me nothing but death.

But from it, there will be life.

I scream and all the magic in me rushes outward, shattering the Decay's hold on me. I drop, catching myself on the ground before more injuries can reverberate through me, and the moment I'm down I reach out to Mather, filling him with healing waves of pure ice. He bolts upright, the magic swarming him, his eyes on mine.

My attention snaps past him, to Theron, swinging his blade at Mather's neck.

Mather darts to the left. The cut on his stomach is just a smear of bloodied cloth now, the skin healed and the muscles new as he lands on his elbows, bends, and misses

Theron's sword by a breath. The blade lances across the bag strapped to Mather's back, so when he spins to kick Theron's legs out from under him, items fly in a gust of rope and packets of food and—

A dagger, the hilt softly glowing purple. Cordell's conduit?

I don't have time to think about it. The particles of air shift around me, tingling along my arms in waves of warning. The magic here is the opposite of Angra's—pure and untouched. And now, awoken, unleashed, with that same magic threading through my veins, I can feel the changes, when Angra's Decay barrels at me.

So I move before he strikes me, and the blast of shadow he sends smashes into the wall. Chunks of rock scatter, but I whirl, punching a hand at Angra in a swift snap of defense, the one glorious loophole that lets me fight him, that let Oana fling bolts of lightning at me without feeding the Decay.

The source of magic hanging just beyond snaps and pops in response to my call, and it isn't snow or ice I punch at Angra. It's magic in its most basic form, a coiling strand that I redirect from the chaotic, striking path it had been on to explode the ground at Angra's feet. He stumbles back, shouting in pain.

A grunt pulls my attention to Mather and Theron. Theron drops, his sword launching from his hand when his arm smacks into the ground. Mather leaps on him, one solid blow knocking Theron's head back into a rock and sending him bobbing in a dizzy swirl.

"You cannot take my power," Angra declares, balling his hand, the Decay building around his fist in what will be a deathblow. "No one can take my power. This world is free, finally, from people like *you* who seek to stifle it."

He thrusts forward. Shadow fills the air, rotating strands of it that break apart into dozens of cloudy, dark fingers, all spiraling for me, all bent on destruction.

"I couldn't have said it better myself," I mutter.

All I feel as Angra's magic dives for me is adrenaline, the resounding, delirious joy of this being over.

Because in two breaths, it will be.

I kick off a nearby stalagmite and leap over the first few funnels of Decay, curving my body in the air to avoid another. As I jump, I thrust my hand at Angra, channeling another bolt of magic that connects with the ground and propels him, faltering, to the very edge of the magic chasm's cliff.

I'm still airborne, pushing myself on by a final surge of magic that floods my being with ice and snow. That chill whirls out of me, latches onto the nearest weapon— the dagger that fell out of Mather's pack—and snatches it to me.

Through the sweat and blood that coat my face, I look down at where Angra wavers on the edge of the cliff.

And I smile.

The dagger's hilt slams into my palm, magic bursting up my arm in a whirl of images and emotions. But they all fall silent in the face of my determination. There is nothing here—no distraction, no thought, only Angra and me and the end of the world.

The dagger shimmers purple in the dimness, reflecting the magic behind Angra. That flash draws his eyes, but too late, time morphing around this moment as if all the world holds its breath to watch me leap across the cliff, raise the dagger, and land, sinking the blade into Angra's chest.

I send one last command at Mather. All too similar to the one his father shouted as the room crumbled around us.

Run!

Angra stumbles back, stunned enough for me to knock him off-balance even more. He teeters, trips, hands scrabbling fruitlessly at the air as I gain my footing on the cliff and push with every bit of strength I've ever possessed.

We teeter, both of us, my momentum and Angra's weight dragging us over the edge.

A movement makes me look over my shoulder one last time. Mather, Theron's arm draped around his neck, drags the half-conscious king for the exit. He doesn't stop to look back at me, doesn't pause to try to join me. He just obeys, tearing out of the chasm with one of his greatest adversaries leaning against him.

My feet leave the cliff with one final shove.

Angra screeches, dark magic streaming from him in a desperate attempt to pull himself back up. But the closer we draw to the magic source, the more electrifying fingers of it snap out and sizzle his attempts. I'm ready too—I will not let him stop me, and for every trembling grasp at salvation he unleashes, I slam into him with waves of my own magic. Light and dark, purity and decay, as the source of magic grows brighter and closer and hotter.

There was a time in my life when I would have given anything for magic. I *did* give anything for magic—I threw myself headlong into a centuries-old war. But I did it also for Winter, for the people I loved, because that was what they needed to live a safe and healthy life.

And once I got magic, once I had far, far too much of it, I hated and feared it. I couldn't fathom how our world could be so dependent on something that had done so much bad. But there was good in it, such wondrous good that the bad was almost understandable.

That is what I see as I plunge toward the source. The brilliance of it hurts my eyes, makes me unable to distinguish one color from the next until all I see is the most searing, perfect light. Beautiful and painful and unmarred and flawed. And while these extremes have made my world a realm of chaos and uncertainty, the answer is so simple:

The good and the bad that the magic gives us are equally unnecessary.

All my life, magic has been a driving force. All my life, I've fought and bled and wept for a future when those I love are safe and happy.

And so I close my eyes and let the magic bring about a new world.

Mather

MATHER TOLD HIMSELF it was Meira's final burst of magic that made him leave the chasm. That she infused her will into him, a single command drumming at his heart until he couldn't conceive of any other option.

But that was a lie.

She had told him to run with such a distinct crack of her voice that he wanted to drop Theron's wobbling form and dash back for her. No, something more powerful made him keep the Cordellan prince—*king*—around his neck and sprint up the exit tunnel. Something that, once he saw it, shocked an even stronger sensation into his body: hope.

He and Phil had carried Cordell's conduit all around this world. From Rintiero up to Paisly and down to the Rania Plains, all the way from there to Autumn. Mather had taken it into the labyrinth because he'd expected Theron to appear in the battle above, and he didn't want any of the Thaw to have it lest Theron somehow manage to take it from them. Mather hadn't considered the conduit more than that, mostly due to the hatred that filled his veins whenever he even thought the word *Cordell*, but now he realized just how blind he'd been.

That was the solution. Cordell's conduit.

Theron had surrendered it. He'd *given it up* in Rintiero. That was what had to happen—a conduit had to be sacrificed and returned to the chasm. Cordell's conduit had been sacrificed, and it was now returning to the chasm—only by Meira's hands, not its own bearer's.

Would that be enough to destroy all magic? Would it allow Meira to survive? It had to work. It *had* to.

The only light in the exit tunnel came from the magic chasm below, so as Mather dragged Theron up, darkness swallowed them whole. He paused just inside the tunnel His ears strained for any sign of Meira behind him, racing up the exit. But all he heard was the continuing sizzle and crack of the magic electrifying the chasm—

Then a rumble. As if the Klaryn Mountains were awakening after a long slumber, shaking their shoulders back as they rose from the depths of the earth. The tunnel vibrated so hard, rocks tumbled from the ceiling and walls, a few stones cracking on Mather's head and arms. He staggered, Theron moaning in a half-conscious gurgle as they slammed into the wall. The vibrations didn't let up, and in the wake of the initial rumble, an explosion ripped through the chasm and up the tunnel.

Mather didn't turn to see what came at them. Survival instinct overtook him, and never had he been more grateful for that numbness. Clarity only, no thoughts that would destroy him.

Thoughts like: *The magic is exploding. Because Cordell's conduit fell into it?*

Or because of Winter's?

He shifted Theron over his shoulder and ran like he'd never run before, legs pumping as if his speed might make everything all right. But even that failed him, and when a flare of painfully white light illuminated the tunnel, charged heat slammed into his back. He cried out, legs giving way under the bombardment of prickling fire crawling over his body, burrowing into his muscles.

But when he dropped, he didn't hit the ground.

He fell *upward*, carried on that wave of magic with Theron hurtling through the air ahead of him. The magic surged beneath them, like a wave relentlessly crashing for the shore. Blood roared through Mather's head, or maybe it was the magic, or the continuing explosions beneath them—the deafening intensity of the tunnel was matched only by the brilliance of the white light. It grew the longer they flew, gleaming brighter and brighter, the magic burning hotter and hotter. . . .

The magic relinquished his body to the surface. Drifts of snow caught him as he dropped to the ground, flipping and rolling down a sharp slope peppered with boulders and tufts of grass. He slammed into a tree trunk, shaking loose a deluge of golden leaves and ice. The tunnel had dumped them somewhere between Autumn and Winter in the Klaryns' foothills. They had to be close to the battle.

These details registered in Mather's mind, but barely, a flicker of fact that vanished as he found himself staring up at the mountains beyond.

The explosion that had ejected him and Theron from the tunnel raged on. The ground shook so hard, he had to steady himself on the tree to stand, and Theron, waking slowly, braced his hands on a rock and bowed his head to block out the rising noise. Because rise it did—the vibrations retracted, the deep breath before the war cry, and as Mather watched, golden leaves raining through the air, the mountains exploded.

Red, orange, silver, green—tendrils of color fanned across the clear blue sky, bursting up as if a volcano had shot a rainbow into the world. Rock cracked in earsplitting shatters; the spark and hiss of the magic evaporating lit the air like the fuses of a thousand cannons readying for battle. But no battle came on the wake of their spark—this *was* the battle, this great explosion that drowned out the blue of the sky in favor of streams of color and magic that made every nerve in Mather's body swirl under his skin.

The absence of emotion let him have one moment of watching this display unburdened. And in that moment, he almost thought it looked beautiful, the destruction of magic—

But there it ended.

This explosion was the magic disintegrating. The colors that swirled out of the mountain dissolved against the air, and each breath that passed brought with it less and less of that sparking sensation, the feel of the air saturated by magic. It was leaving, as Meira had wanted.

Mather flung himself away from the tree. Stones barred the exit tunnel now, thrown there during the continuing eruption. He tugged on one, but it didn't budge. No—she had to have gotten out. Maybe the magic threw her elsewhere, farther down. . . .

Though the earth still shook with the aftershocks of the chaos, Mather scrambled down the incline, hurling himself from rock to tree to rock again. His palms tore against the sharp stones, but he couldn't stop, wouldn't stop, his heart vibrating right alongside the earth.

"Meira!" he screamed. Desperation gurgled through him, the aching grief that had sprouted in his gut the moment he had watched his father die. He clung to his tiny well of hope, but even that darkened, melting like ice in his palm.

He staggered out from behind one last cluster of trees and into the battlefield. Or what had once been the battlefield.

Soldiers from each side stood motionless, gaping up at the continuing eruption of fading magic. Most dropped to their knees as if they had all been driven to the ground by the same life-altering revelation. A few wept, staring at their hands as if seeing them for the first time. Most simply knelt there, soaking in the emptiness that permeated the air.

Mather felt it, too. Even those on the field who hadn't been possessed by Angra's magic felt it, their eyes widening and their chests heaving with the deep breath reserved for inhaling pure air after too long spent in squalor. They turned to those who knelt, and joyous cries began, just as they had in Abril, when he'd first thought all this was over and Meira had stood triumphant over Angra's work camps.

"MEIRA!" The agony in his own voice echoed back to him, countering the happiness of the field. It should have worked—Cordell's dagger should have been a good enough sacrifice. . . .

Maybe it had been, but she had been too close to the destruction.

Maybe Angra had managed one final blow before the end.

Mather tripped into a boulder and smacked his palm against it, beating his sorrow out on the stone. "NO!" he screamed, shoving that word into the mountain, forcing it to feel everything it had taken from him.

A hand on his shoulder. "Mather?"

He spun, launched away, tears blurring his sight—no, despair blurring his sight, making him blind with need so he breathed her name, "Meira," in one quiet, hopeful plea.

But it was Trace. And Hollis behind him, Kiefer, Eli, Feige.

His Thaw.

He hadn't lost them too.

Mather dropped to the ground, doubled over near the rocks that led up to where the chasm's exit had once been. Trace knelt with him and said something, quiet words that Mather refused to hear. Someday, maybe, he'd be able to hear them—but now, all he could do was unravel on this field, in the midst of celebrations and relief and the victory Meira had wanted.

She should be here. If anyone was to survive that labyrinth, it should have been her.

Somehow Mather found himself upright, maybe urged by Trace or Hollis. Ceridwen stood behind them now, battle beaten, her brows pinched over teary eyes. She already knew—everyone who gathered did. Caspar, his generals; Rares and Oana—how had they gotten here? Dendera, her face contorted as if she had been weeping for hours—and Henn wasn't with her.

No. Ice above, no more loss.

Mather studied their faces.

"The world will need you after this."

It had been one of Meira's last pleas to him, and he grabbed onto it, willing the order to consume his every emotion. Something to do past his grief, while everyone around looked to him for explanation or leadership.

Mather shifted forward. Eyes brightened at his movement. He cleared his throat, and Ceridwen clamped her hands over her mouth, her eyes welling with tears that made her shoulders jerk forward in a sob.

Caspar smiled. Rares laughed, no, *bellowed*, nearly toppling to the ground as Oana held him up and joined his laughter. Even Dendera smiled, but smiled through tears and closed her eyes to brace herself.

Mather frowned and looked to his Thaw for explanation.

But none of them offered any words, too shocked to speak.

Two fingers pressed against the back of Mather's neck.

It had been a game when they were children. One he'd played on her, mostly, sneaking up and pressing two fingers on her neck in place of a weapon.

"You're dead!" he'd shout to her shrieks that it wasn't fair, that she'd take him in a real fight, that she hadn't been ready.

He wasn't ready. He was never ready, and every time he snuck up on her, her violent swirl of confidence stunned him speechless. No matter how many times he saw her fight, he was always struck dumb with wonder that someone could be so unapologetically *strong*.

So he shouldn't have been surprised at all when those fingers landed on his neck. He shouldn't have doubted her ability to survive, not for one second.

Everything in him heaved from grieving to numb to vibrant as a he spun around.

Meira. Blanketed with the thick gray dust of the chasm and streaked with blood.

But Meira.

Alive.

She smiled, fighting exhaustion as she wobbled forward. He didn't hesitate, couldn't have even if he'd wanted to—he swept in to catch her as she strung her arms around his neck. Her head bent into his chest, each warm breath from her coating his heart with the purest, most unbelievably perfect waves of joy.

A thousand things rammed against his mouth, but all he said was "Cordell's conduit."

Meira nodded. Ice, every movement from her made him want to cry out.

"I didn't realize what it would do until we were falling," she said, keeping her face tucked against him as if she needed to touch him as much as he needed her. "But we hit the magic, and I watched Angra disintegrate. I expected the magic to burn me up as well—but the dagger touched it before I did. Then everything went white, and I was flying up through the mountains. I thought . . . I thought I was dead . . . but it saved me. The dagger."

She shook her head, unable to say more as she tightened

her hold in one resilient squeeze before she pulled back, laughing. Her laugh made him light enough to float into the now-clear sky. Any remnants of magic were gone; any echoing vibrations had faded.

It was over.

Ceridwen dove forward to throw herself around Meira, who still had Mather's hands on her waist. The Thaw joined next, laughing and colliding in a mess of arms and smiles and tears as Dendera, Oana, and Rares swept in too. They became nothing but a tangle of happiness, grabbing onto their victory through the loss, their triumph through the grief.

Mather's eyes connected with something outside their group.

Cordellan soldiers clustered around a stand of trees not far down. Theron limped toward them, one hand wrapped around his side, his face void of . . . everything.

He was free of Angra's darkness now. How would he react to what he had done?

And how much of what he had done had actually been *him*?

Theron must have felt eyes on him, because he instinctively turned, then immediately winced in regret. He didn't want to face them yet—Mather couldn't blame him.

But the reason Mather's arms weren't empty right now was because of Theron. All the hatred he'd felt toward

Cordell, all the anger at Noam and jealousy at Theron—it had all given him Meira back.

So before Theron looked away, Mather bowed his head.

Theron blinked. His jaw shifted. He closed his eyes and nodded in return.

Meira's mouth grazed Mather's ear. "Thank you. For saving him."

Mather smiled, jostled as more people joined the celebration. He lifted a hand to cup her head, holding her face just down from his. "Thank you for saving *us*."

She grew solemn, and he saw one distinct thought cross her face: William.

"We're free now," Meira said, to Mather, to herself. She turned to face part of the celebrating crowd, one hand on his chest. Brightness returned to her eyes, beautiful resilience that Mather wanted to spend the rest of his life basking in. "We are free!"

Her cry shot out into the air, egging other shouts higher. It was hard to feel anything but joy here, an infectious wonder that every person in the valley dove into headfirst.

Meira pivoted back to him, her grin radiant, and didn't give him a word of warning or a chance to kiss her first— she leaped on him, pressing her lips to his. He hadn't thought he'd ever get to do this again. Hold her, kiss her, know her lips by anything other than memory. The kiss echoed through his every nerve, tangling around the grief knotted in his gut and easing it looser.

Mather laughed against her mouth and swept her into his arms again, lifting her so he could spin as she kissed him, surrounded by chaos and happiness and laughter, the start of their new beginning.

Meira

Six Months Later

AS WE PASS through the great gates that guard Bithai, I bear down so hard on my horse's reins that I'm surprised he doesn't bolt into the crowd.

The streets turn in such sharp angles that I swear I can hear them snapping into place. Merchants shout from their stalls, waving their wares to attract customers under the noon sky. The curved brown tiles of the roofs still sit on foundations of gray stone; vines still scramble up walls in bursts of foliage. Flags wave high in the breeze, hunter-green backgrounds bearing Cordell's golden maple leaf and lavender stalk.

I catch Mather's eye. "Everyone looks happy."

He pitches one shoulder up, thinks better of whatever he was about to say, and nods to my saddlebag. "What did the letter say again?"

Ahead of us, Trace groans. "You don't have it memorized by now?"

But Mather holds my gaze. He does have the letter memorized; I do too. It's the only contact I've had with Theron since I sent Greer to check on him a month after . . . everything.

I'd hoped Greer would return with something more than political reports—something that would let me know how Theron truly was. For the hundredth time, I wonder if I should have gone, or if I should have followed Theron out of that valley after the battle and made sure he was all right.

My body sways toward Mather instinctively.

No—I had my own kingdom to repair. Angra's Decay had infected every Winterian in Jannuari, and when the magic disappeared, they were left hurting and filled with regret over the things they had let Angra make them do. My place after the war was in Winter.

I draw out the letter, the parchment unrolling in my fingers.

To the queen of the Kingdom of Winter:
In the wake of magic's destruction, our world has returned to a state of normalcy. But it will take many years before all wounds are healed.

Which is why I call on you now. A similar letter is at this moment being read by every monarch in Primoria. I beseech you all with the same request: to gather in Bithai in three weeks' time to put into effect the treaty that many of you signed before the war. The principles of that treaty are needed now more than *ever—principles that will help us sculpt a Primoria comprised of eight united kingdoms.*

Only together can we rebuild the world.

Theron's signature swirls across the bottom, capped with Cordell's seal.

I straighten and smile at Mather. "It says that everything will be all right."

He gives me an uncertain look but nods. "It already is."

Maple branches arch over us as we pull onto a wide road. The canopy above lets golden light filter through, making the last few moments of our trip serene, almost dreamlike.

We reach the gate leading to the palace and I smile. This used to be the site of two golden trees. Noam's doing, a display of Cordell's wealth. But they're gone, and a chain holds the gate open in a permanent state of welcome.

Theron has opened the palace to his kingdom.

This image makes me ride into the courtyard with more confidence. We dismount, and Mather instantly sets to work passing out orders to the guards who came with us. Greer and Conall bear the symbol of Winter, a snowflake, on their chests, while Trace, Hollis, and Feige wear the uniform of the Thaw, a snowflake-wildflower hybrid emblazoned on their shoulders—a mark of my elite personal guard, which the Thaw has become.

When everyone is sorted, Mather pushes his fists into his pockets, and I can't help but smile. I still have trouble grasping how easily my Winterians have adapted to normal life.

Mather's eye catches on something behind me and he smiles. "Looks like we aren't the only ones who decided to come."

I can't ask what he means before a body slams me forward.

"How dare you?" Ceridwen shouts, punching me lightly. "It's been *six weeks* since you visited. You abandoned me, you awful girl."

I turn and punch her back, but I'm smiling too. "It was your turn to come to Winter!"

Ceridwen sighs dramatically as another familiar face emerges from the grove. Jesse nods at Mather, sees the fit Ceridwen seems to be having, and shakes his head at me.

"Getting you two together never ends well for me," Jesse says.

Ceridwen ignores him and links her arm through mine. "Regardless of whose turn it was to visit whom, it's been six weeks since we've talked." She pivots us toward the palace, Jesse and my retinue falling in behind. Her eyes linger on the gray stones and glittering windows that tower in a suddenly intimidating wave. "And apparently a lot has happened."

She looks at me, and I wave my hand dismissively.

"I have no idea what this is about, aside from what the letter said."

Ceridwen grunts, unconvinced. "Well. There's other

news to share in the meantime."

We enter the palace. The warm polished wood of the walls wraps around us, a cozy contrast to the vibrancy outside. My eyes flit of their own volition to our right, where the paneled walls hide a doorway and an office beyond. Noam's old office. Did Theron take it as his?

A servant appears and beckons us to our rooms.

"We received word from Ventralli," Ceridwen starts as we trail the servant. "They've settled on a system of elections. The whole process is fascinating—they're to run the kingdom completely under the leadership of someone selected by the people."

I pull my voice low. "Jesse doesn't regret ceding the kingdom to his advisers?"

She shakes her head. "I've never seen him so happy. Knowing Ventralli will progress beyond what he could have done . . . we're both pleased with what's developing."

"Thinking of instating such elections in Summer?" I tease, only because it does, in fact, sound like something both she and I would wholeheartedly support.

She grunts. "Maybe, once the kingdom is in a better state of mind. Speaking of—we've set up an honest trade with Yakim. It appears Giselle has given up her goal of overtaking Summer now that there's no magic in the Klaryns. I've almost gone from loathing her to only hating her."

"That's wonderful!" My smile softens. "I'm happy for you."

She nudges me. "The feeling is mutual, Winter queen."

We follow a staircase up and pass into a hallway that looks familiar, crystal chandeliers and plush maroon carpet.

"I believe you enjoyed this room last time," the servant says, stopping next to an open door.

I glance into the room and recognition flares—it's the room I stayed in when I first came to Bithai, with the canopy bed and lavender rug and heavy white curtains.

"I'm so blind," I say. *"Mona?"*

The servant who attended me when I was last here. She giggles. "You remember!"

"Of course!" I look around. "Where is—"

"Rose got married. Lives on the coast now. But it got me a promotion!" Mona sweeps into a curtsy. "If you need anything, let me know. I'm so happy you're here, *Queen* Meira." She winks, her emphasis on my title bringing up all those Cordellan etiquette classes.

I smile. "Me too." And I mean it, more than I realized I would.

"The rest of your party has been given the rooms around yours," Mona continues. "You've a few hours before the evening meal commences with music in the ballroom. Enjoy your stay."

As she leaves, Jesse turns to Ceridwen. "We should let them rest. Tonight will most likely be long."

Ceridwen agrees with a halfhearted groan and jabs a finger at me. "Find us when you're done resting." Her lips curve into a sly grin as she nods at Mather. "Or whatever you're planning to do."

Mather laughs and dives forward, burying his face in my neck with a bearlike growl as he pushes us through the door. Poor Conall and Greer scramble for their rooms, and the reactions of Mather's Thaw range from giggling to hiccup laughing.

Mather kicks the door shut as I manage to disentangle from him.

He catches my arm. "Wait—Ceridwen had a good idea. . . ."

I smile. "To *rest*. We'll need all the strength we can get for tonight."

Mather moves toward me again, but his playfulness is gone. "Are you all right?"

What a question. "Yes. No." I wrap my arms around myself. A love of the cold still resonates in all Winterians, but it was a trait that sprouted after years of magical influence. Will it now slowly fade? All I know is that I think I'm uncomfortably chilly. Or maybe just overwhelmed.

Mather puts his hands on my shoulders, his forehead to mine. "You're not alone."

I curl in, tucking my arms around Mather's waist. With my head bent along his chest, my eyes land on a painting beside the wardrobe.

Morning light catches banks of snow, the bending bows of snow-laden tree branches, the dripping daggers of icicles.

This painting is as familiar as the city, as the palace.

Theron showed me this painting. One of my first glimpses of Winter.

"I can have it hung in your room if you wish."

I nestle my cheek against Mather, breathing in time with him.

Theron is all right. He has to be.

Banners drape from the ballroom's ceiling—eight different colors with eight different symbols. The theme carries throughout the room, from the vases filled with eight flowers, one of each color, to the clusters of food on eight trays, one delicacy from each kingdom.

I dig my fingers into the indigo sleeve of Mather's coat as we descend the staircase. Hollis and Trace, a few paces behind us, scan the room with the practiced air of security.

"It's beautiful," I say.

One corner of Mather's mouth lifts and he glances at me, his eyes trailing down my pleated ivory dress. He swings in front of me at the bottom of the staircase and loops his fingers through the straps of my chakram's holster. The leather shows a pattern of snowflakes, a far more ceremonial holster than what I'm used to—but the chakram it holds is worthy of such beauty. Polished wood makes up the curving handle, and the blade itself is etched with the bare branches of Winterian trees. A gift from Caspar and Nikoletta, one I haven't been able to bring myself to throw.

Having it is a reminder of what I am, a warrior queen, just like the locket I still wear.

But I like not having to use it. I like that my weapon is purely decorative.

Mather presses his lips to my forehead. *"You're* beautiful," he says into my skin.

We're distracted by a high-pitched squeal I know all too well. I turn in time to see a small black-and-scarlet blur tumble out of the crowd.

"Shazi!" I cry, and bend to intercept her.

Nikoletta emerges from the crowd and smiles her apology as she disentangles Shazi from me. "She isn't yet four and I've already given up on corralling her."

Behind us, Trace leans in to ask Mather a question, which pulls his attention away from the look Nikoletta suddenly gives me.

"Have you spoken with him?"

The change in topic lances through me and I involuntarily straighten.

Nikoletta reads that as my answer and juts her chin toward the glass doors. "He's in the golden forest. Past the maze." She reaches out to clasp my hand. "I know he wants to see you."

I nod, but one question makes me lean closer to her. "Is he all right?"

The grief on Nikoletta's face doesn't wane. "As much as we all are."

She leaves to find Caspar, and I head for the glass doors, linking my arm through Mather's as I pass. He stumbles alongside me, leaving Trace and Hollis with a confused yelp.

But he sees the look on my face, notes the approaching doors.

"Are you sure you're ready?" In his voice is nothing but warmth and support and everything that I love about him.

I draw my lips into a smile. "Ready for anything."

The golden forest appears, as Nikoletta said, at the end of the hedge maze. Dusk has fallen by this time, coating the area in the hazy gray of night, lit only by lanterns that glow along the path.

Mather stops next to me. "What is this?" he whispers.

Ahead of us, golden maple saplings stand in perfect rows over arching grassy mounds. Small gold leaves clink from their thin branches, each tree no taller than I am, dozens of them swaying within a waist-high stone fence that keeps them separated from the rest of the garden.

I step up to the iron gate, my fingers looping through the sculpted metal. Mather waits beside me, willing to follow me wherever I need him to go.

I press my hand to his chest. "Wait for me here?"

He bows his head. "Always, my queen."

I kiss him quickly and enter the forest.

The gate squeals shut behind me, cutting through the melody of the golden leaves hitting their golden branches.

Every tree I pass has carvings on the trunk, names and dates and bits of poetry. No—one poem in particular, one I heard long ago, from dying lips that ring through my memory.

Cordell's poem. Sir recited it on the battlefield outside Bithai before I thought he died the first time, before I was captured, before my life changed in ways I'm still discovering.

> *"Cordell, Cordell, if we must leave*
> *To battle, travel, or to die,*
> *Let those who do not come again*
> *Forever in your presence lie."*

And beneath those lines of poetry, the phrase *Here lies* proclaims that Cordell buries its royal dead under golden maple trees. Such a place exists in Jannuari, only with simple markers for the bodies we burn. Sir has a marker there. And Nessa, and Garrigan, so many stones carved with snowflakes.

So I know where Theron is, whose grave he's standing over, before I reach him. I know whose grave I'd be standing over, where my heart would go.

And when I turn down the row of saplings with the freshest mounds of earth, he's there.

One arm crosses over his chest, the other cups the back of his neck as he bows his head, his eyes closed where he stands before two golden saplings in dirt mounds. One, older; the other, far too fresh. Lanterns spaced along the pathway shine light onto us, but shadows still seep in, warping details. He doesn't move at my approach, and it gives me time to study him.

His once long hair has been cropped short, feeding into a beard that roughens his face. His Cordellan uniform bears more medals than when last I saw it, and the material is finer, a weave of deep-emerald velvet with gold accents.

All in all, he looks far more like his father, in only the best ways. Noam's surety and confidence and control, but none of his harshness or pomposity.

I stop two paces back from Theron, clinging to handfuls of my skirt.

Breathe, Meira. "Nikoletta said you'd be here."

Theron, eyes still closed, smiles, but it doesn't stay when he looks at me.

"She's become far too protective," he says. "Did she send you to check on me?"

"It was heavily implied." I try to smile. "But I've been wanting to speak to you anyway."

Theron drops his gaze back to one of the trees. Noam's sapling, his name showing in the hazy light. Theron stays silent, massaging the back of his neck, before he pulls upright and drops his thumbs into the belt that holds a decorative sword at his waist.

"Well, as I told Nikoletta, and Jesse, *and* my advisers,

I'm fine." He meets my eyes again. "You owe me nothing, Your Highness. I'm pleased simply that you have come to participate in the world's unification."

"Theron." The bite in my voice rumbles up from the complicated tangle in my gut. "You don't have to treat me like that."

His laugh is bitter. "I said something similar to you once. Do you remember what you said in return? *'You are Cordell, just as much as I am Winter. You'll always have to choose your kingdom over me.'* Well, my lady—you have chosen correctly."

I don't respond, opening the silence like a door flooding light into a dark room.

Theron keeps his eyes on me, the hard laughter slipping off his face in favor of a broken grunt. He licks his lips, shaking his head at me, at himself, at the graves before us.

"I remember everything," he starts, a soft whisper. "And I'm so sorry, Meira. I don't know where to begin with apologies. That's part of why I invited everyone here—I helped destroy this world, so I will help rebuild it. But you— golden leaves, I owe you so much more than that."

"I didn't come here for an apology." My voice breaks. "I came here to . . . well, to apologize to *you*, for not coming sooner. For not checking on you. This war began as Winter's problem, and I pulled you into it, *I* put you in Angra's path, and—"

"Angra." Theron practically sobs the name, a violent wince making him fold his chin to his chest. "You may have put me in his path, but I chose to walk down it."

My heart sinks into my stomach. I've feared that from the start, that the things Theron did were more him than Angra. But the look in his eyes chases away my concern.

"The Decay made me want things I never dared let myself admit. It was so freeing." He stops, folds his arms over his chest. "Until Angra . . ."

His tears break free. He scrubs at them, laughing at himself, eyes on the darkening sky.

"I killed my father because of him. I did terrible things because of him. And yet I admired him. I worshipped him. He was so strong, and I had felt weak for so long."

Theron looks at me.

"But I will be strong now. On my own." His words are a promise, the most alive he's sounded yet.

I move without thought, putting my hand on his arm. "You have the greatest capacity to love of anyone I've ever known. You loved your father despite his flaws; you loved *me* even when you knew nothing about me, other than that I was just as unseen as you were. You are so much stronger than me. Stronger than Angra too. And with you guiding us, I know Primoria will achieve a state of peace and equality that will honor everyone we lost."

Theron doesn't move, tears still glistening in his eyes.

"I'm sorry I couldn't be enough for you," he whispers.

My fingers tighten against him. "I'm sorry I couldn't be enough for you either."

Theron pulls away to rub the last few tears off his face. "We should gather with the rest," he says, voice clear now. "There are many important things to discuss."

I nod and take one step back, but Theron doesn't follow me. "Are you coming?" I ask.

He blinks up at me, his lips quirking. "A few more moments. Go on without me."

When I raise my brows, he dips into a bow.

"On my honor as the Cordellan king, I promise, I'm fine. I just need a moment."

"All right." I pause. "We will be. Fine, I mean."

Theron tips his head. "Lady Meira," he says.

I turn, leaving him standing over his parents' graves.

The important thing, though, is that he's standing.

The ballroom is packed by the time Mather and I return. Musicians play lively tunes from a platform between the staircases, complementing the hum of chatting dignitaries. Ceridwen, Lekan, and Kaleo stand with Caspar and Nikoletta; Giselle talks with the Spring general, a man I met when he came to Winter a few weeks ago to bridge the hurt between our two kingdoms. A group of Ventrallans has arrived, talking in animated tones to Jesse.

But they aren't the only ones who have arrived late.

Someone moves toward us. I spot his robe, the scar stretching through his dark skin, and I drop Mather's hand to collide with Rares. "You came!"

Rares squeezes me so tight I cough in protest. "Of course, dear heart! Paisly must be represented." He sets me down, his hands on my shoulders. "And I hold you responsible for the sheer misery of traveling now. I specifically remember telling you how I much *hated* traveling, and one of the few good things that magic gave us was the ability to get anywhere instantly. But no, you had to go and take it all away—and give us something far better in return."

At that, he pivots to reveal Oana behind him.

I smack my hands over my mouth and yelp into my palms. "You're—"

She hugs me, the slight bulge in her stomach pressing between us. "Four months now."

I can't do more than screech, my hands fluttering from her shoulders to her belly and back again. Rares hoots at my speechlessness and swoops in to plant a kiss on top of my head.

"I imagine you've been busy these past months as well." He nods at Mather and leans in to flick him in the forehead. "Treat her well."

Mather rubs the spot, stifling a laugh. "I do, I promise."

Rares looks at me for confirmation, and I smile, sliding my arm around Mather's waist.

"Not that I ever thought you'd pick someone who wouldn't," he tells me with a wink. "I believe we should make the rounds. Quite the gathering we've got here. Downright magical."

"There's nothing magical about this," Oana says. "We've earned all that happens here."

Rares nods his head. "Which seems magical to me, my love." He gives me one more hug. "Where is King Jesse? I hear Ventralli is evolving most curiously."

Mather points into the throng. "He's across the room—I'll show you."

He leads them away. So many people catch my eye—representatives from every kingdom, all gathered to negotiate the best way to continue our peace.

And that unity makes the holes in the crowd feel complete. Where Sir should be standing next to Mather as he talks with Jesse, Rares, and Oana; where Nessa and Garrigan should be following Conall as he weaves toward me through the crowd; where Henn and Finn should be talking with Greer at the edge of the room; where Noam should be laughing with Nikoletta and Caspar.

I don't fight the smile that eases across my lips, the tears that blur the colors and light of the ballroom into a shifting, sparkling kaleidoscope.

Rares and Oana were both right. We are our own magic now. And nothing can stop us.

ACKNOWLEDGMENTS

IF YOU READ my acknowledgments for *Snow Like Ashes* and *Ice Like Fire*, you know that I like to babble and basically thank every person I've ever known. And by this point in the series, a LOT of people have come into my life who have impacted this book, soooo . . .

LOTS OF PEOPLE TO THANK.

LET'S GET STARTED.

Mackenzie Brady Watson. Agent of my dreams. The combination of you + New Leaf is perfection of the highest caliber, and I am grateful every day to be your client.

HarperCollins. Yes, the entire company. But particularly: Kristin Rens, of course, always, forever, for finagling a coherent book out of whatever it is I first give you (which could usually be classified firmly under "hot mess"); Erin Fitzsimmons; Caroline Sun; Nina; Megan; Gina; Kelsey;

Margot; Nellie; and every other person who helped not only this book, but this whole series. Cheesy and clichéd as it is, you have all made my dreams come true, and for that there aren't enough thanks in the world.

Jeff Huang. Seriously now, LOOK AT THIS COVER. I am so honored my books get to wear your art.

Kate Rudd and Nick Podehl. You both gave voice to this series in an utterly mesmerizing way.

Shifting gears to the more personal side of things: Kelson. At the risk of getting too mushy, I'll just immortalize here that I love you, and I'm so happy I get to live this life with you.

My parents—I gave this book to you, but I still owe you far, far more.

Melinda. Okay, so your character's bits got edited out of *Frost Like Night*. You are a crazy whirlwind of energy and beauty, and honestly, Character Melinda got scared she couldn't compare to you.

To the rest of my ever-growing family: Annette, Dan, Trenton, Caro, John, Karen, Mike, and Haydin; Grandma and Grandpa, Debbie, Dan, Aunt Brenda, Lisa, Eddie, Mike, Grandma Connie, Suzanne, Lillian, William, Brady, Hunter, Lauren, Luke, Delaney, Garrett, Krissy, Wyatt, Ivy, Brandi, Mason, and Kayla the Librarian.

To my writer friends, near and far: J. R. Johansson, Kasie West, Renee Collins, Natalie Whipple, Bree Despain, Michelle D. Argyle, Candice Kennington, LT Elliot,

Samantha Vérant, Kathryn Rose, Jillian Schmidt, Claire Legrand, Jodi Meadows, Anne Blankman, Lisa Maxwell, Kristen Lippert-Martin, Sabaa Tahir, Sarah J Maas, Susan Dennard, Evelyn Skye; Akshaya, Madeleine, and Janella; and, always, Cousin Nicole.

Special thanks to my writer-wife, Kristen Simmons. I still can't believe I didn't get to thank you in *Ice Like Fire*. Our friendship may be new, but god, darling. You've changed my life.

Now for perhaps the hardest yet most rewarding part: thanking all of YOU.

In *Ice Like Fire*'s acknowledgments, I blubbered on about many of the bloggers/reviewers/fans who have made my life so freaking magical. If I did that again, I fear this section would be as long as *Frost Like Night* itself, so I'm going to sum up as best I can:

You know how in this trilogy, everyone is always struggling so hard to get magic? They fight and they suffer and they sacrifice, all for this elusive, sparkling thing that promises to make their lives better. Then, as in Meira's case (and as also happens so often in real life), they get it, and it isn't quite as wonderful as they expected.

You guys have been nothing like that.

As I said in *Snow Like Ashes*'s acknowledgments, you are, each of you, better than any conduit. You're better than the most fantastic magic I could conceive of. One of the biggest themes of this trilogy has, for me, been the idea of being *enough*—of not needing outside influences to make you "better" or "worthy." And while I hope I have imparted that belief to at least some of you, I am not at all too proud to say that I've failed myself in that belief. Because I wholly, irrevocably admit that I need each and every one of you. This publishing journey is fraught with so many high highs and low lows, but having you guys there, my little Winterian fandom, has made each moment not only worthwhile but utterly enchanting.

I am so honored I got to share this story with you. Twelve-year-old Sara, scribbling in notebooks, dreaming dreams of a white-haired girl and a wintry kingdom, did not dare fathom the absolute wonder that would come about, more than a decade later.

And it's because of you, and all the magic created just by being *you*.

So, thank you.

Turn the page for "The Crowning of a Queen,"
a never-before-published short
story set in the world of *SNOW LIKE ASHES*.

William

Eleven years before Winter's fall

FLAKES OF SNOW lanced across William's cheeks. Frost bound the trees in white coats and gray washed the sky—the perfect ivory camouflage for the battalion of Winterian soldiers.

On their side of the boundary, at least.

Beyond the wall of snow, a different forest sat close enough for William to see the blizzard's gale ruffle cherry blossoms, the grass so green and the sky so blue they assaulted his eyes. His queen would not be able to bring the blizzard she had created into Spring; King Angra's own power pounded at Winter's border with sickening warmth. But when the Winterian army crossed, the queen would be with them, healing where she could, infusing them with strength and agility.

William's chest cramped with unease. He glanced to the right, picking through the ivory and snowflakes to spot a group of soldiers, the queen at their center, her own silver armor tucked beneath a loose ivory cloak. She gripped the locket at her throat and the sword at her waist with equal fervor, as though she could not decide which would be more vital in the coming fight.

William had served in Winter's army since he was sixteen, first as a soldier, now as a captain. At twenty-one, with dozens of battles under his belt, many led by his queen, he could not stop fearing for her. Her job as Winter's ruler was to be back in Jannuari, not risking herself on the frontlines.

But he couldn't deny how much more confident he felt having her here, and he leaned selfishly into the feeling as the frigid air burned his lungs.

A horn bleated through the forest, and more Winterian soldiers burst from behind the trees, stampeding toward Spring with war cries that mimicked the horn. William followed, a short sword in each fist, snowdrifts crunching under his boots.

Spring soldiers peeled out of their own hiding spots, flooding their side of the once-quiet forest. William tucked his body into a smaller target, counting breaths as the snow beneath his feet gave way to a gentle swoop of velvet grass.

Then, chaos.

William's body jolted from armor striking armor; his shoulder hummed as he caught three consecutive blows before sliding a blade across a Spring soldier's neck. All so fast, everything happened so fast, the movements as fleeting as the breaths puffing out of his mouth—until a shriek shattered his heart.

William pivoted, his boots losing traction on the slick Spring grass and sending him to his knees. There—the queen's soldiers, all but two fallen, and the queen fending off attackers amid their bodies.

William took off, using the slippery grass to his advantage. He slid past swinging blades, propelling himself faster, faster. Now only one Winterian soldier stood between the queen and a relentless group of attackers, three moving toward the Winterian fighter, three toward her.

Two more seconds, and William would be there.

The last soldier in the queen's retinue went down, a blade piercing through a gap in his armor. The queen's attention flicked away from the Spring soldiers to her dying companion. If the wound wasn't too severe, she could heal him, but she was too late.

No—William was too late.

By the time the queen realized her mistake, she had a knife in her gut, beneath her breastplate. The Spring soldier who stabbed her twisted the blade with a sadistic smirk.

William dropped one of his swords, wrapped both his hands around the other, and channeled his force into slicing the soldier's neck. His blade bit through sinew and bone, and the man fell.

Other Winterians closed in around their queen, who crumpled to her knees, then to the ground. William cast away his other sword, moving on instinct to get her to safety—but she stopped him with a hand on his shoulder.

"No." She coughed, and William's face tightened at the blood dribbling down her chin. "Take . . . to Jannuari."

She pulled at the locket, fumbling to open the clasp. William heard a desperate intake of breath from the soldiers shielding the queen, and acidic bile climbed his throat.

She had removed the Royal Conduit.

"Take it . . ." She gasped, forcing words past the impending darkness. "To . . . Hannah."

Grief split William's chest. An unsteady breath, and Queen Eliana Dynam slipped away.

Leaning against the staircase that fanned into the ballroom, William winced at every chiming laugh, every tinkle of music, and wondered how he had made it through Hannah's coronation.

Winter's new queen moved through the crowd with ease. A smile here, a delicate hug there, a laugh so cheerful none would have guessed that her mother had so recently died. She had been this way all day, from the moment officials had clasped the locket around her throat as a symbol of her new role.

William envied her. And, if he was being honest, wanted to yell at her. How could she be at ease when just a week ago that locket had laid over her mother's beating heart?

He took a swig of the dry wine, willing it to erase the

memory of Queen Eliana's body wilting on the Spring grass. He closed his eyes and he was there—soldiers shrieking in battle; the air sour with blood and sweat; weapons ready and body strong, but years of training failing him. He could not do what he had always sworn to do: protect Winter's queen.

"Enjoying yourself, Captain?"

William started at Hannah's sudden appearance by his side, her hands folded against her ivory gown.

He had not resolved the two images that warred in his mind—one of Winter's queen, the severe and sturdy older woman to whom he had always looked with the greatest respect; the other of Winter's princess, a flighty and passionate girl who had always managed to make him smile even while she defied her mother's every wish.

But now that same princess was his queen. He had renewed his oath hours before, to protect and serve her as he had served her mother. Responsibility agitated an emotion he was ill equipped to handle: fear.

"How can you be happy?" he asked, his tone harsher than he had intended. She was his queen, but he couldn't get all the years he had seen her grow up out of his mind, though he was only two years older than her nineteen.

She stiffened. "You're being miserable enough for the both of us, hiding in the shadows, glaring at everyone who talks too loudly."

"We should be in mourning."

"Yes." Her agreement made him frown. Her icy blue eyes shot over the crowd as though she searched for someone. "But Winter didn't need help mourning my father when he died. What my people need now is to see that I can survive this, and they can as well."

By the time she finished speaking, William saw the sheen in her eyes, how her hand crept up to encircle the locket.

He couldn't remember Eliana being so raw. Or perhaps he hadn't been able to see her as more than a queen.

"I'm sorry," he whispered.

With a sniff and a smile, Hannah's tears were gone. "You should be, after everything I did for you and Lady Alysson."

William fumbled his goblet, dribbling wine on the floor. "Lady Alysson? What about her?"

"I'm queen now, and as such, I find I need more support." Hannah's smile turned mischievous. "Alysson has always been a close friend. I invited her to take up permanent residence here, as one of my ladies."

"You—no. You invited her—but her family—"

"Oversees the Tadil Mine, yes. But she is not the heir to her family's estate, and I figured she might be able to make a suitable match here." Hannah put a finger on her chin, pretending to think. "Now, who would be good for her? I was thinking Captain Henn. He has a sturdy career ahead of him and would be most able to provide for her."

William glowered. Alysson had come to Jannuari with

her family to celebrate Queen Eliana's birthday months ago, and the sight of her in the ballroom's light, her cheeks tinged pink from dancing, had struck William immobile. She had been quiet yet fiercely aware, with a focus most soldiers could only hope to learn, effortlessly following every movement in the room.

Including how William had leaned too far in his chair to look at her, lost his balance, and landed flat on his back.

The memory made heat creep up William's face. Hannah giggled.

"You're cruel," he said.

"I don't know what you're talking about. If Henn is not a proper fit, then maybe Finn Whalen. He's only fifteen, but age hardly matters when—"

"If you don't stop, I'll tell everyone who was responsible for the missing wine casks before the Proper Winter celebration last year."

Hannah's amusement cracked. "You drank them too!"

"But I didn't steal them."

She stopped, her mouth hanging open, the closest she came to surrender.

William caught someone in his peripheral vision. She stood with other partygoers, a champagne flute pinched in her slender fingers. The gold color of her pleated gown gave her whole body a soft radiance, and when she laughed, ivory hair rippled across her bare shoulders.

Alysson.

Instinct sent William's body to attention as though one of his commanders had passed by. She looked like a coin he'd gotten in a handful from a vendor, the only one in a dozen that was new and unmarred and caught the light from every angle.

That was terrible. William grimaced, glad he hadn't said that aloud. He wasn't good at romance.

But snow above, Alysson made him want to try.

"Shall I go and fetch her?" Hannah started walking.

William lurched after her. "But—"

Hannah stopped. "You can face Spring armies on countless battlefields, yet a woman undoes you?"

William's pulse heaved. There are many ways to be undone.

But he stayed quiet. A chorus of reasons not to get Alysson played through his mind—loudest was one that fueled his every other action.

Queen Eliana had wanted a different path for him: to be Hannah's husband. Hannah had refused the proposition over and over, but her refusal had never felt like a snub; it had been as expected as William's obedience. Not that Hannah wasn't beautiful, nor desirable. But what he admired about her also exhausted him, and he imagined linking himself to her would be as tiresome as climbing up a waterfall.

But he would have married her, had she agreed.

"Your mother wanted you married by now," he managed.

Hannah scowled. "My mother wanted to live to see the war with Spring ended. She got neither of those things."

William caught the pain that smudged her anger, the quick pull of regret. She may not have been as steady as Eliana, but Hannah was strong in her own way.

"My apologies, my queen," he said. "I only want to serve Winter."

That brought a smile. "You're a good soldier, Will. One of the best, in fact, and that's part of the reason my mother thought you were suited to me. I love you, but not as a husband. You deserve to be happy."

This time, when Hannah walked away, William didn't stop her. He stayed by the staircase, straightened his blue tunic, and slicked strands of hair back across his head, unsure of what to do with the childish anxiety fizzing in his abdomen.

Nervousness was a wondrously different emotion than terror or guilt or responsibility.

His throat tightened. He'd known how to serve Queen Eliana—he knew how to be a Winterian soldier. But how could he be a friend of the queen and a servant of the kingdom? How could he be a focused soldier, yet be blinded by the way Alysson grinned at Hannah before looking across the room at him?

William's mind went blank. Alysson smiled, careful and soft, lasting for hours, though the expression stayed on her lips for a moment. He couldn't breathe, not as she tucked a piece of hair back, and William was entranced by the spot below her ear, the divot where her fingers touched her jaw.

She spoke to Hannah, and William's eyes found her again.

Hannah wasn't looking at him or Alysson. She cast her eyes around the room as if she could take account of everyone in the ballroom. That was what she was doing, he realized—watching over them, searching for trouble.

William's tension eased. Hannah loved her people, her war-torn kingdom, as much as Eliana had—and William could depend on that love to always help her do what was best for Winter.

Hannah would be a great queen.